SPELLS OF SUMMER

INHERITANCE, BOOK EIGHT

AK FAULKNER

SPELLS of SUMMER

A.K. FAULKNER

CONTENTS

PROLOGUE

ERIC KNEW BETTER THAN TO GET UNDER MYRIAM'S FEET WHEN she was cooking, so he sat out on the porch to supervise the kids.

This farm had always been Myriam's dream. Well, the store was her dream, but the farm was a necessary part of it. There wasn't much to look at right now, but he had no doubt they'd be able to transform it into the paradise she deserved over the next few years. Eventually she might even be able to cut out her reliance on third-party growers and produce all her own stock.

The growing was her gift. All Eric could really do was provide the rain, keep their son Bambi out of the machinery, and help her with manual labor.

Bambi was running around with his friends, going off like a little firecracker, and Eric grinned. The kid was full of laughter and energy.

And magic.

One day, Eric would be able to teach him. When Bambi was old enough to know how to keep a secret. Not from his mom, of course, but definitely from strangers, and maybe even his friends.

"Hey. Thought I'd bring you a drink." Paula stepped out onto the porch with a glass of lemonade, and offered it to him, grinning. "You sure you don't want me to take over?"

Eric laughed and accepted the glass. "I'm good, thanks. This is a privilege, not a chore."

Paula chuckled and sat on the seat next to him, wiping the condensation on her hand off onto her skirt. "Rufus hasn't turned your herb garden into a pocket realm yet?"

"Nah, we're cool. He hasn't even tried to summon a god or anything." Eric sipped, and the sour tang of the lemonade was absolutely perfect on such a hot day.

Rufus was only a couple of years older than Bambi, and Paula was already teaching him. Hard not to, Eric supposed, when she and Todd had cut their entire house out of the world and made it their sanctum. They probably had to explain magic to the kid right from the start, so it was lucky Rufus had inherited the affinity, not just the books.

Paula and Todd had kind of shot themselves in the foot there, what with their enormous magic house, and Eric didn't like to think how things might have gone if Rufus was born without the gift.

"Todd still entertaining the grownups?"

Paula nodded. "Everyone's going over your family photos. They'll be in your medicine cabinet next."

"They better not steal my weed." Eric chuckled again, but turned serious a moment later. "Whatever happened with that dude who was bugging you, anyway?"

Paula's smile faded and she hunched forward, watching her son intently as he dithered on the edge of the group trying to be a wallflower in a space without walls. "Comes and goes," she murmured. "Keeps trying to recruit us to his coven, sulks away again when we say we're not interested, reappears a year or two later with the same offer." She crinkled her nose. "He's kinda sketchy. I don't want anything to do with him. I just get this weird vibe, you know?"

Eric nodded. He absolutely understood weird vibes, and they were a totally valid reason to stay the hell away from someone who clearly couldn't take *no* for an answer. "If there's ever anything I can do, just say the word and I'm there." He paused. "You know, so long as what you need is rain, or a song, or some chocolate…"

"Uh, when does anyone ever *not* need chocolate?" Paula sat up again with a smile, eyes sparkling.

"Oh, man, you have *got* to try this." Eric put his glass down so he could use both his hands to punctuate his words. "Get a bar of candy, yeah, but don't open it. Just snap it into pieces inside the bag, and then put the bag in your freezer. Give it a few hours, then you open the bag and you've got little pieces of frozen heaven just waiting to melt in your mouth!"

She looked at him with the suspicion most people gave him when he tried to explain this to them. "Frozen chocolate?"

"The best!" Eric threw his hands up in the air. "I can't even describe how good it is."

They were interrupted by tapping from the kitchen window, and Eric turned to grin at Myriam and give her a thumbs up. Dinner would be ready soon, so it was time to set the table.

He picked up his drink and drained it, then stood up. "Okay. Duty calls. Can you watch the rugrats while I get everything ready?"

"Sure." Paula smiled and stood up. "Myriam still doesn't know, right?"

Eric shrugged. "About me? Yeah. About Bambi?" He shook his head. "Time's not right."

"How do you know?"

He blinked at her, but her question wasn't a demand or

anything. She wasn't interrogating him or accusing him of making a mistake. There was a sadness in her eyes, and her tone was wistful.

Did she *regret* telling Rufus so young?

Paula and Todd both had the gift, and they both treated it like it was something academic. They'd spent years collecting all kinds of books, trinkets, and whatever else was stowed away in that house of theirs, and they were still at it, traveling the country and digging through thrift stores, flea markets, auction rooms, and used bookstores. Todd was absolutely loaded, so money never seemed to be any object when it came to buying up whatever they could find.

It was like they were searching for something, and they still hadn't found it.

Maybe they never would. Maybe they were raising Rufus to carry on the search after they were gone.

Maybe they were greedy.

"I just do," Eric sighed, sorry that he couldn't explain it any better than that. "My gut says no, and I listen to it."

His gut, of course, was steered by his heritage. But that was a secret he only shared with Myriam, and only because she was a Child of Herne too. He would know when the time was right to teach Bambi, and that's when he'd start, but for Paula and Todd — who liked to do everything by the book and make sure it was all perfect — the lack of certainty was probably hellish.

"Your gut says to freeze chocolate," Paula teased.

Eric snorted and waved over his shoulder as he headed for the door. "You're gonna thank me one day," he called to her.

But that day would not be today, because he'd already eaten his chocolate for breakfast.

1

LAURENCE

"You did *what?*"

Laurence stared at Freddy and didn't know whether to laugh in his face or slap him. Either way, he really hoped Freddy was kidding.

Quentin cleared his throat softly and placed a hand on Laurence's thigh, but he too was watching Freddy. "Are you quite serious?"

They sat on stone benches in the courtyard between the La Jolla mansion's front door and the gate to the outside world. Surrounded by the brightly colored flowers which climbed trellises around them, warmed by glorious early summer sun from the blue sky above, and occasionally buzzed by tiny hummingbirds which sought nectar, they were secluded in a private paradise which Laurence was all too aware that Freddy owned. The irony of not letting the landlord inside the house wasn't lost on him, and he doubted it was lost on Freddy, either, but Freddy hadn't complained about Laurence's rule.

The complaint was Laurence's, and it came the moment Freddy sat his ass on a bench and told them one of his two 'presents' for them was a full, grown-ass human being, waiting in Freddy's car out on the street.

"A butler," Freddy repeated. "Don't fret, dear boy, I've vetted him thoroughly. He's exceptionally suited to this household."

"Why? Is he psychic?" Laurence scowled. "Goddess, dude, did you find a random psychic and convince him he's a butler now?"

"Don't be so ridiculous." Freddy's drawl was in full force, which just meant that he was fully convinced he was in the right. "Icky asked me for help finding domestic staff, and that is what I have done. He is not psychic, nor sorcerous. He's simply an excellent, well-trained, professional butler. He'll be an asset to you."

Laurence rocked his jaw, then turned to face Quentin, to try and see whether he was alone in finding this super weird.

Quentin's face carried a faint frown, but his shoulders were relaxed.

Oh yeah. He thinks this is normal, Laurence realized.

He was on his own with this one.

"I did ask," Quentin agreed. "This is very kind of you Fred, but I didn't expect it."

"Right, but I thought we were just looking for a maid," Laurence blurted. "Someone to help keep the place clean, maybe cook now and then."

He could feel Freddy's shit-eating grin even before he turned back to face it.

"Is your problem that a butler is traditionally male, whereas a maid is traditionally female?" Freddy cooed.

The heat that rose to Laurence's cheeks came from more than just the sunlight, and he gripped Quentin's hand to remind himself not to punch Freddy while his brother was looking. "Don't be an ass. My problem is that you've gone and arranged all this for us and we don't even get to meet the guy first."

"That is what makes it a present, yes," Freddy agreed. "And the second gift which I promised you is here." He reached into the inner pocket of his pale cream jacket and withdrew an envelope, which he held toward Laurence between two fingers.

It had to be a spell. Freddy told Laurence weeks ago that he'd found it in a book, but he hadn't had time to stop off in San Diego back when he'd arrived in the US. He'd come to oversee the lawyers handling the defense of Delaney and the Marlowes, and it had been almost two months before he was able to leave Arizona and pay Laurence a visit.

Laurence bit his lip briefly, then slipped free of Quentin's hand to cross the courtyard and take the envelope. Hummingbirds zipped away quickly at his sudden movement, but didn't take long to come back again.

Freddy smiled faintly as he dropped his hand to his lap. "The initial version I found was in Latin, but that was very short-term, intended for use as and when required. But this version is to be... what's the word? Anchored to an item? Imbued? It's a much more elegant solution, but it's in an archaic form of German, so I have included pronunciation notes for you."

"You speak ancient German," Laurence muttered as he withdrew to his seat and felt the weight of the envelope in his hand.

"I speak whatever languages I can scoop out of the minds of anyone nearby," Freddy chuckled. "Finding an expert was not difficult."

Laurence tried not to let his teeth grind together too loudly. "Where'd you even get this? From your dad?"

"Heavens, no. I wouldn't piss on his library if it was on fire.

No, I made an acquaintance in London with a collection of his own. Don't worry, I had his permission."

"What is it?" The disdain in Quentin's voice was all too easy for Laurence to detect.

"It does magically what I do the hard way." Freddy gestured toward the envelope. "Allows the user to comprehend and communicate in any language."

Laurence blinked and held his breath a few seconds while he let himself work through the ramifications, but ultimately they were obvious.

He'd just been handed the key to Rufus' whole library.

Did it matter who Freddy got it from, or even how? Was it remotely okay to use this spell, or would Ru kick him out the moment he detected it?

Was it dark magic?

"I met a fellow who required translation assistance," Freddy continued, as though aware of all of Laurence's concerns, despite being unable to read his thoughts. "His situation was pressing, and so I chose to aid him until I found a spell within his very obviously stolen collection which would allow him to read them himself. I later found another, which would make the spell permanent on an external item, as with your talismans." He nodded toward the pentagram-laced thong around Laurence's left wrist.

Laurence didn't detect so much as a whiff of a lie. Without Freddy inside his head to distort his perception, he felt able to rely on his senses, but there was nothing to suggest that Freddy was embellishing the truth. No hesitation, no pupillary response, no unusual eye movements or body language.

If Freddy was lying, it was a lie he believed.

"And he just let you go through his spell books?"

"He had no choice," Freddy murmured. "And in return for my aid I have gained a local ally should Father decide to try to kill me again. This—" his hand gestured gently toward the envelope "—is simply an olive branch to you."

"This and a butler." Laurence sighed.

"Yes, indeed." Freddy eased to his feet and hopped lightly up the steps toward the gate, then placed his hand on it and turned to face Laurence with a grin. "Come along. You should meet him."

Laurence groaned to himself and looked to Quentin, but Quentin was already up on his feet. He likely would have offered his hand to Laurence, too, if Laurence wasn't holding a spell, so Laurence stood and tucked it into a pocket in his shorts.

"Fine," he said. "Let's do this."

LAURENCE DIDN'T KNOW what he'd expected. A middle-aged balding guy, maybe. Or an old one on his last legs, like poor Higson, still working for Quentin's dad even though he looked at least eighty.

The man who stepped out of the back of Freddy's waiting car was neither. Hell, he was barely into his twenties. He was tall and slim and handsome, with chestnut-brown hair that was slicked into the sharpest side-part Laurence had ever seen short of Quentin's own hair, and deep blue eyes the color of the ocean. He still dressed like a butler though, with a tailored black suit and pristine white gloves which he promptly clasped together in front of himself as he bowed politely.

On the damn sidewalk.

Laurence felt his blush return. There was no stopping it. Goddess, was this what life was going to be like from now on?

The Brits were invading his whole life.

"Martin Flynn," Freddy said by way of introduction. He didn't introduce Laurence and Quentin *to* Flynn, though, which Laurence figured must mean the butler already knew who they were.

It seemed creepy, but then anyone who followed him on social media knew as well. It took some getting used to.

"Lord Banbury," Martin began.

"Can I just stop you right there?" Laurence crossed his arms and lightly — almost coincidentally — nudged Quentin with his elbow in the process to stop him falling into any kind of traditional earl role right off the bat. "I'm not comfortable with these levels of formality. You can call me Laurence. Do you have luggage with you?"

To his credit, Martin didn't bat an eyelid. "I do, sir."

"Great. Bring it in, we'll find a room for you."

"Certainly, sir."

Laurence gave Freddy the stink-eye the moment Martin turned away, but he eased an arm around Quentin's. "Help Martin with his stuff," he said to Freddy. "We'll figure it out from there. Goddess, Freddy, what were you thinking?"

"I was thinking that you need staff," Freddy said without any sign of apology at all. "Go, shoo. I'll get the poor boy situated."

The urge to reach out and throttle Freddy where he stood was strong, so Laurence turned away and steered Quentin back inside. He left the gate open even though Freddy had his own keys, because slamming it shut on their new butler seemed really rude.

Almost as rude as springing a total stranger onto their whole house in the first place.

"Darling?" Quentin breathed it softly as they stepped over the threshold and into the cool interior of the house. "If you don't want him here, we can simply say so."

Laurence felt his eye twitch. Was he the only person around here who thought Viscounts turning up out of the blue with butlers to insert into a household was weird?

One look at Quentin assured him that the answer to that question was 'yes.'

He sighed and tried to let go of his frustration, but this one might take him a while, so he shook his head. "Nah. He's flown all the way here from London. It probably took a while to arrange work visas and whatever. The least we can do is try this out for a while and see if it works for us, and for the kids."

Quentin inclined his head, then leaned in to brush his lips against Laurence's cheek. "I concur," he murmured. "Frederick should have forewarned us. Sought our permission. But I don't have the wherewithal to fight him on this."

Laurence bit the inside of his cheek and watched Quentin a while.

He looked defeated, like he'd already decided this wasn't worth arguing over and that his limited energies were better spent elsewhere.

They probably were.

Laurence sighed and slid an arm around Quentin's waist to hold him close for a moment, to reassure him that his choice was the right one, and then he stepped back. "Do you want to go sit down? I'll sort this out then come find you."

"Would you mind?"

"Hey, if you find Freddy's head on a spike out in the courtyard, don't blame me." Laurence smiled gently at him and traced fingers along his jaw, then stepped aside so that Quentin could run for cover.

Whatever torture the Marlowes had inflicted on Quen had left him so subdued that he had to pick his battles with care, and Laurence had no intention of letting anything drain those energy levels. He could handle Freddy, and Martin, and whatever else the world threw at them until Quentin was back on his feet properly.

Laurence considered Freddy's behavior as Quen vanished into the house. While there was no way Freddy could read any of the Marlowes' minds, he could definitely read Delaney's, and Laurence had no doubt whatsoever that he would have done. Freddy couldn't hesitate to get inside the thoughts and memories of everyone he met. It was like a compulsion, which Laurence at least understood, having met their vile excuse of a father. Laurence couldn't even begin to imagine what horrible memories Freddy might have seen.

Maybe Quentin wasn't the only twin who could use some therapy, though he doubted Freddy would accept any such suggestion.

He turned in time to meet Martin and Freddy at the door, and made a note to grab Freddy after to discuss Delaney. For now, his task was far more mundane: find a spare bedroom, install a butler into it, and somehow find a way to make it not weird.

He could deal with Freddy later.

2

LAURENCE

THE ONLY REMAINING UNOCCUPIED BEDROOM WITH ITS OWN EN suite bathroom was on the top floor, and Laurence supposed that was better than making Martin cross a hallway for a bath, even if it left him right at the top of the mansion. He suggested using the small elevator for Martin's suitcase, but Martin politely insisted on carrying it up the stairs himself, and wouldn't let Laurence do it for him.

This was going to take some getting used to, for sure.

He opened the door for Martin and gestured to the room, then grimaced as he quickly realized it was going to need fresh bedding, towels, toilet paper, and everything else necessary for basic levels of habitability.

"Ah, shit," he breathed. "I'm sorry. Freddy didn't give us any warning. I'll rustle up sheets and stuff." Laurence paused as yet more reality hit him. "You're gonna need keys."

"Lord d'Arcy provided me with a full set of keys to the property," Martin said as he wheeled his suitcase to a corner and slid the handle away. "If you have a vehicle available, I can take care of the room myself, sir."

"Can you, like, not call me 'sir'?" Laurence dipped his

hands into his pockets, and the envelope crinkled. "I don't think I'm comfortable with that. Laurence is fine."

"Certainly, Master Laurence—"

"Goddess, no!" There were several reasons that felt horribly wrong, and Laurence didn't want to think about any of them. "Just Laurence. Please."

"As you wish. Laurence." Martin smiled, and though it was reserved, it was genuine. If Laurence was wrecking butler protocol, Martin didn't seem to mind.

"Great. Thanks. And, um, what do you want to be called?"

"Mr. Flynn would be the traditional form of address," Martin advised without any hint of annoyance for Laurence's lack of expertise. "But it is entirely up to you."

Laurence wasn't sure he was happy with either the stiff formality *or* the implications of it being wholly his choice of what to call his butler, but he didn't have time to go further with it right this moment. "Do you mind if I leave you to unpack for now? I wanna catch Freddy before he disappears, then I'll be back to show you around the house and stuff." Laurence thumbed over his shoulder toward the door.

"I don't mind at all."

"Awesome." Laurence debated letting more words tumble out of his mouth, then he decided it was better to just do what he'd said he was going to and not dither around any longer.

He left Martin, made his way downstairs, and wondered how long this situation would last.

"Does being an asshole run in your family?"

Laurence heard Soraya's question before he'd even hopped off the bottom stair, and he picked up the pace in case he needed to defuse an argument.

"I would like to think that I am only a part-time arsehole," Quentin said gently.

"And Nicky isn't an arsehole in the slightest," Freddy said. "Honestly, I think most families would be quite satisfied with only a fifty percent arsehole contingent."

"Fifty percent suggests it's a dominant gene, though," Laurence said as he slowed down to saunter into the living room. "If it was recessive, it'd skip a generation now and then."

Soraya clicked her tongue and pointed finger guns toward him. "See, Florist Dad knows what's up."

Quentin, Laurence noted, had placed himself in an armchair. It was his preferred way of ensuring that nobody sat next to him so that he didn't have unintended physical contact with anyone he didn't want to, and Windsor had even settled on the chair back like an omen of doom to warn interlopers away. Freddy, naturally, had settled on one end of a couch instead, and Soraya and Kim were squeezed together down the other end of it, which meant Freddy had chosen to join them instead of pick an unoccupied seat. Mia loomed like a shadow with her back to the windows and her arms crossed while she stared daggers at the back of Freddy's head.

Clifton and Felipe were at work, Estelita was at school, and Lisa was at the farm, so at least Freddy's unannounced arrival hadn't attracted the entire household.

Laurence stepped over Pepper's sprawled body and hoped she wasn't going to leap to her feet while he was halfway over her, but all she did was open an eye and wag her tail briefly at him before she dozed off again.

"I don't know how I feel about 'Florist Dad'," Laurence chuckled. He perched on the arm of Quentin's chair and rested his hands on one knee, and Windsor hopped over to land on his shoulder. "What does that make Quen?"

"Asshole Dad," Soraya said without missing a beat.

Quentin's lips quirked into a faint smile. "It could be worse."

If Quentin wasn't offended by it, Laurence wasn't going to white knight on his behalf, even though he wasn't convinced 'Asshole Dad' was either fair or acceptable.

"Soraya, Kim, do you mind if British Dad and I talk to Freddy without a peanut gallery for a few minutes?"

Soraya and Kim exchanged a look, then Kim slid off the couch and took Soraya's hand. "Okay."

"Sure," Soraya said. "But you figure out how to tell Lisa there's a stranger in this house, or I'll tell her my way."

"I'll take care of it," Quentin said.

Soraya relaxed at his promise, and the teens nodded to Laurence on their way out the door, but Laurence tilted his head so he could listen to their retreating footsteps and make sure they weren't lingering to eavesdrop. Not that he could stop Soraya from poking her nose in once they were upstairs in their room anyway.

He huffed to himself then faced Freddy. "She's right, you know. What were you thinking?"

Freddy sprawled slightly, splaying one arm out across the back of the couch and crossing his legs. "I was thinking that you had a business to run, Icky had a kidnapping to recover from, and Mia is not your skivvy. Therefore I took it upon myself to perform a time-consuming task to save you the trouble."

"It's not the effort which is unappreciated," Quentin murmured.

"Right. It's the whole turning up out of the blue with an entire person and expecting us to drop everything to find him a place. Couldn't you have given us a choice? Some warning?" Laurence patted his curls back from his face and tried not to lose his shit at Freddy, but there had to be some way to make him see that his constant inability to view other people as anything other than toys was really fucking rude. "You've got to stop thinking you're the center of the universe, man."

Freddy's grey eyes lingered on Laurence a while before he spoke, and when he finally did, it was without any trace of humor he might normally try to inject. "You're right. I have stood my ground against Father alone for so long that I am unaccustomed to..." His fingers flexed briefly while he searched for a word.

"Empathy," Quentin supplied. "You did everything that you could to survive. But you're beyond that now. You have the opportunity to thrive instead, and for that we must recognize and accept that we are not islands."

Laurence kept his features neutral. This wasn't the time to gush with pride over not only how far Quentin had come, or his bottomless pit of kindness in spite of everything he'd been through. Laurence was surrounded by Brits, and they weren't into that kind of emotiveness.

He'd save it for later.

Freddy slumped dramatically against the arm of the couch, rolling his eyes and releasing a sigh of deep, faux ennui at the same time, and he let his head loll to one side as though Quentin's words were a deep, personal attack on his very nature. "I suppose."

Mia shifted her hands to her hips and raised her chin toward Freddy, but if she had a scathing comment brewing, she kept it to herself. Laurence could almost feel her desire to electrocute Freddy and be done with him from all the way across the room, though.

"So what do we do?" Laurence decided to steer the conversation away from feelings — where neither of the twins were particularly literate — and back onto the matter at hand. "He lives here now? He gets time off, right? Does he need a car? What does he even do?"

Freddy righted himself and ran a hand through his sleek

yellow hair. "Hours traditionally are six in the morning until six or seven in the evening, but unless on holiday, he is considered to be on call at all times. He'll provide you with his phone number so that you can text him for anything you need. You can discuss the hours you require him to work directly." He let his hand fall to the arm of the couch. "He should be the first point of contact for anyone reaching the house, whether by phone or at the door. He'll take care of your food and household shopping, prepare meals, lay tables, and clean up after. He'll launder and iron clothing. And, should you hire further staff, he'll manage them too. Do be sure to give him a tour of the house and let him know if any rooms are off-limits to him."

"Right." Laurence was almost overwhelmed with the deluge of information, and the ways in which it was going to impact his life. He remembered Quentin once making some comment about living without a butler on hand, but Laurence had chalked it up to one more way in which Quentin was out of touch with reality.

Now, instead, it was Laurence who was out of touch with Quentin's reality. Just like flying first class or living in a mansion, having someone running around after Laurence to tidy and clean and cook and do all the other things he should be able to do for himself was weird, and he didn't know whether it was something he wanted to get used to.

"Okay," he added, trying to push it all aside for now. "Fine. So what's happening with the Marlowes and Delaney?"

"It's delicate work, but there is progress." Freddy followed the change of subject smoothly. "I have no doubt that the Marlowes will be released soon enough."

"And Delaney?" Mia prompted.

"I'm working on him."

"On freeing him, you mean," Mia said.

"Absolutely." Freddy rose from the couch and straightened

his jacket. "Now if you'll excuse me, I must crack on. Michael is waiting." He cast a glance to Laurence and made eye contact. "I'll see myself out," he added.

He wanted Laurence to go with him. Laurence wasn't a telepath, and he wore a talisman to keep Freddy out of his head, but his own instincts made it clear as day that Freddy's words were at odds with his intent.

Laurence debated, then his curiosity won out, and he stood. "Nah, man, gotta make sure you actually leave, right?"

Freddy clicked his tongue. "Really?"

Laurence went along with it, and steered Freddy out of the living room with a hand against his back. He led all the way to the front door and out into the courtyard, where Freddy paused to don sunglasses.

"Okay. Spit it out."

"Cameron Delaney witnessed a great deal of what Katharine Marlowe did to Icky," Freddy said, his voice so quiet that only Laurence could hear him.

Laurence licked his lips, then realized what Freddy was implying.

He *had* checked out Delaney's memories.

Was he offering Laurence that information, or explaining why he hadn't arranged for Delaney's freedom yet? There was no way for Laurence to ask that question without the potential for Soraya nosing in on them with her gifts, and Freddy knew it too or he wouldn't be dancing around his point like this.

Laurence gnawed briefly on the inside of his cheek, then nodded. "We should catch up sometime. Text me when you're free."

"I shall. Take care."

Laurence saw him out the gate and made sure it locked after Freddy was gone, then made his way back down the steps to the courtyard and mulled the fresh information over.

He thought he wanted to know what Kathy had done, but now he had the chance, did he really need that information, or would it just make him angry? But if it was worth his anger, it was worth him knowing the truth first, so that he knew exactly what to be angry about.

Right?

He was the Hunter, and if he didn't hunt under his own control it would take him over. If he could sate his need with a hunt for the truth, maybe that would be enough for a while.

Satisfied with his decision, he stepped back into the mansion, and closed the door.

3

MYRIAM

MYRIAM WASN'T SURE WHETHER HER GIFTS WERE BECOMING sharper now that Bambi was in near-constant trouble, or if it was simply that she was listening to them more now that the future she'd spent so long trying not to derail had finally come to pass. Whichever it was, she'd begun to view her instincts not so much as serendipity and more like the remnants of Herne in her veins, guiding her in more subtle but no less powerful ways than they steered her son.

So when the urgent sense came that she needed to retreat into the back room of the Jack in the Green, despite being mid-conversation with a customer, she paid attention.

The joy of being a middle-aged woman speaking to other middle-aged women was, of course, that she could subtly imply a bladder emergency as she steered Ethan in to replace her, and her customers would rush her to the bead curtain as though she were a patient surrounded by paramedics.

She idly checked that the pendants Bambi had given her were still hanging from the thong around her neck, as though they might have fallen off, but no. They was still there.

Although Myriam couldn't see the magic imbued into them, she knew what they did.

Most protected her from magic, but the one her fingers had rested on was the one which specifically protected her from telepathy, and that meant she knew who was in the car which pulled into the alley behind the shop before he got out of it.

There was no sense of warning in her gut, but that didn't mean she had to be thrilled about the unannounced visit.

Myriam filled the kettle and switched it on, then fetched cups and milk. By the time the back door opened, she had distributed tea bags and returned the milk to the fridge, so that she was free to face her visitor with all the hostility that he deserved.

"How dare you come here."

Freddy closed the door behind himself. At least he had the good sense to leave Mikey out in the alley, but Myriam cast the drug dealer a withering stare anyway. Hiding behind the wheel of the car wasn't going to save him.

"I owe you an apology," Freddy murmured.

"You used your gifts to make me think that you were Quentin, and then you kidnapped my son, right here in my own shop." Myriam poured water into teacups and then stirred each one in turn, wondering for just one moment what it might be like if she was the one who could set things on fire with her mind.

It was probably for the best that she couldn't.

"I'm sorry." Freddy didn't come any further into the room. Instead, he lingered by the door like a bad smell. "I have excuses, of course, but none of them are remotely valid. Suffice it to say that I would like to make amends."

"For kidnapping my son," she said, glancing up at him. If she could make him see just how absolutely outrageous that sounded, maybe he had a chance at improving himself.

"I don't expect it to be an easy path," he admitted. "I don't anticipate forgiveness, to be honest." Freddy's gaze slid away from her and out of the window, to the car outside, and then he took a breath. "I don't consider myself to be a good person, Mrs. Riley. However, I would like to try to be a better one than I have been in the past." He tore his eyes from the outside world and set them on her again with a soft frown. "I can't promise to be any good at it, of course, but—"

Myriam fished tea bags out of the mugs, then thrust one into his hands. "Stop talking and take this out front to Ethan."

Freddy took it graciously and disappeared through the curtain without argument, which gave Myriam time to take her own mug to the table and perch on a stool. She used the movements, the space, to settle herself and smooth over the anger which ruffled her feathers at his bald-faced arrogance.

He hadn't even knocked, or otherwise asked for permission to enter.

She sighed and sipped her tea, even though it was almost too hot to drink. It helped her focus her thoughts, and by the time Freddy returned empty-handed, she'd reached a clearer idea of where to go from here.

"In that cupboard behind you — the one above the fridge, that's the one — there is a tarot deck. Bring it here, please."

Freddy's eyebrows lifted, but he did as he was asked, and he leaned across the table to set the deck down in front of her.

"Sit down."

He did.

Myriam had much more experience with time through the medium of tarot than she did without. Bambi had learned to conjure up visions of past and future alike, and he could see them as clearly as if he were there in person, but that had never been Myriam's way. No, the tarot was clear enough for her, and it had never failed her.

She slid the deck out of the pack and passed it to Freddy.

"Shuffle them, and think about what you hope to get out of coming here today."

"Very well." Freddy's large hands moved the cards with ease, and Myriam noted that he had no hesitation in performing several skilled riffle shuffles as part of his process.

He had more than a little experience in handling cards, then. Most likely playing cards, and probably while reading his opponents' thoughts to take all the risk out of any games.

Myriam kept her observation to herself. Freddy had made it more than clear that he was highly risk-averse. Coming here, knowing that he couldn't get inside her mind, but asking for her benevolence all the same was a big step for him, but that wasn't enough for her to forgive. It was barely enough for her to even listen to what he had to say.

"Cut the deck, and then deal four cards, please, in whatever direction or arrangement you would like."

Four cards was ideal. It would allow her to divine some clarity from Freddy's intentions, as well as offer some advice on where exactly he should stick them.

Freddy quirked an eyebrow in a gesture so like his twin that — even though they looked so dissimilar — it was obvious they were two peas in a pod in more ways than Myriam might like to admit to herself sometimes. "All right."

He laid them in a straight line, from his left to his right, with extremely precise placement that set them all in a perfectly aligned row with one inch between each one, and he set the rest of the deck to his right and pursed his lips. Then he reached for the third card and hovered his hand over it uncertainly.

Myriam could see the problem right away. With how neat and efficient Freddy was in everything that he did, and how obsessed he was over controlling every aspect of his life, having two reversed cards in his spread — the third and fourth — likely bothered him.

"They aren't upside down," she said before he could make up his mind to rotate the cards. "The direction they face is as relevant as what's on them."

He eyed her, then retracted his hand and inclined his head. "I see."

She nodded, satisfied that he wasn't about to fiddle with the layout, and turned her attention to his cards. They *were* upside down to her, but that was hardly a problem. She was used to doing readings for querents across a table.

Four of Pentacles, Queen of Cups, Ten of Swords, and Nine of Wands, with the latter two reversed.

On the surface, there was nothing surprising present, but Myriam's task — and the task of any good reader — was to see beyond the obvious, to interpret the cards as a whole rather than their individual parts. A beginner looked at the usual meanings of each card, but an experienced reader absorbed the very art of the cards themselves. Myriam had chosen her deck — with its vibrant colors and meaningful floral designs — and she was intimately familiar with it, but every spread and every situation was unique.

So what *did* Freddy hope to get out of coming to see her today?

The Four of Pentacles could have misled another reader, but not Myriam. Her gifts combined fluently with tarot and she was attuned to her instincts. Its presence here was not about wealth, though Freddy certainly had plenty of that. No. Here, it was about control, and his need to micromanage everyone in his life, because it interacted with the Queen of Cups so neatly. The roses on this card were not about the thorns, but the way some gardeners would over-prune them.

"You must be more aware of your obsession with controlling those around you," Myriam murmured, letting herself vocalize the cards only once she was certain herself. "It will hold you back in what you need to achieve in life. And what you need might not necessarily be what you think you want, but you know that." She tapped the Queen of Cups. "You care deeply, but you need to learn to embrace your empathy, your compassion, rather than hiding it away like a guilty secret, if you really want to move forward." Her hand moved on to the Ten of Swords. "You're resisting those feelings because you are afraid of losing control, but you have to let go of that fight, or you will never grow into who you want to become. You have clung to your suffering for too long. Release it."

Myriam pursed her lips faintly and tried not to frown as the truth of her own words resonated deep within her very core. It was a stark reminder that, for all the animosity she bore toward him, she really had no idea about his upbringing or his circumstances, or how they had affected him. She only saw what he wanted her to.

He *wanted* people to see that he was an asshole.

Myriam clicked her tongue and dipped her fingers to the Nine of Wands. "It's going to be difficult. You will suffer setbacks that make you question time and again whether your efforts are worthwhile, whether your goal is attainable. You are resilient and you are brave, and you must draw on both aspects of yourself to persist if you are to succeed." Finally, she looked up at him, and added, "And get therapy."

Freddy's expression was unreadable. He had mastered the art of resting vacant face, as though the whole outside world was less interesting than the one that existed between his ears. "Do the cards say that, or is that an added extra?"

Myriam laughed and drank some of her tea before she responded. "The cards heavily suggest it; I'm only putting into words what they say. And they say you need to deal with your trauma."

At that, Freddy scoffed and shuffled the cards back into the deck, then reached for the box and eased them back into it for her. "What trauma?"

Myriam shrugged and watched him. His deflection was easy to spot, in part because Quentin did it so often, too. The boys had learned the same coping strategies, it seemed.

"I don't know. The trauma of seeing your brother hurting so often, with no way for you to stop it or to make it better. Or the trauma of knowing that everyone around you thinks one thing but says another. The trauma of being away when your mother died, of finding out second-hand. The created paradigm whereby if you control everyone and everything around you, none of it can hurt you." She sipped her tea slowly to give Freddy a small break from her flensing the armor from his wounds. "You cannot have forgiveness unless you do the work."

Freddy rose to his feet. It wasn't a swift, angry motion. Instead it was slow and calm.

Controlled.

Myriam wasn't fooled.

"Thank you for your time, Mrs. Riley," he murmured.

"You kidnapped my son," she said bluntly. "You played with our minds and our hearts. Now you bring my son's dealer to my door, and you ask what it will take to make amends." Myriam set her empty mug down on the table and stared up at him. "A lot, Freddy. It's going to take a lot. If it's what you really want, you'll do it. But if you give up, if you decide that the hill is too steep for you to climb, it's over. Do I make myself clear?"

Freddy gazed down at her, and a muscle twitched in his jaw, but then he bowed his head slightly.

"Perfectly," he said.

"Good. Now get out of my shop."

He left without another word, and Ethan promptly appeared through the curtains, carrying his own mug.

"Well," he said.

Myriam took a deep breath, and let her animosity flow from her with the air that she exhaled until it was gone, and she was herself again. That was not a feeling she wished to carry inside herself, because it would only attract more.

"Well, indeed," she said. She was grateful for Ethan's simple reminder to let go of her negativity and return to work, regardless of whether or not that was what he meant to do.

What we imagine, we create.

Perhaps if Myriam imagined a better Freddy, she could manifest one.

She snorted at herself. Ten minutes in his presence and she'd already started to think that she could change other people to suit herself. His very existence was a danger, and he was an agent of chaos, despite all his attempts at control.

Chaos was neither good nor evil. It was simply nature. But that didn't mean she wanted to embrace it.

Only time would tell how this was going to play out.

4

QUENTIN

QUENTIN HAD NO DESIRE TO DEAL WITH THE FUSS OF GETTING A butler settled in, and Laurence had already volunteered himself for that task. That meant that Quentin was able to retreat for the rest of the afternoon — or at least until Estelita came home. It was only fair that he explain the new situation to her before she bumped into Flynn in the hallway, though he suspected that Soraya had already sent a furious flurry of text messages.

Better to be safe than sorry.

He switched into jogging bottoms and a t-shirt and then shut himself away in the gym, where he could run mindlessly on a treadmill for half an hour or so. It was meditative, allowing thoughts to come and go without the need for them to be addressed or solved in any way.

Violeta, his therapist, had suggested that his renewed fixation on his fitness —and particularly his drive to practice Aikido more diligently — was a coping strategy.

He disagreed. He needed to do better, to *be* better, if he was to defend himself or — heaven forbid — protect Laurence or the children. He couldn't assume that the Marlowes were alone in their abilities.

He was the Warrior, and he'd failed.

Some days, that didn't weigh so heavily on his shoulders. Violeta was right: it was not his fault, and life was not fair. He had been outmatched, and that was that.

Other days, he knew that he simply wasn't good enough, and he needed to accept his narrow escape for the warning that it was.

It was difficult, trying to remember that only one of those statements was true. The whispering doubt which plagued him was so deeply rooted in his childhood that it was hard to close the door on. Violeta wanted to begin a different type of therapy to address that, something she called EMDR, but their goal in the short term had been tightly focused on diagnosis and on helping Quentin to deal with being tortured half to death, so he dealt with the ridiculous self-esteem days as and when they came. Each and every one was noted diligently on his phone and confessed to as soon as he next saw Violeta.

He heard the door open, and it drew him sharply out of his thoughts and back into the room in time to see Soraya close the door after herself. She, too, had switched into clothing suitable for the gym, though she had the facility to wear shorts, whereas he did not.

Quentin nodded to her, then returned his attention to thin air while she hopped up onto the treadmill beside him.

That was unusual. She usually favored more distance.

"I'm sorry I called you Asshole Dad," she said once she'd started a light, warm-up walk. "You're not an asshole. You didn't deserve that."

He considered telling her that it was all right, or that he didn't mind. Those were the British responses, the ones he'd had ingrained into him his entire life. But he'd learned a lot since he'd met Laurence, and one of the things he'd learned was not to reject compliments or apologies so swiftly.

Instead, he glanced to her and inclined his head. "Thank you."

He continued to run while she warmed up, and she didn't speak again until she, too, was jogging.

"You just keep disappearing on us, you know?"

Quentin nodded again. "I know. I apologize."

Every absence was unavoidable, but she was eighteen years old and she'd already lost her family. Every time he failed to return home in a timely manner had to be distressing for her, no matter how much she tried to act as though she didn't need anyone else.

He knew all too well what it was like to lose a parent at her age.

"I care about you, okay?" Soraya huffed at him and jabbed at her treadmill to make it go faster. "And I've been worried about you. You need a vacation."

Quentin gave a wry smile at the suggestion. "My life is a holiday. I don't work, I have glorious sunshine almost all year round, and I play the piano every day. Where would I go from there?"

He heard her sniff. "Disneyland," she said.

He glanced across to her. "I'm sorry?"

Soraya rolled her eyes and had to grab at the handrails on her treadmill to keep from falling off it. "Oh come on, you must know what Disneyland is."

"In Paris?" Quentin blinked.

"Anaheim! Near Los Angeles," she added when he didn't answer.

"Oh." He supposed that made more sense than flying to Paris for a theme park, though he didn't really have a great deal of experience with such things. He assumed that if one were more invested in cartoon mice with strangely large ears they might be appealing, but he had only seen a small handful of Disney films, and only within the last year. They were the sort of thing Laurence usually deemed safe for Quentin to watch, which made Quentin worry about what was in the films Laurence determined to be unsafe.

But Soraya was American, and younger than Quentin, and perhaps she had the investment that he lacked.

He glanced across to her and caught the hopeful look in her eyes, then laughed softly. "Would *you* like to go to Disneyland?"

"I mean, I guess?" She raised her chin like it was an afterthought to her, but she wasn't fooling anyone. "Like, someone's gotta keep you out of trouble, right?"

"I see." Quentin laughed again, then shook his head faintly. "If you wish to go, ask the others if they would like to come, too, and then work out a date which suits you all."

"All right!" Soraya punched the air and grinned. "Do we get to stay in a hotel?"

"If you wish."

"Sweet! Thanks!" She hit the emergency stop on her treadmill and bounced off it. "I better go and, like, organize this thing!"

Quentin watched as she darted off out of the gym, and was still smiling faintly to himself when Laurence came in.

"Hey baby." Laurence sauntered over and draped his arm over the handrail so that he could grin up at Quentin. "Soraya's running around telling everyone who'll listen that you're taking them to Disneyland?"

"Mmm." He chuckled and idly rested a hand over Laurence's arm. It skewed his gait off balance, but he could handle it. "She came bearing an apology for calling me an arsehole, which was a thinly-veiled cover for suggesting a holiday. For my own good, of course."

"Of course," Laurence laughed. "So what's the deal?"

"Soraya will arrange a date and let me know who is interested, and then I'll make sure that it happens." Quentin slowed the treadmill down so that he could begin cooling off. "I'll speak to Myriam about taking care of the dogs while we're gone."

"I don't mind staying behind if I can't get the time off work," Laurence said.

Quentin eyed him, but Laurence's expression was sincere, and Quentin had to push down the sudden stab of worry that suggested that Laurence didn't want to go with him.

"Hey." Laurence grinned and leaned over to press soft lips against the back of Quentin's hand. "Stop it. I'd love to go. But I've got work, and it's okay for you to take some time out with the kids if I can't make it." He paused, then rested his other elbow on the handrail and his chin in his hand, giving Quentin his best sultry eyes.

They really were *very* good.

"You're super sexy when you're sweaty, you know."

Quentin burst out laughing and slowed to a halt with the treadmill. "You are terrible."

"Uh huh." Laurence pointed up at him. "But you can't deny it."

He opened his mouth and sucked in a breath to argue, then faltered. He really *couldn't* deny it. Part of accepting compliments was to actually accept them, no matter how much his brain liked to argue that his whole body made him the exact opposite of what Laurence claimed, and there was no denying the look in Laurence's eyes or the way he gladly tumbled into bed with Quentin the moment Quentin so much as hinted that he'd like to.

Instead, he reached for his towel and lightly patted his face dry, partially so that he could hide in the cotton for a few extra seconds. Once he was done, he met Laurence's look — which still waited for him, patient as ever — and dipped his head. "I cannot," he agreed. "It would be rude of me."

"That's right." Laurence stretched over to kiss him, and while the contact began lightly, it lingered and deepened until Laurence's fingers were in his hair, and Quentin's were coiled around Laurence's curls in return.

For now, his doubts and his fears were silenced.

It was moments like these in which he felt he glimpsed who he truly was, buried beneath all the layers of lies; some he told himself, others the world told for him. A burning core of humanity which shone bright when it was not smothered. He could inhabit himself without shame and be loved rather than reviled.

Laurence broke free and gasped for breath. His cheeks were as pink as his lips, his hair mussed and cascading over his forehead. He was wild and beautiful and perfect, and Quentin needed him.

"You wanna go be rude someplace else?" Laurence's voice came out husky and hopeful.

"I insist," Quentin answered.

They scrambled out of the gym in a race for the bedroom that was both playful and deadly serious at once, and the world ceased to exist once the door was locked behind them.

For now.

5

LAURENCE

The next morning, Laurence got up when Quentin did. He had two goals, and a bonus treat, except the bonus treat happened first. He ogled Quentin's ass while they got dressed, and it was so distracting he almost forgot the reason he'd leaped out of bed in the first place.

The first goal was to join Quentin for breakfast to see if he could get used to this whole butler thing.

It wasn't too unnerving, walking into the kitchen to find the table already set and a breakfast selection neatly arranged along the center. There was fruit, toast, jars of jam and honey, a couple cereal boxes, and a jug of water. Martin hadn't turned the table into an enormous medieval banquet.

"Good morning, Lord Banbury, Laurence," Martin greeted. "Would you like something hot?"

Laurence gently squeezed the tip of his tongue between his teeth as he sat down at the table. Quentin obviously hadn't given Martin the same instructions regarding desired lack of formality, but Laurence had to remind himself that Quen had gone straight to the gym while Laurence showed Martin around, and then they'd spent the time after that fucking like bunnies.

"Tea, please," Quentin murmured as he sat.

Laurence eyed him, then smiled to Martin. "Yeah, I'll take tea as well. Thanks."

Martin bobbed his head and switched the kettle on, then readied the teapot and poured milk from the fridge into a smaller jug suitable for the table.

It was still weird. It felt like his home had turned into a hotel, and Laurence patted his curls absently while he tried to deal with his discomfort.

Quentin clearly had no such problem. He helped himself to a slice of toast and a banana like all this was fine, and he rested a hand on Pepper's head while she in turn rested her head on his thigh to stare adoringly up at his toast.

"You're up early, darling," Quentin prompted, looking Laurence in the eye.

His question remained unspoken, which was super British of him, but Laurence had learned to speak British over the past year or so, and he laughed.

"Yeah, figured I'd get a head start. I want to read Freddy's letter, make sure it's nothing crazy."

Great, now he had to dance around sensitive subjects in his own home.

Quentin simply nodded. "And if it is not?"

Laurence shrugged. "I guess I'll go along with it. It's worth a shot. But I might run it past Angela first, get a second pair of eyes on it."

The teapot appeared on the table as if by magic. Martin placed teacups by their plates, then backed away to give them space, and Quentin automatically reached out to pour the tea for Laurence and then himself.

"That seems reasonable," Quentin murmured. "Will you be home late, do you think?"

"Possibly?" Laurence grabbed an apple and took a bite. "I owe Ru a favor, and I figure it's probably time I repaid him. It's not gonna be pleasant, but..." He shrugged. "I knew that when I made the deal, and I think I'm in a place right now where I can handle it."

He knew Quentin understood him from the soft set of his eyebrows, the slight press of his lips as he regarded Laurence. The worry was subtle but clear.

"So long as you are certain?"

"Yeah." Laurence raised his chin. "I'm ready as I'll ever be. Things are quiet. I'll just get it over with and then it won't be hanging over my head any more."

Quentin set down his half-finished toast and wiped his fingers on a napkin so that he could then reach out and take Laurence's hand, and he squeezed Laurence's fingers gently. "All right. And you'll call me if you need anything?"

"I will." Laurence raised Quentin's hand and kissed his knuckles, then grinned. "Anyway, what're you gonna do while I'm having all the fun?"

"I'll walk the girls, and then Mr. Flynn and I can sit down and go through some basic scheduling and administration together. After that, who knows?" Quentin's lips twitched into a small smile as he gazed at Laurence.

"Yeah, yeah, you're gonna bask by the pool all day, I know it baby." Laurence grinned and ate more of his apple. "Work on that tan of yours."

Quentin scoffed and withdrew his fingers so that he could go back to forcing food into his mouth. "Absurd."

Laurence laughed and drank his tea. He could pass the rest of breakfast by teasing Quentin and still have plenty of time for magic before he had to leave for work.

He could almost forget Martin was even there.

Sooner or later, Laurence would have to figure out how to introduce the existence of an illegal not-a-pet-raven to Martin, but for now he was grateful that Windsor took his new role seriously — or as seriously as Win was able to take things, at least — and was flying high above Quentin to make sure Laurence knew if anything bad happened. He could touch base with his familiar or look through his eyes if necessary, and Windsor would alert him to any danger Quentin might get himself into. Likewise, if it was Laurence in trouble, Windsor could yell at Quentin about it. That was the theory, anyway. Laurence really hoped it never got put into practice.

He headed to his sanctum at the top of the house and shut himself inside, taking a moment to lock the door so that nobody could barge in and interrupt his work.

This room wasn't ideal for his needs, but it was the best he could do right now, and it was better than nothing. There wasn't much here that could upset Quentin; he kept any spell books in his old apartment, over the shop. His sanctum was mostly for prayer or meditation, not magic.

More than other spaces in the mansion, the sanctum was home to an abundance of plants in large pots, and it smelled of earth and fresh growth. Laurence took the time to check each plant was healthy, dip a finger in the soil and top up any that needed water, and to attune himself to the energy of the space he was in before he began to cleanse it.

The atmosphere was subdued today. Gentle, at rest, as though it were happy to bask in the warmth of summer and enjoy the life that it brought. It made Laurence smile as he settled cross-legged before his altar.

Once he was comfortable, he took the lighter from on top of his personal grimoire and lit the candles, then he picked up a bundle of dried sage which had already been burned and extinguished countless times before. He held the blackened ends over a flame until they caught, blew them out again, and gently passed the lightly-smoking sticks back and forth to cleanse any remaining negative energy from his space. With that done, he set the sage down in his offerings dish and used his athame to cast a circle around himself.

Finally, he set the athame down beside the raven feather on his altar and rested his hands on his knees.

"Beloved ancestor," he murmured. "Master of the wild hunt, king of the forest, lord of ravens, I offer you my sacrifice. I ask for your wisdom." He smiled slightly, and added, "Mighty Herne, I hear your hounds throughout the ancient woods. All of nature sings your name, as you nurture it in return."

Laurence allowed his eyes to drift closed when it felt right, and fell silent, inhaling the sage-tinged air and releasing it through parted lips.

"Bambi," Herne rumbled warmly, his deep voice enveloping Laurence like an old, familiar blanket. "Merry meet."

His eyes drifted open to an ancient forest, the vast oaks towering overhead and the air fresh and unsullied by pollution. Rays of light streamed through the spaces between leaves, though Laurence knew there to be no sun.

"Merry meet," he said through a broad smile. "It's good to see you."

Herne laughed and offered Laurence his hand. "And you also, my child," he rumbled as he hauled Laurence to his feet and into a tight hug. He pulled Laurence clear off the forest floor for a few seconds, then set him down again and fondly patted his hair.

Laurence wheezed faintly as the enormous hand covered the top of his head.

"The veil weakens once more," Herne said as he crossed to

a log and sat down, patting it for Laurence to join him. "You were successful in your quest to rescue your lover."

"How—" Laurence broke off, and sat down on the log. He faced the god, whose antlers towered above them and yet never touched the trees, and groaned. "No, don't tell me."

He'd sent Windsor to ask Herne for help in how to track down Quentin after Marlowe took him, but Windsor hadn't gone back after to let Herne know everything was okay. He didn't need to. Herne could sense whether or not Laurence was at his peak, and since his peak required sex, the answer must have been obvious. Of course Laurence had reunited with Quentin, otherwise he wouldn't even be able to reach across the veil like this.

Herne chuckled. "There. You find truth."

"Yeah, yeah." Laurence smirked briefly, then his smile faded and he shook his head. "We got him back. He's not himself, but he's getting there, I think." He licked his lips. "Can I ask you something?"

"Of course."

The trouble with being in Otherworld like this was that Laurence was butt naked. Nothing could cross the veil with him unless it belonged to both worlds, so he couldn't show Herne the spell. Hell, Laurence hadn't even looked at it himself yet.

"How can you tell whether magic is bad?" He bit his lip, then leaned toward Herne and gazed up at him. "I've got one teacher who insists that the magic my other teacher used to find Quentin is dark, but she sees nothing bad about it. I've got a spell in my pocket which should let me understand any language, but I don't want to cast it if it's a warlock's spell. How do I know?"

Herne frowned and shifted to face Laurence more squarely. "Allow your instinct to guide you. You seek truth, and you will always find it. That is the way of the Hunter." He ran fingers through his beard, then added, "What was this magic?"

"She summoned a psychopomp and asked it to find Quen. She said they could find people from pictures, where most other beings can't." Laurence rested his elbows on his knees. "If she hadn't done it, he'd be dead. I can't overlook that. She paid him — Mu'ut, I mean. She paid him for his help."

Herne's lips pursed, and he lowered his hand to his own, thickly-furred knee. "I do not know of Mu'ut. The people whose souls he cares for, they are local to you in your world?"

Laurence nodded. "Yeah. Physically. But they're native to the continent I live on." He placed his hand against his own chest. "We're the settlers on their lands, from centuries ago."

Herne smiled. "And you share their lands with them?"

"Uh. Not really. Not at all." Laurence winced. "The settlers brought disease with them and the local people didn't have any resistance to that disease, so it tore through them. Then we kinda just went on a murder spree to try and finish the job. It wasn't a good time. The colonists almost wiped the native peoples out completely."

"Ah." Herne glanced up to the trees, to the score of ravens preening in the branches overhead and then he nodded. "Then you already know the answer, in your heart, do you not?"

Laurence jutted his lip out a little.

Herne was right.

"I think it's complicated," he sighed. "I watched her cast her spell, she paid Mu'ut for his help, but we still called on something that didn't belong to us, and I don't know whether the spell she used was a transaction he had any say in."

"And you don't know whether it pulled him away from his duties to the people to whom he does belong," Herne agreed. "The only way for you to know is to evaluate the spell and find out whether or not it was a bargain struck or chains imposed."

"Urgh." Laurence hung his head for a moment, then lifted it and took a deep breath. "And just ask Ru why he thinks it's dark in the first place. Thanks, I hate it."

Herne laughed and squeezed Laurence's shoulder. "You say that, but you do not. Not really." His dark eyes shone with affection. "We must part. The veil interferes. But we will speak again, my child."

"Okay." Laurence leaned across to hug him again, and barely managed to say, "Merry part," before he was back in his own body.

"Merry part, Bambi." Herne's words drifted to him from across the veil, like the last hints of burning sage on the air.

Laurence felt for the envelope in his pocket, but left it there. He had to get to work. After, he'd go see Rufus and ask his opinion.

And — finally — do the thing he'd promised a year ago.

He uncrossed his legs, stood up, and tried not to think about the car crash he was going to have to watch.

6

LAURENCE

"I THINK I'M READY."

Ru eyed him and paused what he was doing, and since what he was doing was handing Laurence a glass of water, he just stopped with his hand halfway between them and looked mildly annoyed.

Laurence couldn't blame him. After all this time, Ru was probably wanting to make real sure that he hadn't misheard.

"To look," Laurence clarified. "To try and find out who killed your parents." He licked his lips quickly. "If you're ready, too? Like, I don't want to dump this on you just because it's convenient for *me* right now. I can wait, if you don't want me to start yet."

He was half throwing Ru that lifeline, and half hoping Ru would take it for Laurence's sake.

Rufus flexed his jaw, then moved again, and the glass finally came close enough for Laurence to take. "If I wait, you'll get caught up in something else. Now is fine."

Laurence nodded and sipped his water to try and hide his disappointment.

He'd done this before, to try to work out who had killed

Quentin's mom, and all it led to was him watching helplessly as she collapsed of a heart attack in her own rose garden. It turned out the duke had used magic to kill her, but Laurence hadn't *seen* it.

All he saw was a woman he could never help, while she died years before Laurence met her son.

"Okay," he said, like he could put it off some more, but he was too wise to time these days, too aware of how crushingly inevitable it became whenever he took his eye off it. There was no way around, only through.

"Do you need anything?" Ru raised his chin and crossed his arms.

At least he had clothes on today.

"No. Just… No." Laurence finally made it past the kitchen, but he ignored the stairs that went up to the second floor and the library he usually spent his time here in. Instead he went for the living room, with its outdated decor and untouched appearance.

He didn't see the living room often. If he was in this house, it was because he'd come here to learn, and only when Amy brought baked goods over to force them both to try and socialize did Laurence get to know this room even existed.

It looked like Ru didn't bother with it much, either, but Laurence supposed getting people in to redecorate was tricky when your whole home was in its own, private spiritual realm.

Laurence sat on a slightly dated but perfectly clean couch and put his water down on the side table at his elbow. He watched the still branches of trees beyond the window and tried to think of anything to say, but nothing came to mind. Ru had seen him use this gift before, so Laurence didn't even have to explain what to expect.

Ru sat on a couch across from him and leaned forward, elbows on his knees.

Waiting, like he had done for a whole year now.

"Okay." Laurence exhaled and closed his eyes. He got comfortable while he started the process of baiting his gift. He knew who he was looking for: Todd and Paula Grant. He'd seen photographs of them online, back when he'd been trying to find Rufus to teach him magic. He even, thanks to the press, knew exactly when and where the accident took place, and the name of the truck driver who had killed them.

But Rufus suspected murder, and that was what Laurence needed to either confirm or refute.

Laurence allowed the visions to come to him, and his instinct to steer him toward the one which held answers, and then — albeit reluctantly — he bit the bullet and dived in.

He recognized Rufus' parents immediately. Todd, tall and lanky, with his wavy hair that Rufus had inherited, and his easy smile which Ru had not. Paula was almost as tall, with her SoCal tan and her hair in a messy bun, freckles dotting her cheeks and forearms.

Laurence saw near-perfect starry skies overhead, and only the faintest smudge of cloud at the horizon. The beach he stood on was not immediately recognizable to him, but there were people on it who he knew. Amy, with her shower of red curls, a decade younger than Laurence was used to. A handful of people from the Facebook group Laurence had joined while he was tracking Ru down.

Mom and Dad.

Laurence gasped in shock at the sight of his own parents.

And himself.

His head was spinning. This all felt so familiar, and he'd figured it was because it was a moot, with Pagans from up and down the coast coming together for an evening of socializing and friendship out in the warm summer air. Laurence had been to so many as a child — far fewer once he hit his teen years — that he recognized it for what it was immediately.

But there he was, his gold curls unmistakable, as he chased other children around in the sand.

Laurence held his breath. Just for a moment.

Most of his childhood dwelled behind a barrier: there was this, when he was free, and then there was after, when there was heroin.

He had all but forgotten his life before drugs.

He felt hot tears swell into his eyes. They turned his vision into a blur, and he quickly wiped them away.

He needed to see.

There he was, the child who would one day be a Hunter. He was hunting now, waving his arms and roaring like a lion, laughing as he chased friends whose names he'd since forgotten, until they all ran out of steam and fell to the sand to stargaze together.

Laurence remembered none of it. Not this specific night. Only vague impressions of having done this forever, on beaches and in parks, in cities and in deserts. Fun, friends, food, and fire, back before he'd learned to fear fire.

He tore his attention away from himself and back to Mom and Dad. Dad had his guitar across his lap as he played quietly so that the music was a soft backdrop to the adults chatting around the bonfire. Mom held marshmallows near the heat, then blew on one before offering it to her husband.

It was a tiny, perfect moment, and Laurence wanted to live in it forever, but it wasn't what he was here for.

Where was Rufus?

Everyone else seemed to bring their kids along. Surely Paula and Todd hadn't left their boy at home?

Laurence moved away from the fire, searching. And there, away from the other children, were two who sat together, their backs to the adults while they gazed out to sea. He approached, and saw tumbling curls, far longer on the child than they would be on the man he became.

The other was a girl, years older than Ru but not yet an adult. Laurence thought he recognized her, but her name didn't come to him.

They laughed together as Laurence moved around them so that he could see their faces.

"This isn't magic," Ru spluttered.

The girl laughed and picked a small teddy bear up off the beach between them. She brushed sand from it with care, then pressed it against his chest. "It is. And I made it for you."

He sniffed at her, but his hand closed around it as she let go, and he glanced down to the little thing that was barely bigger than his own fist. "If it was magic, I'd be able to see it."

"Oh, you can see all magic, can you?" She grinned at him and elbowed him in the ribs. "Dork."

Rufus rolled his eyes, then chuckled. "Sure, okay. You've got a point." He smoothed the bear's fur with his fingers, easing it back from the tiny little bead eyes, as if he could help it to see. "What's it for?"

"Protection," she said, still smiling. "Hold it close and it'll keep you safe. I promise."

"From what?"

The girl shrugged. "Hopefully? Everything." Her smile became strained, and she glanced over her shoulder toward the adults. "Promise me you'll hang onto it."

"Yeah, of course."

She turned back to him, her features suddenly fixed. Almost emotionless.

"Promise me," she said.

Laurence's heart thudded in his chest. Blood buzzed in his ears. He felt lightheaded.

She was young, and she had been laughing, but now that she'd switched it off like a lightbulb he finally recognized her.

She was Angela.

Both Laurence's future teachers sat here, ten years in the past, away from the adults as they talked of magic.

Rufus looked her in the eye, then clutched the bear tighter. "I promise," he swore.

Angela's expressions returned, just like that. Her smile lit up the night, and she leaned in to quickly hug Rufus. "We should get back. We don't want anyone to worry."

"Yeah," Rufus agreed. He stood up and held the bear to his chest like he meant to show her just how much his promise meant. "We have to get back to Carlsbad, so we're probably leaving soon anyway." He licked his lips, then added, "Thanks for the bear. Next time, will you show me how you made it?"

Angela bounced up and grinned. "Sure thing. C'mon, let's go."

She took his hand, like a responsible older sister, and guided Rufus back to his parents.

Laurence stuck with them through what came next. The happy farewells. The offers to host the next moot. The hugs and kisses and waves as Paula and Todd broke away and made sure Rufus had his seatbelt on before they left the beach for good. Todd was a good driver, a cautious driver. A man who seemed conscious that his wife and child were in the vehicle, and who wanted them to get home in one piece.

They didn't, of course.

Laurence was almost numb when it came. He didn't want to be. He was still reeling from the proof of just how distant from his own past he'd become, from seeing Dad alive and vibrant and young, and from seeing Angela hand Rufus the bear which the boy was now hugging in the back seat while he smiled to himself.

But he had to pay attention. Anything could be the clue he was here for, and that meant Laurence needed to be present.

He had to watch as the truck up ahead jumped the median. It swerved to avoid a car on its own side of the interstate, but the driver lost control. Laurence could see it in his eyes from three hundred yards away: sheer panic as he wrestled with a steering wheel that didn't seem to do a whole hell of a lot.

It came almost in slow motion. The truck's wheels finally turned, but they hit a dip in the median, and a second later the cab pointed one way while the trailer just kept on coming.

Todd was on the ball. He hit the brakes, hard. The truck jackknifed and the trailer slid across all three lanes of the interstate.

It looked like they were going to make it.

Laurence could almost see how this should go. The trailer sliding to a halt, the car screeching but stopping feet away, Todd scrambling out to help the stricken cab driver escape his own vehicle.

But it didn't.

Fate snatched death from the jaws of life. A blare of a horn, and Laurence turned to see the car behind Todd's come in far too fast, a split second before it rammed into them and robbed Todd's car of the ability to stop in time.

Paula screamed.

Rufus' hold on his teddy bear tightened.

And Todd reached for Paula's hand as their car slammed into the stricken trailer.

Laurence tore himself free and gasped for air. He did *not* want to see what would come a second later. His own imagination could supply crushed bodies and a crying teen without needing the visuals to really hammer them home.

He grabbed his glass and drained the rest of the water in two huge gulps that were too big and made his chest burn on their way down, then he fought to get a grip, because there was so much going on in his head right now, and all of it screamed for his attention.

Rufus was still there. Still waiting, though there was a sharpness to his stare that hadn't been there before Laurence closed his eyes.

It was the look of a man who finally had answers within his reach.

Laurence licked his lips and put the glass down, then met Rufus' gaze.

"Angela Tate gave you a teddy bear," he said. His voice croaked a little, but he continued. "Where is it?"

Rufus frowned at him. "What? I don't know. In the house somewhere. Why?"

Laurence grit his teeth and stood, and his hands formed fists at his sides. "Because I think that bear is why you're still alive."

The truth hit him like a ton of bricks.

Angela knew.

She *knew* the accident was coming, and she'd made a charm to protect Rufus. Either she knew who had orchestrated the crash, or she'd done it herself.

Laurence felt sick. She was his teacher, for crying out loud. She'd saved Quentin's life. Rufus', too. But if she'd killed Todd and Paula, Laurence didn't know whose side he'd be on.

His goals do not align with yours.

His mom's voice echoed in his ears from the reading she did for him, back when he'd wanted to know whether Rufus was the right teacher for Laurence to learn magic from.

If this was where he and Ru were going to part ways, Laurence had to be extra sure he knew what the fuck was going on, and that meant they needed to examine the bear to see whether it really had saved Ru's life, or if it was just an inert toy without any magic behind it.

He'd save the decisions for later.

7

QUENTIN

"Hey, Banbury! Long time, no see! Nice crib!"

Quentin smiled faintly as Neil Storm crossed the lawn toward him. The dogs wagged their tails as they sniffed Neil's knees. "Neil! Still talking gibberish?"

Neil scoffed and stepped into the shade of the parasol Quentin waited under. He pulled his sunglasses off, then grabbed Quentin for a tight hug that squeezed the breath out of his lungs. "'Long time, no see,' like, it's been a while since I saw you last, dumbass."

He wheezed until Neil let him go, then straightened his shirt and crinkled his nose. "Yes, I got that part."

"Crib!" Neil waved an arm toward the back of the mansion. "And you finally got that butler you were always moaning about not having, yo."

"Only yesterday," Quentin said dryly. "Lemonade?"

"Got anything harder?"

Quentin shook his head. "No. There is no alcohol in the house."

If Neil thought that was at all odd, he didn't say so. "Then lemonade's great, thanks."

Quentin nodded slightly to Flynn, who took the hint and disappeared discreetly back indoors, then he backed away to the table and poured them each a glass. "It's good to see you. Did you manage to write enough songs?"

Neil laughed so hard he almost spilled his drink. "Dude. I wrote them, cut the album, released it, went platinum *again*, went on tour to promote it, had a wild time. You know how it is."

He had absolutely no idea how it was, but as he settled down into a chair across the table from Neil, he had to marvel at how vibrant his friend seemed. The tour, however it had actually gone, seemed to have worked wonders for his wellbeing. Neil's hair had somehow grown even longer, and he still insisted on wearing jeans and enormous leather boots despite the San Diego heat, but there was a level of happiness to him that Quentin couldn't help but envy.

Neil sipped the lemonade and pointed toward the pool. "So what's the deal? Get bored of apartment living and decide to blow the savings on something more to your liking?"

Quentin shook his head faintly. He should have anticipated this line of questioning. Neil had texted him in the morning and suggested that they meet up for lunch, and instead Quentin had provided his home address and proposed that Neil pay a visit. He preferred to avoid any risk that they might start drinking together, especially since it was how they'd spent all their previous social time before Neil had to go and tour Europe. This way he could catch Neil up on a few things in a private space and avoid the booze altogether.

"It belongs to my brother, Frederick," Quentin murmured. "Quite a lot has happened since we last saw one another."

"Yeah?" Neil grinned at him and leaned back, tossing an ankle over his knee and sitting there like he owned the place. "You got the hang of those awesome gifts of yours yet?"

"More or less." Quentin placed his glass on the table. "How long do you have?"

"For you? All day." Neil shrugged. "You tell me what you did, then I'll tell you what I did. Deal?"

"Deal. And for a start, how about you call me Quentin, rather than Banbury?"

Neil's eyebrows climbed as his eyes widened. "Whoa, did I just get my friendship level upgraded, or what?"

"No, it was upgraded a while ago. I just neglected to tell you."

Neil laughed and reclined his chair so he could stretch out and get his booted feet off the ground. "Okay, Quentin. Your turn. From the top."

Quentin debated reclining his own seat. Being more comfortable might help him get through the next hour or two, so he did the same and gazed to the ocean beyond the pool.

"All right," he murmured. "We may as well start with my father, I suppose."

THEY TALKED for so long that the dogs fell asleep, and even Windsor had settled in Quentin's lap and nodded off. After Quentin filled Neil in on everything that had happened since they'd last spoken, Neil talked about the ups and downs of trying to write his album on time, and then the rigors of touring across Europe. Usually he would brag about sleeping with women he met in bars and clubs, but this time he concentrated more on the work: rehearsals, hotels, venues, and the concerts themselves.

Although Quentin had never doubted it, it became increasingly clear just how hard Neil worked, despite how laid-back he seemed in social settings.

"So, in short, you've got a magic bird, I'm running out of

wall space for all my shiny accolades, and life is okay-ish." Neil stretched his arms over his head, then got up and paced slowly as though he was reminding his legs how they worked. "I still want to get you in the studio, you know. I wasn't joking about that."

A year ago, Quentin had scoffed at the idea.

Now, though, it wasn't so fanciful. Not if he truly intended to accept Neil's compliment for what it was.

"All right," he said, letting the words out of his mouth before his brain could step in and stop them. "I have no experience whatsoever in your genre, though."

"That's a given. You're still a snob, duh." Neil laughed. "But give it a try. You might enjoy it, you might not, but until you *try* you won't ever know, will you?"

Quentin raised his hands in surrender. "That is a fair assessment."

"Right on. And then we can talk about magic."

Windsor shook himself awake and clacked his beak, then hopped onto the arm of Quentin's chair. He settled a beady, judgmental glare on Quentin.

Quentin did scoff this time, and pushed himself to his feet. Pepper cracked open one eye, then closed it again, satisfied that this didn't mean he was about to feed her.

"I'm not going to learn magic."

"Yeah, I hear you." Neil planted hands on his hips and raised his chin as he came to a stop. He gazed directly at Quentin. "You don't wanna turn into your dad. But you're working your ass off on that already. You're in therapy, and it's going good, right?"

Quentin crossed his arms tightly. "I am, and it is, yes."

"Cool. Cool, cool cool, cool, cooooool. Totally cool." Neil clicked his tongue. "And have you talked to her yet about how you're always holding yourself back?"

He opened his mouth, then shut it again, trying to quash

the irritation that flickered to life in his chest. "Somewhat," he muttered.

"Quentin. Buddy. Bro. Dude. My man." Neil dropped his hands to his side and closed the distance, walking around the table until he could put his hand on Quentin's shoulder. He squeezed lightly for a moment, then let go again. "I get it. I really do. I can't even begin to imagine how scared you are, all day, every day."

Quentin shifted position slightly, adjusting his center of balance, and tightening his arms together as though he could simply convey to Neil how uncomfortable this had all suddenly become.

"Let me tell you something. And, I know, it's not *the exact same thing*. But you're a smart guy. You can see parallels." Neil, thankfully, backed off again and gestured expansively toward the mansion. "My house is bigger."

"I, um…" Quentin blinked at him. "I'm not quite sure that I follow."

Neil just smiled faintly. "Get this. My mom and dad weren't loaded. They worked hard, supported me when I wanted to learn the guitar, but I knew they were putting in the hours so we could afford tuition. Twice as hard when Sis said she wanted to be an actress. Can you imagine?" He laughed fondly. "There you are working your fingers to the bone, and *both* your kids wanna go into the arts. But they never said no, never told us to lower our sights and settle for something less."

At the very least, Quentin could picture supportive parents, so he nodded as he listened.

"Turned out I could pretty much learn any instrument I put my mind to," Neil continued. "And Ames is a *great* actress. I can't tell you whether that's because we're naturally talented, or because we had all the support we needed. Maybe it's both. Talent plus privilege equals success, yo." He pushed long, wavy hair back over his shoulder in an exaggerated flick of his hand. "But here's a fact. Success, wealth, and talent combine into power. Oh, sure, I can't summon gods, or uproot trees with my mind, or any of that shit. But I have a global audience. Millions of followers on Twitter, TikTok, Weibo, Sonico, Mixi… It goes on. I've got so many accounts in so many languages I have a whole team just to manage it all. I send them my posts, they translate and share." Neil paused and glanced back to Quentin. "I've got a voice. When I say something, there's a good chance that someone out there in the big bad world will hear it. I can influence whole groups of people with my words, and that's before I even put them to music."

Quentin didn't feel like lowering his own guard right now, but he did at least loosen his arms. He knew that Neil was famous, of course, largely because Neil told him so. But Quentin was so far removed from what most people would call 'the real world' — usually in a sneering, dismissive tone — that he hadn't at all considered what that fame *meant*. Now that he had some understanding of Twitter thanks to Laurence, he had seen the effects of even minor celebrity; there were people who messaged Laurence out of the blue as though they were old friends, or those who turned up at the shop and knew his name and wanted to take photos with him. Laurence had long since been forced to give up using it for meeting up with his friends or sharing where he would be going in the evening.

But Laurence only had a few thousand followers, and most of those seemed to be people who wanted to know more about Laurence's famous friends, like Neil. And, if he were to be honest, like Quentin himself. He had very little fame that he was aware of, but as he socialized with people like Neil, with all his awards and followers, a little interest had rubbed off on him. Since he abhorred most forms of media, he remained largely oblivious to it.

Neil had thousands of times the level of fame that Laurence did, and until now, Quentin had never really understood that fact.

"And how do you choose to influence them?" he murmured.

"That right there is the million dollar question, isn't it?" Neil replied, his voice softening. "You and me both, we gotta know everything there is to know about ourselves, because we've got power and there is no way of telling what damage we can do if we use it unwisely. If I get all up my feelings then sound off online, I can hurt people I'll never even meet. What's the point of that? We both know anger is contagious. My job is to be the very best version of me, because there are kids out there who look up to me. I'm either a role model, a hero, or a pawn in a culture war, but whatever I am, my words can help people or they can hurt them, and I've said enough dumb shit in my life already. What you gotta do, ol' buddy, ol' pal, is you gotta fully inhabit your power so that you can knowingly use it for good. Because if you deny it, if you keep turning your back on accepting who you are and what you can do, someone's gonna pay. And it'll never be you, because you're the one with the privilege." Neil grimaced. "We get to walk away, totally unscathed. Maybe a few people don't like us any more, but we're too big and too powerful to fall. It'll be other people who suffer, whose lives we make more painful without even knowing their names. Is that who you want to be?"

Quentin sucked in a breath and tried not to respond on autopilot. Neil's point was extremely logical, and made altogether far too much sense. He was right. Although their power was worlds apart, Quentin's had the very real potential to do lasting physical harm. It was one of the first points he had raised in his therapy with Violeta.

Hell, he'd almost killed Laurence in a drunken panic. One look at his talisman and Quentin nearly threw him clear off the building from the Altitude Sky Lounge. Only the safety glass — and Neil's fist — had saved Laurence's life.

All this time he worried about the potential for losing control, and he'd already done it.

"We can't go through life just burying our weaknesses." Neil shrugged at him. "They become blind spots. Then, when they bite us in the ass, we get defensive and lash out. We do even *more* harm. You—" he pointed right at Quentin's face "— have got to stop hiding from what you can do. So it's just as well I'm back in town, 'cause it's time we put your ass to work."

Quentin debated whether or not to crack a facetious remark, but Neil cast him a withering stare before he could even think about getting that far, and he sighed.

He was going to regret this. He knew it.

But he would regret it more if he *did* hurt someone.

"All right," he said. "Let's try it your way."

8

LAURENCE

Rufus wasn't budging an inch. He stood in the doorway, hands clenched into fists, and glared at Laurence as though Laurence was suddenly his mortal enemy.

Laurence tried to see it from Ru's point of view. The guy *had* waited a whole year for this, and now it was here it had to be pretty disappointing. Ru must've pinned his hopes on one vision being all it took even though Laurence had tried to warn him it never worked out that way, so his empathy came easy.

But he was still being stared down by a witch who was far more powerful than Laurence was.

"I'm telling you," he said slowly, "I saw you on a beach at a moot. You were sitting with Angela Tate and she gave you a teddy bear. She said it would protect you."

"The *crash*," Rufus snarled.

"It looked like an accident—"

"No!"

"Ru!" Laurence bared his teeth and took a step closer. His own anger flared at being cut off before he could finish what he'd been trying to say, and he only stopped when they were almost touching. "I said it *looked* like an accident! I didn't say it *was* one. You need to dial it down, because I'm here to help you get to the bottom of this. This is what I do. I hunt truth, and once I start, I don't stop."

Rufus' pupils were wide, and his skin pale. Laurence could see the fight in every inch of the witch's body, the pent-up grief and anger and frustration that all threatened to boil over, and he prayed that Ru wasn't loaded with spells that would only take a word to tear Laurence apart.

"Listen to me. Magic can be hard to pick up on, you know that." Laurence licked his lips and pushed his own irritation back down so he could try and talk sense into Ru. "Even for me. I can see wards, you can't. But that doesn't mean I can see everything. Not without some kind of perception spell." He left off *which you haven't taught me yet*, because now really wasn't the time. "So let's find the bear, and we can look at it properly and see if it really did save your life, or whether Angela was just being a kid doing something nice for a friend."

It took a few more seconds for the tension to bleed out of Rufus' stance, and he dipped his chin briefly. It was as much of an apology as Laurence was likely to get, but that was fine. It beat getting magically murdered where he stood.

"I don't know where it is," Rufus muttered. He stepped out of the room as he turned away. "I don't remember the crash, not really, and not much of what happened straight after. But I think it's in the house somewhere."

Laurence nodded and tailed after him. "It's fine," he said, trying to be as gentle as he could while coming down from his own rollercoaster. "We'll find it."

If they didn't, his only option would be to get Ru to teach him some perception spells, then go back into the vision, and that sounded way less fun than digging through parts of the house he didn't normally get to see.

It took them much of the day to all but tear Rufus' house apart, and Laurence saw way more of the property than he ever had in the past. There was more to it than a library and a yard, and while Laurence wasn't there to pry into Ru's private business, this was the first real opportunity he'd had to see how his teacher really lived.

It wasn't a life that would have suited Laurence, that was for sure. While Ru might have a nice big house, it was dead in a way Laurence hadn't been able to put a finger on before now. Sure, he knew it was only tenuously linked to the real world, but it became clear throughout the day just how deeply that disconnect ran. Rufus had fresh water that came in through a space beneath the house which Ru still wouldn't let Laurence see, and air was exchanged whenever the front gate was opened, but there was more to it. Tradespeople couldn't come here, or they'd see a house magically appear out of nowhere the moment they stepped over the threshold. That meant there was nothing modern about the interior. Everything from carpets to furniture to white goods were at least twenty years old. None of the life subtly present in most houses was here at all; no flies, no traces of spider webs even in the most distant closets, nothing. The yard was a mess when Laurence first came here a year ago, but since he'd fixed it up, it was stagnating. There were no insects out there to pollinate, no birds to sing.

He figured anything that had been brought into this realm with the house had died without that connection to nature. Not right away, but little by little, until only the plants remained. And in time they would die too, without fresh nutrients sinking into the soil to sustain them.

Amy Jenkins once said it was Ru's mom, Paula, who had been the expert at hiding things away from the real world.

She'd called it Occultation, which implied there was a whole branch of magic and theory dedicated to more than the intricacies of planar engineering, but maybe some part of Paula's skill had been in sustaining a sanctum realm once it was snipped neatly away from the world and — without her to tend to it — the whole thing was slowly falling apart.

Laurence followed Rufus from room to room while they methodically searched every nook and cranny, and they had begun on the first floor. He didn't want to question Ru about why. Maybe the witch wanted to put off searching bedrooms for as long as possible, or maybe he was being thorough. Either way, Laurence figured it was none of his business. He was poking his nose into corners of Ru's life that nobody had seen since Todd and Paula died, he could keep his mouth shut if it helped Ru deal with it.

The kitchen and the living room, he already knew, but there was a whole other world Laurence was only now finding out about. The living room led into a games room, dominated both by the pool table in the center, and the folding glass doors that opened out onto a dirt-strewn patio whose wicker furniture had been bleached by the sun. From the kitchen, a door led through into a garage that practically oozed disuse. There was no car. The car that used to be stored here never made it back, and Ru had obviously not bought a new one. Laurence doubted he even knew how to drive.

When they went upstairs, they searched the library first. There was no teddy bear in there, of course. Not even in the locked closet where Rufus imprisoned books he considered too dangerous to be out on the shelves.

Laurence doubted the bear was hidden in a bathroom, but those got searched too. And finally the bedrooms — far too many for two parents and one kid. Maybe Paula and Todd had meant to have a bigger family, but life didn't work out that way.

He did his best to make small talk now and then, to try and make it less painful for Rufus, but ultimately he knew the only thing that'd make it better was answers, and the sooner they found them the better.

It was obvious which bedroom was Rufus'. Not only because it bore the scent of a room which received fresh laundry and air and a human body every night, but also it just seemed so obviously the room of a pre-teen kid which was now occupied by an adult. A few small, plastic trophies for swimming were on a shelf, along with rows of paperback children's novels and a couple of old toys. If there used to be posters on the walls there weren't any more. The bed was a twin, and had dull blue sheets on it.

Laurence sighed softly. Ru might be an incredibly powerful witch, but at what cost? He was a man whose whole existence was pinned to one single point in time, like an iridescent beetle under glass. Ten years had passed, but Rufus still inhabited his childhood.

It was time to set him free.

They all but turned the bedroom upside down as they dug through drawers and into cubbyholes. Ru only owned adult clothes, which meant everything he'd grown out of through the years must've been taken away, likely by Amy. If she'd taken away his childhood toys, too, the bear could be long gone by now, which meant Laurence would have to start fishing through time again to try and find more information. It wouldn't be so easy, but he'd do it if he had to, and keep his complaining to himself.

"This is a waste of time." Rufus scowled. "I don't even remember what it looked like."

"Yep, well, fortunately I do." Laurence poked his tongue out while he felt around at the back of a closet that was too high up for him to see that far into. His fingers found cardboard, so he tugged, and dragged out a battered old box the size of a microwave, though it was pretty light. The faded print on it didn't give away what might have been in it once, it only listed information like "fragile" and "this way up."

He lowered the box to an empty spot on Rufus' bed and opened it, and he held his breath with hope.

Inside was a treasure trove of abandoned plush toys.

Laurence pulled each one out with care and set them onto the bed. He still had a whole bunch of his own out at the farm, so he wasn't going to pass comment, not even as a joke.

Finally, his fingers closed around a little bear, slightly squashed from its time in a closet, but otherwise pristine.

This was it.

He recognized everything about it, from the meticulously hand-stitched body to the way the fur half-covered the tiny black bead eyes.

"Ru."

Rufus looked to Laurence, then to the bear in his hand, and he stared at it for what felt like a whole minute before he breathed, "Oh. *That* bear?"

Laurence huffed and held it out. "Now do you remember it?"

Ru shook his head slowly as he accepted the bear and brushed the fur away from its eyes just as he had ten years ago. "Vaguely? But…" He pursed his lips at it. "It's so small."

Laurence nodded. He totally got what Rufus meant. The bear which once fit neatly into Ru's hand was now almost obscured by it. "But is it magic?"

"Yes." Rufus frowned and turned the little bear in his hands, examining it from every angle. "There are at least five protection spells. I'd have to separate them out to try and identify them."

That made Laurence frown faintly. "It can't have five spells, right? In a single item?"

"It's clever," Ru mused. "It must be stuffed with talismans.

It isn't the bear that's imbued, it's whatever's inside that's holding the spells." He glanced up at Laurence. "Angela Tate?"

Laurence nodded briefly. "Yeah."

"Great." Ru turned on his heel and strode for the door before Laurence could say another word. "Let's go dissect this bear, then we can track her down and find out what she knows."

"Whoa. Wait!" Laurence ran after him. "We? Leave it to me, I'll get to the bottom of it!"

"You think I'm going to sit back and do nothing while you go dig up the person who knew my parents were going to die and didn't save them?" Rufus snorted as he barged his way into the library. "No. I want to be there. I haven't waited all these years just to get left on the sidelines. I'm going with you." He slapped the bear on the desk, then glowered at Laurence. "Unless you're protecting her for some reason."

"Maybe the one I'm protecting is you, dumbass!" Laurence planted his own hand down on the desk and leaned across it to point at his teacher. "You'd be dead if it wasn't for this bear, and if you go out there to the one person who knew what was coming, someone might finish the job!"

"I can take care of myself!"

"Can you?"

They both leaned toward each other, both with hands on the desk, like it was a battle of wills and if they could just out-stare each other the winner would be chosen. Except Laurence never felt all that well-equipped when it came to willpower, and Rufus might throw him out and ban him from ever coming back if he *did* somehow win it.

Rufus curled his lip. "We could take Quentin with us."

It *sounded* like a suggestion, but Laurence saw right through it to what it really was: an admission that Laurence might be right, that they might need some heavier firepower if they were going into this together.

He didn't like that Ru seemed to view Quentin as a weapon.

"Quen doesn't do magic," Laurence murmured, softening his posture to go with his tone. "And he doesn't like being around it. I can handle this. I'll find Tate, talk to her, then come back here and we can figure out our next step. Okay?"

It took another minute for Rufus to huff and sit down. "Fine."

"Great." Laurence slumped into a seat opposite him. "Let's see what's in the bear."

He tried not to count all the bullets he was dodging, but one thing was for sure. He wasn't going to get to ask Rufus about the spell that still sat in his pocket. Not now, and — if this all went horribly wrong — maybe not ever.

Fuck.

9

LAURENCE

"Just teach me the spell, Ru."

Rufus scowled at him. "You think this is the time?"

"Yeah. I do." Laurence crossed his arms and sat his butt on the library's long, heavy table, careful not to scatter the eviscerated bear or its talisman guts.

He didn't want to say the obvious, but that didn't stop him thinking it.

It's not like your parents are gonna get any more dead if we take another half hour.

Rufus curled his lip and looked down at the assorted pieces. He'd used small nail scissors to snip the threads at one of the bear's longer seams, so while the bear didn't have a gaping wound, it still looked deflated after its stuffing was pulled out.

Laurence regarded them, too. There were tiny segments of thread on the desk, off-white fluff, and a scattering of items Ru had pulled out: a metal thimble so small that Laurence suspected it had come from a Monopoly set, a square yellow Lego brick, a woven friendship bracelet that could only fit a child, a tiny white plastic wishbone, and a black plastic rook from a travel chess set — complete with magnetized base.

Though he couldn't see the magic, he understood how it had lasted all these years. Spells imbued into items which didn't represent the intent of the magic would wear off over time, but this assortment of children's toy pieces were well chosen.

He used his fingers to scatter them a little further apart. "Come on," he murmured. "Show me. When are we going to get a better opportunity to do this?"

Rufus sniffed at him. "Fine. Whatever."

That was as close to *you're right* as Laurence was going to get, and he was willing to take it if it meant finally learning how to see the magic he couldn't naturally detect.

***

THERE WAS no way Laurence was going to admit that this hadn't helped.

Rufus walked him through a spell, which didn't take too long, but now Laurence could see far more than his own eyes could make out, and what he saw was nonsense.

He grit his teeth. Ru knew this would be the result. Of course he did. He had at least a ten year head start on Laurence, and hadn't exactly been sharing his knowledge at speed. Laurence wasn't even a full-time student, whereas Ru had nothing but time on his hands.

Great. I couldn't even catch up if I was full-time.

The nonsense wrapped around the little talismans, woven through them in dark red filaments which were finer than hair. Laurence was only used to detecting a glow, but what he saw now was far more detailed, and he raised his wrist to look at his own talismans.

They, too, bore the threads of magic, bright with the green he was familiar with.

Laurence turned his attention to Rufus and did his best not to stare.

Ru was riddled head to toe with strands of magic in his own turquoise. They wreathed him, threaded through him, and ultimately seemed to be part of his very structure.

"Goddess," Laurence breathed. "How many spells have you got on?"

"Enough," Rufus said.

"Why don't you just imbue them into something?"

"Because whatever you put them into can always be taken off you."

Laurence nodded slowly. "But they all fade when you sleep, right? You have to re-cast them all every morning?"

Rufus shrugged at him. "I don't need most of them when I'm asleep."

Laurence didn't push it. He turned his attention back to the talismans whose threads matched the color of Angela's magic and slid off the table to drop into a chair so he was closer to them. "Okay. Now I can see, but how do I know what it *means*?"

"Well, either you spend a century or two learning to identify different types of spell by their weave, or you can use identification spells. The most accurate way is to use a top level spell like this one, apply your knowledge, then switch to a more granular spell to dig deeper." Rufus sat beside him and reached for the thimble. "These are all protection spells, one way or another," he muttered. "We can extrapolate a lot from what they're imbued into when the spells are this old. A thimble's obviously physical protection. Armor, even. That's what thimbles do." He passed it to Laurence, then picked up the wishbone. "This is harder. Make a wish, I guess. A wish for safety? I'd have to dig deeper. You don't have to, though. You can look back in time and watch it being cast, and identify the spell that way."

"Assuming I'm not shut out somehow," Laurence cautioned. He'd been unable to see Quentin get kidnapped off the street by Kathy Marlowe, and the helplessness it'd left him with was something he wasn't eager to experience again.

"Why assume when you can check?"

Laurence felt like he should argue, but Rufus had a point, so he squashed his pride and closed his eyes.

Nothing.

He could find visions of Angela as a child, no problem at all. But the specific incidents where she made these talismans or put them in the bear? No. It was like they didn't even exist.

"Okay," he huffed. He kept his eyes closed a few seconds longer, because he would be opening them onto a world which had gotten smaller for him. Suspecting that there were other ways to block his gift and finding proof were very different, especially as Angela knew everything about Laurence's abilities.

That was the price of her help in saving Quentin's life.

She knew what he could do, and she could block him from doing it, and he wanted to walk on over there and confront her?

"No dice, huh?" Rufus clicked his tongue. "No problem. Let's go digging."

Laurence grimaced as he finally let his eyes drift open. Rufus' idea of digging meant sifting through yet more books, and Laurence could only help with that if he used the spell that seemed to be weighing heavier in his pocket with every passing hour.

Fuck it.

Laurence slid his hand into his pocket, then made up his mind, and stood.

"Right. You get the books," he said. "I'm gonna use the bathroom."

He left Rufus searching shelves, and darted across the hall before he could change his mind.

———

Once he was locked away in the bathroom, Laurence dug out his phone and the envelope. He placed his phone on the closed toilet seat, then tore open the envelope and checked the sheets of precisely folded paper inside.

As Freddy had promised, while there was a printout of the original spell, he'd also included pronunciation notes and a translation, as well as a breakdown of how to cast it. Laurence skim-read what he could, but nothing dangerous leaped out. In fact, if Freddy hadn't said it was a spell, he wouldn't have thought it was one at all. It seemed so casual, especially once translated into English.

As Hermóðr rode in the forest
he met a stranger from the south.
The stranger spoke and Hermóðr listened
and became wise in his words.
Like Hermóðr flee
the chains of tongues.

Even the physical component was a simple one. All he had to do was have the object to be imbued in his hands when he cast the spell. It was such a contrast to all the Latin Laurence had been entrenched in over the last year, with its obsession over oratory gestures and precise sigils. Maybe if Rufus had started him out on *this* kind of magic, Laurence would be further ahead by now.

Or possibly he could only think that way because he'd worked so hard trying to understand the basics.

Laurence re-read the instructions, more slowly this time,

until he was sure he was ready to give it a try, then he sat on the toilet seat with the phone in his hand: the spell required that he be seated and comfortable, and that he cast as though he were relaying a story to a friend, so he settled in and leaned back against the wall as he held the phone loosely in his lap.

He took a breath, and so did the universe.

"Did you just do magic on the toilet?" Rufus scoffed as Laurence wandered back into the library.

Laurence eyed him. "Yeah. Do you watch me pee when I'm in there?"

"No. But obviously I know whenever there's magic cast inside my own house that I didn't do." Rufus crossed his arms. "What was it?"

"Just a translation spell." Laurence shifted his weight from one foot to the other, and he felt like he was about to get sent to the principal's office even though his high school years were behind him. "I figure I can't help you unless I can read whatever you give me."

"Where'd you get it?"

"Quentin's brother. He found it." Laurence took the spell out of his pocket and placed it on the desk in front of Rufus. "Here. It's pretty simple, if you wanna look it over."

Rufus unpicked sheets from the envelope like they might be doused in anthrax, pored over them for a couple of minutes, then pushed them away. "Just ask next time. It can be suicide to use magic in someone else's sanctum without permission. Plenty of witches might kill you for trying."

"Okay." Laurence paused, then realized what was missing, and he added, "I'm sorry. I didn't think."

"You rarely do."

Laurence glared at Rufus, but there didn't seem to be any malice in Ru's words, and there sure wasn't any in his expression either. To Rufus, it was just a fact, and Laurence frowned slowly.

Was that how everyone saw him? As someone who didn't stop to think about the things he did?

"You're a creature of instinct," Ru muttered. "It's infuriating. Doubly so because it seems to work for you. But if you could apply that brain of yours once in a while it could save you a lot of trouble. That's all I'm saying." He passed the spell back to Laurence, then pushed a stack of books toward him, too. "You don't trust people. Not even the ones who are helping you."

"People who help me have their own agenda, and it always costs me more than I ever wanted to pay." Laurence flashed his teeth briefly as he folded the spell back into the envelope and stuffed it into his pocket.

Ru eyed him, then nodded. "That's why you put this off so long," he surmised.

Laurence shrugged. "I knew what I agreed to. But I've seen so many people die, and…" He swallowed as he grabbed the first book to take his eyes off Rufus. "Worse," he said, his voice thick.

Rufus didn't respond right away, and when he did, it was to change the subject completely, for which Laurence was grateful.

"Since we already know we want to identify protection spells, let's go through what you'll see once you start narrowing it down."

The whole thing seemed to have steered Rufus away from the idea of barging right on over to Angela's house right away, for which Laurence was grateful. If he could just keep his worlds from attacking each other he might be able to magic up enough breathing room in which to figure out what had happened all those years ago, before Ru decided to take matters into his own hands.

The idea of a witch as powerful as Rufus leaving his sanctum in anger didn't fill Laurence with optimism, and if nudging him into teacher mode was what it took to defuse him, then Laurence was more than happy to do it.

He settled in to pay attention to the lesson, and tried to push his mom's prophecy to the back of his mind.

10

LAURENCE

He didn't get home until late, and he wasn't all that sure he'd learned a whole lot, but what Laurence had succeeded in doing was stopping Ru from trying to track Angela down, so he counted it as a win.

Dinner was long gone, but Martin offered to assemble something for him, and Laurence was too tired to refuse.

The moment he stepped into the living room, though, any hope of relaxation evaporated.

"Quentin's going off in a helicopter tomorrow," Soraya groused at him.

Windsor cawed in amusement and flew to Laurence's shoulder from the back of Quentin's armchair, while Quentin was still getting to his feet. The dogs crowded around Laurence's legs, and for a moment he was overwhelmed by the rush to his senses after spending the day cut off from the world. Windsor was in his thoughts, chattering excitedly to welcome him home. The dogs smelled like they'd been bathed recently, but there was always the underlying odor of dog that nobody else seemed able to detect. He could hear the faint sounds of Martin chopping vegetables from the kitchen, behind the aural barrage from four teenage girls who were all insisting that a helicopter ride without them was unfair.

And then there was the looming presence of Quentin, forever tugging at Laurence's core, as he stepped into Laurence's personal space and brought the familiar scent of oud wood with him. He placed his hands lightly on Laurence's hips and made eye contact, then waited.

Warmth radiated from his palms and into Laurence's skin. Laurence fixed his own gaze on Quentin's and let the storm clouds there anchor him before he could fall apart.

"Are you all right, darling?" Quentin asked softly, eyes flickering back and forth as he checked Laurence's features closely.

"Yeah. It was just… a lot." Laurence gripped Quentin's elbows as the sensory overload either settled down or he acclimatized to it. He wasn't sure which. "Kiss?"

Quentin inclined his head and leaned up to brush his lips against Laurence's, and Laurence exhaled against them. He let his eyes drift closed a few seconds, then opened them when he was ready to face the chaos.

"Okay. One thing at a time. Helicopter?"

"Neil's suggestion, not mine," Quentin murmured, looking pretty sheepish about it.

"I think we should go too," Soraya said, and Laurence could hear the stubbornness in her tone, but also the faintest edge of worry.

She was scared, and he couldn't blame her. Quen had a habit of going missing whenever he went outside on his own.

Laurence drew his brows together and stepped back so that he could look past Quentin's shoulder to where the girls were spread out across sofas. Soraya and Kim sat close together as usual. Estelita and Lisa shared another couch, which was huge progress for Lisa, even if she did have her feet up on the cushion and her arms around her knees.

"You know," Laurence said slowly, "if the girls go with you, they can make sure you and Neil don't stay out too late."

Soraya eyed Laurence, and her crossed arms loosened a little as she gave the back of Quentin's head an *I knew he'd be on my side* stare.

"I hadn't even decided on whether or not I was willing to go at all," Quentin spluttered. "It was an invitation, it hadn't got any further than that."

"I didn't hear you say no," said Estelita.

"Eavesdropping is rude," Quentin replied.

"I can't help it," she muttered. "And anyway, if you're going out into the desert to practice, we should go too. That way we can all practice together. It just makes sense."

"And I've never been in a helicopter," Lisa said. "I could just go and watch."

Laurence glanced her way, but she wasn't looking up at him. Instead she was watching Pepper and Grace as they settled at his feet.

She still hadn't talked about her gift. Not to anyone who'd shared that information with Laurence, anyway. He knew she had one, but he had no idea what it was, and he wasn't going to pry until she was ready to tell him.

"It's not my decision," he finally said. "How many people can get in a helicopter, anyway?"

That was a mistake. The teenagers erupted into another cacophony of cross-talk. Soraya rattled off facts about different civilian helicopter models and their carrying capacities, while Estelita complained that without an adult present, Quentin and Neil could get into trouble. Lisa interjected now and then that they were all small so surely they could fit in anything, and Kim — as usual — kept her thoughts to herself while she observed everyone else.

Thank the Goddess that Clifton and Felipe weren't in on this too.

"It seems to me," Laurence said, raising his voice to cut through the noise, "that it's down to Neil, right? I assume he's the one providing this helicopter?"

Quentin nodded faintly.

"Right. Case closed. If Quentin decides he's going, he'll speak to Neil, and then Neil can figure out the logistics. Clear?"

Windsor stretched out his wings for dramatic effect, and Laurence felt the bird's smugness through their bond.

"Okay."

"Fine."

"Got it."

"Okay." Laurence smiled, then stepped over Grace. "I'm gonna go eat, and tomorrow we'll find out whether or not you're having an adventure."

He'd only just got home and already he was putting out fires when all he'd wanted was food and sleep.

Silently, he cursed Neil for the mess, but he couldn't be too angry. After all, Neil's drunken quick thinking had once saved Laurence's life. Laurence owed him, and dealing with a few raucous teens was a very fair price to pay.

***

"I ASSUME there's more to the whole helicopter thing?" Laurence patted the worst of the water from his curls once he was out of the shower, and looked to Quentin's reflection in the bathroom mirror. "What's the actual plan?"

Quentin finished brushing his teeth before he answered. "Neil thinks that I'm holding back," he murmured. "He suggested that we go somewhere to practice the extent of my gifts without being a danger to others, and since that means the middle of nowhere, he offered to hire a helicopter to halve the travel time." He made eye contact with Laurence's reflection and pressed his lips together faintly. "Little did I know that Estelita was home by the time that part of the conversation occurred, and I was mobbed at the dinner table over it."

Laurence used the towel to pat his chest down lightly, and he let his eyes wander from the mirror down to Quentin's ass, hidden in another towel that was wrapped around his waist. "I thought Neil didn't want to get involved?"

"Indeed. But without his input, I would not have worked out that I could freeze things." Quentin turned and crossed his arms loosely. He leaned against the sink to watch Laurence. "Perhaps he has other ideas that could prove equally fruitful. And speaking of fruitful—"

"Uh huh." Laurence didn't lift his gaze, and he let out a lewd grin to make it clear he was totally happy staring at the outline of Quentin's cock through his towel. "Yeah, baby. Full of fruit."

Quentin snorted. "I'm not certain that sounded quite as seductive as you may have intended, darling."

"Did it work though? That's what matters." Laurence grinned up at him at last, while simultaneously dabbing the water from his own dick.

Quentin heaved a long-suffering sigh to hide the amused twitch of his lips. "You are *awful*. As I was saying: speaking of fruitful, was today productive?"

Laurence wetted his lips with the tip of his tongue while he fished his thoughts out of the gutter. The fact that Quentin wasn't shying away was good, but mingling talk of Laurence's day with Rufus with flirting would be a spectacularly bad idea, so he wrapped the towel around himself and stepped around Quentin to fetch his own toothbrush. "In the end, yeah. It was touch and go for a while, but..." He sighed while he squirted toothpaste onto the bristles. "I think Angela knew the accident was going to happen, and I can't look back and see anything useful. Either she was in a place that was shielded, or she was with someone who blocks that kind of stuff."

Quentin's humor faded and he turned to face Laurence, straightening up with a frown. "Marlowe, do you think?"

Laurence shook his head. "Nah. She would've killed Angela, and being there would've stopped anyone from using magic. Could've been in Otherworld, or some other realm, or she could have been in a place that was warded, but it means she — or someone she was with at the time — knows how to block me. And probably you, too." He pointed to Quentin's reflection with his toothbrush. "I'm gonna go see her tomorrow and ask outright. I don't see any point messing around."

Quentin's dark brows furrowed as his frown grew deeper. "What makes you think that she was involved?"

"I looked back at the accident. Then before it." Laurence lowered the toothbrush with a slow sigh. "I saw Mom and Dad, and Paula and Todd, and Rufus and Angela. And... me." He ran his thumb slowly over the toothbrush's on switch, but didn't press it. "I looked so happy."

Quentin's touch was light, but firm, as his fingers curled around Laurence's arm and drew it toward himself.

Laurence relented to the unspoken suggestion without any resistance. He set the toothbrush down and turned to face Quentin, and let Quentin steer him closer, until their bodies met and Quentin's arms curled around him.

He draped his own around Quentin's waist, careful not to brush over his scars, and rested a chin on his shoulder.

They stood there a while, saying nothing. Laurence let his eyes drift closed, and allowed himself to accept the strength and the protection Quentin offered to him. The tug on Laurence's energy was just as comforting as the warmth he received from Quentin's skin, and he basked in both as they soothed him.

Sometimes, touch was way more important than words, and Quentin was getting good at knowing what Laurence needed from one minute to the next.

Laurence smiled to himself and drew a deep, relaxed breath. "Thanks, hon."

"You are most welcome."

He remained where he was, holding Quentin and being held in return. "We were all at a moot on a beach. I was, like, thirteen, and playing with the other kids. Mom and Dad were hanging out with the other adults, and Angela was with Rufus. She gave him talismans to protect him, and that's how he survived the crash, which suggests she knew it was coming."

Quentin's fingertips traced slowly up Laurence's spine, starting in the small of his back and drifting inch by inch up to a spot between his shoulder blades. "I thought she told you that she did not know Eric?"

Laurence pursed his lips and pressed them to Quentin's skin while he dredged up the memories he was looking for.

She *had* said that, way back when he first went to meet her at the Harbor House restaurant.

"You think she was lying right from the start?"

"It is possible, I suppose, that she simply does not remember him," Quentin murmured. "But I do not think Eric is all that forgettable."

"Yeah." Laurence laughed a little. "He's not. I mean, he wasn't…" He hummed briefly to himself as he began the slow, reluctant process of pulling back from Quentin's arms. "I need to talk to her, and Ru suggested I take you with me as backup, but…" He licked his lips again. "It's going to be a lot of talk about magic, and if she can block your psychokinesis it just seems like we're telling her we don't trust her and not getting any benefits out of it that make it worthwhile."

Quentin smiled faintly, though Laurence could see the

strain around his eyes at all the talk about magic. "If you wish me to be there, I shall."

"But Neil—"

"You take precedence," Quentin said, so firmly that it made Laurence's skin tingle.

He searched Quentin's gaze, and found nothing but sincerity.

"No," Laurence sighed. "We'd just be exposing you to a trigger and potentially making Angela defensive, all for no reason. I don't think she'd attack me. That's not her style. The worst she'd do is cut me out of her life and disappear."

"You're certain?"

Laurence prodded at his instincts, but no alarm bells rang. He couldn't even hold a little white lie against her. Not after he'd withheld significant information from her when he'd sought her help rescuing Quentin from Marlowe. If he was totally honest with himself, he felt like Rufus was more likely to attack him than Angela ever was.

He nodded. "Totally," he said. "You go have fun blowing up the desert with Neil, I'll talk to Angela, and we can catch up over dinner after."

Something about the whole situation was tugging on Laurence's subconscious, trying to be heard, but it was too far away and Laurence knew better than to try and dig for it. That would just make it bury itself even deeper. All he could do was let it percolate on its own, and it would bubble to the surface in its own time.

Until then, he had a better idea for how to handle tomorrow.

11

MYRIAM

"Is that everything?" Ethan stepped back from the truck and slapped his hands together to shake dirt loose.

Maria consulted the clipboard in her hand and ran her finger down each page as she made sure each checkbox was ticked off, then she nodded with a smile. "Yeah, that's it."

"Great!" He grinned and turned to Myriam. "Any more heavy lifting before we roll out?"

Myriam watched Maria close the truck's doors. "No, we'll be fine. You two take care."

Aiden scurried out from the back door to quickly hug and kiss Ethan goodbye, and soon both Maria and Ethan were in the truck.

Myriam didn't often send her staff out in pairs. Deliveries were usually a solo job, but there were a couple of two-person lifts in today's orders, which meant spending the day short-staffed.

She had a feeling Ethan wasn't going to be the only member of staff she was down today.

"Everything okay?" Aiden asked after he'd waved goodbye to the departing truck.

"Yes," she said without hesitation. She smiled to Aiden and then ushered him back inside. As glorious as the sunshine was, they couldn't linger in the alley all day. They had work to do.

Rodger was in the back room, and in the space between Ethan loading the last pot onto the truck and Myriam returning, he'd already got his laptop out onto the table and fired it up. "Chupacabra sighting on Pacific Beach."

"No," Myriam murmured. It didn't grab her attention, and almost all chupacabra sightings were stray dogs with mange. If this one was real, her instincts would have risen to the bait.

"Okay. How about the return of the Proctor Valley Monster?"

Myriam snorted and filled the kettle.

"Yet another haunting at the Whaley House?" Even Rodger didn't sound convinced by that one.

Aiden began assembling everything he'd need to get to work making this afternoon's floral arrangements. "We don't do ghosts, right?"

"We don't," Myriam agreed.

"But we all know not every haunting is really a ghost." Rodger paused. "Well, most aren't anyway, but... You know what I mean."

Myriam chuckled as she distributed teabags among cups. "We do," she assured him.

Now that Rodger had decided that his job included keeping up to date on local weird happenings, he'd managed to become a lot more focused on his work in the store, too, and Myriam occasionally wondered whether this was why she'd hired him in the first place. Had her instincts honed in on him because they'd detected this hidden competence just waiting for the chance to blossom?

Regardless, she was grateful, both to her gut, and for the fact that Rodger was finally earning his wages. He seemed happier as well, like searching for things that went bump in the night had given him purpose, and it was wonderful to see him smile now and then.

"Are you two going to be okay on your own today?" she added, stirring milk into their tea.

"Yeah, of course," Rodger muttered.

Aiden raised his eyebrows. "Are there more deliveries? I can do those, if you'd prefer?"

Myriam shook her head and distributed the cups. "No, no more deliveries. Just a hunch."

It wasn't until she turned back to the window that she realized she'd only made two cups of tea, and as she gazed thoughtfully down the alleyway, she saw Bambi turn down it and pull up where Maria had been parked only minutes ago.

"Hm." She took her apron off and went to hang it on a hook.

The hunch was growing stronger by the moment.

Myriam washed her hands as her son locked the truck and came in through the back door, and by the time he was over the threshold she was in a position to hug him tightly. "Bambi!"

"Mom!" He laughed and returned her hug, before he peeled away to nod toward Aiden and Rodger. "Hey. What's up?"

"Myriam won't let us investigate anything interesting," Rodger said with a sigh.

"It's not interesting if it's not real," Aiden countered.

"Oh, man. I spend my whole life trying to avoid trouble, and you two are *looking* for it?" Bambi laughed easily as he sat at the table, then his gaze fell on Aiden's orders list, and he began to flick through it.

Myriam smiled wryly. "Yes, you can have the day off," she murmured.

Bambi groaned at getting caught out so fast, and the guilty

look he cast her as he gave Aiden the clipboard back told Myriam her guess was right on the money.

"When do we get as much time off as Laurence does?" Rodger drank some of his tea while he tried to look innocent.

Bambi's guilty look only worsened, and he frowned to himself.

"I don't pay him for his days off, if that's what you're asking," Myriam replied.

Everyone other than Maria knew that Bambi would occasionally get into trouble. Or, more likely, Quentin would get into trouble and poor Bambi would have to find a way to go rescue him. But Myriam wasn't unsympathetic to her staff's perspective, either. Bambi had a lot of unplanned absences and the whole team pulled together to cover his workload, so it was only fair for them to know that he wasn't being paid when he wasn't working.

Maybe it was time to consider having a serious conversation with her son about whether or not he really wanted to try and maintain a job.

Rodger nodded like he was satisfied with her answer.

"All right, Bambi." Myriam turned her attention back to her son, who wasn't dressed for work, and hadn't put on an apron. He'd turned up in summery shorts and a muted yellow t-shirt, and if he meant to work today he would've worn pants. "What's on your mind?"

Bambi gave her a hand-caught-in-cookie-jar look that hadn't changed since he was four, and she tried not to laugh.

"Angela Tate turned up to at least one moot when I was a kid," he murmured, "but I don't remember her from them, and nor do you, right? Or you would've recognized her name when she first came by the store."

Myriam pressed her lips together lightly as she considered the implications. Bambi's mysterious mentor had approached him on the request of a third party, and to call her secretive would be putting it mildly. "Maybe she used a different name back then?"

Bambi's eyes — so like Eric's — narrowed. "I didn't see her give a name," he admitted. "But she did tell me she never knew Dad, that she only knew of him by reputation."

"Evil twin," Rodger declared.

Aiden sensibly chose to sip his tea rather than add to Rodger's statement, though his eyes were wide as he looked between Rodger and Bambi.

"Evil twin," Bambi echoed.

Rodger gave a swift nod. "Or a body swap, or possession, or amnesia, but I'm gonna vote for evil twin."

"I don't think evil twin would account for nobody remembering her *and* for her not knowing Eric despite attending the same events," Myriam murmured dryly. "So what do you propose, Bambi?"

She already suspected, of course. Bambi was going to go see Angela and ask her questions, but he didn't have Quentin with him, so either he trusted Angela or didn't want to upset Quentin with talk of magic, and the truth was likely a little of both. He needn't have come all the way here just to ask her a couple of questions that could readily have been answered on the phone, and Myriam instinctively hadn't made tea for either of them.

Whether or not he'd been consciously aware of his intentions in coming to the store, they were obvious now.

Bambi licked his lips briefly and looked up to her. "Would you mind coming with me to go talk to her?"

Going was the right thing to do. That much was obvious. Myriam was already prepared for it. But it would be useful to try and pin down why exactly she'd allowed herself to be guided this way.

"What do you hope that would achieve?"

He let out a soft humming sound for a second while he

gathered his thoughts. "What I really hope is you both might recognize each other and, together, we can all figure out why none of us seem to remember her from back then. But if not, I think introducing her to you will show her that I do trust her, I'm not accusing her of anything." He hesitated. "I mean, I kinda *am* accusing her of knowing Ru's parents were going to die, but I don't want it to become this antagonistic thing where she just walks away from us all and we get nothing." He leaned an elbow on the table and ran fingers through his hair, idly scratching his scalp in the process. "She really values knowledge, and she might want to know why she's missing some. That or she was lying about never having met Dad, but I don't know. She's really hard to get a read on when she wants to be, but why would she lie about that?"

Myriam nodded along as he spoke. She didn't disagree with any of his points, even though he was clearly clutching at straws.

"All right," she murmured. "You'd best ask her if she's willing to meet me, and where, as I doubt she'll appreciate it if we turn up on her doorstep together."

Bambi smiled slightly and raised his chin. "Yeah, I already checked. In case you said yes."

Myriam laughed softly and stood. She smoothed out her dress, then looked to Aiden. "I won't be long."

Aiden smiled. "All right. I'll stay at the register until you get back."

Rodger closed his laptop. "Then I'd better get out front, too, and tidy the place up."

"Call me if you need me." Myriam eyed the skeleton staff she was leaving her store to, then followed Bambi to the back door.

"Ten bucks says evil twin," Rodger called after them.

"Goddess," Bambi muttered under his breath, "I sure hope not."

Myriam said nothing, but she had the uncomfortable feeling that Rodger might be half right.

There might not be a twin, but someone had murdered Paula and Todd, and that meant there was evil.

All she could do was find out whether they were heading straight for it.

12

LAURENCE

LAURENCE PARKED THE TRUCK AND TURNED THE ENGINE OFF, then looked across at his mom in the passenger seat. She had the faintest glimmer of amusement in her eyes.

"This is where she wants to meet?"

Laurence nodded. He'd parked in a lot at the eastern edge of the Mission Valley Mall, right by a nail spa. "I mean, not in the spa," he clarified.

"Then where? In-N-Out?" Myriam laughed warmly as they left the truck.

"El Pollo Loco," Laurence said.

"When she wants to meet you alone she picks the Harbor House, but when I'm invited it's a five dollar combo?"

Laurence chuckled as they crossed the parking lot and approached the concrete benches outside the dusty pink walls of the fast food joint. It was a beautiful, sunny day, with the lightest of breezes to make the palm leaves and the shadows they cast dance slowly together. "Angela likes to mix it up. I think it's to give away as little about her own tastes as possible, if she even has any."

Myriam nodded and waited for Laurence to open the door for her. "Are we eating, or just getting drinks?"

"We usually eat, but, uh…" Laurence scanned the small fast-food joint's interior and raised his chin when he spotted Angela near the back. She didn't have a tray in front of her, only a drink, so he smiled quickly to her then looked back to his mom. "It's too early for lunch. We should just get drinks."

"All right. Why don't you go join her, and I'll catch up?"

Laurence weighed his options. The whole point of Mom being here was so the two women had time to figure out if they recognized each other. But maybe Angela would appreciate finding that out before she was trapped in a corner with Myriam, so he smiled gratefully. "Thanks."

He left her there as she ordered soda and crossed quickly to Angela's table, sliding into a seat facing her and offering a smile. "Hey. Thanks for agreeing to this. I know it's short notice."

Angela's features were relaxed, and as neutral as they usually were, though she watched Myriam rather than Laurence. "Why am I meeting your mother?"

Straight to it. He didn't expect anything else, so Laurence licked his lips and then rested his hands on the table where Angela could see them if she wanted to. "The abridged version is that my other teacher, Rufus, was in an auto accident ten years ago that killed his parents. He's always suspected foul play but couldn't prove it, and the price for his mentorship is that I work on figuring out whether his suspicion is right." He hesitated a moment, just to get his facts lined up before he spoke again. "I looked back in time and saw you give him something for his protection right before he got into that car. You were both at a moot, and my mom and dad were there. So was I. But I don't remember you, and nor does Mom, and you said you'd never met Dad when you first came to see me."

Angela refocused her attention onto him. She made direct eye contact, and her emotionless facade cracked faintly around the edges, allowing a faint crease of curiosity to peek through. It was there in the slight press of her lips, and the minuscule dip of her eyebrows. "You are not accusing me of lying," she surmised.

"No," Laurence agreed. "Why would you? So I was hoping maybe if you and Mom were in the same place together, it might help one or both of you remember something."

"And you're absolutely certain it was me?"

Laurence nodded and withdrew a hand from the table. He dipped it below, to the pocket of his shorts, to ease out the little thimble from Ru's bear, then he slid his hand back across the table's surface and settled the thimble down on a napkin by Angela's drink. "This is your magic, isn't it?"

Myriam settled in the seat by Laurence's side and placed one soda in front of him as she smiled politely to Angela, but Angela didn't respond. Instead, she reached for the thimble and turned it slowly in her fingers.

"This is… improbable," she said. Her curiosity bled slowly into caution.

Laurence felt his hopes begin to sink. "Improbable that you made it?"

"Improbable that I don't remember doing so. But you're correct in that this *is* my magic." She finally looked across to Myriam and scrutinized her, eyes scanning her features for several seconds. "I can only apologize for my rudeness in not remembering you at all. You are a very memorable person."

"I could say the same, dear," Myriam mused. "Although you must have been much younger in appearance, yes?"

Angela gave a short nod. "I am not older than I look, no. I would have been fifteen at the time. But I don't know you, or Rufus, and I did not know Laurence until I introduced myself a few months ago. If I was the only person to have forgotten then I would suspect I had simply ditched the information as irrelevant, but for us all to have been affected?" She idly nudged the thimble back toward Laurence, then picked up her soda and sipped through her straw.

Laurence narrowed his eyes as he took the thimble. "You think someone did this to all of us."

"It's the only conclusion that makes sense," Angela murmured. She set her drink down and let her fingers linger at the base of the cup while she raised her head to regard Laurence. "That thimble isn't enough to save someone from a fatal crash."

"There were other charms. You made five in total, then hid them inside a small teddy bear, and you told Ru not to let go of it. It's a lot of preparation, casting, and sewing to go through, and you don't remember any of it?"

"A bear," she mused, and then shook her head. "I did used to have a teddy bear, but I lost it… Or rather, I thought I had lost it. Evidently I gave it away."

Laurence tried not to grind his teeth. Angela was the last person he'd think could have memory problems, and this conversation just confirmed his worst fears.

Someone had done this to them all, for whatever reason. Angela and Dad were both capable of magic at the time, yet they'd both been affected, and now Angela had no idea why she'd protected Ru, or who from.

This was going to turn into a hunt. He could feel it, deep down. The itch, the flutter of excitement at bringing his instincts to bear on prey that was well-hidden, the wildness in his heart roaring to be let loose.

He sucked on his straw to avoid looking like he was excited about charging into another situation with mind-altering bastards who might fuck them all over. "You were good enough at the time to make all these charms and save Ru's life," he said. "I figure it was probably easy to change the memories of people who couldn't use magic, but you had all those skills and you were only fifteen. Who could get around your defenses back then?"

Angela's jaw flexed slightly, and her gaze became haunted. "I can think of one person who both could and would have done it."

Laurence had to push aside the mental image of tearing out that person's entrails for now. He'd need more information to make *that* happen.

"Who?"

"The man who sent me to help you in the first place," she said. "His name is Vincent Harrow."

Her tone, her posture, and her expression were all in perfect alignment. Angela radiated a grim horror that Laurence never expected to come from a sorcerer with her skills or experience, and she wasn't even trying to hide it.

That could only mean one thing.

"He's a warlock," Laurence breathed.

Angela dipped her head. "Among other things."

He stared at her, and for once she was readable enough. Whatever else Harrow was, Angela arguably thought he was somehow worse than a warlock.

"Like what?" He had to ask, but he wasn't sure he wanted to know the answer.

She glanced around the inside of the restaurant, either checking they were still alone or buying herself a little more time. But in the end, she returned her attention to him and drew a breath.

"He's my father," she sighed.

13

———

QUENTIN

QUENTIN HAD BARELY STEPPED OUT OF THE SHOWER WHEN NEIL arrived, and only found out because Neil had sent him a photo of the dogs in Quentin's own kitchen, and a message which read *I'm stealing them, you can't stop me.*

He snorted and replied *I don't recommend it,* then hurried to make himself presentable enough to head downstairs.

The noise of teens haranguing an adult was spilling out of the kitchen, and Quentin darted through to try and mitigate it all somehow, though he wasn't sure exactly what could alleviate this level of excitement.

It was as though almost everyone in his life was squeezed into the kitchen all at once. The dogs, Windsor, Mia, Neil, Flynn, and half a dozen teenagers.

"I only brought a Lamborghini," Neil said as he stuffed toast into his mouth. Then, around the chewing, he added, "I can't fit you all into that."

"It's okay, I can drive," Soraya announced. "We've got an SUV. We'll follow you."

"I have to go to work." Felipe rolled his eyes. "Why would you even want to go all the way out into the desert anyway?"

"Uh, hello? Helicopter?" Estelita said it like she thought he was missing something very obvious.

"Mm." Clifton didn't seem convinced, either. "I'll pass."

"So four of us," Soraya declared. "Easy. The Airbus H175 is a good choice."

Mia clicked her tongue. "Soraya. You can't just *tell* someone who hasn't agreed to take you anywhere what vehicle they should rent to take you a place they didn't agree to take you to."

Quentin sat in a spare seat and reached down to pet the dogs as they leaned against his legs. Flynn poured him a cup of tea without a word, and Quentin nodded his thanks, then made eye contact with Neil.

To his credit, Neil just looked amused by it all. Quentin supposed that touring and being famous was likely a lot more hectic than this, but it was still altogether a little too much, so he cleared his throat.

Windsor hopped across the backs of chairs until he was up on Quentin's shoulder, and clacked his beak as though he was calling the table to order.

"All right," Quentin murmured once he had everyone's attention. "Neil, I do apologize. Our conversation was overheard, and everyone seems to have got a little over-eager."

Faces around the table turned toward Neil in an aching silence that was almost physical.

"Yeah, it's Gucci," Neil said. "I get it. Look, if you all want to come, it's cool with me so long as it's cool with your dad."

The faces swiveled in unison toward Quentin, eyes all so wide that they must have been taking begging lessons from the dogs.

"But we're not flying today anyway," Neil added.

"Oh?" Quentin reached for some toast and buttered it. "Why not?"

"Because I refuse to believe you have any clothes that are

remotely suitable for a desert." Neil smirked at him. "Or were you going to dress like that?" He used his coffee cup to point toward Quentin's chest.

Quentin glanced down at himself. This was very casual wear, so far as he was concerned. A loose-fitting white shirt and black trousers. It was as lightweight as he could get in the summer months without exposing skin. "Yes?"

"No. So we're going shopping and we're gonna get you something way more sensible. And *then* we can pick a day for flying."

Quentin crinkled his nose and started to pick at his toast. He could hardly protest about shopping, even though the idea of allowing someone else to choose clothes for him made him bristle, but if Neil had expertise in this area it would be ungracious to disregard it.

"We will only be there for a day," he murmured.

"And a day in the desert without the right clothes or equipment can do a lot of damage, especially in the summer," Mia chipped in.

Quentin frowned faintly in her direction, but Windsor let out a raucous stream of chatter that sounded very much like he, too, was in agreement with Neil and Mia, and so he relented.

"All right," he said.

He was probably going to regret it.

***

ALTHOUGH SORAYA HAD RECENTLY OBTAINED her driving license, Quentin was somewhat apprehensive about handing her the keys to the SUV, but ultimately realized that he had no choice in the matter. She needed access to a vehicle if she was to keep her skills sharp, and he could not drive. At what point would he begin to gain confidence in her ability if he did not allow her to exercise it?

Neil was far more relaxed, of course. He was content to sit up front with Soraya and chat with the kids while she concentrated on the road, which gave Quentin the freedom to pay attention to the traffic around them — something he usually did, but which he was well aware had worsened after his run-in with Katharine Marlowe. Violeta said that a heightened situational awareness was a normal response to trauma, which only made him rethink advice from the Book of Five Rings.

On the whole, in strategy, it is most important that you regard your normal bearing as the same as your bearing at a time of fighting, and your bearing at a time of fighting as the same as your normal bearing.

The more he mulled it over, the more it seemed as though Musashi had always been on tenterhooks because his world was so deadly.

"Q. Hey. Earth calling Q." Neil leaned over the back of his chair and waved his hand an inch from Quentin's nose. "I said, the butler doesn't know, right?"

Quentin blinked and refocused on Neil while Neil slid back into his seat and adjusted his seatbelt. "Know... what?" Then the rest of it caught up to him, and he crinkled his nose. "Q?"

Windsor cackled, and Quentin gently petted the bird in his lap, hoping that would shush him.

"You get a nickname now. That's what friends do, and Q is cool, man." Neil ran a hand through his hair and tossed a lock back over his shoulder. "The kids all know—"

"The 'kids' are mostly adults, and all have their own gifts too," Kimberly mumbled.

"Noice," Neil said. "What about Mia?"

"She also knows," Quentin said. "But you are correct. Mr. Flynn does not."

"Don't talk superpowers in front of the butler, got it. You know, you should tell Ames about all this. She'd love to get in on it. Then she can be here when I'm touring, and I can be here when she's filming. It's win-win."

Quentin raised his eyebrows at the suggestion they drop all this into Neil's sister's lap. "I would not wish to impose—"

"Amy Storm?" Soraya butted in. "We could hang out with Amy Storm?"

"Oh, yeah, sure, she's way cooler than me." Neil rolled his eyes, smiling with amusement.

"No she's not," said Estelita.

"I mean, she *is*," said Soraya.

"Neil is right here," Quentin chided.

"Sorry." Soraya cast Neil a shy smile for a second before she returned her eyes to the road ahead.

Neil just laughed it off, then pointed toward a strip mall they were drawing near. "It's right there. The one with the green sign."

Soraya nodded and approached the mall, then pulled in and parked up without incident, and Quentin had to admit — if only to himself — that she had done an admirable job.

They all piled out and crossed the car park while Windsor flew off to sit on a signpost so that he could keep watch.

Once they were all inside the store, Neil waved the kids ahead and said, "Go absolutely feral. I want a word with your dad."

Quentin paused to one side of the door and tried not to look too dismayed by the shop interior. Almost everything on display was in shades of sand or beige, regardless of whether they were items of clothing or camping goods.

Beige was *not* his color.

The girls fanned out along the aisles and began chattering

amongst themselves, and Neil stepped over to stand by Quentin's side.

"So what actually happened?"

Quentin pursed his lips and glanced across to Neil. "I suppose everyone got a little excited by the thought of a helicopter ride." He hesitated, then added, "And in their defense, I go missing quite often. It must be terrifying for them. Perhaps they believe that if they accompany us, I shan't get myself into trouble again."

Neil nodded slowly and ran fingers through his short beard. "I get it," he rumbled softly. "It's up to you. I'm more than happy to hire a bigger chopper to get us all in and out, but if we're all going, they'll need suitable gear too. A desert's risky enough, but at this time of year you and Kimberly are gonna burn to a crisp in less than an hour if we don't go properly prepared."

Quentin inclined his head a touch. "I'll cover the cost of whatever they need, if you'll lend your expertise in the selection?"

"You're on." Neil clasped a hand down on Quentin's shoulder and gave it a companionable squeeze. "Shop today, fly tomorrow?"

"If that's all right with you?"

"Sure it is. I wouldn't offer otherwise." Neil grinned. "Want me to ask Ames if she'll join us?"

Quentin hesitated. "That does mean revealing certain information," he said.

"Yeah. How about you talk it over with the kids and text me later, okay?"

He nodded, grateful that Neil understood. "I shall. Thank you."

"No worries. Now let's get that poker outta your ass." He began to haul Quentin deeper into the store with a grin that Quentin could only describe as maniacal.

Neil was, Quentin decided, enjoying this *far* too much.

———

THE SHOP only had a handful of changing rooms, and so Quentin tried on ankle boots that looked like they would have been incredibly useful for walking up and down mountains in Annwn had he known such things existed half a year ago. Neil assured him that they should all wear boots rather than shoes lest they encounter an angry rattlesnake, but Quentin really hoped that they would not. After all, the whole purpose of heading all the way out into somewhere so desolate was to do as little damage as possible. If the area was littered with wildlife, he wouldn't be able to test himself to the fullest extent for fear of harming any nearby animals.

By the time his turn for the changing room came up, he was reasonably apprehensive. Everything in his arms was so far out of his comfort zone that he had come close to calling the whole thing off, but now that the teens were excited, it would be mean of him to cancel the trip. And besides, as he had told himself so often lately, he was no coward.

"I can't believe you've taken so much in there, dude," Neil said from the other side of the curtain once Quentin was inside. "This isn't fashion week."

"I am doing the best that I can." Quentin huffed as he checked the edge of the curtain for gaps until he was satisfied that he was safe.

God, he wished Laurence were here.

He rifled through the collection of trousers and shirts and paired them off as best as he could, but it was a lost cause. These items were the epitome of function over form, and he would clearly have to sacrifice silhouette and fit to wear any of them.

Quentin closed his eyes briefly and prepared himself, then

unbuttoned his shirt with swift, mechanical fingers. He shed it while his eyes were still closed, and turned away from the mirror to hang it on an available hook.

This could be over and done with quickly if he just got to it and didn't fret so much, so he stripped off his trousers as perfunctorily and draped them over a stool, then grabbed the first pair to try on and slithered into them like they might bite him.

They're only trousers, for god's sake. Grow up.

He grimaced. The material was stiffer than he was used to, and a little heavier, but at least the label was accurate about the size, and when he pulled the shirt on and turned to regard himself in the mirror he had to admit that it wasn't a complete disaster. No, he wouldn't wish to attend any events dressed like this, but for desert exercises?

If he could manage going for a run in athletic wear, he could absolutely bring himself to wear moisture-wicking shirts and convertible trousers.

But not these ones.

QUENTIN WENT AS QUICKLY as he was able, spurred along by the occasional bored sigh from Soraya, or an "Are you done yet?" from Neil. If he were able to choose darker colors he would, but Neil was set against them, insisting that they would absorb heat from the sun more quickly than light ones.

In the end, he pieced together a combination that would work best with the boots he had already selected and returned to his own clothes, only to step out of the changing room and into a trap.

Neil was there, waiting, with an almost Panama-style hat in his hands, which he immediately dropped onto Quentin's head. "Boom! Never leave home without one!"

"No."

"Yes."

"Neil—"

Neil waggled a finger at him. "You have got to protect the top of your head, bro. This is the best option. Wide brim, vented for air flow, comes in khaki to match the rest of your stuff, looks less shit than a bucket hat. It's perfect."

"I rescind my upgrade," Quentin groused. "You may call me Banbury."

"Dude, you're such a sourpuss." Neil laughed and propelled Quentin back to the shop floor. "You look great. You'd look great in a burlap sack, for crying out loud. Some of us have to work to look half as good as you, so stop wailing and get to the checkout. I think you're about to make these folks' day."

Soraya looked up as Quentin passed her, and her eyes went wide while she clamped her mouth shut. Her cheeks darkened, and she was clearly struggling not to laugh.

He raised his chin and continued on to the counter, where everyone else's purchases were already piled high, waiting for Quentin to pay for them. Soraya could have her amusement for now, because tomorrow they would all be in the same boat, with their UV-protective clothing and factor 50 sunscreen and regrettable fashion choices.

And then, after tomorrow, he could tuck it all away in the closet and forget that it existed.

14

LAURENCE

"GREAT." LAURENCE WAS ONLY HALF SARCASTIC. "LET'S GO HAVE a word with your dad."

"No."

Angela was slowly turning placid again, shutting down in front of his eyes, and Laurence stopped himself from reacting to that. He knew this sign all too well, he'd just never expected to see it from Angela.

It was a trauma defense.

Laurence let go of a breath slowly and bobbed his head. "You're right," he murmured. "He's a warlock. We can't just rush in."

Myriam slurped her drink loudly, then looked at him with wide-eyed innocence when he turned to face her. "I am so sorry, dear. Please, go on."

He knew damn well that she was implying that he was a reckless hothead, but he wasn't going to rise to the bait. A whole lifetime of impatience was still something he struggled to overcome, but he *was* getting better at it.

Sometimes.

"He isn't my biological father," Angela sighed as though

this was just high school gossip. "I know that he adopted me, though I don't know whether he did it legally."

"Were you..." Laurence hesitated, then licked his lips before he continued with the utmost care. "Were you already capable of magic when he took you in?"

"Yes. Thankfully."

She knew what he'd just asked her, then: whether or not Harrow had 'gifted' her with her magic the way only warlocks knew how.

"And you got away, right?" Laurence kept his voice gentle, his features sympathetic. "You're not a warlock."

"I did. Mostly. And no, I am a sorcerer, not a warlock. There are lines I am unwilling to cross." Angela hesitated, then added, "He knows about you, of course, since it was he who sent me to teach you."

There was something left unsaid. Laurence could almost taste it. The words she didn't use, the sentence she didn't continue on to say, like this was one of her lessons and she expected him to piece together the answer from what she had already taught him.

"And he's asked you how it's going?"

It was, Laurence figured, a reasonable conclusion to draw. He wouldn't send his own daughter off to teach someone without then keeping tabs on the progress, would he? Otherwise why send her at all?

Angela bobbed her head.

Laurence leaned back in his chair and tapped his fingers slowly against the side of his cup.

"It's fair to say that he knows the limits of Bambi's magical education, then?" Myriam asked.

"Yes. But he knows more. I have seen photographs of you in his possession. You are often alone and in San Diego, but there are some of you with Quentin, in New York."

Laurence felt his eyebrows climb halfway to his hairline. "I have a warlock for a stalker? That's not creepy at all."

Another warlock for a stalker, he reminded himself. Quentin's dad had already nosed into Laurence's life from half the world away, but what had Laurence done to attract the attention of Vincent Harrow, a guy he'd never met and whose child Laurence was not dating? Was Harrow so cut-off that it really had taken him years to hear of Eric's death? But even if that was the case, why did he care whether or not Laurence had a teacher?

Like all warlocks, Harrow wanted something. Laurence had no clue what it was, but it involved him, and that meant he'd have to find out.

"You say you only mostly got away," he said, thinking out loud. "Why not completely?"

"Warlocks like to think they own and control everything in their lives, including their children. We never really break free until they are gone, and even then..." She paused and looked toward another customer who was busy grabbing condiments from the end of the counter. "I don't know," she admitted. "I am not in a position to imagine my own freedom."

"Have you considered killing him?" There wasn't any gentle or kind way to suggest it, so Laurence just let it all out with a calm tone and watched her response.

She barely flickered. "Of course. But I would have to be sure that I could succeed, because the price of failure would be slavery."

Laurence sat back and frowned at her, but she still watched the customer who was now carrying their tray away from the counter and picking out a table for themselves. "Not death?"

"He only kills the slaves he has no further use for." She finally turned her placid gaze back to Laurence and met his eyes. "He has other slaves discard their carcasses like meat. He lives his whole life within his sanctum, where he is simultaneously at his most powerful and most heavily fortified, and he is surrounded by the people he has stolen from their own lives to service his. Some of them retain a semblance of personality and thought, others are hollowed-out shells of human beings who are nothing more than organic robots to him. Many are capable of magic themselves, but are only allowed to use it to serve his will. He is a monster, Laurence, the like of which I promise that you have never seen."

He was about to open his mouth, to protest, to insist that he'd seen that exact kind of monster, but the truth was that he hadn't. The duke had his own way of working, and this wasn't it.

But Laurence was a monster-slayer.

"Is he human?" he asked.

"To my knowledge, yes." Angela nodded. "And he knows nothing of your gifts, only your magic." She paused again, and then added, "Did anything unusual occur while you were in New York?"

"Yeah, absolutely it did." Laurence scowled and leaned forward to rest an elbow on the table. "A Black Dog took Quen to Annwn, and I had to go get him back."

Angela slowly lifted an eyebrow. "You lack the magical knowledge required to do that," she said.

"Yeah. I had help."

She pursed her lips a little and glanced off to one side, then back at him. "He was testing your limits," she murmured.

Laurence felt his heart thump and the hairs on his forearms lift. He sucked in air as the weight of her words hit him and left him floundering. "He sent the Black Dog to take Quentin," he breathed in shock. "Just to see what I'd do about it?"

"And it transpired that you could handle a ghost problem," Angela said.

Ghost problem.

Had Harrow put Delaney on their tail, too? Was Marlowe's involvement purely accidental, or had she been maneuvered into place like a chess piece? Just how far was Harrow going to go in his efforts to probe Laurence's skills?

Would he test them to destruction?

"Setting this aside, just for a moment," Myriam said softly as she squeezed Laurence's arm, "is there a way to recover memories once they're lost? If we undo whatever he did, will we also find out how he did it in the first place?"

"I have a few avenues that I can explore," Angela replied, nodding to Myriam across the table. "I will test them out."

"I'll see if Ru has anything that can help," Laurence offered. "Maybe you two should meet? Again, I mean. If we all work together on this, we can get to the bottom of it faster, right?"

Angela shook her head. "He is a witch."

"Uh huh," Laurence said slowly, not sure what her problem was. "So am I," he reminded her.

"Yes," she said. "And there will be aspects of my craft which a witch will consider to be magic darker than he is willing to engage with."

Laurence wanted to object, but he knew she was right. Hell, even *he* knew what the problem was with the magic she'd used to save Quentin's life, even if he wasn't as violently opposed to it as Rufus was.

Rufus would've let Quentin die rather than cross that line. Angela was right. It was better to keep them both apart for as long as possible, because who knew how Ru would react to having her on the case? And even if he tolerated her long enough to solve the murder, what then, once he knew who she was and what she was capable of?

Laurence ran fingertips through his stubble and scratched his jaw. "Is it possible Vincent Harrow murdered Rufus' parents?"

Angela's emotions finally seeped back into existence with an amused snort. "Of course. He's a killer. Murder is just one tool in his kit. Who knows who he's disposed of over the years? The question is does Rufus seek knowledge, or does he want vengeance too?"

"I don't—" He stopped himself right there.

He *did* know. His gut absolutely knew without a shadow of a doubt that all Ru's barely-contained rage, all his conviction that the accident was not accidental, and his willingness to teach Laurence in exchange for answers even though he had no interest in being a teacher all pointed to one inescapable truth.

Ru would not be satisfied with knowledge alone. It was one small step toward a goal that was too far away for him to reach right now.

"Revenge," Laurence sighed. "He'll want revenge."

Angela nodded curtly and rose to her feet. "Then I'll do what I can to help him get it. Give me a couple of days and I'll let you know what I find."

"Thanks. I mean it." Laurence stood too, but Myriam didn't, so he just stood there waving goodbye while Angela stalked out of the restaurant. "Mom?"

She finally stood. Her hazel eyes creased in thought, and she pressed her lips tightly together. "Mmm?"

"Shall we, uh…" He tilted his head slowly. "What is it?"

"Nothing," she said as she patted his arm again. "We should go."

Laurence tailed his mom to the exit, and then back across the parking lot, but she wouldn't say anything more and he knew there was no point in trying to push. She'd held out on him about Herne's dream his whole life, she could totally keep her mouth shut about whatever had occurred to her, and nothing he could say would force her hand.

He just wished he could shake the feeling that he wouldn't like it.

15

FREDERICK

FREDERICK SIPPED TEA AND SIFTED THROUGH THE LOCAL lawyer's notes on his tablet while Michael scoured the hotel suite to ensure that their bags were packed and nothing was left behind.

He disliked what he had experienced thus far of Arizona, but he disliked all the driving back and forth to San Diego even more — not that he was the one doing it, but it was tiresome nonetheless. Still, after today, he hoped all that would be at an end.

One look out of the window could fool anyone into believing Phoenix wasn't so bad. It was a beautiful morning, with a bright and clear sky, and gorgeous dusky mountains on the far side of the skyscrapers, but he knew damn well that beyond the hotel's front door was an oven, with humidity so low that the air actively leeched moisture out of one's body. He drank twice as much water whenever he was here compared to just about anywhere else in the world, and he'd be glad to see the back of the place.

"All clear," Michael said as he wheeled the luggage to the door.

Frederick set his cup down, turned the tablet off, and stood. He cast his own eyes over what he could see, but he knew Michael had been thorough. It was simply force of habit.

"Very well," he murmured. "Shall we get it over with?"

Michael gave a grim nod. "You're sure you want to do this?"

"No," Frederick groused. "But I see little choice."

It was time to meet a Marlowe face to face.

THE MARICOPA COUNTY Fourth Avenue Jail was right in the middle of downtown Phoenix, sitting like a particularly forbidding windowless office block among multi story car parks and the equally forbidding sheriff's office headquarters.

Frederick wasn't fond of the legal system in the United States, let alone the idea of black-clad, heavily armed police officers on the streets. It all felt highly adversarial, and he'd come to suspect that Icky had no idea of the level of favor he was asking Frederick to perform here. Delving into the memories of the defense attorneys he'd hired on behalf of the Marlowes every time they left this place was dismal enough, but to be here in person, knowing full well that once the Marlowes exited those glass doors he would be utterly powerless, was the very definition of terrifying.

Challenging, he reminded himself. He had come this far. He had to trust his skills to see him through what was to come, because he was more than the sum of his gifts, and he knew it. Hell, it was why he'd pushed so hard to play rugby, to hit the gym, to take up boxing.

In the matter of getting his hands dirty versus remaining at a safe distance, the former was going to win out today.

Michael parked on the street so that Frederick could

observe the doors. There were two sets, facing one another: one for visitors, and the other for releases, and Frederick watched them like a hawk until, finally, the door marked RELEASE cracked open.

There she was. Katharine Marlowe. She carried no possessions, and looked for all the world like she just hopped off a bus instead of out of a maximum security jail as she descended the handful of steps to street level.

"Showtime," Frederick muttered.

He didn't need to tell Michael to stay here. The plan had already been thoroughly worked out in advance. Still, they exchanged a concerned glance with one another before Frederick left the car and crossed the street at the intersection. The last thing he bloody needed was to get himself fined outside a jail for the absurd American crime of jaywalking.

His connection to Michael shut down abruptly when he was a few feet away from Katharine. He expected it, he'd seen how it felt to Laurence in Laurence's memories, but still it was jarring to be disarmed so bluntly in a public place, and he relied on his sunglasses to hide any involuntary reaction he might have given.

She eyed his approach, but said nothing.

"Katharine Marlowe," he began as he stopped well within murdering range. "I'm Frederick d'Arcy. Quentin's brother." He offered his hand, and added, "I have been overseeing the legal effort to have you and your brothers released."

She took his hand and attempted to crush it. "So where are they?"

Frederick waited until she let go before he answered. "I believe the jail processes releases in an order which suits them, and while I do not know what time precisely that may be, I do know that all three of you should be set free today. If not, I shall be quite irate." He gestured to the car. "Would you care to wait with me? I don't believe they're keen on people lingering on their doorstep."

Marlowe curled her lip into a sneer. "Are you a witch?"

"No. I'm afraid that only seems to manifest itself in the first born in our family, although I should caution that Quentin very much dislikes that word."

"I don't give a shit," she said. "Okay. I'll wait with you. But if you try anything, I'll kill you."

"Aren't you charming," Frederick said smoothly. "I can see why my brother was so eager to let you back out into the wild."

She snorted, and as he led her to the car he felt as though he were being tailed by a particularly hungry tiger.

KATHARINE SAT in the seat nearest to the jail so that she had clear line of sight, which Frederick had anticipated. With her military background, it seemed an obvious choice, and it gave him some comfort to have accurately predicted such a small thing.

Frederick eased his tablet from the seat pocket in front of him and tapped away at it. It would give her the impression that he required external storage for information, which should render him less intimidating. He removed his sunglasses, too, since soldiers were trained to do so when making contact with civilians. It would help convince her that he had nothing to hide.

"I must apologize for the time taken to secure your release," he drawled. "The FBI were quite keen on continuing their charges against you even without my brother's willingness to give evidence, and so I had to engage the services of a local firm to progress the matter."

Katharine merely grunted. She didn't take her eyes off the doors.

"I do have some questions of my own, however," Frederick continued. "Completely off-record, I assure you."

"I don't owe you shit," she said.

"That's as may be," he agreed. "But you tortured my brother, and I would like to know whether he's completely lost his marbles in forgiving you for it." Frederick paused to adjust his position a little, to hide how much saying those words out loud to the perpetrator's face had lit a flare of rage in his chest.

He'd failed to protect Icky from their father, and now he'd failed to protect Icky from the Marlowes, and here he was doing everything in his considerable power to let both sets of perpetrators walk free.

It did worse than rankle. It burned.

Katharine finally turned away from the jail and regarded him with all the detached disinterest of a fully-fledged superiority complex. He should know. He'd given plenty of people that exact same look.

"He lost his marbles years ago," Katharine said bluntly. "You haven't lost yours, though. Do you know what your father did to him?"

Frederick felt a muscle twitch in his jaw. "Yes," he said.

"But he didn't do it to you," she mused.

"No."

She searched his gaze, then nodded to herself. "First born," she said.

Frederick said nothing. She might be ex military, but she clearly wasn't a fool, and if her deduction supported his own claim that only Icky bore any gifts, then so much the better.

"You want us to kill your father," she concluded.

Frederick was so surprised by her statement that he

couldn't keep his eyes from widening, nor his eyebrows from inching up. His failure to predict *this* line of conversation would have to take a back seat to his brain whirring into action to assemble the new variable into his day. "I beg your pardon?"

"That's the real reason you've come all the way to this country and paid lawyers to get us out, isn't it?" Katharine raised her chin toward him. "I can smell hidden motive a mile away, d'Arcy, and you're full of it." She barked a short laugh. "The irony. One brother thinks he's a monster, the other *is* one."

"Rude," Frederick said, sniffing dismissively. "You are correct that I am a monster, but, no. I did not intend to conscript you for murder, although now that you've presented the possibility perhaps we can explore it in the future. I actually wished to seek assurances from you that you are not in fact about to go off torturing and murdering whomsoever you deem deserves it yet again."

"You'd rather I tortured and murdered who *you* deem fit?"

Frederick shrugged faintly. The very real possibility of having experienced killers at his disposal hadn't really reared itself before, but he far favored the idea of not having to deal with the Marlowes ever again. If he wanted someone offed, he could take care of it without relying on someone he couldn't protect himself from.

Though that wasn't strictly true, and he knew it. He was all too aware that only Katharine stood a chance of killing the duke, since Icky refused to.

"I would rather you not do it at all," he sighed. "As would Quentin, obviously, since he facilitated this whole arrangement. He's willing to take you at your word."

She eyed him thoughtfully, then nodded. "But you know that I can just disappear and continue my work, and so long as neither of you saw me again you'd never know whether I'd lied to you."

"That is correct."

"Then what do you want? Some kind of custody arrangement?" She laughed again. "An ankle monitor? You've got no legal right to enforce one, and you can't stop me taking it off when you're gone."

"Goodness, no." Frederick rolled his eyes and waved his free hand dismissively. "Nothing so useless. I would like to give you a home and a job."

It wasn't strictly what he would like to do, but Icky hadn't come up with any plan beyond *don't let them go to prison*, which was too short-sighted for Frederick's liking. He had created this part of the solution himself, because leaving the Marlowes at a loose end would only give them time and opportunity to get back into their usual routine of murdering innocent people, but it definitely rankled.

"You can't expect me to move to England," Katharine said slowly. It wasn't a question. "What, then?"

"What I can offer you is a new identity," Frederick murmured, "and the funding necessary for both a property and to set yourselves up in business as bounty hunters in whatever state you wish to, though some states — such as Michigan — require very little in the way of training or licensing to do such work."

"And, conveniently, Michigan is over two thousand miles away from San Diego," Katharine replied.

"Very convenient." Frederick allowed a ghost of a smile to grace his lips, and then he tapped at his tablet to wake it again and scrolled through her files. "You must admit that your skillsets are eminently suited to such work."

She shrugged and went back to gazing across the street, turning her back on him and crossing her arms. "I'm not going to make any promises. But I'll talk it over and see what they have to say."

He knew she meant with her brothers, but he meant for

things to be crystal clear, so he murmured, "With Stephen and Adam?"

"Yes."

"All right." He nodded to himself and tucked the tablet away. "I can arrange for a hotel for all of you for a while so that you can find your feet and take as long as you need to reach your decision."

"So you can keep tabs on us," she corrected him.

"I realize that it has already been said, but it does bear repeating: you *tortured my brother*." Frederick kept a firm hold on his anger. Now was not the time to allow it to break free. He might not be able to use his gifts this very moment, but he was an aristocrat and a lawyer, and he both could and would control himself so that he could present his argument. "You tortured him, and then you left him to die, and it was only through circumstances that you had not foreseen that he is alive today. You intended to murder him, but he is doing everything in his power to protect you from the consequences of your actions when you and I both know that he isn't the first. How many times have you succeeded, Katharine? How many have you tortured and killed on this vendetta which doesn't even belong to you?"

"I don't answer to you," she sneered.

"You don't answer to anyone," he replied smoothly. "And here you are, yet again, not answering for your crimes, with my assistance. So either you draw a line under all of the murdering you've been up to and walk out of here into a new life, or you can go right back to it and sooner or later it will catch up with you."

Katharine swiveled slowly in her seat to face him, and her gaze was hard. "Are you threatening me?"

How typical, he thought. *The murderer doesn't like to be on the back foot.*

She wasn't the only one. This was madness, being here

without his telepathy to protect him. *Challenging* didn't even begin to skim the surface of how naked he felt, but the Marlowes' power also robbed him of his ability to check whether or not Katharine were truly capable of the change Icky believed possible, and the idea that everyone else lived their whole lives just relying on the words that came out of each others' mouths was frankly horrifying.

"You've already threatened me." Frederick gave her a lazy smile and a raised eyebrow. "Turnabout is fair play, don't you think?" He leaned in slowly. It was a calculated risk, to show that he wasn't remotely frightened by her, and it was a lie. Any sensible person would be terrified to share a space with a serial killer. "I may be a monster, but *you* are evil. Pure, unmitigated, rancid evil. You are no better than my father, and this line you draw to pretend otherwise — your insistence that you will not harm children — is a lie you tell yourself to pretend that you are still human. But you and I know that you would wait until the day they turn eighteen then murder them on their birthdays. That's unconscionable, Katharine, and if you can't see why, then you are beyond the redemption which Quentin believes you to be capable of."

The glint in her steel eyes suggested that she might be considering killing him right then and there, and Frederick was more than willing to fight like a cornered cat in the enclosed space if he had to, but after a long, drawn-out staring contest, Katharine sniffed and held a hand out toward him. "Give me your phone number. I'll call you when we've made our decision."

Frederick leaned back, smothered his relief with a judicious application of stiff upper lip, and withdrew his card case and a pen. He turned one of his business cards over so that he could write his American phone number on the back, then he blew on the ink to dry it and handed it over.

She examined it. "You're a lawyer? Why'd you hire others to do this for you?"

"Because I am not qualified to work with American law, and because it would represent a conflict of interest regardless." Frederick capped the pen and returned it to his inner pocket, then tucked the card case alongside it. "I have flown here to handle this situation, and once you have made your decision I shall return home. There is no need for you to ever see me again." He tugged out his wallet this time, and flipped it open, then grabbed the notes inside and offered them to her. He'd calculated a thousand dollars to be more than enough for them to spend a while in a cheap motel while they all planned their next move. "Here. For tonight."

Katharine's lips peeled back from her teeth like she might hiss at him for offering cash, but then she took it from his hand and stuffed it inside the pocket of her trousers. "We're done here."

"The doors are not locked," Frederick replied, which was the politest way to say *fuck off* that he was willing to offer.

Katharine let herself out and slammed the door shut. She jaywalked right back to where he'd picked her up from, clearly not giving a damn about getting caught either drifting across the road or loitering outside a jail, and didn't once look back.

"Go," Frederick ordered the moment she was gone.

Michael didn't say a word. He started the car and pulled away from the curb, and it wasn't until they hit the westbound interstate that he finally opened his mouth.

"Well, she seemed nice," he said tersely.

Michael's thoughts were clear as a bell, though. He'd spent the whole time scared for them both, frightened that Marlowe was about to lose it and lash out, and he'd already endured enough horror at the duke's hands without another of Icky's enemies trying to kill him.

"Didn't she?" Frederick murmured. "Still, done now. With any luck that'll be the end of it."

Jesus, I fucking hope so, Michael thought, though he didn't say it out loud.

Frederick was about to agree, but the vibration of his phone against his chest derailed him. Katharine hadn't already decided, surely?

The caller ID did not answer his question, so he thumbed the green button and answered. "Hello?"

"Frederick."

Ah. He knew that voice very well.

"Myriam," he said, adopting a far warmer tone. "This is an unexpected pleasure. How may I be of assistance?"

"I would like your help," she said briskly. "If I text you my address, could you meet me there this evening? I'm afraid I won't be home until seven."

Frederick pursed his lips faintly. Myriam, calling *him* for help? This was peculiar, and his curiosity was readily piqued.

"That's quite all right," Frederick said. "It will take me that long to get to you anyway. May I ask the nature of the problem?"

"I've forgotten something," Myriam said. "We all have. And I think you might be the only person who can recover it."

He blinked slowly. This had to be something big for her to ask for *that* kind of help, especially so soon after chewing him up and spitting him out yesterday.

"All right," he said. "We're on our way."

"No," Myriam cut in. "No 'we.' Just you."

He understood her meaning. Michael would not be welcome, and that was fair. He may well no longer be the teenager Myriam used to know, but she had yet to see it, and now was not the time.

"I'm on my way," Frederick assured her.

Myriam hung up without saying goodbye, and Frederick

pursed his lips while he watched the other cars on the interstate.

Did he really want to be sucked into more of this nonsense?

Problem? Michael's mind was filled with concern. The poor boy worried an awful lot.

Potentially, Frederick replied, slipping his response directly into Michael's thoughts without saying a word. *There's only one way to find out.*

He couldn't help but feel that he was spending all this time and money on helping Icky make a terrible mistake.

16

MYRIAM

"Have you lost your mind?" Bambi was pacing the back room of the store and tugging on his curls in frustration. His cheeks were flushed, and he was obviously doing his best not to completely blow his top.

Myriam slipped her phone into the pocket of her apron and picked up the list of orders that were still waiting on fulfillment. "He wants to make amends," she said coolly as she flipped through the papers to do a quick estimate of how long this would take. "If we don't give him that opportunity, how will he prove that he has the will to back up his intentions?"

"Mom, he—" Bambi huffed and threw himself onto a stool so hard it wobbled, and he grabbed the table to stop himself falling right off it again. "He's not okay."

"He kidnapped you from right in front of me," she agreed. "Took you to England without your permission. He's a liar, a manipulator, and a megalomaniac. I'm not disputing any of that."

"Then—"

"Bambi." She spoke firmly, to let him know that she

wouldn't be having her decision changed by any further argument, and he huffed angrily at her.

The truth was that he was absolutely right to be concerned. Freddy was all those things, and possibly more. Bambi hadn't said too much about what had happened in London, and since he talked openly about most other things in his life these days, his silence spoke volumes.

But Freddy wanted to make amends. He wanted to become a better person. And Myriam had enough experience raising a child to know that, sooner or later, you had to trust them to make their own futures.

If everyone rejected Freddy, who knew what he might become?

"Have you considered," Myriam said quietly, "what growing up in that family might have done to him?"

Bambi's face reddened with anger. "It's not like he's the one who—" He shut himself off and dug fingernails into the surface of the desk.

Myriam knew what he meant. Freddy wasn't the one who had endured their father's abuse firsthand. That was Quentin's sorrow to bear.

"He's not," she agreed. "But he loves Quentin a great deal, and had to grow up unable to protect him. Can you imagine the helplessness? I see it in his obsessive need to control everything, but I also see it in his physique. Bambi, he's done everything he possibly can to defend himself from whatever was happening to his brother, and only now does he know that he was never in danger anyway." She took a breath and let it go, using it as a four second meditation to exhale her upset. "Those boys all lost their mother," she finally added. "Even Freddy."

Bambi curled his lip. "She wasn't exactly innocent."

"But they didn't know that at the time." Myriam walked around the desk and settled a hand on Bambi's shoulder and then, when he looked up at her, she leaned in to hug him around his shoulders. "I love you, Bambi. You are a blessing, and I'm proud of you every single day."

He sighed and curled his arms around her waist as he buried his face against her shoulder. "I love you, Mom. I don't want you to get hurt."

"I know, dear," she murmured. "Stick around and help me with today's orders, then you can come home with me this evening and make sure he doesn't get up to any funny business, all right?"

Bambi nodded. "And if he does, I'll fucking stab him."

"That's only fair."

<hr>

AFTER THEY CLOSED THE SHOP, they shared a truck out to the farm. They had plenty of time to greet Ellie and become covered head to toe in stray dog hairs, but also to ascertain that Lisa wasn't home. The teen might still be with Quentin, but Myriam texted her just to be sure.

She'd never thought she'd have a teenager under her roof again, and sometimes Lisa spent the night with the other girls at Bambi's home instead, but for once Myriam was grateful that the house was empty. She didn't want to spring Freddy — of all people — onto the poor dear.

While Bambi started weighing up kitchen knives in his hands, Myriam fetched a can of dog food from the pantry and spooned it into Ellie's bowl. Ellie, for her part, was able to sit still for the few seconds the process took, which was the only time the dynamo of a border collie was able to remain unmoving when she wasn't asleep.

"There," Myriam said as she pointed to the bowl with her spoon. "Eat up."

Ellie darted in, and Myriam took can and spoon to the sink and washed both.

Bambi was still selecting knives. He would balance one in his hand, his fingers loose, then tighten his grip and thrust toward the window with the blade. If he seemed satisfied with the motion, he'd then turn the hilt so that the flat spine of the blade rested against his forearm, and purse his lips in thought.

"You are not going to stab Freddy with that," Myriam advised him. "That's my best chef's knife. I don't want to prepare vegetables with something you've used to murder Quentin's brother." She patted her hands dry on a towel and began to fill the kettle.

Bambi bared his teeth, but put it back in the knife rack. "Fine," he growled. "Something smaller would be better anyway. Easier to hide, quicker to use."

Myriam lifted her eyebrows as she glanced up at him. "If you do so much stabbing, why don't you have your own knife?" She paused briefly, then added, "Not that I mean to encourage it."

"It's not worth it." He sighed as he turned his back on the knives and crossed his arms. "Even if it's a legal carry, all it takes is a cop to not know the difference between a legal knife and an illegal one and I get arrested for it. Even if I get released later, it's a pain in the ass. Besides…" Bambi tailed off a while and watched Ellie eat, then huffed and met Myriam's gaze. "Open carry means I gotta have the hilt visible everywhere I go, and that would make me look like a serial killer."

Myriam nodded thoughtfully. Bambi was right, but it was also a relief that he wasn't ready to go out into the world armed at all times. For all the trouble he got caught up in, he was still her son, and nobody wanted their baby to get hurt.

"I could ask Ru if there's some way of hiding it with magic, though," Bambi mused.

Well, there went the relief. Myriam puffed out her cheeks and made tea for them both before she changed the subject. "What did Freddy do?"

Bambi eyed her briefly, but turned away with his mug of tea and made his way to the kitchen table. He sat slowly in a chair and cradled the mug in his hands, even though it had to be piping hot, and avoided looking at her. "What do you mean?"

"I wasn't born yesterday, dear." Myriam sat opposite him and put her mug to one side so it could cool a little.

Bambi had a posture he adopted whenever he had something to hide. He would shrink in on himself, his shoulders hunched and his lips turned down like he could become invisible if he tried hard enough. And he almost could, too; he could disappear in a crowd if he wanted, sneak his way past everyone the way Eric used to whenever he wanted to smuggle his own snacks into the movie theater. It was a wonder that it ever worked. Eric had never been a small man, and Bambi was almost as tall as his father, and yet Herne's gifts meant they could pull it off.

In *public*.

Not here, at Myriam's table.

She wasn't a fool. She'd seen her son leave her store with Freddy — though she'd thought he was Quentin at the time — and by the time Bambi returned, he'd brought an abiding loathing for Quentin's brother with him. Sure, they were cordial enough with each other, but something had obviously happened, and if Myriam was about to allow Freddy into her home, it was time to know what it was.

"In England," she clarified. "What happened?"

Bambi's hunker shifted into a full-on slouch and he gulped down tea, then hissed at it. "Fuck. Look, it's nothing. You know what happened. He kidnapped me, forced Quentin to go home, thought he was cleverer than everyone else, and ended up nearly getting Mikey killed because he's too much of a selfish prick to work with us." He glared at the mug like he could kill it with his mind. "Their dad made him do it, but he could've come to us, offered to work with us, and he was so sure he knew best."

Myriam nodded thoughtfully. She *had* heard this part before. But she knew there was something else, too, and now was the time to find out what it was. She knew it in her heart, and her instincts were never wrong.

"What else?" She asked it softly, watching her own mug now to take the pressure off Bambi. She blew on her tea a while before taking a slow sip.

Bambi knocked back the rest of his tea in a couple of gulps, then slammed the mug down on the heavy wooden table with a *thunk*. "He tortured me, Mom," he said, his voice thick as molasses. "He wanted to make Quen angry enough to kill the duke, and he figured the most *efficient—*" he said the word with the utmost bitterness "—way was to break me as fast and as inhumanely as he could." He balled his hands into fists and used those fists to wipe tears from his eyes while they were still forming. "And then when I managed to get to Avalon to recover, he shot me up with heroin. I wasn't even *there*, I was in Otherworld, and he just put heroin in my body without my permission and I—" He collapsed into hiccups as his words failed him.

The rage which flushed Myriam boiled in her veins and made her skin feel incandescent. She thought she could have been prepared for whatever Bambi said, but she'd been wrong, and now she wanted to be the one to stab Freddy so that Bambi didn't have to.

She stood with all the control that she could muster and hurried around the table so that she could settle back down in the chair beside her son, and then she curled her arms around him and held him to her chest, because it was what she could do. More than that, it was what she should do. She might feel anger, but whatever had happened had been done to Bambi, not to her, and she wasn't about to center herself in *his* pain.

He leaned into her and wrapped his arms around her waist, then sobbed against her shoulder, and she wished that she could make his hiccups turn to laughter the way that Eric used to, but that had been his way, and this was hers. Sometimes it was better to get the poison out than to slap a Band-Aid on it, and all Myriam could do was hope that she was taking the right path.

The man who had hurt her son was on his way over, and she had to decide whether he was the lesser of two evils, but one thing was certain.

If he messed with them again, she wouldn't give a damn *which* knife Bambi used to gut him with.

17

FREDERICK

"I COULD DRIVE YOU MOST OF THE WAY, THEN WAIT AT A GAS station or something," Michael offered. His frown was petulant on the surface, but the undercurrent of concern seethed through his thoughts, and his emotions were buffeted by them.

"I would rather you remain here," Frederick replied as he ditched his towel and reached for a fresh shirt. "Where you are safe," he added, glancing to Michael, who had already picked up the towel to fold it.

It had taken so long for Michael to recover from the thrashing the duke had put him through. He could have died, and all because Frederick's father wanted to force him out of hiding and into the light, and Frederick was about to head into another situation where he would be exposed. While he did not expect Myriam to assault Michael, he also saw no need to allow the opportunity to even arise.

No, it was best to keep Michael at the hotel, where nobody wished him any harm, and where he could rest after two back-to-back days of driving.

Michael's gaze drifted down Frederick's body and lingered

with hope at his crotch, then he forced himself to turn away so he could lay the towel down and hide his own reaction, though it was burning bright in his thoughts.

Frederick just smiled dryly and pulled his boxer shorts on. "Utterly filthy," he murmured. "Whatever shall I do with you?"

"Literally anything you want to," Michael said. He cleared his throat and turned back to face Frederick, his cheeks almost as red as his hair.

"Agreed. But later. For now, promise me one thing."

"Of course. What?"

Frederick pulled his trousers up and tucked his shirt in, then fastened the fly as he made eye contact with Michael. "If Mrs. Riley sees fit to murder me horribly, do me a favor and avenge my death, would you?"

Michael's frown returned, and he swatted lightly at Frederick's arm. "Fuck off. Don't you dare get murdered, or I won't forgive you."

Frederick laughed as he pulled Michael close for a kiss and held him tightly until he was done, then he let go with a brief squeeze of Michael's arse. "Very well."

It derailed Michael as intended, and left him torn between concern and arousal, which would do nicely until Frederick returned tonight.

THE FREEWAY WAS QUITE IRRITATING. Having returned to the hotel to shower before setting off again, it meant that Frederick was now trapped in rush hour traffic on his way north, and while it hardly compared to London, it still meant that his top speed was capped at forty miles an hour for half of his journey.

Things improved once he was on the smaller roads, though, from traffic to scenery, and the summer sky was still clear and blue even though he didn't reach the address Myriam had sent him until around half past seven. The route the SatNav guided him along matched Michael's memories of this place, so that when he finally reached the single track dirt road which led to the farmhouse, Frederick's natural suspicions of being led on a wild goose chase were all but contained.

The building revealed itself like the sun peeking out from behind clouds as Frederick turned the final bend around the edges of a wooded area, and it hadn't changed a bit since Michael's memories of his last visit here several years ago. The cream walls picked up the evening light and infused it with additional warmth, while the two-story house was itself dwarfed by the vast greenhouses behind it.

Frederick parked neatly alongside the Jack in the Green truck by the front door, and was ready for the streak of black and white border collie before she even reached him. He calmed her down and convinced her that he was a friend with hardly any effort at all, and allowed her to lead him around the house to a rear porch.

Laurence was there, waiting for him like a bouncer.

"Laurence," Frederick said as he stepped up onto the porch. He kept his greeting neutral, since Laurence looked reasonably unhappy.

"Freddy," Laurence answered, his voice low. "Mom says you want to start making amends."

He eyed Laurence and shrugged slowly while he took in as much about Laurence's body language and facial expression as he could within the extra second that the movement gave him. The lad was taut as a mousetrap, his eyes dark and narrowed, with a slight curl to his lip. It was reasonable to deduce that Laurence was unconvinced by whatever Myriam had truly said to him.

"That is correct," Frederick murmured.

Laurence leaned a fraction closer. His eye contact was surprisingly aggressive. "Look, man, I appreciate everything you've done for us — you know, other than the kidnapping and the drugging and the torture — but if you do *anything* to fuck with my mom, I will tear your kidneys out with my bare hands and watch you bleed to death. You get me?"

The image Frederick conjured from Laurence's words was all too vivid, and he considered protesting, but Laurence clearly cared more for his mother's safety than he did for his own. To push back against that courted disaster.

"I understand completely," he said, gazing evenly into Laurence's eyes.

Laurence sniffed the air, then backed off and opened the back door. He let the dog inside first, then gestured for Frederick to go next.

"After you," he said, and somehow it sounded like a threat.

Not for the first time, Frederick silently cursed the existence of the talisman which protected Laurence's thoughts, and he stepped into the wolf's den.

***

HERBS HUNG from a rail across the kitchen windows as they dried in the summer sun, and their aroma filled the room with rosemary and sage, a scent combination which Frederick instinctively associated with Christmas rather than midsummer.

Myriam did not rise from her seat at the dining table. Instead, she gestured for Frederick to sit across from her, so he did so, settling down on the rustic wooden chair and propping one elbow onto the arm.

Laurence lingered behind Frederick's shoulder, so quiet that the only way Frederick was aware of him was the shadow cast across the room.

It was best to get straight to business, then. This was not an atmosphere for conviviality.

Frederick met Myriam's gaze across the table and raised his chin a little. "Would you be so kind as to detail the nature and scope of the problem, please?"

Myriam pressed her lips together before she spoke. "There's someone from Bambi's childhood we've all forgotten, but she was there. I would like you to see if you can uncover those memories and figure out what made us forget her in the first place. Can you do that?"

Normally, uncovering a forgotten memory was hardly a challenge. Things were rarely truly forgotten, merely buried behind the most tenuous and underused neural pathways. But this wasn't an individual case. For multiple people to have mislaid the same information there had to be an external force involved, and until Frederick could work out who or what it was, there were no guarantees.

Instead, he pursed his lips and answered more carefully.

"Potentially. I will do my utmost."

Myriam dipped her head and removed a thong from around her neck, then she laid the talisman as far away from herself on the table as she could reach.

When she sat back and crossed her arms, Frederick already knew that it was far enough. Suddenly the dog was not the only other consciousness sharing the kitchen with him, and he didn't wait for Myriam to backtrack on her decision.

He slipped into her thoughts, dissociated her mind from her body, and wrapped them both inside a construct so that Myriam couldn't do anything to make Laurence go digging for his kidneys.

MYRIAM WAS ALREADY FROWNING. Her instincts were every bit as strong as her son's, and without Frederick suppressing them as he had when he first met her, they had already keyed her in to the change in her surroundings. Subtle details which Frederick had altered to give her those clues, of course, but most people would take a few minutes to realize that the old house's creaks and groans had gone away, or that the dog laying on the floor by their side was no longer breathing.

By the time Myriam considered asking whether or not Frederick was inside her mind, he had already dug up more context on what she wanted of him. The woman, Angela Tate, and her own inability to recall meeting Myriam or Laurence. The fact that Tate's father was a powerful warlock. The likelihood that their memories were buried by magic.

The moment that Myriam stood up for Frederick against Laurence's doubts.

Frederick had never before attempted to recover memories which were magically erased, and had absolutely no idea whether it was possible for him to achieve, but he did relish a challenge.

"Yes," he said, before Myriam formed words. "We are inside your mind. It allows me to work without distraction. Are you comfortable for me to proceed?"

Her comfort was absolutely in flux, no matter how evenly she composed her features. "I would like you to continue," she replied.

They both knew that she was sidestepping answering his question, but pushing for an answer would be counterproductive. How *could* she be comfortable with this? Only Michael was so completely at ease with having a telepath in his life, and Frederick was well aware of how repulsed everyone else was by the idea that their thoughts might not be private.

It would help if Frederick could see Laurence's vision from

the inside. Knowing exactly which moot on which beach at what time would have been useful. But as he rifled through Myriam's conversations with her son he realized that Myriam had that information.

It was the night Todd and Paula Grant died.

"One moment," he murmured.

Myriam folded her hands together on the table and waited.

<hr>

"Next time, we'll do this at our place," Paula Grant said with a grin as she hugged Myriam tightly. "We've got plenty of room at the house."

"And I know you'd love to get a good look at how it all works," Todd added with a smile to Eric.

"Nah, all that's behind me now." Eric chuckled and set his guitar down in the sand so that he could shake Todd's hand. "Though, I mean, I guess I could just look it over. You know, to make you happy."

Todd and Eric both laughed, and Myriam—

—as Paula and Todd led their son, Rufus, to their car.

Frederick frowned at the blip. It was as though someone was careless with the remote and had accidentally nudged the fast-forward button.

Memories were simultaneously intricate and yet staggeringly simple things. Some were constructed with care, and others got stored like a bundle of index cards, patched together out of fragments of previous knowledge to save the brain from saving sufficiently similar information twice. Lesser detail was often dropped, difficult to retrieve for the owner of the brain in question but not too hard for Frederick to dredge up once he followed all the placeholders and expanded all the shortcuts.

The blip shouldn't happen.

He ran back over the sequence of events, right from the start this time. The trickle of people arriving and parking their cars, making their way onto the beach, and greeting friends and loved ones after weeks or months apart. A bonfire was lit, and the children — including Laurence, Frederick noted — were the first to stuff their faces with as much food as they could squeeze inside themselves before they ran rampant across the sand.

The adults lingered by the fire, for the most part, first offering prayers to gods Frederick cared very little about, and then socializing over meals.

The further detail he dug up, the more blips he noticed.

And there was nothing behind them.

This went beyond disused and dusty neural pathways. There were no strands drifting in the metaphorical breeze, no buried placeholders lurking like archaeological finds waiting to happen. If the missing memories still existed at all, they were locked away, floating in the ether with nothing to tether them to the rest of Myriam's mind.

"This is going to be a real needle in a haystack situation," he sighed as he withdrew to the constructed illusion of Myriam's kitchen. "It may take a while."

Myriam gazed at him while her mind joined the dots. *He doesn't mean a few minutes, or he would have continued. This is British understatement at work. He means hours. Days. Months, maybe?* She consulted her gut instinct, and her mood began to sour as it agreed with the way her thoughts were headed. *Years. There are whole years of my life to turn over, piece by piece, just to find a single memory.*

"Worse," Frederick said. "The memories we're looking for aren't connected to any moment in your life. They're free-floating, if they exist at all."

"Sounds like we just need a little luck," Myriam said as her lips curved into a wry smile.

Frederick raised himself to her surface thoughts to see whether she was being sardonic, but she was utterly serious. She could not see through time the way that Laurence could, but she *did* experience a high degree of serendipity.

Her gift was good fortune.

He allowed himself a broad grin. He could use her power as easily as he had controlled Laurence's, and allow her instinct and luck to guide his hand. The applications were endless. His telepathy *and* pure, raw fortune? He could be unstoppable!

Frederick cleared his throat and leaned forward. Now was the time to focus, not to lose himself in a fantasy.

He closed his eyes and shut out all but the most essential of his senses so that he could coil himself around Myriam's gifts and wear them like a cloak. It was almost a merging, in a way, and he had to pay close attention to avoid losing track of who was who.

Then he began to skim-read, and allowed Myriam to take the lead on what was worth a deeper dive.

---

*"*NEXT TIME, *we'll do this at our place," Paula Grant said with a grin as she hugged Myriam tightly. "We've got plenty of room at the house."*

"And I know you'd love to get a good look at how it all works," Todd added with a smile to Eric.

"Nah, all that's behind me now." Eric chuckled and set his guitar down in the sand so that he could shake Todd's hand. "Though, I mean, I guess I could just look it over. You know, to make you happy."

Todd and Eric both laughed, and Myriam waved welcomingly to Rufus and Angela as they approached. Rufus clutched a tiny teddy bear to his chest as though he never wanted to let it go, and Angela's arm was looped loosely through his elbow.

"There you are!" Paula turned to face her son and beamed at him. "Did you have fun?"

"I guess." Rufus blushed like he was suddenly embarrassed.

"Thanks for keeping an eye on him," Todd said to Angela.

"Always," Angela replied, and even Frederick couldn't read her expression to guess at what she meant by it.

"Here I am again. How unexpected." The voice wasn't one he recognized. It seemed feminine, and only vaguely interested in conversation.

There was no mind he could touch which accompanied it.

The words pulled on his consciousness and tugged Frederick out of the memory, but he was not at Myriam's table, and Myriam's gift was no longer intertwined with his own.

Instead, he was nowhere.

There was no light, no sound, no sensation. He certainly wasn't breathing, even though he knew he had to be. He felt no chair under himself, nor table beneath his hands, but he refused to listen to the prickle of panic in his gut.

No. This was the kind of situation he put others through. He would *not* fall for it being done to him.

Who are you? He tried to voice the words, but in the end there was only thought.

"I am memory's end, Trickster," the voice came, the only sound in the nothingness.

Frederick did everything he could to pull a construct together, to replace the nothing with even a shred of imaginary surroundings, but all he succeeded in doing was breaking the chains on his fear.

It crawled up his spine, fizzing and stabbing as it went, until his lack of breath began to suffocate him.

He had to get out.

He *needed* to get out.

You are in over your head, he realized.

"Drink," the voice purred around him.

Drink what?

What if I refuse?

There was laughter, and it wasn't his own.

"Then you remain here. You cannot move on until you drink, but you are under no obligation. Stay, if that is your wish."

Stay here. Alone. In this void, bereft of sensation, of stimulation, of power.

How long until staying here drove him irreversibly insane? Solitary confinement might sound like a blessed relief from the constant torrent of thoughts battering at his defenses twenty-four hours a day, but the truth was that it was a very effective means of torture, and Frederick didn't fancy enduring it for too long.

"Tricksters," the voice chuckled, somewhat affectionately. "They are always looking for ways to bend rules, to slip through cracks, to find an escape. You are weighing up how long you can endure this to give your friends time to save you from it. But when you are ready, the river will be here for you, and you will drink of its waters and be returned to your life."

At what cost? If Frederick could feel his teeth right now he was sure he'd be grinding them, but all he had was the fear which was transmuting into terror, and he had no idea how to deal with such an unfamiliar emotion.

"The cost is this memory, nothing more. It does not belong to you, and you will leave it behind."

And you?

Another laugh. "You will also leave me behind. But I am a god, Trickster, and you are merely human. I do not belong to you, and you may not hold onto me."

There was too much valuable information here to

abandon. Myriam's memory itself seemed almost inconsequential now. They all knew Angela had been present, and while all Myriam had asked of Frederick was for him to see whether the information could be recovered, what he'd stumbled into was far too important to let go of without a fight.

They were up against a *god*. Laurence would know what to do about that. The boy might run on pure instinct, but those instincts never steered him wrong, and Frederick could see why Icky put so much faith in him.

Now it was Frederick's time to do the same.

All he had to do was wait, for as long as he could, here in the darkness which slithered through his core and dug claws into his consciousness. Wait, and Laurence would find a way out, and then Frederick could tell them what he'd discovered. So what if it took days? Frederick would wait.

What if it takes weeks?

Months?

Years?

"Bold choice," the voice drawled.

He had the distinct sense that whoever — *whatever* — was there had gone now, and left him alone to his fate, insensate in the void. The one thing he might have been able to influence, or even just use to keep from going insane, had disappeared, and the last shred of power he might have convinced himself he had was gone with it.

There was silence. Not the quiet of an empty room, but a desolate nothingness he doubted even existed anywhere on Earth, and the longer he spent in it, the more it crowded him. Smothered him. Suffocated him.

He thought he tried to scream, but heard nothing, *felt* nothing, and the last vestiges of self-control were ripped from his non-existent hands.

18

LAURENCE

When Freddy slumped like his muscles had all been sucked out of him, Laurence barely remembered to drop the knife he was holding before he darted in to catch the falling body. The blade clattered on the tile floor, and Laurence grunted at Freddy's weight as he shoved Quentin's brother upright then propped him against the table instead.

Freddy began to slide sideways in his chair the moment Laurence tried to let go.

"Shit," Laurence breathed. He glanced across the table to his mom, but Myriam was alert, her eyes open and creased in concern. "What happened?"

"Nothing," Myriam said. "He was inside my mind, and then he wasn't, and…" She gestured to the room around herself, then stood and crossed to Laurence's side. She felt for Freddy's pulse at his throat. "He's breathing, at least."

Laurence wasn't wholly sure if he should be worried. He had no idea whether this was a side-effect of Freddy being busy or if it meant something was wrong, but Freddy was a control freak. Would he sit on a chair if falling off it was a risk?

"Freddy," Laurence said, leaning forward to Freddy's ear. "Hey. Freddy! Wake up, man."

Nothing.

Myriam disappeared from Laurence's periphery, then returned with the knife he'd dropped clasped in her hand. Laurence was half convinced she was about to stab Freddy for fun before he realized what she was getting at.

They were both trained in first aid because working in a shop with sharp objects on the daily pretty much required it.

She meant to test Freddy's pain response to check whether he was asleep or unconscious.

"Whoa. Mom." Laurence eyed the knife, and shook his head, then took the more sensible and less pointy option.

He slapped Freddy's cheek.

Then he did it again, harder.

Nothing.

"Fuck."

"On the floor," Myriam said. "I'll call an ambulance."

"Yeah."

He carefully eased Freddy to the ground while his mom called 911, arranged the big guy into the recovery position, then checked his breathing again to make sure nothing had changed.

Then he sat back on his heels, rested his elbows on his knees, and exhaled slowly.

What the hell had gone wrong? Had Freddy had a stroke and this was just really bad timing, or did Myriam have some kind of telepath-killing brain defenses Laurence didn't know about? Was he fucking with them for a joke?

Laurence closed his eyes and smelled the air. He waited for his gut to process the information available and he listened to its soft, worried clench.

His instincts agreed with his senses: Freddy was in trouble. But there was nothing Laurence could do about it. He was all out of telepaths now, and even if he could find another, the d'Arcys were all telepath-proof. Nobody would be able to get into Freddy's head and fish him out of whatever difficulty he'd got mired in.

What would Quentin think?

Laurence exhaled and pushed himself to his feet so he could put a little distance between himself and Quentin's brother. There was something disquieting about seeing such a confident, powerful man in such a helpless position, and Laurence didn't have time right now to try and unpick all of his conflicting feelings about it. That or he just didn't want to, and was intentionally keeping himself busy.

He took out his phone and called Quentin.

"Darling?" Quentin answered quickly, and sounded like he'd been expecting Laurence's call. "What's happening?"

I help! Windsor declared proudly over their bond.

Laurence sighed softly. His familiar was with Quentin so that Laurence could be warned if anyone attacked Quen. This side-effect was unintentional.

Thanks, he sent to the bird. Then to Quentin, he murmured, "I'm okay, baby. But Freddy... I don't think he is. He was trying to help Mom uncover some buried memories, but he's just like... Passed out? He didn't say anything, he just lost consciousness and now we're waiting on an ambulance. He's breathing," he added quickly. "But I can't wake him up."

"Is it a coma, do you think?" Quentin asked softly.

"Too soon to tell. We're gonna keep tabs on him until the ambulance gets here." He let out a breath and, as it trembled, realized that he'd started shaking a little. "It can't be magic," he added. "Mom's house is protected *and* Freddy's got the talisman I gave him."

Quentin was quiet a moment, then murmured, "Let me know what hospital they take him to, and I will meet you there."

Laurence nodded. He hadn't planned on accompanying Freddy to the ER, but now Quentin said it, it seemed like he should have. "Sure thing, baby. See you soon."

He hung up and dangled the phone between his fingers as he eyed the unconscious body on his mom's kitchen floor, and the mess of feelings Laurence had tried to ignore pushed their way out of the prison of distractions he'd built for them.

Could this have happened to his mom, instead of Freddy?

Was it callous of him to think that way? A human being was lying helpless at his feet, and Laurence was pretty sure he didn't really care about Freddy's well-being at all. The only way he could stir some sympathy was if he thought too hard about whether it might affect Myriam too, or what Quentin might be feeling about his brother being incapacitated.

And what about Mikey?

Laurence cursed under his breath.

He should tell Mikey. Laurence would hit the roof if their situations were reversed and Mikey didn't reach out to him if this happened to Quentin.

That was it. The realization that hit him at last, no longer trapped behind the wall Laurence had shoved it over.

For all that Freddy might have done in the past, he was a human being with people who cared about him, and if Laurence let his coldness toward Freddy creep any further, *they* would be the ones who suffered for it.

Urgh. Why was being a good person so hard?

Laurence grit his teeth, dug up Mikey's phone number, and called it, because only an asshole would text this kind of stuff.

THE NEAREST EMERGENCY room was also the biggest in East County, and Laurence sat waiting with his mom to find out who would be first to arrive: Mikey or Quen.

It was Mikey.

Myriam's face was a picture of frozen politeness, which Laurence knew damn well she reserved for people she didn't think too highly of, so he bounced out of his seat to go intercept the redhead before Mikey could come any closer.

Mikey's cheeks were a pinched pink that clashed with the orange of his curls, and he looked like a man trying really hard not to panic. "Hey. Laurence. Where is he?"

Laurence gestured to the doors beyond the waiting room's brown and white reception desk. "They've taken him through. C'mon, I'll let them know you're his partner, they might let you in to see him."

Mikey's throat bobbed as he swallowed. "What the fuck happened?"

"We don't know." Laurence took Mikey's arm and steered him to the desk. "He just passed out. No warning, no nothing. We couldn't wake him, so we called 911."

"I should've come with him," Mikey said.

Laurence shook his head. "Hey. No guilt, okay? Hopefully this is just a—" He waved his fingers toward his own temple vaguely. "Thing."

"Never seen anything like it," Mikey argued with a scowl. He glanced toward Myriam, then back to Laurence. "Did she hurt him?"

"What?" Laurence stared at Mikey and tried to imagine where *that* suggestion could've come from. "No!"

Mikey curled his lip for a second, then turned his attention on the receptionist and switched to a strained smile. "Hi. You have Frederick d'Arcy here? I'm his partner, Michael Brennan. I'd like to see him, please."

Laurence nodded to confirm that what Mikey had said was true.

"Right this way, Mr. Brennan." She smiled and rose from

her seat to lead Mikey to the doors Laurence couldn't pass, and Laurence sighed as he returned to his seat.

This shouldn't have happened. They shouldn't be here. And he shouldn't feel so irritated that Mikey was allowed back there but Laurence wasn't. Instead he'd had to sit out here in the waiting room while a doctor asked him all the usual questions. Were there drugs? Was there alcohol? Did Freddy have any known medical history that could've caused this? And Laurence had to admit that while nothing had been ingested on his watch, and Freddy didn't strike him as the kind of person who would allow narcotics into his body, he didn't actually *know*.

Freddy had passed out in front of him and Laurence didn't have a clue whether this was normal for him.

He sat in sulky silence as the minutes limped by and tried not to think about it, but he knew what the problem was. Freddy had gone down on Laurence's watch, and he couldn't do a thing about it, regardless of whether or not he liked the guy. He couldn't help, and didn't even know where to begin trying.

When Quentin arrived, Laurence felt it, as though the undertow which churned away inside the man he loved had reached through the walls of the hospital to drag on Laurence's soul. The sensation of his own familiar flying nearby was almost secondary. He raised his head and turned in time to see Quentin stride in through the entrance like he was about to storm a castle, a black stain against the hospital's white walls, and Laurence's breath fled his lungs as all his blood rushed to his dick.

Not now! Goddess, focus!

He sprang to his feet and hurried to intercept Quentin, drawn to him so forcefully that they almost collided.

Quentin hadn't eaten. Not dinner, and maybe not lunch, either. No way would his pull be so strong if he had.

"He's alive," Laurence breathed. He knew what he'd want to hear in Quentin's shoes, so he led with that. "Mikey's in with him."

Quentin nodded curtly. His gaze was like glass; hard, yet brittle. "And you are both unharmed?"

Laurence slipped his warm fingers around Quentin's ice cold ones. "We're fine. Take what you need if you're going in."

Quentin's lips parted a touch, and he glanced toward Myriam as though unsure if he should do what Laurence suggested while his mother watched.

"This is a hospital, baby," Laurence whispered.

The implication was brutal, but it needed to be said, because otherwise Quentin would refuse help like he so often did, and then he'd be back there in an emergency room with people who might not survive him leeching their life force, even though he didn't mean to, and even though he took so little.

There was still reluctance in Quentin's eyes, but he tipped his head ever so faintly in a gesture Laurence was willing to bet most other people wouldn't even notice, and he leaned in to press his lips gently to Laurence's.

Laurence tightened his hold on Quen's fingers as he leaned into the kiss. He gave everything he had, without hesitation, and Quentin teased energy out of him slowly and tenderly as the kiss drew on until Laurence managed to forget where they were. Life trickled from his lips like sand through parted fingers, and just as warm.

Quentin hadn't taken from him like this before. This wasn't a desperate refueling, nor life-saving gluttony from a starving man. It was careful and controlled, and it made Laurence's scalp tingle and his forearms fizz.

"Goddess, you can do that again *any* time, hon," he rasped, breathless, as Quentin's lips finally eased free.

"I am not ungrateful," Quentin whispered against his

cheek, "but I must go. I love you." His free hand grasped Laurence's shoulder to steady him. "Will you be all right?"

He was more than all right, and he suspected Quen knew damn well what that kiss had done to him, but this wasn't the time, so Laurence raised his chin. "Yeah. Do you want me to wait?"

"There's no need," Quentin said quietly. "You could be here all night. Until we know more it's best if at least one of us gets some sleep. Go home, darling. Soraya is outside, if either of you need a lift?"

Quentin *had* to be worried if he'd let Soraya drive him here.

"We have my truck," Myriam said softly. Laurence hadn't heard her come near. He was still wrapped up in the flush of Quentin's kiss. "But I'll let Soraya know not to wait."

"Thank you, Myriam."

Laurence swayed as Quentin stepped back. "I love you too, hon. Call me if you need anything."

He knew it was mean of him to hope that Quentin wouldn't be allowed in, but Laurence waited to be sure anyway. And when Quentin disappeared through the ER doors into the world beyond, he felt even more at a loose end than he had before Quentin arrived.

"We've done all we can, Bambi," Mom said as she took his arm. "Quentin's right. You should rest."

"I guess."

All Laurence could do now was go outside, collect Windsor, and hope that whatever had struck Freddy down wasn't coming for Myriam next, because if it did, he wouldn't be anywhere near as calm about it.

19

QUENTIN

This was all wrong.

Freddy was never the one in hospital. This should be the other way around, and to walk in to a room like this, with Freddy unconscious in bed, was such a monumental reframing of a familiar scenario that Quentin's whole gut lurched sideways while the hospital sounds behind him faded into inconsequential babble.

The curls of the man sprawled at Freddy's side were ginger, not blond, but he looked every bit as haggard as Laurence whenever Quentin was injured.

Mikey raised his head. His eyes were reddened and sore, and his hair was a crumpled mess. His hands remained locked around one of Freddy's, tight, like they were glued together.

For all their sins, Quentin had no difficulty recognizing the bond that they shared, and he felt like an outsider at his own brother's bedside.

"I'm sorry to disturb you," he murmured. He stepped closer to the bed, keeping it between himself and Laurence's former drug dealer.

Laurence said that he and Mikey had spoken. He said that

they had cleared the air between them, settled some things from their past, but all Quentin could picture right now was the moment Laurence had bared the scars inside his elbows and begged Quentin not to hate him.

Mikey had done that to Laurence. Long ago, when they were teenagers, when people made mistakes and did idiotic things together, Mikey had taken advantage of Laurence's loneliness and got him addicted to heroin, and now Mikey was here with Freddy when Freddy was at his most vulnerable.

It did not sit quite right. But Quentin could be civil.

For Laurence's sake.

For Freddy's.

"It's okay," Mikey mumbled. He didn't mean it. Of course he didn't. Who wanted to be interrupted at the bedside of the person they loved if it wasn't by the doctor who could make it all go away?

Quentin glanced to the foot of the bed, searching for some sort of chart or document, but there was nothing. The hospital likely kept that information on a computer, which meant picking a clinician's brain at some point. Instead, he looked to Freddy. Leaned in and rested the back of his hand to Freddy's forehead. Watched the rise and fall of his chest.

"Do you know what tests have been done thus far?" Freddy's temperature felt fine now that Quentin's own was back to where it should be. There was very little contrast between them. But Quentin was not a doctor, and the back of his hand was hardly a precise instrument.

"They took some blood, ran a CT. I think they wanna do an EEG next." Mikey rubbed his eyes in a way that made Quentin instinctively want to reach out and stop him from doing damage to his skin. "They think it's a coma."

"Mm." Quentin decided not to mess around testing that theory for himself. Medical staff would already have checked whether or not Freddy responded to stimuli. Instead he sighed and placed a hand against Freddy's shoulder, and gazed down at his brother. "All right," he murmured. "I'm not going anywhere, Fred. Understood? We'll figure this out. You're not alone."

Freddy, of course, refused to answer him. He looked for all the world as though he were merely asleep, and all the fuss was for naught.

If this were indeed a coma, though, Freddy would be shuffled out of the emergency room and onto a ward. He'd be hooked up to monitors and machines, fed and watered through tubes and cannulae. He would grow a beard, and his hair would lose its shape.

Quentin blinked as his brain slotted all those pieces together.

He had his mental image of this room all wrong, substituting himself for Frederick, and Laurence for Mikey, but what if it should be the other way around?

Quentin had been in Mikey's position, and Laurence had been in Freddy's.

He sucked in a breath and allowed his train of thought to fully complete its journey before he spoke it out loud.

"Is he in Otherworld?"

Mikey sniffed a little. "What?"

"I mean, I don't know how he could get there," Quentin said. "But that doesn't make it impossible." He took a step away from the bed and drew his phone, hoping that Laurence hadn't got too far away just yet as he scrolled through his admittedly small list of contacts.

"Hey, baby." Laurence answered quickly. "Did something happen?"

"Is there a way to test whether or not someone is in Otherworld?" Quentin cut to the chase.

He heard Laurence's sharp breath. "Uh. There has to be, right? I'll check in with Ru."

"Will he be available this time of night, do you think?"

"He's always available. It's whether or not he bothers getting dressed that's the question."

"Er."

"Ru's basically a hermit, baby," Laurence groused. "Social graces aren't his forte. I am *way* past used to it."

Quentin couldn't help but scowl faintly. "But you shouldn't have to be, darling. You didn't ask to see any of that."

Laurence paused for so long that Quentin wondered whether the line had lost connection, but then he spoke again. "You know what? You're right. I never really thought about it that way but… Yeah. I don't fuckin' consent to seeing his ass, actually." He huffed. "Okay. I'll get over to Carlsbad and see what I can find. You gonna stay there?"

"Unless Freddy's situation changes, absolutely," Quentin replied. "Thank you, darling."

"Any time. I'm on it. Speak soon."

Quentin hung up before he could offer to visit Rufus himself and offer a few words of polite encouragement to never expose himself to Laurence ever again, and he turned to regard Freddy and Mikey. "Laurence will be in touch," he explained.

Mikey nodded and laid his head back down against Freddy's hand, so Quentin retired to a nearby sofa and settled in for a long wait.

THE NIGHT WAS no different from one in any other hospital. Staff came and went. Sometimes they wheeled Freddy away for tests or scans which couldn't be done in the room.

Sometimes they came to check his heart rate or blood pressure.

Nobody had answers.

Quentin passed his time as best he could, whether with meditation or with juggling the unusual position of attempting to provide some comfort to Mikey, though he felt inadequate at the latter. He had to balance his own dread at Freddy's condition with understanding the fear Mikey must be feeling, and at times it seemed too large a task.

He would manage, though. For Freddy's sake.

It was a little past five o'clock in the morning when they decided to move Freddy onto a ward. Quentin accompanied him, with Mikey following, and they trailed along corridors behind the bed then sat patiently to one side as Freddy was settled into a new room with a new sofa and a window view of a city which the first splinters of daybreak were beginning to touch.

"What if they can't figure this out?" Mikey balled his hands into fists, and then crossed his arms to shove those fists under his armpits. It made his shoulders hunch forward into a posture which was either defensive, self-comforting, or both. "What if it's just a stroke and he's never coming back from it?"

"We can't…" Quentin cleared his throat as his voice came out in a rasp, and he tried again. "We can't assume the worst," he said, more steadily this time.

"But we can plan for it," Mikey countered.

Quentin shook his head faintly. The cobwebs were trying to settle in, and he needed to shake them loose.

What he wouldn't do to have Freddy's logic available to him right now.

He blinked and looked to Freddy, the most organized man Quentin had ever known — short of their own father, of course, but Quentin didn't wish to allow that man to creep back into his consciousness. It had been bad enough hallucinating him near-constantly for the first few weeks after escaping Marlowe's clutches, and Quentin didn't need any more of that right now.

If there was a worst-case scenario, Frederick had already planned for it, and that meant there were legal frameworks in place.

"You should contact Freddy's staff," Quentin said as he looked back toward Mikey. "Advise them of the current situation. If he has any mechanisms in place to handle this scenario, they should be activated, even if that's as little as notifying his employer and providing you with a stipend."

Mikey's green eyes widened. "You think I'm worried about money right now?"

Everything Mikey had ever done before now had been for money, up to and including getting his best friend hooked on heroin.

Quentin was too tired to prevent the flash of anger which roared to life in his chest, but he wasn't too tired to keep from saying anything out loud. Still, Mikey's expression shifted from resentment to fear, so clearly enough of it had evidenced itself through Quentin's features or body to make a mark.

"I think," he growled with all the care that he could muster, "that Frederick would like to ensure that you *needn't* worry." He sucked in air, then added, "I am going outside to get a little fresh air. Would you like coffee? Or food, perhaps, if I can find some?"

Mikey swallowed so hard that his whole head bobbed, and he croaked, "Sure. Yes. Please. Coffee. Thank you."

Quentin dipped his chin faintly and turned on his heel.

On his way out of the room, he realized that the last person to loom menacingly over Mikey was probably the duke, who had beaten the poor boy so thoroughly that he'd been hospitalized. At night, separated from Frederick's protection, alone with a d'Arcy who could kill him with a thought, it was no wonder Mikey seemed so terrified.

Quentin ground his teeth and stalked away from the room as briskly as he could, and counted down from ten several times as he took the stairs to the ground floor in search of somewhere he could be alone, if only for a minute.

IT WAS FAR LONGER than a minute.

There was a pretty little outdoor seating area just beyond the entrance to the emergency department, with a couple of stone tables and benches and — more vitally, so far as Quentin was concerned — plentiful signage to indicate that smoking was not allowed in the area.

He sat until the sky was a washed-out, watery blue and the temperature had crept up to pleasantly warm. Perhaps Mikey was still waiting for coffee, or perhaps he was hoping that Quentin would take even longer to return, but for now Quentin just appreciated the peace and quiet, punctuated only occasionally by the arrival of another ambulance screaming its way through the early morning and to the emergency room.

And that was all Freddy was to them, he supposed. Another body in the night, another stranger who may or may not make it to tomorrow. A man who had stood by Quentin's side since birth was now in the hands of people who couldn't possibly know him, monitored by a drug dealer who had only been part of his life for a year.

It was absurd.

Quentin sighed softly and withdrew his phone. It was nearly six o'clock now, but there were no messages from Laurence yet, so Quentin stood and sauntered toward the steps at the end of the small garden and typed out a text.

No change. I'll likely remain here a few more hours until we're certain that he is stable.

The message was barely sent when a shadow flit into his field of view, and his attention snapped to it. He needn't have been concerned. There was no monster, no black dog, and certainly no assailant. Merely a teenage girl. A little grubby, perhaps, her pale white skin duller than it might be if she'd had a good night's sleep, and wisps of short, fair hair poking out from under her dark hoodie. He gave her a polite smile as he passed her on the steps, part in sympathy with another person who had clearly been up all night, and partly to show her that he was no threat.

She rolled her eyes at him as most teenagers might, bumping against him as she went past. "Sorry," she grunted.

She didn't sound terribly sorry.

Quentin was about to apologize himself, even though there was no real fault to be had on either part. The steps were narrow, and they were both tired.

But the phone he'd been tucking away into his jacket was no longer in his hand, and nor was it in his pocket, though he ran his fingers across the material just to be certain.

He paused in mild confusion, and turned to look back into the garden.

Had the young lady just *stolen* from him?

Quentin wasn't sure anyone had ever stolen something from him before, but he definitely no longer had his phone, and she was the only other person around. And she *had* just come into contact with him.

He cleared his throat. "Excuse me?"

She checked back over her shoulder, then accelerated like a bloody gazelle and disappeared around the corner of the hospital in a flash.

Adrenaline flooded his limbs, and the world shifted into sharp focus as he broke into a run and raced after her, but the little bugger was already out of the garden and sprinting across the street.

Quentin vaulted over the fence to the pavement below. The landing reverberated up through his ankles and knees, but he pushed off and did his damndest to close the distance between them.

He didn't dare use telekinesis to trip her in case she broke his phone in her fall, and if he did anything more obvious there would be no way she wouldn't notice it.

All he could do was run her down, and hope he caught up with her before she did something daft.

2 0

———

LAURENCE

Laurence wasn't too happy discussing Ru's constant nudity with Quen, and *especially* not in front of his mom, so the sooner he ended this call the better. "Okay. I'll get over to Carlsbad and see what I can find. You gonna stay there?"

"Unless Freddy's situation changes, absolutely," Quentin replied. "Thank you, darling."

"Any time," Laurence said. "I'm on it. Speak soon."

He sighed as he thumbed the hang up button on the steering wheel, and began mentally planning his route. The farm was between him and Carlsbad, so he could drop Mom off home and just carry on to Rufus' place, but he'd really been looking forward to just sleeping all night and worrying about shit in the morning.

His mom gave a little sigh too, from the passenger seat, and her hand moved to pet Windsor's head while the bird cooed in her lap. "Do you think Quentin could be right?"

"I mean, we know he is," Laurence muttered. "Ru's a grown-ass adult. I know he's been living alone all these years, but he *does* know he can't just go to the store without clothes on, so he should know nobody wants to see his junk unless they asked to."

Myriam nodded. "I meant about Otherworld."

"Oh." *Duh.* He sucked his teeth. "No idea. I've never seen anyone *else* spiritually enter Otherworld, only physically. Quen's the one with that experience. Either he's seen something he recognized, or he's clutching at straws. Either way, no sleep for me."

"Would you like me to come with you?"

Laurence glanced across to her for a moment, but had to get his eyes back on the road. "You've got a store to run, Mom."

She scritched Windsor under his chin, and the cooing sounds turned even more smug. "We only have one truck," she reasoned.

He grit his teeth. Either he left his mom at the farm without transport, or she drove back from La Jolla on her own. Maybe she could stay the night in La Jolla, but there were still ridiculous logistical problems, unless Freddy had dropped the keys to his rental car in Mom's kitchen and nobody had noticed.

"Okay," he decided. "We'll stop at the farm, get you an overnight bag, then take it from there, yeah?"

"Perfect!"

Windsor cawed in agreement.

***

IT WAS CLOSING IN ON HALF past ten when Laurence heaved Rufus' gate closed and turned to face the mansion. At night, the golden sheen of the bubble overhead was barely visible, even to Laurence's eyes, adding only a faint tint to the twinkling stars and thin sliver of moon in the sky.

He held his arm out for Windsor, who swooped across

from the truck once Myriam opened her door, and hopped up to sit on Laurence's shoulder like an omen of doom.

"Put some pants on, Ru," Laurence said as he grabbed his mom's overnight bag and made his way to the front door. "My mom's here."

He mentally kicked himself for adding the excuse. *Because I don't want to see it* was more than enough. Quentin was right, and yet Laurence was still trying to use his mom as a shield for setting boundaries.

He'd have to talk to his therapist about it some time, but right now he had bigger fish to fry. He stood on the doorstep, bag in hand, and waited.

They had to wait a couple of minutes before Ru opened the door, but he did at least have pants on. He gave Laurence the stinkeye before turning a warm smile on Myriam and offering his hand to her.

"Mrs. Riley. We've met before when I was a kid, but it's a pleasure to do it as an adult."

Myriam smiled in return and gripped his hand. "Thank you, Rufus. Merry meet, dear."

"Merry meet. Come in." He pointed to the bag as he backed out of the doorway. "What's going on?"

Laurence stared hard at Ru and tried to think of literally any time when Rufus had been remotely this polite to anyone, ever. He *did* have a protective streak over Amy Jenkins, Laurence supposed, but even that was different to this.

"It's my fault," Myriam gushed as she stepped inside. "I asked someone to help us try and figure out why none of us could remember Angela Tate giving you that bear of yours, and now he's in the hospital."

"Quen's brother," Laurence added as he followed Mom inside. "He just collapsed outta nowhere. I was wondering if you had a spell for figuring out whether or not someone was in Otherworld?"

"Oh," Rufus said lightly. He closed the front door. "Will that tell you who killed my parents?"

"It might," Myriam said before Laurence could put his foot in it. "After all, it was trying to figure that out that landed Freddy in the hospital. If he's in Otherworld, he can't get there himself, which means someone did it to him." Her smile was sweet and innocent, the kind of smile that came before a dagger to the diaphragm. "My house is under the protection of the wards you taught Bambi, so if something slipped past them, you're the best person to figure out who or what that could be, aren't you?"

Rufus gnawed on his lip. "Psychopomp," he said. "God. Daemon. Psychic." He gnawed some more as he padded past them toward the kitchen. "Potentially any number of mythological creatures. Those wards specifically protect against magic."

Laurence put the bag down on the floor, out of the way up against a wall, and tailed Ru. "So we know what *didn't* do this," he agreed now that Rufus' brain had engaged with the problem.

"How was this Freddy going to help?" Rufus countered. Then he looked to Myriam and added, "Coffee? Tea?"

"I will have an herbal tea if you have any, thank you."

Ru nodded as he opened a cupboard and offered Myriam a couple of boxes to choose from.

"He's a telepath," Laurence sighed. "Angela's looking for a magical way to recover all our lost memories, Freddy was trying the psychic way. He went in to Mom's mind and... I don't know. Never came out again. Just lost consciousness right there in Mom's kitchen, and now he's in the hospital. Quen suggested it might be Otherworld, but..." He gave a one-shouldered shrug so he didn't disturb Windsor. "I don't know how to test that theory, so I came here. I'm sorry, I know it's late."

"It's fine." Rufus sounded like he meant it. He put the box Myriam didn't choose back in the cupboard, then filled the kettle. "You're pulling in everyone you can to try and get to the bottom of this. The least I can do is help out."

Laurence felt his forehead crease as his eyebrows shot up. It was a rare patch of maturity from Ru, and Laurence didn't want to punish him for it with a snippy response, so instead he took his time and turned away. "The bag is in case it takes us all night," he said. "Mom has to get to work in the morning, and we only have the one vehicle between us right now."

"It's not like I don't have spare bedrooms," Ru agreed. "Why don't I show you to one, Myriam? Then Laurence and I can take to the books."

"That would be very kind of you, Rufus." Myriam smiled again, and patted his forearm. "A nice cup of tea and a warm bed sounds like a perfect end to an unexpected evening. Thank you."

All Laurence could do was keep his mouth shut. Whatever magic Myriam was working, it had turned Rufus from surly shut-in witch to charming host, and Laurence had no intention of popping that balloon.

"So your mom can't use magic," Rufus stated.

Laurence wasn't sure whether it was a question, but he nodded anyway. "That's right. Only Dad could."

Ru hummed to himself as he perused the shelves of his library from his position perched on the end of the table in the center of the room. "Freddy can't use magic."

"Nope. Quen can, but he won't." Laurence leaned against a window frame and turned his attention out to the yard below. He really should bring Ru some plant food and fresh soil some day.

Windsor ruffled his feathers and hunkered down against Laurence's shoulder. Laurence felt the bird's exhaustion, but Win was too stubborn to leave for a more stable perch. He'd spent all day flying around the city after Quen and the kids, so Laurence wasn't surprised that he was having trouble keeping his eyes open this late at night.

"Their dad wasn't willing to invest all that effort twice, huh?"

Laurence's heart thudded, and a bubble of nausea rocked his gut. He knew what Ru meant — that the duke hadn't tortured and abused *both* sons for thirteen years — but he'd never thought of it that way before. "I guess not," he muttered.

"They must be twins," Ru concluded.

Laurence peeled himself away from the window and turned to face the witch. "What makes you say that?"

Rufus shrugged. "Those things need precise timing. The only reason not to take the same lengths with your second child to provide yourself with a backup if you somehow lose the first is that there's a clash in the timing. Twins would cause that clash."

Several things hit Laurence all at once. The awful calmness of Rufus' statement came first, washing over him with pure horror at how clinical, how reasonable it sounded. Then came understanding; realization that a man who was willing to do all that to one child just to perpetuate a bloodline would absolutely consider creating a backup.

The third thing that hit him made his knees buckle, and he lurched into a chair to stop himself falling over.

Nicky.

Why else would the duke make a third child six years after the first two?

Backup.

Neither Quen nor Freddy had ever mentioned Nicky having accidents or being hospitalized. Did that mean the duke found another way in those intervening six years? Or had he changed his mind?

Memories clashed for Laurence's attention. Black Annis, trying to tell him something about Quentin's youngest brother, and the duke offering Quentin tests throughout his childhood: tests to see whether he was capable of magic, and the disappointment when Quentin failed those tests.

Had Nicky *passed* them?

Was that why the duke had been willing to kill the twins to force compliance? Because he *had* his backup already?

Windsor squawked and made his way across to the back of another chair so that he could roost in peace, and Rufus turned to regard the bird before switching his focus to Laurence.

"You look like you want to throw up," Ru observed.

"Yeah," Laurence grunted. "I think I do. But it's… It's not anything that matters right now. You just connected a few dots for me, that's all."

Rufus blinked, then his chin lifted. "There's another brother," he surmised.

Fuck, Ru was too damn smart.

"Yep." Laurence sighed and shook his head. "Can't do anything about that right now. How do we figure out what's wrong with Freddy?"

"Same way we always do," Rufus said. He eased off the desk and walked toward the section Laurence knew to contain all his books on healing. "We read."

Laurence groaned. It turned out the flip side of knowing how to read all these books now was that Rufus expected him to read all these books, and the trick would be to not get caught up in random stuff he found interesting.

They had a target, and Laurence had to stay on it. Maybe if he viewed the spells he needed as prey, his instincts would guide him to them, and he could cut out a few hours of skim-reading.

"Hey," he said slowly as Ru started to pile books on the table. "Is Otherworld stuff in your healing section?"

"No, but diagnosis is," Ru replied. "Just in case Quentin's wrong." He walked away to another part of the library and collected an armful of books from there, too. "Otherworld," he explained. "In case he's right."

The books were gathering mass on the table and Laurence's gut sank with each new pile. At least with his own gifts he knew what they could do, and what their limits were, but with magic there were endless applications, combinations, and complications. It was potentially incredibly powerful, but Goddess, the *time* it all took was exhausting.

"Right," Laurence sighed and pulled the nearest book toward him, then began to skim it like a flipbook, praying that his gut would stop him the moment something useful whizzed past.

Otherwise this was going to be a long night.

21

QUENTIN

The girl was like lightning, zipping down a hill at a pace Quentin had to push himself to maintain. She ran in the road rather than on the pavement, and her rationale quickly became apparent.

This road was short, and ended at traffic lights crossing a far wider one. If she committed to a pavement, she would have less time to make any decisions when she reached the end of it. Staying in the road allowed her to remain nimble, so long as nobody ran her over.

Beyond the lanes of the wider road spread the buildings of a mall and its mostly-empty car park. It would be a poor tactical choice for the girl to make, since the mall was clearly closed this early and offered very little cover. She might try to find a security guard to help her, but ran the risk of Quentin exposing her as a thief.

If she was sensible, she wouldn't take that route.

That left her with running alongside the main road. The traffic was light right now, and it put Quentin at definite risk of being spotted by a driver who might call the police about a man chasing a teenager in the wee small hours.

She reached the intersection, and turned right.

Quentin swore under his breath and pushed harder so that he could try to keep eyes on her, and rounded the bend onto pavement lined with a leafy embankment on his right which sloped sharply up to a row of trees, beyond which were squat, sandy buildings. On his left, five lanes of road separated him from the mall. And ahead, there she was again, sprinting still.

She couldn't maintain this pace, surely? Sooner or later she would need to settle in for a marathon, and that was when he would gain on her, assuming that she was even aware of how to pace herself for an endurance run.

Still, he'd allowed his confidence to get the better of him in the past. Best not to let it do so again.

"I'm not going to hurt you," he called out, just in case words would end this sooner than exhaustion, but she didn't bother to answer, and he wasn't going to waste more energy on it.

This hill was less aggressive than the last one, and it gave them both less of a boost, so Quentin focused all his attention on assessing each and every factor of their environment, both searching for an advantage and making sure neither of them got bloody killed by something so silly as a stray car.

The lights at the next intersection were not in the girl's favor, but she didn't stop. Instead she switched directions, turning right.

It led uphill, and slowed her.

Quentin was gaining.

They ran across streets, through car parks, and up and down embankments until they closed in on a residential area the far side of what looked to be a railway line, and by the time he reached it, she'd already jumped over a wire fence on the far side. She landed on pavement and turned to stare back at him, her cheeks flushed and chest heaving. Her eyes were wild, almost panicked, but then she looked to the fence again, and she stopped.

Quentin saw no train coming, so he bolted across the tracks and reached for the fence.

So did she.

He heard a crackle as he was halfway through vaulting it. His muscles seized up, and he crashed to the ground at her feet.

He'd been tasered enough bloody times to know what was happening, but she had no such device. There was just her hand, and the fence.

"I'm gonna stop, and so are you," she panted. "Leave me alone!"

Quentin couldn't answer. Not with words. But she wasn't Marlowe, and he wasn't powerless.

He flexed his telekinesis and pushed her away until she couldn't reach the fence any more, and the voltage locking his body in place cut out. He rolled as far from the metal as he could, and staggered to his feet. "All right," he rasped. "I suppose neither of us are hiding anything now."

She stumbled back from him and raised her hands in surrender. "I don't want any trouble."

"Nor do I. I just need my phone, I'm afraid." Quentin patted dust from his jacket, then tugged his shirt back into place. "This really doesn't need to get out of hand."

She wiped the back of her mouth with her hand and eyed him. He could almost see her trying to reach a decision, weighing up all the odds and figuring out how to make sure she came out ahead.

Then she dropped her hands to her sides, and sparks flared around her fingers.

Quentin sighed. "My phone," he reiterated. "If you would be so kind."

"I don't want to hurt you," she snapped. "Just get lost. Leave me alone!"

He glanced around, to the palm trees and the block of apartments rising above them. This was *not* a place to unleash a clash of titans. Anyone could be watching them, or even recording them.

"Please," Quentin murmured as he returned his focus to her. "My brother is in the hospital. I need my phone. If it's money you want, let's go to a cash machine and get some."

Her tongue darted out between her lips for a fleeting moment. She narrowed her eyes. "You want me to go with you to an ATM, and you're just gonna, what, *give* me money?"

Quentin nodded. "That is correct, yes." He hesitated, then took a guess, based on her general state of grubby disarray. "But I can offer more than money."

She blinked at him, then her nose creased up. "Ew! *Ew!* Gross! Fuck off!" She raised a hand into a fist, and the sparks grew brighter, more furious.

He swore he heard them fizz.

Quentin spread his hands, palms toward her. "Friends your own age," he clarified. "With gifts, like yours. And like mine."

He waited. She *had* to have felt him pull her off the fence. He just needed her to connect the dots.

Her hand lowered a little.

"A safe place," Quentin said softly. "Somewhere you can visit, come and go freely, with no obligation, but which will always be open to you. Food, shelter, hot water. And yes, if you need it, money."

Now her hand came back up, and she snarled at him. "I'm not stupid!"

"I never so much as implied it."

"And I'm not letting anyone fuck me!"

Quentin blinked owlishly. "I, er..." His mouth worked while he tried to figure out how to respond to that.

Oh. Oh, *god*, no wonder she'd been disgusted by his offer of money.

"No," he said. "That's not, um… Goodness, no, absolutely not!"

"You think I'm just going to go anywhere with you? What the hell?"

Quentin blinked again, and took a slow breath. He had been awake all night, and while the sprint had shaken loose some of the sleepiness, it still took a little longer than hoped for to cajole his brain into action. When it finally helped him out, though, he lowered his hands. "If you give me my phone, I can call people who will assure you that I am *not* who you think I am."

"The cops," she prompted.

"Absolutely not." No, he'd been shot at by police, and learned rapidly why Laurence wasn't too keen on them. They were all a little trigger-happy for his liking over here. "No, the house. So that you can speak to them for yourself."

She stared at him like he was insane, which was very reasonable, he thought. And after some decision was reached, she dropped her hands and pulled his phone out from the depths of her shapeless hoodie, turning it in her hands until she had it the right way up. "Facial recognition, right?"

"Yes." Quentin had set it up after Mia scolded him for the lack of security on his device.

The girl pursed her lips, then came closer and held the phone up toward him. "Unlock it, but if you try and take it I'll zap you."

Quentin inclined his head and stepped forward until his phone recognized him. "There."

She snatched it away again and started thumbing at the screen. "Who do I call?" Then she blinked. "Neil Storm? You know *Neil Storm*? Not *the* Neil Storm, right?"

Quentin shrugged. "Yes, Neil Storm. He's a musician."

The girl let out a strangled scream. "Neil *Storm?*"

"Er..." Quentin had to disengage from his idea of Neil, and remember instead how excited the girls at the house had got the first time they heard his name. "Yes," he said, more assuredly. "Although I doubt he would appreciate a call this early in the day."

The strangled scream became a strangely panicked noise.

Quentin tipped his head as he watched her, but she didn't seem as though she were about to pass out or become violent. "The one you want is listed as 'Home.' Ask to speak with Soraya, if possible."

The girl just tapped away at his phone, then held it to her ear as she backed away again. "Oh. Yeah. Hey. No, this isn't, uh —" she glanced to him. "Your fuckin' *lord* or whatever the hell, you weirdo."

Quentin groaned inwardly. Of *course* Flynn was the one to answer.

"He gave me his phone," she said, turning defensive. "I wanna speak to Soraya. My name? I'm not giving you my fuckin' name. Is *everyone* British in this house of yours?"

Quentin shook his head. "No."

She huffed and began to pace while she waited, then she stopped again. "Hey, is that Soraya? Yeah. Look. I'm with this guy, and he says you're..." She tailed off, then huffed again. "Look, he's *weird*, and British, and he says he's got some kind of house or something? Where people like me... uh..."

Then she stopped, and listened. Occasionally, she looked toward Quentin.

Quentin had chosen Soraya because she would be blunt. There would be no sugar-coating from her, but she also wouldn't take any nonsense over the phone, and it certainly looked as though she were giving this young lady an earful right now if the wince she gave was any indicator.

"So he's *not* a pervert?"

He felt the heat in his cheeks as he forced himself to not look away, and fervently hoped Soraya didn't choose this moment to crack a joke. It was intensely frustrating to not be in control of this situation, but what else could he do other than exercise patience?

The girl huffed and started to pace some more, but slowly this time. "I can make electricity," she mumbled. Then, "Huh. That's cool. So you can see me?" She looked up into the clear blue sky. "Huh." Then she gestured toward the sun with her middle finger. "What'm I doing right now?"

Quentin took a moment to tuck his shirt back into his trousers, then checked that he hadn't lost any buttons.

"That's kinda cool," the girl muttered. "Fine. Thanks. Sorry I called so early." She hung up quickly, and crossed the asphalt, holding Quentin's phone out toward him with a sullen frown. "Where's this house of yours?"

"La Jolla," Quentin said. He took the phone slowly so as not to spook her, and checked it to see whether Laurence had replied to his earlier text message, but there was nothing, so he put it in his pocket where it belonged.

She snorted at him. "Okay," she said slowly. "So you meant it about just handing me a big wad of cash, huh?"

Quentin inclined his head. "I did."

She clicked her tongue a few times in a row while she considered again, then she nodded. "Okay, sure. We'll go to an ATM, you get cash, then you tell me the address of this place and I'll think it over in my own time."

"I presume there's one at the mall?" Quentin eyed the fence, and finally there was something approaching on the rails behind it.

It was the trolley.

There had to be another way around. While the trolley was moving slowly enough as it entered what looked like a small, elevated station, he was sure that crossing the rails in front of it would draw unwanted attention.

"Yeah, there is. This way." She jerked a thumb over her shoulder, and turned on her heel to stride away from him.

Quentin hurried to catch up, then strolled alongside her. "My name is Quentin," he said, since introductions seemed to be in order. "What's yours?"

She wiped her nose on the cuff of her hoodie, and didn't answer him until they reached the street. "Mel," she finally said.

"Well then. It's a pleasure to meet you, Mel. I only wish it could have been under nicer circumstances."

"Oh, like, without the pickpocketing?"

Quentin smiled wryly. "I *meant* without my brother being in a hospital, but that too, I suppose."

Mel snorted at him and started to stride back up the hill to where they'd come from. "I should've taken your wallet," she groused.

"Little point," Quentin said cheerfully. "I rarely carry cash. I don't think I have any on me right now."

"Oh my god." Mel threw her hands up and her head back. "Fine! Let's just go hit up an ATM and then I'm gonna go away and hopefully never see you again."

Quentin ran his tongue along his teeth as he considered playing his ace, and then he shrugged affably enough. "That's fair. The girls and I were heading out on a helicopter trip with Neil later today, so we would probably miss you if you did pop over."

Her eyes bulged and she ground her teeth while jamming her fists into the pockets of her hoodie, and she sped up slightly.

"Neil *actual* Storm?" Mel finally asked, once they reached an intersection.

"Yes."

Mel huffed. "Fine," she muttered. "I'm sticking with you. But no funny business."

"I assure you that I am not remotely amusing," Quentin murmured.

They climbed the hill back to the mall in silence, which gave Quentin plenty of time to worry about letting the girls know that he might not be able to leave Freddy's side long enough for the promised trip, and even more time in which to fret over why Laurence hadn't replied yet.

Rufus' home had no signal, that was all. Quentin simply had to wait until Laurence popped outside, and then everything would be resolved.

As Mel led him across the road toward the mall, all he could do was check his phone again, but there was still no reply. He did his level best to quash his concern, but everything around him was out of his hands, and he had no say in what happened next whatsoever.

Things rarely went well when he was not in control.

22

LAURENCE

Laurence jerked awake as sunlight streamed in through a crack in the curtains, and he took a quick moment to work out where he was.

A soft bed he was half-sure he'd sunk into, a faintly dusty smell to the air, and warm grey walls were signs that he wasn't at home. No, this was Rufus' place, one of the unused bedrooms they'd searched the other day, and now Laurence vaguely recalled falling into bed after he and Ru stayed up reading half the night.

He groaned and pulled Windsor closer for a brief snuggle, scritching the bird's chest through thick feathers, and fumbled around for his phone to check the time.

It was dead.

"Ah, fuck."

Windsor cawed and rolled onto his feet. *What is wrong?*

"I haven't got a damn charger with me and now my phone's out of battery," he explained, showing Windsor the blank screen. "Urgh, I should keep, like, an overnight bag in the truck or something." He blinked, then added, "Ah, shit."

An overnight bag would be a great idea, because now he had no charger *and* no clean clothes for the day.

Windsor clacked his beak. *Hungry.*

"Same. Let me shower, and I'll see what Ru's got, okay?"

Okay!

Laurence fought his way out of the mattress' evil clutches, and stumbled off to find a bathroom, all while trying not to think too hard about the logistics of getting his mom to work from Carlsbad in time to open the store.

Assuming she hadn't already gone and left him here without the truck.

THE SMELLS EMANATING from the kitchen wafted through the entire house, or so it seemed to Laurence's nose as he followed it down the wide staircase. He smelled freshly brewed coffee, the sweetness of syrup, and the unmistakable mouth-watering waft of pancakes and butter.

Windsor chattered excitedly and launched from Laurence's shoulder to get there first, so he picked up the pace and trotted the last few steps to catch up.

"You must have got *some* sleep," Myriam chided from inside the kitchen.

"No," Rufus said stubbornly. "Your son might give up easily, but I don't."

Myriam snorted before Laurence could argue. "My son knows how to take care of himself. What are you going to achieve if you're dead on your feet?"

"Wow. What a conversation to wake up to," Laurence said dryly as he walked on in.

The kitchen looked like someone *used* it. Myriam had made a stack of pancakes, and was at the stove making more. The table was dressed and laid out, with orange juice and coffee, butter and syrup, fresh fruit and and a can of whipped cream. His mom had obviously done the best she could with whatever Ru had in cupboards, but it was more than Laurence had ever seen Ru do for himself.

Windsor had perched on the back of a chair and was eyeing the pancakes. His desire to eat everything laid out in front of him reverberated across their bond, and only emphasized Laurence's own empty stomach.

"Ru," Laurence said before Rufus could say something sarcastic about self-care. "Can I use your phone charger?"

Rufus gestured to the wall near a window. "Sure."

"Thanks, man." Laurence plugged his phone in, made sure it was charging, then sat himself at the table and poured coffee. "Okay, what time is it, and how're we gonna get you to the store on time, Mom?"

"It's half past seven, and we're not," Myriam said as she brought the last pancakes to the table and settled down with them. "It's too much fuss. We'll go straight to the hospital first, then I can go to work after I've dropped you off."

Laurence wasn't going to argue. Not with his mom when her mind was made up. He helped himself to pancakes and dropped hunks of butter on top, then added what was probably far too much syrup. He topped it all off with a handful of berries, which totally made it health food all of a sudden. "Okay. And we've got all the spells we need?"

Rufus shrugged. "Impossible to know. But we've got all the spells we *should* need."

Laurence raised an eyebrow as he stuffed a forkful into his mouth, but got distracted by the mixture of warm, sweet, buttery pancake on his tongue. "Oh Goddess, Mom, I forgot how amazing your pancakes are!"

"That's what you get for moving out," she chuckled as she helped herself from the pile.

He grunted, then refocused on Ru's use of *we*. "You're coming to the hospital?"

Rufus shrugged, and his gaze drifted toward Myriam for a second before he mumbled around a mouthful. "It's a long way to go to find out we need more information or took the wrong spells. If I come with you, we stand more of a chance of figuring it out faster."

Laurence ate some more rather than answer right away. Mom was looking innocent, which meant she wasn't, and Ru's look carried way more information than he might have wanted it to. It seemed pretty obvious to Laurence that Mom had spoken to Ru and maybe talked him into coming along. What Laurence wanted to know was how. What had she said to coax the recluse out of hiding long enough to go visit a hospital forty miles away, to help someone he'd never even met?

He doubted it would be anything he could replicate, no matter how much he silvered his own tongue. Myriam just exuded mom energy, and Ru seemed to respond well to it, so Laurence decided it was best left alone and just accepted for what it was: help from an expert.

"Thanks, man," Laurence said. "We'll get you home straight after."

Windsor cawed a complaint, so Laurence pulled the remaining fruit closer, and Win helped himself to the leftovers. He finished off his own pancakes while he watched the bird stuff himself on berries.

Taking Ru out into the world felt weird, but it really would cut out a lot of hassle if whatever was wrong with Freddy wasn't quick or easy to diagnose, so Laurence quashed the disquiet back down and took his empty plate to the sink. After Mom cooked and Ru agreed to come out with them, washing up was the least Laurence could do to help out around here.

"WHAT'S THE PLAN?" Myriam asked as she pulled the truck onto the freeway.

Laurence dug his phone out of his pocket and plugged it into the cable between the front seats, and switched it on. It had picked up enough juice from Rufus' kitchen to at least power on. "I think we're just gonna try the Otherworld theory first, right?" He looked into the back, to Rufus, who was scowling in the middle of the rear seat.

"It's the potential problem doctors can't fix, so it's better if we check it out first," Ru agreed with a grunt. He glanced out of the windows as Myriam drove, eyeing other vehicles with deep suspicion.

Laurence's heart sank.

Goddess, he was such a dumbass. Of *course* Ru never left the fucking house unless he had to. He'd survived an auto wreck that killed his parents, and now Laurence was taking him out on the exact same freeway that they'd died on.

Shit.

"Thank you," Laurence said softly. "I know you don't even know Freddy, and — if I'm honest — he's kinda an asshole, so I really appreciate you doing this."

Rufus rubbed his nose and shifted in his seat, then he glanced toward Laurence. "We all knew finding out who killed them wouldn't be easy. I can't ask you to do all the work without help."

Laurence's phone began to vibrate with a barrage of missed notifications, so he nodded gratefully to Ru and turned his attention back to his phone. A few emails, a bunch of social media notifications, and some text messages from Quentin. He read through those first.

"Okay," he breathed. "Quen says there's no change with Freddy."

He tapped out a response.

Hey baby. Good morning. We're on our way. Ru's coming with, and we have a few ideas, so if you want to head off that's fine.

The response came quickly.

I will wait. Thank you. I have an additional matter to discuss at some stage.

Laurence raised an eyebrow as he thumbed his response. *What is it, baby?*

I encountered a gifted young lady, and she has remained here with me.

Laurence let out a breath.

"What is it, dear?" Mom kept her eyes on the road as she asked.

"Quen managed to get himself into trouble in a hospital, of all places. How does he do it? He's fine," he added, before his mom could worry. "But now he's got some kid with powers hanging around him. He's like the Pied Piper."

"The Pied Piper lured children to their deaths," Rufus intoned.

"Bad analogy." Laurence shook his head, still bewildered that in less than twenty-four hours Quen had somehow had a run-in with another psychic miles away from home. "This is fine, though. He can look out for her while we work, and that'll give him an excuse to be out of the room."

"It's only magic," Rufus muttered.

"And this is only a car," Myriam said quietly.

Ru glowered at the back of her head, then his shoulders slumped. "Fair point. I'm sorry."

Laurence cradled an arm around Windsor while he thumbed out another message, then he leaned back in silence and watched the cars go by.

He had a bad feeling about all of this, and the closer they got to Grossmont, the stronger it got.

If only he could put a finger on *why*.

2 3

LAURENCE

Quentin let him know what ward Freddy was on, and Laurence checked out the hospital map so they could all look like they knew where they were going. It worked: nobody stopped them or asked questions, and Laurence got everyone into Freddy's room without incident.

It *was* kind of cramped in there, though. They wouldn't be able to hang around too long.

Laurence eyed Mikey without comment, then nodded a greeting to the grubby white girl he didn't know before he turned his attention to Quen. "Hey, baby." He glanced to the shadow along Quentin's jaw and the darkness under his eyes, and added, "You should get some rest."

Quentin stepped in for a light kiss, and his fingertips lingered at Laurence's hips. "I'm quite all right."

There was no arguing with him, so Laurence changed tack. "Ru's here to help. Do you want to go get a cup of tea?"

Quentin's eyes creased faintly and his gaze slid aside. "That would be wise," he conceded. Then he turned to the girl and said, "Would you like some breakfast?"

She sniffed. "Yeah, sure."

Quentin dipped his head and brushed his lips against Laurence's cheek. "Thank you, darling." He stepped away, nodded politely to Rufus, offered Myriam a warm but thin smile, then led the teenager out of the room.

Mikey sat up on the couch and rubbed his eyes. "What's going on?"

"You need to leave," Ru said.

Mikey stood slowly, and Laurence could see the look in his eyes as he switched from curious to murderous, so he stepped in fast and put a hand against Mikey's chest.

"You've got to trust me, man," Laurence said, as gently as he could. "I need you to keep watch, make sure nobody comes in here until we've figured this out. We can't have some nurse finding us in here doing magic."

It took a few seconds for Mikey to dial down the murder, but in the end he sagged. "Fine. But if you hurt him—"

Laurence sympathized. He really did. He knew what it was like to be helpless when the man he loved was in a hospital bed and there was nothing he could do about it. But he needed to balance Mikey's fears against Rufus' desire to get home fast and — though it felt cruel — Rufus' needs were going to come first. That was just basic triage.

He held up a hand. "The longer you argue, the longer Freddy's in a coma."

Mikey chewed on his lip, but the decision was already made. Laurence could see it in his posture.

"I'll wait with you, dear," Myriam said. "I'll only be in the way in here." She gestured for Mikey to go with her as she moved toward the door.

"Fine." Mikey stalked out of the room, and drew the door shut quietly behind them both.

Laurence exhaled, but he didn't wait around. He checked that the blinds were closed so nobody could spy on them, and by the time he turned back, Rufus was already reading a spell off his phone. It was a basic check to see whether Freddy's mind was still in his body, and the universe paused for breath and ground to a halt as Rufus reached the final word then kicked back into action like nothing had happened. Laurence was used to it by now, but it still gave him tingles up the back of his neck every time.

"Well?"

Rufus sniffed. "Quentin's right," he admitted. "Fine. He *might* be smarter than he looks."

Laurence grit his teeth. Now was not the time to get into a fight. "Okay, so we can pull him back out to his body, right?"

"It would be safer for him if we went in," Rufus sighed. "If we tear him away from whatever's holding him, we might do damage. If we go in and find out what's keeping him there, we can extract him more delicately."

Although Laurence was pretty open to the idea of spiritually dragging Freddy through a hedge backwards, he really didn't know what that might do. When he'd been in Avalon while Freddy tortured him, Freddy's telepathy hadn't been enough to cross into Otherworld. He'd resorted to injecting Laurence with heroin, and that wasn't something Laurence felt even slightly comfortable with suggesting here, but if there were less morally horrific options, what could that do to someone? Could they leave a piece of themselves behind? Would it shred their mind and leave them in a permanent vegetative state?

Freddy might be willing to do it to him, but Laurence couldn't bring himself to take the risk, especially if Freddy was serious about turning over a new leaf.

"Fine." He sighed heavily and unwrapped the thong around his left wrist, slowly peeling away all his magical protections until they were no longer a part of him. He dropped them into the drawer by Freddy's bed, and put his phone in there for good measure in case the translation spell on it conflicted with the magic Ru was about to cast.

Once he closed the drawer, he stepped around to the other side of the bed so the talismans were well out of range of his aura, then nodded to Ru. "Let's go."

Rufus dug whiteboard markers out of his pocket and tossed one to Laurence. He dug up a spell on his phone and walked through where they'd need to place sigils, and then they both got to work, splitting the room into halves and focusing only on their own half to get the job done. Laurence had to refer back to the phone a few times, but he was way more confident about his sigil work than he would have been a few months ago, and when they were done, they swapped sides to inspect each others' work.

The room was dotted with markings which Laurence really hoped they'd be able to clean off again once they were finished. They spiraled out across the floor then ran up the walls and windows, without any circle to contain them.

"Great," Ru declared, evidently happy with what they'd done. "Now we lie down on the floor."

Laurence didn't try to hide the disgust that writhed up from his throat. "Ew. No. This is a hospital. The floors are probably gross."

"Lie down or fall down, your choice."

Rufus had a point. They were about to ditch their bodies, so they were going to end up laying down whether they started there or not.

Laurence sighed. "Fine."

They settled down on either side of the bed, careful not to smudge any sigils, then Rufus began to intone the spell, and because Laurence's phone was in a drawer, he had no idea what Ru was saying. It didn't sound Latin, and it definitely wasn't Spanish, and that was the end of Laurence's linguistic expertise.

The universe took another breath, and this time when it exhaled, the hospital room was gone.

———

INITIALLY, Laurence thought that everything was gray. The sky, the air, the ground, it all seemed to be a mix of dreary shades of blue-green soot. As he sat up and took a better look, though, he began to make out more color and texture.

He sat — naked — on a riverbank, with limp, pewter-green grass underneath him which faded down to sepia pebbles that disappeared into murky, sludge-green water. The river was only twenty feet wide, and slurped along at a leisurely pace with the occasional shadow bobbing under the surface.

Overhead, the sky was slate behind clouds like smoke from a wood fire. There was no sign of the sun, which didn't surprise Laurence too much; it didn't seem to feature much in Otherworld, that he'd seen.

Beyond the river, the opposite bank rolled off into a field that disappeared into the horizon, also covered with dank grass, but also dotted with tall plants that ended in spears of white or yellow, star-shaped flowers and their filament-like stamens which rendered the edges a little fuzzy. He didn't see a whole lot of them in California, but Laurence recognized asphodel easily enough. They were native to the Mediterranean, especially in and around Greece, and not dangerous in any way.

"I don't see him," Rufus muttered.

Laurence tore his attention from the fields and toward Ru, but looked away quickly. Of *course* Rufus was butt naked. But at least in Ru's defense he had no choice about it this time. "Yeah," Laurence breathed. "Me either."

He stood and brushed dirt off his ass as he turned to examine their surroundings more. A lead-colored mountain sprouted from the ground to his right, and the river was flowing sluggishly from a cave in the foothills which was so dark that even he couldn't see into it. The mouth of the cave was surrounded by bright scarlet splashes of poppies growing with wild abandon, which were towered over by a copse of black poplar trees, with their branches and leaves which looked forever shaped by winds that were no longer around.

At his back, more hills, and more grass. To his left, more of the same.

This place was vast, and yet almost completely uninspiring.

"I don't think this is *our* Otherworld," he said as he looked toward Rufus and did his best not to focus on anything below the nipples. "These plants are all native to the Mediterranean."

Ru grunted. "Yeah," he agreed. "We should go."

Laurence licked his lips and tried to think. "Wait. We followed Freddy, right?"

Ru nodded.

"And the only place we can't see is that cave." Laurence pointed toward it.

"Which means that's probably where Freddy is," Rufus agreed. "But we're not going in. We have to—"

The river began to swirl. An eddy quickly became a whirlpool, and then the whirlpool rose into the air as a column of water, a tornado with no wind that settled into the shape of a woman.

She stepped onto land as her clothes were still forming around her, and her black hair settled into tightly curled ringlets that spilled down to her waist over the pleats and drapes of her pale green dress. The garment flowed like a toga, but she wore various brooches and pins at her shoulders and waist which seemed to cinch the material and hold it in place.

"—go," Rufus finished in a whisper. "Shit," he added.

She looked them over with dull eyes. "Hunter," she said to

Laurence. "Philosopher," she mused as she regarded Rufus. "You come for the Trickster. He may leave whenever he wishes. He chooses to stay."

Laurence narrowed his eyes, but if she was lying, he couldn't detect it.

But why would Freddy want to stay here?

"I don't mean to seem rude," Laurence said, choosing his words carefully, "but why would he do that?"

"I cannot say." She didn't seem too curious about whatever motives Freddy might have, if her flat tone was anything to go by. "You are welcome to ask him yourselves."

Laurence looked up to the cave.

It didn't look welcoming.

"Let's not," Rufus grunted.

Laurence's gut agreed.

"We can just walk right in there?" Laurence asked, just to be clear. It was always worth being super specific in Otherworld. The last thing he wanted was to get tricked by a faerie or something. "Go in, ask him, come out again, no problem?"

She shrugged. "You may go in and speak with him as much as you please, but if he answers, you face the same choice. You might choose to stay too. I cannot say."

Laurence's nose crinkled. He looked to Rufus for any sign, but Ru's lips were clamped tight, and he looked like he'd never regretted leaving his house more than he did right now.

"But I *can* choose to leave?" Laurence crossed his arms.

"Of course. Drink of the waters, and you will be able to leave."

"So he's... not drinking?"

"Correct."

Laurence swallowed tightly as he watched the miserable green water glug along the banks, and couldn't blame Freddy for refusing. It looked nasty as hell. There was no way he was going to put any of that in his mouth. None. The thought of it turned his stomach, and every instinct he had screamed out in warning, begging him not to let so much as a drop of that river touch his lips. And if it was the only way to leave the cave, then he sure wasn't going *in*.

He'd have to apologize to Quen later for failing to rescue his brother, but Laurence was done here, and he wasn't going to hang around any longer and give the mildly horrifying lady any more opportunities to talk him into going against his gut. He was out of his depth, in an Otherworld he had no familiarity with, and there was a very real chance that he could wind up trapped here forever.

"Pull the rip-cord, Ru," he said thickly, his throat closing around the words. "Get us the fuck out of here."

The murk around them blinked out of existence so fast that the sterile, neon light of a hospital room overhead nearly blinded Laurence, and he lay gasping on the cold floor while he waited for his heart to stop racing.

He didn't know how or why Freddy had got trapped in Otherworld just by looking through Mom's memories, but Laurence knew with utter certainty that he'd have to figure it out fast.

Rescue Freddy, defeat his captor, solve a double homicide.

Laurence reached for the nearest sigil and rubbed through it with his hand to break it, then bounced to his feet and looked around for something to clean the rest of the markings up with.

It was time to get to work.

24

MYRIAM

THERE WAS NO CONVENIENT PLACE TO SIT OUTSIDE FREDDY'S room, and so Myriam found a spot she could stand with her back to a wall and keep her eye out as Bambi had requested.

She didn't want to be alone with Mikey, but she was well used to the fact that witches far preferred peace and quiet when they worked, and having to deal with the energies of concerned onlookers would help nobody, so here she was. Standing beside the man who had gotten her son addicted to drugs.

That's not fair, she chided herself. *You didn't want to interfere in Bambi's destiny.*

Myriam sighed softly and adjusted her hold on her purse before she forced herself to look at the young man. Things wouldn't have gone any differently if she had allowed Freddy to bring him along to her home, but at least Mikey could have been there instead of receiving news like this secondhand.

If she was willing to give Freddy a second chance, didn't Mikey deserve one too?

He was hunkered over, his hands deep in the pockets of his undoubtedly expensive pants, his gaze fixed on the door to

Freddy's room. He hadn't even noticed her watching him, or if he had, he didn't respond.

Myriam cleared her throat. "He'll pull through, dear."

Mikey grunted. "You can't know that."

He was half right, and if she wanted to argue the point she'd have to do a reading, but this was not the time, and there wasn't space for Myriam to lay cards out.

She could, she supposed, pull a single card from the deck, but if the answer was complicated it wouldn't be enough, so she just nodded. "I can't," she agreed. "I want to ask you something."

Mikey finally tore his attention from Freddy's room and turned it on her instead, and his eyes looked like he'd spent all night crying and then rubbing the tears away. "Sure."

Myriam did her best to choose her words with care. If she sounded too accusatory, too resentful, he might clam up, and then she wouldn't ever get any sense out of him.

"How did you turn to dealing?"

Mikey's eyes, already dull, turned just a little darker still. He lowered his head until he was looking at her shoes, and his shoulders sagged. "After Mom died, what was I gonna do? I didn't have anyone looking out for me, I was lucky enough I still had a place to live. I needed money, and I wasn't allowed to work enough hours to make it."

Myriam nodded a little as she listened. She was well aware of the labor laws in California, and a teenager couldn't have worked more than three hours a day on school days. For Mikey to buy food, pay bills, and keep the house in order, it wouldn't have been enough.

"So it was do what you had to, or drop out of school," she sighed.

He clicked his tongue. "I didn't want to drop out. I couldn't make what I needed by flipping burgers, and I just kind of fell into it. I only wanted to sell weed, but my supplier knew a guy and—" Mikey huffed. "It's all so fucking dumb. I only needed a little help, and the only people offering it were… Well, you know the kind of people they were. I was a kid, Mrs. Riley, and there was nobody there for me."

The ache which had consumed her for so many years came back in full force, and Myriam held her purse more tightly to her stomach, like she could use it as a hot water bottle, but the ache didn't stop.

Maybe she'd known deep down that this had to be Mikey's truth, but ever since Bambi had started using, her worry had been for her son. She had no room left over to care about her child's dealer.

And that was the problem. Nobody had worried about Mikey. And now, finally, he had someone who did, and that man was lying unconscious in a hospital bed.

The poor boy had to be going out of his mind.

"You're not going back to that life," Myriam declared.

He raised his head again, and held it high. There was, somewhere in his gaze, a light that was struggling to flicker back into life. "I'm not," he stated.

She hesitated at what her gut told her to do next, but she knew that it was right. And, with any luck, it would soothe the ache, so she reached out and rested a hand against his arm. "I am so sorry. I told Freddy that you weren't welcome at my home, and that was unnecessary of me. You had a right to be there."

Mikey sniffed and rubbed the end of his nose with the back of his hand, but he didn't give any indication that he wanted her to stop touching him. "No, you had a right, too. It's your home. We all did dumb, stupid shit when we were kids, and none of us can change the past, but we can make sure we never do it again, right?" He glanced up at her, peeking through rumpled red curls. "I did some bad shit. I was in trouble, but I had no idea how badly I'd hurt everyone around me just trying to get out of it, and they were my friends." He pulled away and leaned back against the wall, resting his head to it and kicking the baseboard with one heel. "They were all my friends," he whispered, "and I fucked them all up."

The ache in Myriam's heart only intensified. She leaned back against the wall by his side and watched the corridor, but nobody was coming their way or heading for Freddy's room. It was just her, Mikey, and the weight of the shared years that they'd both failed in their own ways.

"You didn't," Myriam admitted quietly. "You're right. You were young and alone, and I saw the influence you had on my son, but I didn't understand the influence the world had on you." She pressed her lips together and weighed her thoughts, but the ache that gripped her heart was clear as a bell, and she had to listen to it. "Freddy believes in you, and he can see far beneath the surface. Further than I possibly can."

Mikey's lips curled into a faint, wry smirk, though he remained looking to the door he faced. "And you believe in him?"

Myriam tutted. "That boy is an idiot," she replied. "But, like you, he thought he was alone. People make desperate choices when they are backed into a corner and have nobody to help them. He wants to do better, and I'm willing to give him the space to try. If I can do that for him, I can do it for you, too." Though, she had to admit — if only to herself — she was still intent on giving him a piece of her mind for putting Bambi through hell.

His smirk crumbled into dust. His lip trembled faintly, and Mikey dropped his head again. "I don't deserve that. But I want it. It's wrong to want it, right?"

"To want what?" Myriam tried not to smile. "Forgiveness? Love? We all want those things. What matters is how hard we work to earn them."

"Yeah." Mikey sniffed and rubbed his nose again. "I guess

this is why Laurence turned out okay, huh? Having a mom as wise as you?"

"I'm only human," she countered. "We all are, gifts or no gifts. All we can really do is our best, dear."

She *wanted* to give him a hug, but the opportunity wasn't there, so instead she held her purse to her chest and went back to keeping watch. The ache inside her was slowly subsiding, eased by a sense of relief that soothed it like a balm, and she felt a little better about sharing space with Mikey.

The wait became a comfortable one. They could hold on together instead of apart, and Myriam felt more at ease now. She hoped that Mikey did, too, though of course he would feel far better if Bambi could solve whatever was wrong with Freddy.

She saw the handle turn, the door crack open, and straightened up immediately. Her heart skipped with hope, but as Bambi stepped out into the corridor, she could tell from the darkness in his eyes and the thinness in his lips that it wasn't good news.

"Well?" Mikey demanded. "What happened? Is he gonna be okay?"

Myriam did what she could to prepare herself for the worst, but this was way out of her league, and not for the first time since his death, she wished Eric was still here.

But Bambi had Eric's capacity for magic, and if anyone could help Freddy now, it was her son, not her husband.

"We've got to get outside," Rufus said, pushing past Bambi and out into the corridor. "All of us. Now."

"We'll explain," Bambi promised. "But Ru's right. We've gotta go."

Mikey looked about ready to start something, so Myriam gently took his arm and held it until she had his attention, and when he glared down at her with gritted teeth, she nodded softly to him.

"It's okay," she murmured. "I know you don't want to leave him, but it won't be for long."

A short, brutal war played out across his features. His face creased into anger, then switched to fear, but stoicism washed it all away, and he gave her a short nod.

"Fine," he said.

He left a lot unsaid, but Myriam understood. They were asking him to leave Freddy's side, and Myriam wasn't sure she'd have had his strength if she was in his shoes.

Bambi led the way, and Ru was hot on his heels, so Myriam gently steered Mikey along with them and kept a hold on his arm so that he knew he wasn't alone, because that was what she *could* do.

LAURENCE

WHERE ARE YOU? LAURENCE TEXTED QUENTIN AS HE WALKED, relying on peripheral vision to avoid bumping into anyone.

In the cafeteria, Quentin replied.

On our way.

"Okay," Laurence said as he shoved his phone into the pocket of his cargo pants. "Quen's in the cafeteria, I've told him we'll meet him there."

Rufus pulled a face, but didn't say anything. Instead, Mikey piped up.

"What are we running from?"

"Not gonna discuss it until we're all in one place," Laurence declared. He ignored the elevators and went straight for the stairs to burn off some of the energy that made him feel like he was vibrating. He didn't know if he could stand still, and he didn't want to try it.

They all followed, their footsteps echoing down the staircase like they were a gaggle of schoolchildren on a museum trip, and Laurence burst out of the stairwell once they hit the first floor, searching for signs or smells of the cafeteria.

He picked up the faintest thread of bacon over the perpetual antiseptic aftertaste of every hospital he'd ever been in, and strode toward it.

The cafeteria was quiet. There were a few customers here and there, but it he figured it probably got busier around lunchtime, and it was as good a place as any to talk. Quentin shone like a beacon, against the far wall with the young woman he'd managed to collect, sipping from a mug while she polished off the last of a plate of food.

Laurence led the way around tables and chairs and sat next to Quentin, and Myriam slid in beside the girl before Ru could steal the seat, which left Rufus and Mikey to pull chairs over from nearby tables.

"Darling," Quentin murmured. He looked questioningly to Laurence, eyebrow lifted, gaze patient.

Laurence rested a hand on Quentin's thigh under the table and gave him a gentle nod, then looked to the teen and offered his other hand. "Hey. Sorry, it's pretty hectic around here, I didn't get a chance to say hi. I'm Laurence."

She ignored his hand. "Mel," she mumbled around a chunk of toast.

Laurence wasn't offended. Mel was grubby and eating like she'd been hungry for days. He didn't doubt she was homeless, and homeless kids had good reason not to go around shaking the hands of every stranger they met. "Nice to meet you. This is my mom, Myriam. And this is my friend, Rufus. This is Freddy's boyfriend, Mikey." He gestured to each in turn, and they nodded to Mel and offered varying degrees of greeting, most of which Mel pretty much turned her nose up at.

Still, Quen said she was gifted, and that meant Laurence wasn't going to waste time dancing around with his language.

"You were right," he said to Quentin. "Freddy's in Otherworld, but it's not the one we know. I'm making an educated guess when I say I think it's Ancient Greek, but all the plants and the way she was dressed lean really heavily that way."

Quentin set his mug down. The tea in it was only half-finished. "She?"

"There's a goddess," Laurence explained. "She says Freddy's free to leave any time he wants, but he'd have to drink from a river there, and it looks pretty fucking rank, if I'm honest." He licked his lips as he ran through how urgently Rufus had wanted to leave, and pieced two and two together. Hopefully he'd made four, but he turned to face Ru just to be sure, and asked, "Who was she?"

Rufus laced his fingers together and slowly cracked his knuckles. "Ancient Greek, river coming from a cave, no sun in the sky. That was Hades, the Underworld, and there are five rivers in Hades, but only one of them comes from a cave. The river Lethe flows from the Cave of Hypnos, and Lethe is also the name of the goddess of the river." He shook his head. "The river is the Ameles potamos, the river of unmindfulness. Souls had to drink from it to forget their former lives if they were to continue on their journey to the Fields of Asphodel, or to rebirth. Lethe means "oblivion" in Classical Greek, and what she brings oblivion to is memory. She wants Freddy to forget before she'll allow him to leave."

Laurence gnawed on his thumb while he slotted all the pieces together. Was *that* what Freddy was resisting? Forgetting something?

There was something missing. A piece of the puzzle he couldn't quite see.

Mom had known Freddy was inside her mind.

"I very much doubt that Freddy would willingly relinquish his mind to anyone or anything," Quentin said. "He's really very protective of it."

"He's protective of everything that's his," Mikey said.

"Aren't we all," Quentin murmured as he hid behind his mug of tea.

Laurence waved his hand quickly like he could brush the distractions aside, and he looked across the table to his mom. "Freddy was in your memories," he said slowly.

Myriam nodded. "That's right."

"You saw those memories," he said, struggling to clarify what he meant with words that weren't made for the job. "Like, he was showing them to you while he was looking at them, right? He does that, when he wants you to know he's there."

"Yes," Myriam agreed. "We were looking at them together."

"So you must've seen the same things." Laurence pressed on as the final piece came into view. "Lethe is what made us all forget Angela. We've all been there, we've all drunk from that river, and we don't remember it. Holy shit, Mom." He felt sick at the thought of it, of putting that water in his mouth, but also of having been in that impossibly black cave, in an Otherworld he didn't belong in, and of having had his memories taken from him without ever finding out.

Goddess, he still wouldn't have found out if Freddy had done what Lethe wanted.

His hand tightened on Quentin's thigh as the realization hit him like a freight train. "Freddy's sacrificing himself," he breathed. "If he'd drunk the water, he'd be here now, and we never would've found out any of this. He's refusing because he knows it'll leave him stuck in Otherworld and we'd go digging to find out why."

The truth of his words resonated with such clarity as the puzzle piece slotted into place that he sat back in his chair, dazed by it, his thoughts whirling as they spun through the ramifications of Freddy's choice.

Freddy knew what a person whose mind was in Otherworld

looked like. He knew they were unreachable by anyone without the ability to cross into Otherworld themselves. He knew that by refusing to drink he'd be helpless in Myriam's kitchen, and Laurence knew damn well Freddy *despised* being helpless.

Freddy chose to throw up a signal flare for Laurence.

"Great, so now we know why," Mikey said. He leaned forward in his chair and stared directly at Laurence. "You can get him out."

"We'd have to go into the cave to reach him," Rufus muttered. "And then we'd be in the same boat. Either we drink and forget to be able to come out again, or we hang on to our memories and stay there."

"But we aren't forgetting everything." Myriam frowned. "Just specific things. And knowing about Lethe's existence isn't the memory being protected. If I did drink from the river — if everyone who has forgotten Angela did so — and it wiped all of our memories, things would play out very differently."

"It would raise a great deal more suspicion," Quentin murmured. "This is precise work, targeting a specific memory or group of memories. It should be safe for one person to go in and tell Freddy that he can leave now. Those who don't go can simply fill in the blanks once everyone is safe."

"I'll do it," Mikey declared.

"Absolutely not," said Quentin.

"Great, let's go," Rufus said at the same time.

Rufus and Mikey looked on the verge of starting an argument with Quentin, so Laurence slapped his hand against the table to cut it off before it could begin. "Someone has to go in. Mikey's volunteered. If we argue about it, Freddy just has to wait even longer for his rescue, so can we shelve it for now and get him out first, and *then* do any arguing we want to." He stood up to make it clear he considered the discussion over, and beckoned to Ru and Mikey to do the same. "Wait here," he said to those still seated. "We won't be long."

Quentin opened his mouth, clearly not impressed at being given an order, and probably about to say something he would come to regret, like *no, I volunteer to be present while Rufus performs a magic ritual with me at the center. This totally won't backfire on all of us.*

"Baby," Laurence said softly. He placed a hand on Quentin's shoulder as he leaned across the empty chair, and he pressed his lips to Quentin's forehead. "Mikey needs to do this."

He felt the solidity of Quentin's shoulder under his hand, the urge to fight that was coiled within that frail-seeming body, and he waited.

The tension released. The shoulder slowly lowered.

"Very well," Quentin sighed.

Laurence nodded to him. This was the right thing to do for so many reasons, but there wasn't time to list them all or to discuss the finer points of whose need to help Freddy should come out on top and why, and he was grateful that Quentin had chosen not to fight this battle.

"Thanks, hon. We'll get him back. I promise."

A glint of steel flashed in Quentin's eyes, then it was gone, and he raised his head. "Go."

Laurence squeezed that shoulder before he let go, then he pulled away from the table and made sure Rufus and Mikey were with him before he set off across the cafeteria. Behind him, he heard Mel's voice, demanding to know what was going on, but he trusted Quentin and Mom to handle that mess.

He had his own problem to take care of, and there wasn't any more time to waste.

2 6

MIKEY

Volunteering was crazy, but what else was he going to do? Sit back and let Quentin do everything?

Hell nah.

Frederick saved Mikey, and now it was Mikey's turn to save Frederick, and then they wouldn't be even, because this wasn't some exchange of favors, no score card to be kept. This was life, and it was love, and it had taken him a year of therapy to understand that being there for each other was what love was. It wasn't a series of transactions, it wasn't an obligation.

It was an honor.

And, sure, he was terrified, but so what? Mikey had spent his whole life terrified. Scared of his uncle, scared of the cartels, scared of the cops, and eventually scared of freedom from all of that.

There was nothing wrong with fear. Anyone who wasn't scared of heading off into some magical world of the dead to face a goddess was probably worth staying far, far away from.

He stepped into Frederick's room and pushed past Laurence to get to Frederick's side, to grip his unresponsive hand, to steady himself with it and fight back the lurching in his gut. Everything between his ribs and asshole felt like it had clenched into one huge knot.

Frederick would absolutely hate everyone seeing him this vulnerable.

Rufus grabbed his phone and a whiteboard marker and set to work scribbling all over the place. He didn't say a word. Maybe he thought Mikey was beneath him, or maybe he just wanted everything to be done, but he moved quickly and consulted his phone every step of the way.

"Okay," Laurence said. He stopped at the foot of Frederick's bed and rested his hands on it. "Here's what's going to happen. You'll blink and be somewhere else. It's kind of like an elevator; the doors just open and you're in a new place. It's probably going to seem a bit weird, but it's totally fine."

Mikey nodded faintly. He knew exactly what it was like to be in the real world one second, and in a completely made-up world inside his own head the next. Frederick was a big fan of creating mindscapes that were either drawn from memories or spun like delicate tapestries out of pure imagination, and he would sweep Mikey up in them like a fairy godmother.

"So you said there's a cave," Mikey prompted, turning to face Laurence.

Laurence nodded slightly. "Yeah. You should arrive next to a river. Follow it to the cave, Freddy's inside. You go in, tell him he can leave now, then you both drink from the river and you'll wake up back here again." He took a breath. "Look, man, I know you want to help him, but I can do this. You don't have to."

Mikey snorted at him. "I do have to."

They locked eyes for a few moments and said nothing. Whether Laurence was making his mind up about something or not, Mikey couldn't know, but he didn't care. For the first time in his life Mikey was the one in charge of his own destiny, and this was his choice to make, not Laurence's.

"Okay," Laurence finally breathed. "You'll have to lie down on the floor, 'cause when you enter Otherworld spiritually you leave your body behind—"

"—And I don't wanna knock my head when I fall down," Mikey concluded. "I got it."

Laurence's eyebrows raised, and he smiled faintly. "And you'll be butt naked. I'm gonna wait outside and make sure nobody walks in on you both. Just stick to the plan."

Mikey flipped a casual salute and waited until Laurence was gone, then he watched Rufus work. He was undoubtedly the teacher Laurence had dug up to learn magic from, but he also seemed cold as a fish and utterly disinterested in casual conversation, which Mikey could respect. If it meant that the spell went off without a hitch, he was more than happy to stay silent so Rufus could work.

"Done," Rufus said. "Lie down, don't break any sigils."

Mikey forced himself to let go of the death grip he had on Frederick's hand, and he looked around for somewhere safe to put himself down on the ground.

"I'm not going with you," Rufus added as Mikey got comfortable, "so the only way out is the river."

Mikey blinked. "Wait, what do you mean—"

Rufus started speaking another language, and Mikey clamped his lips together. He knew fuck all about magic, and didn't want to find out the hard way whether talking during spellcasting could screw it all up, so he kept his mouth shut and his questions to himself.

And then, exactly like Laurence said, Mikey wasn't in Kansas anymore.

Nor were his clothes.

He was already assessing his new surroundings while he cautiously stood, and it all seemed pretty innocuous as far as weird otherworldly realms went. Fields, flowers, grass, mountains, and the sluggish, grey-green river that moved past like it had nowhere better to be.

"Nice," he muttered.

He looked to where the river was coming from and saw a pitch-black hole in the nearest mountain, so he set off towards it and broke into a run once he was sure nothing was going to pop out of the grass and bite him.

***

THE CAVE WAS a lot scarier up close.

Mikey stopped at the entrance and tried to look in, but it was like it was night inside. He glanced to the sky overhead and was only mildly unsettled by the lack of sun, but there *was* light. It was some vague approximation of day out here.

In there? Nope. Utter blackness.

Mikey forced himself to step around tall stems with white, star-shaped flowers, and he followed the edge of the river over the threshold which cut like a straight line between day and night. If he'd had any breath he would've held it, but breathing seemed like an afterthought here, something you did if you felt like it but not anything you noticed once it was gone.

The black enveloped him. It shut out sight and sound, it muffled sensation and left Mikey half sure that there wasn't any ground under his feet any more.

Don't panic. Don't panic!

"Frederick?"

He'd tried to say it out loud, but he couldn't feel his tongue or his lips, wasn't sure he'd managed to shape the word at all, and he didn't hear it.

Michael?

Mikey felt like his heart should skip. Maybe, back in his body, it did.

I'm here, he insisted. *I'm real. I've come to get you out of this fucking cave.*

Frederick didn't respond right away, but when he did, it was such a relief that Michael could have sobbed, because the cave disappeared and they were standing together in a hotel room with all the fragmented lights of Hong Kong beyond the windows.

Mikey rushed to Frederick and wrapped arms around his waist, clinging to him like he was a tree in a sandstorm. Past Frederick's shoulder, though, the room was imperfect. Fudged, like Frederick had thrown it up in a rush and not bothered with the details.

Outside, what Mikey had figured was Hong Kong was just multicolored lights, haphazard, shoved together like a Christmas tree decorated by children.

"What cave?" Frederick whispered as he coiled his arms around Mikey's shoulders in return.

"This cave," Mikey said, trying so hard not to babble, and failing. The room was disconcerting, and the inability to look Frederick in the eye somehow made it worse. "You — we — are in Hades. The river is Lethe. This is the cave—"

"—Of Hypnos," Frederick concluded.

Mikey nodded. Whether Frederick had plucked that from his mind or knew it from all those books he read didn't matter. "But it's okay. You can drink now."

Frederick groaned. "You don't understand. If I do, I'll forget. That's what Lethe does. It's the river of oblivion."

"I know. I have to drink it too, or I can't get out." Mikey leaned back as much as he could without letting go, and gazed into Frederick's eyes, searching for any sign that he was okay, that the mess around them was intentional. "Whatever you found, you've got to let go of it."

Frederick's jaw clenched and his eyebrows tugged together. There was something in his expression that took Mikey far too long to identify, and it was because he didn't expect Frederick to ever display it.

It was fear.

"You don't understand," Frederick croaked.

"I *do* understand." Mikey flattened his hands against Frederick's back and mustered a small and hopefully reassuring smile. "You're scared of letting something else tamper with your mind, even though you do it all the time to other people, because you love a good bit of hypocrisy."

Frederick's eyes widened indignantly.

"I know I'm right. *You* know I'm right." Mikey's smile became a grin, a weak tease to wallpaper over his own dread. "You did what you had to for us to figure out what was going on, but you can't stay in here forever. You can't." He felt the grin fade as the thought of Frederick spending the rest of his life in a coma in the hospital swam into his head. "It's not worth it," he added, pleading, praying he could make Frederick see just how dumb it would be to give up everything they had for one little memory that wasn't even his.

"But we could," Frederick breathed. A shadow crossed his gaze as whatever he was afraid of returned, and his grip on Mikey's shoulders tightened. "How long have I been here?"

Mikey frowned at him. "Less than a day."

Frederick laughed, a short bark of bitter humor. "It felt longer." Whether he'd meant to say it out loud — or whatever passed for out loud within a mindscape — was unclear. He didn't seem aware that he'd said anything at all, but then his features lit up like he'd just solved some complex problem. "We *can* stay here. We have everything we need, right here."

He raised a hand to run fingertips across Mikey's temple. "Perfectly safe."

Mikey stared into Frederick's eyes, trying to work out whether this was a joke. Frederick loved playing games with people, getting inside their heads and disrupting their worlds, and Mikey had agreed to allow Frederick to do that to him for as long as they were together. It was completely possible Frederick was fucking with him.

The longer he stared, the less convinced he became that Frederick was messing around.

Mikey felt a flutter of worry. Frederick wasn't *serious*, right?

Was he?

"I mean…" Frederick murmured.

The worry condensed itself into a ball, and it tightened. It twisted and it snarled, and it became something else.

It turned into anger.

Mikey let go of Frederick and shoved him away, hard. "I didn't sign up for this," he spat.

Frederick blinked at him. "What?"

"Don't give me that bullshit!" Mikey pointed directly at Frederick's face. "You're in my head, you know exactly what I mean!" He felt his skin grow hot, even though he wasn't in his body, and he jabbed his finger against Frederick's chest. "You spend less than a day in a dark cave that you can leave at any time, and *this* is what it does to you? You're gonna fall apart because something happened and you weren't in control of it?" This time he did spit — at Frederick's feet — as the anger flourished into pure, terrified rage. "If you can't control yourself, you're in no fit state to control *me*, asshole! How *dare* you! How dare you even *think* about spending the rest of your life in a hospital bed just because you got scared!"

His head swam. He wasn't sure if he'd gone too far, but god damnit, he was so utterly terrified. The thought that Frederick might be *scared* of something, so scared that he was willing to consider hiding out in an imperfect fantasy world of his own making, was boneshakingly horrible. He'd put his whole life in Frederick's hands because those hands were capable. They were strong, and powerful, and they knew what they were doing, and he could *not* go back to living in a drug den getting raped by cops and threatened by cartels just to scrape by day to day putting other people through hell.

He refused. He was better now. Maybe not perfect, but he wasn't a dealer, wasn't a victim, and he sure as fuck wasn't willing to hurt innocent people anymore just so he could get food in his belly and hot water coming out of his faucets.

"You're right," Frederick said quietly.

Mikey glowered at him, but the look of shame in Frederick's eyes was unguarded, honest, and it stabbed through Mikey's rage until it collapsed into a sagging, sad mess of fear and exhaustion.

"I'm sorry," Frederick added, words that he said so rarely that they carried the weight of a singularity. "You are absolutely right. Thank you."

"You mean it?" Mikey jutted his lower lip out and risked letting go of the tightness of his own posture.

Frederick inclined his head and drew himself up to his full height. "I do," he murmured.

Mikey watched him to be sure, then he nodded. "Great. Then get your ass in gear and drink this stanky-ass river water so we can go home."

Frederick stepped in closer and raised a hand to cup Mikey's cheek, and Mikey leaned into the touch and the kiss which followed it.

"Let's go," Frederick whispered against his lips.

Mikey nodded as the hotel room faded away, and wondered just how much they were about to forget.

27

LAURENCE

FREDDY'S ROOM WENT FROM ZERO TO ALL HELL BREAKING LOOSE in the blink of an eye, and Laurence quickly shouldered the door to get inside and shut it after himself as the noise washed over him.

"No, I'm okay!" Mikey was insisting as he hauled himself to his feet.

"You probably have a catheter," Rufus said, sounding vaguely amused.

"Shh!" Laurence raised his hands as he stepped further into the room and took in the scene. "Keep it down in here!"

Freddy was awake, which was a positive result, but he looked pissed as hell, which was absolutely negative. He'd already half-thrown his bedsheets off, and was now fighting with wires and tubes attached to his hands. Mikey had made it up and was trying to stop Freddy tearing things out of himself, and Rufus had his back to a wall well out of Freddy's reach.

"Laurence," Freddy barked. He stopped fussing over the wires, and glared across the room. "What is the meaning of this?"

Laurence shook his head faintly. "You were at Mom's, you fell into a coma, you've been here ever since. C'mon, man, you're in Mikey's head, right? Let him bring you up to speed." *And don't kill Rufus*, he thought, wondering if that was the first thing Freddy had tried after waking up in a hospital bed with a witch looming over him.

Freddy turned his Sauron-like glare onto Mikey, who stood there looking nonplussed until Freddy huffed and reached for his sheets. "I see," he said thickly. "So we don't know what was lost."

"No," Laurence said. "I'm sorry. We had no way of knowing Mom's brain was booby-trapped. We need to clear up all these sigils, then I can get a nurse to get all these tubes out of you, okay?"

Freddy was still frowning as he nodded to Laurence, and he laid back down again. "What will you do?"

Laurence grabbed some tissues from a box by the sofa and crouched down to start wiping sigils off the floor all over again. "I've got to go check on Angela. She was going to see if she could find a spell to do the same thing. If she managed it, she might be just as stuck as you were. Are you going to be okay if I go do that, or do you want me to wait until you get discharged?"

Freddy sighed so faintly that Laurence was probably the only person here who heard it. "Go," he murmured. "If she is in any sort of trouble, it's best to get there sooner rather than later, yes?"

"Yeah," Laurence agreed. "Thanks, man. Quen's downstairs, though. I'll tell him you're awake. He'll probably want to stick around and make sure you're okay."

"You'd best help with these sigils, then," Freddy murmured with a glance to Mikey.

Mikey gave an obedient nod and took some of the tissues, and together they cleaned up fast as they could while

Laurence tried not to think too hard about how often they'd done this kind of thing when they were teenagers.

IF YOU'VE FOUND a way yet, don't do it, Laurence texted Angela as he hurried back downstairs to the cafeteria with Rufus. *We need to talk.*

"You know," Rufus said as they jogged, "Lethe usually obliterates all memory."

"You're saying she's not acting under her own free will." Laurence nodded. He'd figured as much. Nobody who had their memories of Angela tampered with like this was a firm follower of any Ancient Greek faith; if any of them ended up in an Otherworld it should be the one Laurence was used to, where Arawn ruled the dead and Herne hunted in the wilds. "Makes sense. And I think it's fair to say that trapping a goddess into wiping memories and then watching to make sure they're never recovered is a pretty warlocky thing to do, right?"

"Yeah," Rufus agreed.

"Great, so how do we get past this?" Laurence pushed the doors open at the first floor and slowed to a brisk walk to avoid bumping into anyone in a hospital and making their day even worse than it might already be. "Figure out what's holding her, break the spell, get our memories back?"

Rufus clicked his tongue. "Lethe can't restore memory, she can only obliterate it. We'd have to go over her head to get them back."

"Or hope that if we break the spell, Freddy can do that part," Laurence countered, since involving himself with yet more Greek gods sounded like a really bad idea.

Ru just grunted, with no indication of whether or not he

was on board with letting Freddy poke around in his head, and Laurence didn't push it.

They made it to the cafeteria, which was slightly more popular with customers now, and weaved around people to get to Quentin's table.

Quentin, Mom, and Mel had all waited, still in the same place, though Quentin had slumped slightly further into his corner, and Mom seemed to be doing her best to engage Mel in conversation. As Laurence stopped by the table, all three sat up and turned to face him.

"He's awake," Laurence said without hanging around. He offered Quentin a soft smile, and added, "They'll discharge him as soon as they're done getting wires out of him. Do you want to go take care of him, get him home safely?"

Quentin licked his lips faintly. "Is he… all right?"

"He's annoyed, but from his point of view I figure he was at Mom's place then woke up here, and it was a bit of a shock." Laurence winced, knowing all too well what that must have felt like, though he had the added advantage of knowing he'd spent his coma time in Otherworld. Freddy, on the other hand, seemed to have no memory of any of it, which had to be doubly aggravating for a man who spent his time playing with other people's minds. "Mikey's with him, but…"

He tailed off. He couldn't find a good way to say *but I'm going to probably do more magic before all this is over, so maybe you want to stay out of it*, so instead he just left it hanging in mid-air like a bad smell.

"I think that's very sensible," Myriam murmured with a warm smile. "Why don't Mel and I go to your place where she can freshen up and meet other people her own age, and then I can hang around there to make sure Neil doesn't turn up and corrupt the youth in your absence."

Quentin dipped his head and looked to Mel. "If that is acceptable?"

She eyed him like he might be trying to pull a fast one, but then she nodded. "Sure. There's only so much you can wash in a public restroom anyway."

"Great," Laurence said smoothly before Quentin had too much time to work out what Mel was saying. "Nice to meet you, Mel. It'll be good to chat later, when things are less hectic."

"Things are never less hectic, dear," Myriam chuckled as she stood. She stepped in to hug Laurence, and added, "Be careful, Bambi."

He clung to her quickly, trying to make it look cool and casual and not like he desperately wished she could stay. "I will, Mom. Merry part."

"Merry part, dear." Then to Quentin, she added, "And get some sleep."

Quentin actually pouted at her, but nodded. "Very well. I shall."

Laurence smiled to Mel and his mom as they left the cafeteria, then he turned back to Quentin, and allowed his concern to show at last. "Are you okay, baby?"

Quentin slipped free from the table and ran fingers down Laurence's arm until he reached skin. He took Laurence's hand and held it, squeezing a little. "I am fine. Thank you, darling. Is there anything that I can help you with?"

Rufus snorted and crossed his arms, but he had the sense to say nothing, so Laurence ignored him and focused on Quentin.

"Probably going to be a whole lot more magic before all this is dealt with," Laurence explained quietly, leaning against Quentin's chest so that he could lower his voice and still be heard. "If you can find out what Freddy and Mikey remember, though, that would be really helpful. If I can work out what gets erased and what doesn't, I might be able to work around the edges, or find out what spell is keeping Lethe around. You know how it is, hon; literally anything could be the clue we need to solve this."

Quentin dipped his head a little and pressed his lips to Laurence's cheek. "Of course. Thank you. I shall do whatever I can."

"What we really need to know," Rufus muttered, "is why these memories at all? What's in them that this warlock doesn't want anyone to know?"

"We can't find out until we fix this," Laurence said. "So let's do it, then we can go digging." He turned his head to kiss Quentin on the lips, and allowed the contact to linger, wallowing in the tenderness of his lover's presence for as long as he could before he reluctantly pulled back. "See you soon, sexy."

Quentin's cheeks turned pink, and he let go of Laurence's fingers after another squeeze. "Call me if you need me."

"I will."

He gave a lingering glance at Quentin's face as he began to turn away, but he had to go. He still hadn't got a text back from Angela, and if she was in trouble, Rufus was the only one who could help her.

Laurence left the hospital as fast as he could, checking occasionally that Rufus was still at his side, and wished desperately that Quentin was able to come with him.

28

QUENTIN

QUENTIN MADE HIS WAY BACK TO FREDDY'S ROOM ONLY TO FIND that there was already a nurse in there, so he chose to wait outside to give Freddy some dignity.

The blackness at his side was not unexpected, but Quentin did his best to focus on a spot on the wall opposite rather than pay it any mind.

"So now you're putting Frederick in danger too," his father mused.

Quentin said nothing.

"He doesn't have the tools," Father said, as though assessing battlefield tactics rather than talking about his own children. "You cannot drag him into these things if you truly care about him."

What *was* there to say? Why talk to an hallucination? It would only draw attention, possibly even lead to someone calling security or a doctor, and then where would Quentin be? Mired in red tape and unable to help Laurence find the information he required.

No, it was best to try to remain calm and wait for this particular brain malfunction to settle down.

"Speak up, boy."

Quentin ground his teeth and closed his eyes as he counted down from ten to try to get a grip before Freddy came out.

"Such a child," the duke sighed. "First you endanger his career by having him dither around in this country for months on end, and now you put him in the hospital. Was it worth it? Are you getting what you want out of all of this?"

Quentin felt something within him snap. Something small, and distant, suppressed by his knowledge that he was in a hospital and a danger to those who were extremely vulnerable, but it was a distinct sensation, and his eyes flit open.

He turned to face the apparition.

"What I want," he breathed as softly as he could manage, "is to stop seeing you every time I experience the slightest hint of stress. It's exhausting, and you aren't even real. Just piss off, all right? Leave me alone."

His father's eyebrow climbed faintly. "I did not raise you to use language like that, Quentin. Nor did your mother."

Bloody hell, was his brain *trying* to make him lose control?

Quentin sucked in a breath and let it out between clenched teeth. "Mother knew what you were doing, and she didn't do a bloody thing to stop you."

The duke shrugged. "All power comes at a price." He nodded toward Freddy's door, and added, "What have you gotten him into?"

"What do *you* care?" Quentin hissed. He could feel himself fraying, like fumbled notes in the bowels of an orchestra, a tiny element of discord that would unravel the whole piece if not nipped in the bud. "You were willing to kill him with your own hands. You damn near murdered Michael just to force him to come to you. Don't pretend that you care about anyone but yourself."

Father's eyes gleamed with a luminance that didn't match the cold fluorescent hospital lights. "Everything that you have done has been for your own personal interest, boy," he snapped. "You ran away from home at nineteen, traveled the world, lost touch with the brothers you insist that you love, and fell in with a drug addict." He nodded toward Frederick's room. "And now that addict's dealer is entwined with Frederick, and you *still* pretend that you care. You are an infant, Quentin. A toddler in charge of an arsenal, and everyone around you suffers your tantrums. You should be here, with me, learning to control yourself, and instead you are swanning about in America hoarding teenagers and hospitalizing your brother. When will you learn?"

The orchestra was collapsing in on itself.

"Shut up," Quentin seethed. He stepped toward the apparition. "Shut *up!*"

"Is there a problem here?"

The interruption came from a voice Quentin didn't recognize. A steely tone from an unimpressed woman who wore raspberry-colored scrubs and a no-nonsense glare.

"I—" Quentin sucked in a breath and tried to center himself.

"No problem," the duke said smoothly, turning his attention to the doctor. "My son is upset, that's all."

She nodded slightly. "We have other patients," she advised. "Please be more mindful."

"We will. My sincere apologies."

The doctor eyed Quentin and nodded to him, then continued on along the corridor to another patient's room.

The floor fell out of Quentin's world, and he stumbled back until he had the wherewithal to grab the wall and cling onto it for stability.

It wasn't possible. His father *could not* be here. Quentin was warded. This couldn't be happening!

The fluorescent light began to flicker.

"Get a hold of yourself," his father muttered, glancing up toward the tube. "Or do you want to shower a hospital corridor with glass?"

"You can't—" Quentin gasped.

"Silence," Father cut in. "Focus, Quentin. Argue later, once you have control."

He was right. Curse him, curse his entire life, curse the very ground he walked on, but the duke was *right*, and Quentin had no choice but to hold onto his composure and not have an absolute meltdown here of all places.

There was nothing he could do other than close his eyes and focus on one of the grounding exercises Violeta had taught him. He spread his fingers across the wall and allowed himself to latch on to the silky surface of the paint, the cool touch of it against his skin, and the faint but present rippled texture which only made itself known when he was in motion. When his fingers stilled, it melted away as though it were nonexistent.

This was real. Present. He exhaled slowly, drew breath with care, and listened to the hospital. The dull fizz from its lights. The clatter of a wheeled trolley somewhere far away. Footsteps. Conversation between clinicians from a staff station between here and the elevator. Muted beeps and rasping from oxygen machines behind the doors of private patient rooms. His own breath.

No glass fell from above. No light flickered beyond his eyelids.

He had folded himself back inside his own body, where he belonged.

Quentin cleared his throat and straightened himself up as he opened his eyes. He checked that his cuffs were laying correctly, that his shirt was in place, his waistcoat flat, and then he turned to face his father.

"You gave me your word," he said, amazed at how calm and collected he managed to sound.

"I am not breaking it," Father replied, meeting Quentin's gaze. "I have done no harm. This is not my doing."

Quentin glanced toward Freddy's door, but nobody emerged. "Then whose is it?"

"Detail the symptoms," Father said.

He deliberated briefly, but Laurence did have a point. They needed information, and any single clue could be vital. Even if it came from the man Quentin detested with every atom of his being.

"There are memories which have been forgotten," Quentin murmured, finally turning back to look at his father while he detailed what little he knew of the situation.

The duke listened, although he showed little sign that he was doing so. He did not nod, or make a sound, or otherwise indicate that he was paying attention, but this was nothing new. He had been this way for as long as Quentin had been alive, and likely longer, so Quentin outlined what he could and made no apology for any gaps in his information.

Father remained quiet after Quentin finished speaking, so Quentin waited for a response.

"You need to break the spell, oath, geas, or other binding which holds Lethe in place," the duke finally said, "or restoring any missing memories will result in their immediate loss again, and you'll waste time chasing your tails in a cycle of recovering and forgetting. It seems as though once that is taken care of, Frederick will be able to re-establish what was lost using his own gifts. Your priority has to be the Lethe problem."

Quentin bobbed his head faintly. "I concur."

"To ensure any spell would outlive the caster, it would by necessity have been placed upon an object or a place, likely with anchors." The duke sniffed derisively, as though he believed that controlling gods was inferior magic. "I'm sure you understand what needs to be done."

Quentin pursed his lips. "Find the anchors, destroy them, release Lethe." He frowned at his father. "But they could be anywhere. Quite literally. I have no way of knowing where to even begin, let alone what they might look like."

Father's lips twitched into a faint, calculating smirk. "You know the answer to that conundrum, boy."

Oh, he knew it all right. The thing Father had wanted for eight years now.

Come home.

Learn magic.

"I told you," Quentin said coldly. "That is not my home. Not so long as you are there."

"You did," the duke agreed. He stretched an arm out to one side, and a book appeared in his hand, as if he'd just picked it off a shelf.

He probably had.

Quentin eyed it warily. He could see the glow from here, ghostly green like precious jade seeping from the edges of the pages. It was not his father's magic, but it was magic nonetheless.

The duke offered it toward him. "Here," he said. "Take it."

"No." The word was out of him before he was aware of it.

"You are twenty-six years old," the duke sighed. "Act your age and accept some responsibilities. If you will not come here to be taught, you must learn from afar instead. There are locator spells in here. One of them should aid you."

Quentin hissed between his teeth, and he couldn't tear his gaze from the book. It didn't *look* evil, but he was well used to the fact that evil rarely advertised itself.

"This is not warlockry, if that is your concern," his father sighed. "It is sorcery."

Quentin managed to spare him a quick glance. "Then why do you own it?"

"I own many books from many schools of thought," Father replied. "Most handed down to us, some obtained within my lifetime. Knowledge is power; it behooves you to learn as much as you can. Take the book, Quentin."

"I said *no*," Quentin snapped.

"Do you wish to protect Frederick or not?"

Quentin's eyes widened, but the look on Father's face was just as placid as it had been throughout the whole conversation.

This was not a threat. This was not Father breaking the vow that he had made, the one Quentin had dragged out of him while his father was on his knees begging Quentin to kill him.

It was a simple question.

An offer of help.

You don't have to read it, he reminded himself. *Simply pass it to Laurence. You will not have to use magic. You are only a messenger.*

Quentin raised his chin and forced himself to reach toward the book, but he hesitated. "You aren't here," he said. "Nor is that."

The duke snorted at him. "The sooner you stop trying to define what can and cannot be, the sooner you can crack on with things that matter."

He felt like a child. He was hit with an echo of the crushing disappointment that his father stared down at him with whenever Quentin had failed to sense anything magical about an item, the years his father had either caught Quentin looking at books or trinkets in his personal collection and then heaved a sigh of displeasure when Quentin's answers were not those his father sought, and his fingers spasmed.

Before he was fully aware of the choice he'd made, he

gripped the book and held it as far away from himself as he could without dropping it.

Father stepped back and glanced toward Freddy's room, then nodded. "Was that so hard?"

Quentin had words on his tongue that were the sort of language only Laurence usually used, but his father sliced a hand through the air between them and vanished, leaving a dark blot on Quentin's retinas that danced in a mockery of his father's presence until it too was gone.

The book remained.

He held his breath, but the book didn't disappear, and his hand didn't melt. Nobody died — or, at least, that he was aware of. Nothing bit him, nothing hurt.

If anyone saw him like this, they'd think him an absolute fool.

Quentin shook his head and bent his arm, drawing the book closer until he was able to lower it by his side, out of his own line of sight. He tried to look casual with it, and if he convinced himself it was nothing more dangerous than the handle of a briefcase, perhaps he could get away with it.

The door to Freddy's room clicked, and then opened, and the nurse stepped out and smiled to him as she passed, and Quentin ducked inside in time to catch Freddy buttoning his shirt. Thankfully the rest of him was decent, complete with trousers and shoes, and he was sitting on the edge of his bed.

Freddy looked to him, then frowned. "You look like you've seen a ghost."

Quentin made a slightly strangled sound, then cleared his throat and tried again. "Are you free to go?"

"I am." Freddy eased himself to his feet, and Mikey scooped up a hospital-branded bag from the end of the bed. "Are you my chaperone?"

"I am," Quentin replied, intentionally echoing Freddy. "Someone has to make sure you get home in one piece."

"Michael is right here," Freddy drawled.

Quentin clicked his tongue. "Very well," he sighed. "Laurence asked me to pick both your brains about what happened."

Freddy chuckled and patted Quentin on the shoulder. "There we go. And after that, you can tell me how you came by one of Father's books and why you look about ready to piss yourself."

Quentin swallowed and led the way out of the room, not really willing to engage any further until they were well away from here. He eyed the corridor, but of course, Father was nowhere to be seen, so he walked briskly toward the elevators and managed to tuck the book under his arm.

It felt like a loaded gun, and the sooner he could divest himself of it the better.

LAURENCE

There was still no response from Angela, no matter how much Laurence texted her. He even tried calling, but it rang and rang, and she didn't have voicemail switched on.

Laurence cursed under his breath.

She had to be in trouble. He'd never known her go this long without answering a message before.

"Do you have any of her blood?" Rufus asked while he absently petted the raven in his lap.

"No. Nor saliva, or hair, or anything like that. Angela's smart, she doesn't just leave that stuff lying around, and even if she did, I bet she's warded up to the eyeballs anyway." Laurence shook his head, but there was no point finding an exit ramp yet. He still didn't know where he was headed, other than away from La Mesa.

"Do you know where she lives?"

Laurence sucked in air through clenched teeth. "I don't know, man. I've been to a house, she gave me the address, but there was no sign at all that she actually lived there. It was like a show home." He nodded to himself. "But it's worth checking out, just in case. And if not, maybe we can find something there that could lead us to her."

Rufus grimaced and looked to the road ahead, but his gaze kept darting to the mirrors. "Yeah," he agreed, without any enthusiasm.

Laurence understood. He really did. Ru wasn't used to being outside his sanctum this long, and he sure didn't like being in a vehicle. He must be feeling pretty naked right now, and while Laurence was tempted to offer to get Ru home and continue his search for Angela alone, the truth was if she wasn't at the first place he looked, he was going to need Rufus' help.

He weighed up his options, then picked one.

"Look," Laurence said softly, "I know this is hard. If you want me to drop you home first, I will."

He hoped desperately that Rufus wouldn't take him up on his offer, that Ru's intelligence had latched on to a problem to solve and that his need to do that would outweigh his discomfort.

Rufus sighed slowly. "No. She gave me the bear. She saved my life. Even if she didn't know what was going to happen, she's directly responsible for me living and breathing today. If she needs our help, we have to give it. I'll stay."

Laurence did absolutely nothing to show his relief. Instead he just bobbed his head. "Thanks," he murmured. "And there's got to be a reason she went to all that trouble. Five different protection charms? She was covering as many bases as she could, right?"

"It's plausible that she knew something would happen, but not exactly what," Rufus agreed.

"Maybe she had a premonition. Or precognition." Laurence glanced over at Windsor this time. The bird was resting his chin on Ru's knee, enjoying being petted. "What do you think, Win?"

Windsor raised his head and ruffled his feathers before he began to chatter away. *Is she gifted?*

"No. I don't think so, anyway."

Why did she forget?

Laurence hummed to himself, then added, for Ru's benefit, "Win's asking why Angela forgot. I figure because if she remembered and nobody else did, she'd wonder why they all forgot. And if they all remembered but she didn't, they'd ask her, and she'd realize her memories were missing. The question is, I guess, why I was able to look back through time and see it and not have my memories erased, but Freddy got affected by looking at Mom's memories." He bit the tip of his tongue lightly. "That has to be an oversight in the spell that binds Lethe, right? The caster didn't plan for anyone seeing those events from the outside, only from memories?"

"Very few magicians are aware that the gifted exist, and even if we are, we tend not to interact." Rufus shrugged. "You know how insular we are. The warlock probably didn't think any other way of uncovering the truth was even possible. And why should he? This has stayed hidden for years, and if you hadn't turned up on my doorstep, it would have stayed that way. That bear was in my *sanctum* and I just forgot all about it, even though there were spells in it. Do you have any idea how hard that is?"

"I mean, you detected me doing magic in the bathroom," Laurence said dryly.

"Exactly. And those spells were…" Rufus sighed.

"Background noise?" Laurence suggested. "I mean, you were a kid, Ru. Most of what you've learned has been after your parents died, right?"

Rufus nodded.

"So by the time you put all your own magic in place, all your wards and stuff, they were already there. Part of the fabric of the house, in a room you never went in."

"Still," Rufus began.

"No." Laurence cut him right off. "You've got to cut yourself a break. Your parents had just died. You were doing what you could to protect yourself. It's not possible to be perfect a hundred percent of the time, and those were peak extenuating circumstances, man. Sometimes it takes a fresh pair of eyes to spot stuff, that's all."

"Poop," Windsor agreed sympathetically.

Rufus grunted irritably, but he didn't argue, so Laurence drove on and let the other witch stew on it a while.

"OH, YEAH, THIS IS *SOMETHING*," Rufus murmured as Laurence pulled up onto the drive.

Laurence put the truck in park and killed the engine, then turned to check what Ru was talking about, but Ru was staring up at the bland white house with its unremarkable walls and its uninteresting front yard like the building was on fire.

Laurence turned his attention to the house, but all he saw was the dim red glow of subtle wards around the windows and door. If this place was lit up like a Christmas tree, Laurence had no way of knowing.

He *really* needed to learn more of Ru's perception spells.

"What kind of something?" Laurence offered his arm to Windsor, who climbed out of Ru's lap and hopped onto his wrist. "A sanctum?"

"Yeah." Rufus nodded. "We're going to have to tread carefully. If she's not expecting us and any of those wards trip, she might just kill first and ask questions later."

Laurence swallowed slowly, but it didn't seem to shift the sudden tightness in his throat.

"C'mon," he croaked. "Let's go."

They got out and approached the front door slowly. Windsor worked his way up to Laurence's shoulder and made soft, soothing sounds to himself, and Rufus peered up at the building as they got closer to the front door.

Laurence stopped on the doorstep and waited.

"You should be able to knock," Rufus said. "There's no booby trap that I can see on the door itself."

"Okay." Laurence took a deep breath and silently reminded himself that having been here once was no guarantee that he was welcome back, and then he rapped so hard on the door that his knuckles stung. "Angela? It's Laurence! Are you home?"

He didn't hear anything.

"I guess not," Rufus muttered.

"Hang on." Laurence banged again, then tilted his right ear to the door, and pressed fingers against his left to block out the rest of the world.

He closed his eyes, stilled his breath, and listened.

There was… *something*. He couldn't put a finger on what it was, but the house didn't sound empty. Was he really capable of hearing one person breathing at the far end of a house, or was his imagination fucking around with him, making him hope she was in there when she wasn't?

I help? Windsor thought.

Laurence stepped back from the door and nodded. "Yeah," he whispered. "Go check out the windows. Don't get too close, okay?"

Yes!

Windsor launched into the air with a beat of his wings so powerful that it scattered Laurence's curls, and he propelled himself skyward in mere seconds.

Laurence closed his eyes again so that he could ride along inside Windsor's head and see what the bird saw. He had to plant his feet firmly, make sure he was centered and balanced, because otherwise the sudden shift from standing to flying would probably make him fall over.

Windsor reached for him and gleefully pulled him the rest of the way, and then there they were: flying, together, gaining height and enjoying the wind against their feathers.

Laurence kept his joy to himself. Now wasn't the time to start squealing, and Windsor was making enough ruckus for the both of them.

Is fun! Windsor agreed.

Yeah. Yeah, it is.

Can do any time!

Laurence chuckled inwardly. *I'll keep that in mind. Thanks, Win. Let's see if we can find Angela.*

Yes!

Windsor turned on a dime and passed window after window, swooping back and forth so that he could eyeball them from as many directions as he could.

It wasn't until he was at the rear of the house that they spotted something.

Closer? Win asked.

Yeah. Be careful, though.

He knew Windsor understood what he meant. The wards could be anything, but one of the things they might be designed to do was kill a familiar, or at least disperse it. Laurence didn't want a feather on Win's body harmed, and especially not for trying to help someone.

I see! Windsor cried, excited by his own ability to assist.

Closer! Laurence urged at almost exactly the same time.

They'd both spotted the shadow in the corner of a room, and Windsor approached the window until he could perch on the Juliet balcony and hold his eye an inch from the glass.

The wards didn't react. Or, if they did, Windsor wasn't vaporized.

Laurence wanted to be relieved. They'd found Angela. At

least, he hoped it was Angela, and not some random woman who had broken into her home. But the relief didn't come, because the body was huddled in a corner of the room, facing the wall and barely breathing.

There wasn't any blood. No sign of injury. But she wasn't moving, and she hadn't come to the door.

Okay. Thanks, Win!

Yes!

Laurence pulled back and opened his eyes. He took a second to adjust to his own body. And then he looked to Ru. "I'm gonna kick the door in," he said. "Will that kill me?"

Rufus frowned. "I don't *think* it will, but—"

"Yeah, that's good enough for me." Laurence stepped up and raised his foot, but Rufus grabbed him and dragged him back so quick Laurence almost fell over. "What?"

"An external door? With sneakers on?" Rufus snorted at him. "I'm going to convince myself that you're smarter than that."

Laurence eyed him, but Ru had a point.

"I *am* smarter than that," he admitted. "C'mon."

He led the way around the edge of the house and into the back yard. It wasn't wholly private, but it was a start.

"Can you, I don't know..." Laurence huffed. "Check nobody's watching us, or something?"

Rufus eyed him. "Nobody's watching us."

All Laurence could do was take his word for it, so he crouched down and rested his hands against the ground. He nestled his fingers between cool strands of grass and felt for the earth beneath it, and then he pushed his energy out, seeking roots, feeling his way toward something more usable.

He'd done this before. He kept staying small, growing houseplants and controlling flowers, but he *could* push harder. He'd force-grown bamboo to full adulthood in seconds, he'd wrested control of Jack's own vines from him, and he'd turned rosebushes into weapons to try and fight Quentin when Freddy had controlled his body in London.

Maybe Quen wasn't the only one holding himself back, and a helicopter trip to the desert with Neil was what they *all* needed.

Laurence touched strong, vital roots, and he poured himself into them.

Spears of nearby aloe plants stabbed themselves toward the nearest window under his command. They stretched and grew far beyond any height they'd achieve naturally, and the more Laurence drove onward, the more enthusiastically they leaped at the glass and then punched right through it.

It shattered and mostly landed on the far side of the wall. He used the aloe to sweep glass fragments out of the window frame, then didn't wait around. Laurence had the aloe withdraw and clambered in as soon as the sharp leaves were out of his way, got covered in aloe sap, then did what he could to wipe it onto the curtains once he was back on his feet inside the house.

So far, so not dead.

Laurence held an arm out for Windsor, then gestured for Rufus to follow, though it took some cajoling to get the witch to actually come inside.

"I assume you saw her in here somewhere?" Rufus grunted as he tried to redistribute sticky aloe sap off of his hands and onto his pants.

"Yeah. Upstairs. At least, I'm pretty sure it's her. Come on."

He led the way, with Windsor on his shoulder and Rufus at his heels, up the stairs. Everything was just as bland as he remembered from the last time he was here. No personal decor, no sign of this being a place someone lived in, except this time there was the eerie sense that everything was deeply wrong.

The room Angela was in wasn't the same one she'd

summoned Mu'ut from, but Laurence wasn't interested in the exciting revelation of entering yet another uninteresting, barely-decorated room.

All his attention was on her.

She was curled into a corner, facing the wall, her arms cramped into the space between her chest and knees. She was breathing softly, and as Laurence crept silently closer, he realized she was sleeping.

He hadn't busted into her home just to wake her from a nap, surely?

No, he reasoned. *She would've heard the door, or been woken by us breaking her wards.*

There were sigils in the room, chalk marks across the floor, but her circle was well and truly broken. Laurence could see that the center had been in the middle of the room, but the way that the chalk was smeared made it obvious that Angela's body had been dragged through it toward where she lay now, streaks of white pointing toward her like accusatory fingers.

Laurence crouched down behind her shoulders and took note of the chalk dust across her arms and legs. There was even some on her face. But there was no blood, no bruising, no sign that any external force had done this to her.

"Angela?" He reached out and hovered a hand above her shoulder, then glanced at Ru to check it was safe. Ru nodded, so Laurence turned his attention back to Angela and lowered his hand to her shoulder. "Hey. Angela? Are you okay?"

She seemed to rouse slowly, like he'd disturbed a nice, deep sleep that she was right in the middle of enjoying. There was a languorous cascade of little shifts and stretches from head to toe, and once those were done, her eyes drifted open.

"Hey. Wakey wakey, rise and shine." Laurence crinkled his nose and thumbed toward the chalk behind himself. "What happened?"

Angela didn't say anything. Her arms flopped in the small

space between her chest and the wall, and then she wriggled until her legs were straighter. She rolled onto her back so vaguely that it seemed purely accidental, and looked up at him with eyes that didn't quite seem to focus.

She broke into an unguarded smile, which was as uncanny on her face as it was beautiful.

The sense of wrongness twisted itself tighter in Laurence's gut.

"Hey." He moved his hand away and shifted it to rest on her upper arm instead. "Are you okay? What happened? What did you do?"

She *seemed* to be listening to him. Her features were alight with happiness that bordered on wonder, and her smile widened at the sound of his voice, then softened once his questions ended.

What she didn't do was answer. She didn't even nod, or give any other nonverbal clue that she'd understood a single word.

Laurence felt Rufus looming at his back, saw the shadow reach over them both, and Angela's smile turn toward the newcomer. She flailed hands toward him, and then Windsor seemed to capture her attention instead, and she tried to reach for the bird only to accidentally wave a hand against Laurence's face.

"I figure she's not normally like this, right?" Rufus grunted.

Windsor hopped to the floor, then across to where Angela could reach him, and she burbled with delight when her fingers met feathers.

"No," Laurence said thickly. "She's not."

Everything about Angela's conduct was recognizable, but not as Angela.

Laurence gasped in horror as it fell into place. The snuggling into a corner, the unfocused gaze and happy smiling, and the uncoordinated limbs, he'd seen *all* this before, but never in an adult. Not even in a child.

This was *newborn* behavior.

"Oh, Goddess," he groaned. "I think I know what's wrong."

Rufus crouched and rested his elbows on his knees. "Hit me with it."

Laurence swallowed tightly. He felt sick to his stomach, and he wasn't sure he wanted to say the words out loud, but the more he fought it the more convinced he became that he was right.

"She drank from the river," he breathed. "And I don't think it was a little. You said people have to forget their whole lives to get reborn, right?"

Rufus nodded, and then he, too, started to look sick. "Goddess," he choked. "You're right."

Laurence gave a grim nod as he watched Angela fumble at playing with Windsor. "She's been completely erased," he whispered. "Every last memory. She doesn't even remember how to walk or talk." He licked his lips and sat back on his ass on the hard floor. "She's a baby. She's forgotten *everything*."

It looked like Lethe was done playing around.

30

QUENTIN

The taxi was taking them to Myriam's farm rather than Frederick's hotel. Frederick was far more interested in recovering his rental car from where he'd left it than he was in spending any more time resting, it seemed, and Quentin couldn't blame him, but it did mean that their conversation was rather stymied until they could be free of their unwitting eavesdropper. They did what they could to make small-talk, but the weight which bore down on them all was forced to wait until the taxi dropped them off.

Frederick even watched the cab leave before he uttered a word.

"All right," he mused. "How did Father find you?"

"I don't know," Quentin admitted. "I should be warded against that sort of thing." He pulled out his wallet and unfastened the otherwise-unused coin purse, but the pentacle Laurence had given him was still inside. "Perhaps my blood allows him to overpower it."

"Probably," Freddy agreed. He tossed car keys to Michael, who caught them deftly and moved to unlock the waiting vehicle. "He was really *very* keen to get his hands on it, after all."

"Mmm." Quentin preferred not to think about everything they'd gone through just because the duke wanted Freddy to obtain some of Quentin's blood for him, and he supposed that neither Freddy nor Michael were terribly keen to linger on it either. "What do you recall of the whole Lethe situation?"

"Nothing," Freddy muttered, his features darkening with displeasure. "Do you have any idea..." He tailed off, then puffed out his cheeks and rocked on his heels. "My apologies. What a crass question. Of *course* you know what it's like."

Quentin understood. Freddy wasn't at all used to forgetting, but Quentin's whole life was defined by it. That didn't make it any less unsettling.

Freddy headed around the car and eased into the passenger seat, but Quentin paused, then called out for Ellie.

The border collie came charging from afar. He heard her rustling through undergrowth long before she bounded out onto the driveway, and he smiled gently to her, then opened the back door of the car.

"Icky, no," Freddy opined.

"Yes," Quentin replied smoothly. He nodded for Ellie to get into the car, then eased in after her and buckled himself in. He stuffed the book into the back of Freddy's seat, and drew Ellie into his lap so that he could be her seatbelt. "Who knows when she was last fed, or when Myriam will be able to get back to her. Stop off at the house, we can let her out there."

Freddy and Michael exchanged a glance that undoubtedly bore an entire conversation which Quentin was not privy to, and then Michael started the car and they left the farm behind.

"I shall have to have the car valeted, or the rental company will fine me for having a dog in it," Freddy groused.

"And you care about a fine?" Quentin raised his eyebrows toward Freddy's reflection in the rearview mirror.

"It's the principle of the thing," Freddy insisted. "Anyway. Back to the matter at hand. I remember nothing, but Michael retains some information, so it would appear that Lethe is very specific about what must be forgotten."

Quentin nodded a little and shifted his gaze to Michael's reflection instead.

Green eyes flicked to the mirror, then back to the road ahead. "Fields, flowers, the river, and a cave. I followed the river all the way to the cave, but that's it. I couldn't see into the cave, it was too dark. I know I must've gone inside, but that's when I woke up back in the hospital again. I've got nothing more than that."

"I see," Quentin mused.

Freddy pursed his lips. "If there is a cave, then that must be the Cave of Hypnos. The River Lethe flows from it and out into Hades. No light or sound enters it." He grimaced, and added, "It's possible that Hypnos was inside, since he does allegedly live there."

Michael glanced to Freddy. "How do you know all this?"

"Benefits of a classical education," Freddy drawled. "I might have thought that being forced to learn Ancient Greek just to read the Iliad would be worthless in my adult life, but who knew how wrong I was?"

Michael snorted. "You speak Ancient Greek?"

"Freddy speaks far more languages than I do," Quentin murmured. "He has a gift for it." He paused, then blinked. "Literally."

"My secret is out." Freddy sighed dramatically.

Michael looked to Quentin in the mirror. "How many languages do *you* speak?"

Quentin shrugged. "Not many. Latin is my strongest, but I

can get by in French or Italian, and I'm picking up a little American Sign Language. My Ancient Greek is very rusty."

"Icky only cares about languages which can get him to and from fashion week venues," Freddy chuckled. "Paris, Milan, New York, London. Isn't that right, Icky?" He didn't wait for an answer, and instead twisted in his seat so that he could reach back and pluck the spell book out of the pocket Quentin had tucked it into. "Right. What's going on here? Why did he give it to you? That is, I'm assuming you didn't fly home and back while I was conked out, of course. You hadn't the time."

Quentin held Ellie a little tighter in his arms as the book swam past his nose, but she didn't object. All she did was wag her tail and lick his ear. "Father projected himself into the hospital somehow," he stated, trying not to let himself get agitated by the memory. "Well enough that a doctor was able to interact with him. Until then I had supposed him to be an hallucination."

Freddy turned again and scrutinized Quentin's face, frowning softly. "Do you hallucinate often?"

Quentin tipped his head aside as part of a gentle shrug.

"Is it always him, when you do?"

"Mmm." This wasn't really something Quentin discussed with anyone other than Violeta, and even then, sparingly. To have Freddy lay it out — in front of Michael, no less — was quite uncomfortable.

"What triggers it?" At Quentin's scowl, Freddy added, "Come along, Icky, you're smart enough to have already poked at this. I know you are."

"Stress," Quentin said irritably. "Frustration. That sort of thing."

"And this is new," Freddy pressed. "When did it start?"

Quentin glared so hard he was reasonably sure he was showing teeth.

"Mmm." Freddy nodded. "Marlowe, yes?"

"Fred."

"My apologies," Freddy said softly. "I'm simply seeking context. So you had reason to believe that it wasn't really Father, until he proved that it was. And he gave you this." Freddy looked to the book in his hands and started to flip through it. "I assume it glows?"

"Yes." Quentin knew he was being terse, but felt entirely justified after being prodded at about his mental health so rudely.

"How inconvenient. Especially as I thought we were protected from him." Freddy hesitated, then grit his teeth. "He has Michael's blood, too," he sighed.

Quentin blinked slowly while his brain caught up.

The duke had beaten Michael half to death. Of *course* he had collected some of the redhead's blood while he'd been at it.

"Why has he gone to all the trouble of giving it to you?" Freddy held the book up briefly.

"He believes that Lethe is being controlled by a spell which is anchored to an object, and that one of the spells in that book—" Quentin crinkled his nose as he eyed it in Freddy's hands "—can trace the spell to the object."

Freddy nodded as he listened. "And then all we do is destroy the sigils and free Lethe," he concluded. "Why does Father care?"

"I don't know." Quentin huffed. "He has taken to furnishing me with an allowance, too. An olive branch, I suppose."

"Sounds like a manipulative one at best," Michael chimed in.

Quentin nodded slightly. "I concur. As much as I want nothing to do with him, if there truly *is* something useful in there, it would be remiss of me not to pass it on to Laurence."

Freddy snapped the book closed and raised his chin.

"Father isn't wrong. There are two or three spells in here which fit the remit, and none of them require a blood sacrifice or… Whatever other unsavory practices he might engage in."

Quentin blinked at him, startled that Freddy had extracted the relevant information so swiftly, and by skimming pages at that. Was this a facet of his gifts, or was he simply as brilliant as he assured everyone that he was?

"Penny?" Freddy prompted.

"You read the whole thing?"

Freddy shrugged. "I have an eidetic memory. I can recite an entire book after skim-reading it, and I can certainly dedicate processing time to analyzing what I've seen while I continue a conversation in a car." He pursed his lips, and added, "I can access my own memories just as easily as anyone else's, which is why this is all so…" He sighed softly and reached over to stuff the book back where he'd got it from. "Disturbing," he finished.

Quentin soothed himself by fussing Ellie's flank, running fingers through her soft fur and scratching under her chin. "So they are safe to cast?"

"So far as I can tell, yes."

Quentin tried not to grind his teeth, and continued to focus on Ellie in his arms. He had no desire to start viewing his father as helpful in any way, but before he could think of any reasonable response, his phone buzzed.

He extracted it without dislodging Ellie and unlocked it to find a message from Laurence.

If you're still with Freddy, can you bring him with you?

There was an address listed, and then a little emoji of two hands clasped together, followed by one with big, puppy dog eyes that allowed Quentin to picture Laurence's expression with remarkable accuracy.

He typed out his response and sent it.

I can ask. What do you need him for?

The reply was as quick as it was horrific.

I think Angela's lost ALL her memories. Could use help to check.

Quentin swallowed tightly and slipped his phone away, then gazed at Freddy and tried to work out how best to ask yet another favor of him — especially one that was potentially as awful as anyone asking Quentin to use magic.

Freddy met his gaze and his frown slowly returned. "Trouble?"

"A lot, yes."

"Need me to come along?"

"If you wouldn't mind?"

A muscle in Freddy's jaw twitched briefly, and then he nodded. "All right."

"Thank you."

Freddy eyed him, then sat back in his seat and watched the road, and Quentin returned to fussing Ellie, though which one of them was soothed by the touch was no longer clear.

He had asked so much of Freddy of late, and sooner or later Freddy would begin to say no, or ask for something in return.

His father was right. Quentin was so incredibly selfish, and everyone he had surrounded himself with simply enabled his behavior to continue.

How many more people would he harm in pursuit of his own comfort?

Quentin closed his eyes and counted down from ten, grounding himself with the weight of Ellie in his lap, and tried not to dig too deep into whether or not he was remotely as good a person as he'd believed himself to be.

31

LAURENCE

LAURENCE HAD TRIED A COUPLE OF TIMES TO HELP ANGELA TO her feet, but she didn't seem to even understand what he was attempting and — worse — coming away from the wall distressed her too much. In the end he'd let her go back to nuzzling into a corner while she petted Windsor, and instead he assessed what remained of the sigils of her spell on the floor.

With the translation spell attached to his phone, the sigils still didn't read like a language, but they *did* make a kind of sense that they wouldn't have before. Laurence wasn't entirely sure whether it was translation, experience, or a combination of the two, but as he walked around the chalk marks he began to slowly piece together what he could while snapping pictures in case he needed them later.

"This was a summoning, right?" he asked of Rufus.

Rufus nodded as he, too, paced the room to take it all in. "I can't work out who, though. That must've been over here." He gestured to the damage done where Angela had presumably crawled through her own markings.

It could be one of any number of beings, Laurence figured.

If Angela was willing to summon Mu'ut to track Quentin, she had every pantheon in the world to draw on to get whatever she'd been trying to find. It was probably a reasonable guess that she'd managed to recover some memories or face Lethe directly, though. What else would have left her like a newborn?

Laurence sighed and checked his phone, but it had only been a few minutes since he'd texted Quentin. He couldn't expect them to arrive immediately, so instead he turned his attention to the windows, and stepped over to search for sigils there.

Rufus grunted. "We shouldn't touch them. They've let us inside the building, even though we're both carrying live spells around with us. Whatever she's warding against, it's not us."

Laurence grimaced, but nodded to himself.

She was probably far more concerned with keeping warlocks out.

"Okay," he breathed, and turned his attention back to the chalk on the floor. "We'll have to clean all this up before Quen arrives."

Rufus pulled a face, but he didn't say anything. Instead, he made himself useful, and fetched a couple of dampened towels from a bathroom.

Together, they got down on their knees and wiped up the mess.

LAURENCE HEARD the car pull up, and left Ru to keep an eye on Angela so he could go open the front door.

Quentin was already on the doorstep, about to knock, so instead he lowered his hand and gave a quick, tense smile. "We came as quickly as we could."

Laurence nodded and took in the state of Quentin, covered as he was with black and white dog hairs. It was easy to detect the faint whiff of dog on him, too. No wonder it took a while for him to arrive.

He reached out to grip Quentin's hand before it was out of reach. "Thanks, baby."

Quentin's fingers squeezed his briefly, and then he stepped back to allow Frederick room to pass.

Laurence turned his attention to Freddy — who was considerably less dog-marked — after briefly acknowledging Mikey with another nod. "Thanks for coming, man. I know you've got better things to do."

Frederick squared his already impressive shoulders and lifted his head. "It is worth confirming your deduction, Laurence."

Laurence backed inside to give everyone room to enter, but it didn't escape his notice that both the twins were doing pretty badly at disguising their discomfort. Quentin was hanging back and eyeing the doorframe, and Freddy seemed to be steeling himself before he followed Laurence. Only Mikey was at all at ease, and even he was pretty subdued.

Today was turning out unsettling all round, it looked like, but it wasn't over yet.

Laurence cast a reassuring smile toward Quentin, then led Freddy up the stairs. "She's through here."

Freddy didn't enter the bedroom. Instead, he lingered by the doorway, hanging back and regarding Angela from afar. By the time Mikey joined him by his side, Freddy's expression had soured even more, and a ghost of something awful crossed his gaze.

Fear.

Laurence blinked as he worked out what it was.

Freddy was afraid.

"You were correct," Freddy said thickly. "She's a blank

slate. There's nothing there." He swallowed. "I mean, there are emotions, but no memory of anything before…" He shifted his gaze to the floor at Laurence's feet. "You've cleaned up?"

Laurence wetted his lips. They'd dried up as fast as his throat had, and he couldn't shake the realization that all the people he knew who usually exhibited perfect composure had lost control over it at the same time. "Yeah," he croaked. "It was just a summoning circle."

"Summoning what?" Mikey breathed. "What did this to her?"

"We don't know who or what she summoned," Laurence replied. "But we're pretty sure Lethe did this."

"It's the only thing that makes sense," Ru agreed.

Freddy glanced toward Rufus only briefly before he turned his attention on Laurence. "I'll cut to the chase. Our father somehow manifested in the hospital before I was discharged. He gave Icky a book of spells and maintains that one of them should help you track down the sigils holding Lethe to whatever the caster wanted and forcing her to do all of this." He waved idly toward Angela as his mask of control began to reassert itself. "I can't see anything malicious in the spells themselves, but Icky is obviously rattled by the whole affair. We have the book in the car, so I suppose that all which remains to be done is to track down this spell and destroy it, after which we can set about recovering everyone's memories for good."

"Your father," Rufus cut in, his head held high and the most disdainful sneer Laurence had ever seen plastered across his features. "You want us to use a spell from a warlock?"

"Dear boy, I don't care if you use it or not," Freddy said blithely, turning on his heel and heading for the stairs. "But if you don't, you won't find whatever it is you've been butting up against all this for, will you?"

Before Laurence could leave the room, Freddy was

replaced by Quentin in the doorway, his skin pale and eyes wide as he took in the scene. His shoulders were scrunched a little closer to his ears than normal, and the dark stain of a night without shaving was painted across his jaw.

But he *had* made it into the house. Upstairs, even.

His gaze settled on Angela, and he stepped into the room as his unease bled away, replaced by concern. "How long has she been like this?"

"Can't have been more than a day," Laurence reasoned. He didn't say *why* he'd figured that out, but Angela showed no evidence of having soiled herself. Even if she'd made sure not to eat before running the risk of encountering Lethe, surely she'd need the bathroom sooner or later, but there was no mess, and no odor. It was probably far less than a day, but Laurence didn't want to explain his thinking while Quentin was already struggling to hold himself together surrounded by unknown magic.

Quentin crouched slowly behind Angela's back and reached out to place a hand lightly against her shoulder. "Hello? Are you all right there?"

"She's lost her memory," Rufus griped. "Of course she's not okay."

Quentin ignored Rufus entirely, and smiled warmly to Angela when she swiveled to look in his direction. "Hello! What's that you have there? Is that Windsor? He's a very pretty bird, isn't he? Do you see how the light makes his feathers shine in different colors?"

Angela seemed utterly enraptured by Quentin's smile and his words, and she broke into incoherent but happy-sounded burbles in response.

Laurence tipped his head aside slowly as he watched.

Did Quentin know how to deal with babies?

"You can't stay here on the floor forever, can you?"

Quentin said, sounding reasonable. "What shall we do, hmm? Would you like something to eat?"

"She doesn't understand you," Rufus said.

"Shh." Laurence waved a hand at Ru to try and shut him down before he could upset Angela. "It doesn't matter. It's just sound." Then, to Quentin, he murmured, "She doesn't seem to want to come away from the wall."

"Of course not," Quentin replied, still smiling to Angela. "It's a very big world, and it's all a little too much, isn't it?"

Footsteps preceded Freddy's return. "She'll need swaddling if you want to move her," he said, like that was a perfectly normal statement to make about an adult human being. "And you *should* move her. You can't leave her in a room at the top of stairs like this."

"It's all right," Quentin murmured. "We can take her to the house and look after her until the spell is destroyed."

"Mr. Flynn," Freddy prompted.

"Distract him," Quentin replied.

Laurence blinked and finally turned to face Freddy, startled by how readily the twins seemed to know what a newborn's needs might be, but his attention snapped to the book in Freddy's hand. It had an ethereal jade green glow escaping from the pages, and it was modern enough to be bound in green cloth that was worn with age.

Freddy offered the book. He still seemed reluctant to step past the doorway, so Laurence crossed the room and took it before Rufus had a chance to intercept.

"It came from a *warlock*, Laurence!" Rufus seethed, hands balling into fists at his sides.

"Father said that it was sorcery," Quentin murmured, the lightness in his tone dimming to a faint sliver. "Not warlockry." He turned away again and spoke to Angela. "Are you all right if I lift you? Would that be okay? Shall we try?"

He eased his arms gently under Angela and lifted her off

the ground, rolling her to face his chest in the process. It looked easy, but Laurence knew Quentin had to use his telekinesis to lift a whole person, especially a dead weight. He also knew how comforting it was to have the invisible hold coil around him.

Swaddling.

Angela griped a little, but Windsor flapped up and landed on her knees to distract her with his oil-slick feathers, and she settled in with a smile, cooing to the bird.

"There," Quentin said softly. Only then, when she couldn't see his face, did he allow the strain to creep back into the set of his lips, the furrow of his brow. "Can you fix this?" He looked to Laurence as he asked.

"He can fix it," Freddy cut in, with more confidence than Laurence felt. "Come on. Let's go bamboozle your butler."

Laurence gave Quentin what he really hoped was a reassuring nod, then stepped aside so that he could leave the room with Angela in his arms.

I go? Windsor asked.

Yeah. Stay with them, make sure they get home okay, Laurence answered. *If anything happens, call me.*

Yes!

"I'll stay here," Mikey said as the twins headed downstairs. "Keep comms lines open."

Mikey might be the one saying it, but the plan was undoubtedly Freddy's, and Laurence didn't care to argue. What mattered was finding the spell and wrecking the sigils so they could dig up whatever memories everyone had lost, and hopefully that would let them track down the truth about Rufus' parents.

"Sure," Laurence said. He flicked the book open and started to skim-read it, and it was a weird experience knowing how to both spot that there were at least three languages in here *and* understand each one as natively as he did English.

Ru came over to hover at his shoulder, a scowling but silent cloud of objection. Mikey lounged against the doorframe with his hands in his pockets, content to wait for the witches to figure everything out.

There really wasn't anything in the book that called for mutilating children or... any of the other shit Laurence knew the duke to be far too capable of. Sure, the spells lacked that certain cooperative element which was a core of witchcraft, but it also didn't demand the universe bend to its will *or else*. Instead this was more like reading a science textbook, stuffed with formulae and reasoning, observations and data. He almost missed the actual spells at first, because they were just as boring as the rest of the text.

"Ew," he finally muttered. "Sorcery is pretty fucking soulless, huh?"

"Yeah," Rufus agreed. "But the Brits are right, at least. It *is* just sorcery. Nothing worse."

Laurence couldn't keep the grin from his face if he tried, and he didn't try.

"Great. Then let's pick a spell, get whatever ingredients it asks for, then go bust up some sigils."

The hunt was on.

3 2

LAURENCE

"THIS IS ALL NONSENSE, RIGHT?" LAURENCE READ AND RE-READ all the rationale behind why the first spell he'd decided to try should work, and it went right over his head. "'For the success of obtaining a thing denied or hidden, make an image under the ascendant of him who petitions for the thing...'" He paused for breath, then decided not to read the rest of the paragraph out loud anyway. "How is this magic?"

Rufus snorted. "Precisely what a sorcerer would say if they read any of our texts. We should just go to my place and get a better spell."

"Going to yours is like an hour away, and then however long it takes to dig up the right spell from your library," Laurence countered. "Dude, you're amazing, but you have *got* to catalog that shit. It takes us forever whenever we want to find anything." He held up the book. "We're here now, and this is what we've got, and the longer we take, the longer Angela has no way back. I'm not running the risk that this becomes permanent."

"If it isn't already," Rufus said.

"Not going to make that assumption then wait around for

it to become reality," Laurence said. "Okay. What does this recipe call for… Better not be eye of fucking newt."

He ran his finger down the page, but it just kept on listing where exactly images should be placed and how they would relate to one another.

"Blah blah blah," he breathed. "Okay, so basically this is like making a dowsing rod, but on paper, and with some linen and bit of silk to wrap it up. I can't believe we're doing this."

"Linen, silk," Rufus echoed. "I'll see if there's any here."

"I'll find some paper."

They split up. Laurence already knew where Angela kept a bunch of her ingredients, so he passed Mikey, crossed the hallway to the room she'd summoned Mu'ut from, and began searching through drawers.

By the time Laurence unearthed loose sheets of paper, Rufus had wandered in holding a pair of pants and a blouse, and Mikey followed soon after with a pair of scissors. When Laurence blinked at them, Mikey shrugged.

"The spell doesn't call for pants, right?" Mikey waggled the scissors. "Wing of bat, toe of frog, pants of linen…"

Laurence considered it, and had to admit Mikey had a point. "Fair," he said. "Okay. What's next…" He put the paper and the book on top of the chest of drawers. "What *is* an ascendant?"

"Astrology," Rufus said, piling the clothes up next to the book. "We're going to do a lot of math."

"Great," Mikey said as he tossed the scissors onto the clothes. He whipped out his phone and grinned. "That's where I come in."

Rufus eyed Mikey. "You're a mathematician?"

"Close enough." He pulled a pen out of a pocket in his pants and clicked the end. "What are we working out?"

Ru puffed out his cheeks. "Okay. We'll need your exact date and time of birth," he said, pointing to Laurence. "Then we can work out what your ascendant is, and go from there. We're going to have to draw circles, too." He tapped at the diagrams in the book.

Mikey leaned over to peek, then backed toward the door. "I'll see what I can find."

"First of December," Laurence said once Mikey was thundering down the stairs. "Sagittarius. That's all I know. I don't really do the whole Zodiac thing. I'll ask Mom for the time."

He grabbed his phone and decided to call his mom rather than text her, in the hope that it would save some time.

Please, he offered in silent prayer while he waited for her to pick up, *remember this stuff.*

He died a little on the inside at the thought of driving all the way back to the farm just to find his own birth certificate, so when Myriam answered, he didn't hang around.

"Hey, Mom! Weird question: do you know exactly what time of day I was born?"

MIKEY FOUND an assortment of round things from the kitchen they could use as templates for drawing circles. He and Rufus worked out where exactly words and sigils needed to be placed inside those circles, and Laurence cut linen, silk, and paper to the right sizes, then found needle and thread in the drawers to hold everything together with.

Finally they were ready.

Laurence had two circles of paper, the same size as each other, which they'd used a mug as the template for, with wine glasses as templates for the inner circles. Rufus had sketched out the final sigils on sheets of paper, so all that remained was to line circles over sketches and trace them.

There was no verbal component to this spell. The book's

author evidently felt that talking over everything was hardly scientific, and they'd managed to get the universe to agree with them at some point.

"Okay," Laurence breathed, mostly to himself. "Let's do this."

He lined up his first circle and leaned closer so that he could make out the ghost of Rufus' sketch below, and then he worked with a steady hand to trace the markings.

Slowly but surely, the universe began to hold its breath.

It was weird, using magic like this, and Laurence wasn't anywhere near as proficient a witch as Rufus was. In a way it was comforting to have it confirmed that his own preferred style of magic was the right one for him, because *this* felt unnatural.

He finished the first circle and lined up the second, and the universe slowed further, as though it was reaching full capacity.

With a few stitches, he attached both pieces of paper to the strip of linen he had cut, and then closed them together — face to face — like a book.

The universe had almost ground to a halt.

Laurence's final step was to wrap the paper talisman in silk and stitch the edges of the material together to make a pouch, sealing the talisman inside.

He knotted the thread and snipped it free, and the faintest wisp of green curled from his hands and swam around the silk until it sank through the threads and disappeared.

The universe exhaled. The world jerked back into motion.

Laurence weighed the pouch in his hand, then grinned slowly. "Let's go find a spell," he said.

"Let's go find some maps," Rufus added. At Laurence's raised eyebrow, he clarified, "If we follow it like a dowsing rod and the spell is miles away, we'd be wasting time."

Laurence grimaced. He remembered all too well what it

was like trying to follow Quentin's scent when it turned out Quentin was all the way over in Arizona. "You think it'll work with maps?"

"I hope so," Ru said, "or we're going to be driving around for Goddess knows how long."

Laurence grabbed his keys and headed for the stairs. "Great. Let's go."

THEY MADE it to the nearest chain bookstore in record time. Laurence figured they'd draw less attention at B&N than they might in any of San Diego's independent booksellers, and as he ushered everyone in through the wide front doors, he went on a charm offensive to deflect staff and assure them he'd call right away if he needed any help.

They found the travel section, tucked away beyond all the rows of fiction and autobiographies — not that Laurence was sure they weren't really the same thing — near the back of the store, and Mikey went and stood too close to the only other customer in the aisle until she put down the book she was looking at and left.

The coast was clear.

Rufus grabbed the biggest atlas he could find off the shelves, opened it to a double-page spread of the whole world, and held the pages by the corners.

It made sense to start at the absolute biggest level they could, even though Laurence really hoped the spell's anchors weren't in South Africa. He took another look around to make sure they didn't have onlookers, then licked his lips and debated how to do this.

If he looked as he threw the silk pouch, did he run the risk of altering the outcome, or would the magic override any subconscious control he tried to exert over its path?

It was, he figured, better to be sure first time, so he closed his eyes and tossed the pouch toward the book, only opening them again once he heard the soft pat of its landing.

The pouch had landed over half of California.

Mikey blinked. "Are you sure about this?"

"Process of elimination," Rufus said. He set the pouch aside, returned the atlas to a shelf, then pulled down a much more local guidebook.

They repeated the process, but this time when Laurence opened his eyes, he'd missed.

"Again," Rufus said.

Laurence threw it again.

It landed on the exact same spot on the floor.

"What does that mean?" Mikey leaned closer.

"Does the talisman only work once?" Laurence groaned at the thought of having to make more of them, but at least they'd done all the math already. All he'd have to do was trace a few more pieces of paper.

Rufus shook his head. "It's landing in the same place."

Laurence gazed down at the map, and the location of the pouch, and he let out a grunt. "Shit. It's in the sea, isn't it?"

Ru put the book back, and together they scoured more pages in more books to find a map which included more of the sea, but short of zooming back out to atlas size, they weren't having a whole lot of luck.

"This is a waste of time," Rufus sighed.

An idea was scratching at the back of Laurence's mind. His hunter instincts weren't giving up so easily, so he closed his eyes and slowed his breath to let the thought come to him.

If the spell is in the sea, then that's where we need to go.

He grinned as he opened his eyes and the solution came to him, in time to find both Rufus and Mikey looking at him in bewilderment.

"Mikey, have you got a spending limit?"

"Uh…" Mikey shook his head. "Not really. Why?"

Laurence rubbed his hands together with glee. "We're going to rent a boat."

He took their stunned silence as confirmation of the brilliance of his plan.

33

LAURENCE

"Do you even know how to drive a boat?" Rufus looked skeptical.

"Pilot," Mikey said. "And give me a few minutes."

Ru gave Laurence a hefty side-eye, but Laurence held up his hands.

"Do you know how to scuba dive?" Ru asked, looking at Laurence this time.

"Sure!" said Laurence, with far more confidence than he felt. "Ethan and I go diving, like, all the time. Some of the time. Twice. But it was great!"

They'd already picked up the scuba gear, which took a half hour for them to check everything fit Laurence properly and fill the tank with air, and then it had been a slog to Google up a boat rental place that would actually rent them a boat without any staff. Laurence had to phone ahead to make a same-day reservation, and then drive out to Coronado Island for them to go get their yacht, because anything smaller wouldn't be allowed to leave the bay.

He didn't wig out at the price since that was coming off Mikey's card, but at close to a grand for three hours bareboat this was obviously a toy for the rich, not for people like Laurence.

He hefted his scuba gear up onto the back of the little yacht while Mikey headed into the pilot's seat.

"He doesn't know how to pilot it," Rufus insisted, joining Laurence on the rear deck which was just about big enough to seat four people who were pretty fond of each other.

"Freddy will pick someone's brains," Laurence sighed. "Then he'll dump that knowledge into Mikey. It's weird, but it seems to work."

The engine fired up, and the yacht purred like a tiger.

"I guess that means we're a go," Laurence added.

"Thanks, I hate it." Rufus ducked into the cabin and slumped down in a seat.

Laurence moved along the railing to cast off their mooring rope, and then he too headed inside, grabbing the back of Mikey's chair to hold himself stable as the yacht slowly chugged away from the dock.

The cabin was much quieter than he'd imagined it could be, even when Mikey picked up the speed as they got out into the bay. Laurence worried that they'd spend the whole trip yelling over the engines to be heard, but they were barely louder than a car's.

"Which way?" Mikey asked.

Laurence fished the talisman out of his pants and held it by the little bit of thread poking out from the knot he'd tied in it, then he let it sway in his fingers and under the motion of the boat until he was sure it was definitely leaning the same way after every bump or jolt. He pointed forward, past Mikey's shoulder. "That way."

Mikey didn't argue. He aimed the yacht at the open sea and steered the boat toward it.

LAURENCE ALTERNATED between getting changed into his rented wetsuit and holding the talisman up to confirm that Mikey was still on the right bearing, and by the time he had the oxygen tank firmly strapped on, they were well out into open sea. The screen above Mikey's wheel displayed fewer other boats, and the water was much choppier, though still not too bad.

"Can't we go any faster?" Rufus asked from his seat by a small table behind Laurence.

Mikey shook his head. "No. Over about thirty knots the fuel consumption shoots way up high, and since we don't know how far we need to go, I want to conserve it as much as we can." He glanced back over his shoulder up at Laurence, and added, "We better find this soon."

Laurence frowned. "We've only been going an hour; we can't be out already."

"It's not that." Mikey turned back to his screen and gestured at a dotted line across it. "That's the border. Any further south than that and we're in Mexico."

Laurence eyed the screen while he turned the problem over in his mind. Obviously they weren't carrying passports, and the boat rental place had reminded them not to go into restricted waters or cross into Mexico, but he hadn't really thought either would be a real problem. They were creeping closer to the line, though, and crossing it would get them snarled up in red tape — likely overnight — if they got hauled ashore by the Mexican navy.

The only solution would be to turn around, go all the way back to Coronado, then drive over the border and rent a boat in Mexico, and it was getting too late in the day for that to work out.

Both turning around and plowing on led to an overnight delay, but Laurence wasn't a confident enough diver to go to the sea bed after dark, and that was what cinched it.

He sighed softly and shared his decision.

"Okay. If we reach the border, we turn back."

"You're the boss," Mikey said.

———

THERE WASN'T a whole lot of other marine traffic to avoid. The occasional tourist ship, out hoping to see whales and other sea life, but not much more than that. The navy ships were further out to the west, and most small fishing boats were closer to the shore.

Now and then a dolphin or porpoise pod entertained itself by swimming alongside their yacht, but they would soon grow bored and disappear. Laurence wasn't too sure of the differences between dolphins and porpoises, or even whether they were just the same animal under different names. That was Quentin's area of expertise, not his.

He felt a soft pang. Quentin would adore seeing the chattery sea mammals having fun racing a yacht, but instead he was at home, and Laurence was here without him. He had to remind himself that it was for the best, that Quentin was not suited to bumping into the amount of magic involved in all of this, but Laurence still missed being at his side.

Soon, he told himself. *Soon this'll be over and everything will get back to normal.*

Laurence snorted to himself. 'Normal' was a concept he was steadily losing touch with, no matter how much he thought he missed it.

The talisman lurched to the left.

"Stop!" Laurence yelled. He grabbed Mikey's shoulder as the talisman swung back to point behind them.

Mikey grabbed the throttle and turned the wheel, and Laurence hung onto the back of his chair to stay upright.

Rufus cursed loudly, but managed to grip onto the table and stay in his seat.

Mikey slowed the yacht to a crawl and they crept around in a decreasing circle, trying to pin down the talisman's directions. They were so close to the line of the Mexican border that everyone's phones were beeping either roaming alerts or welcome messages to Mexican cellphone networks, and Laurence bit his lip praying they didn't attract the attention of anyone who might try to herd them north.

"Here," Laurence said as they finally coasted over a spot where the talisman hung directly down.

Mikey flipped something, and the anchor at the bow of the yacht dropped out of sight. He killed the engines, and Laurence heard the soft, steady ratcheting of the anchor chain.

Then everything stopped, and the only sound was the water lapping against their hull.

Laurence watched the talisman just to be absolutely sure, but it only swayed slightly as the boat bobbed on the ocean, doing its best to hang straight down despite the motion. He put it down on Rufus' little table, tucked a last strand of hair back under his hood, and picked up his goggles.

"Okay," Mickey said as he got out of his chair and walked through the cabin. He squeezed past Laurence to the back door and opened it. "Anchor has stopped at just under fifty-four feet, but don't hang around, okay? Freddy says your no-decompression limit is going to be fifty minutes. Any longer than that and you'll have to stop every five minutes on the way back up to off-gas all the nitrogen you've built up in your body."

Laurence just stared at him. "Fifty minutes limit or I have to fart my way to freedom, got it."

Mikey rolled his eyes and headed out onto the rear deck, then checked over Laurence's tank and waited for Laurence to pop the mouthpiece in before he checked it again. "Don't forget the talisman."

"It's no use," Rufus explained, while Laurence flapped his way down the steps to the small boarding platform next to the twin engines. "It's made out of paper. It'll get soaked, the ink will run, it'll stop working. Not worth cluttering his hands with."

Laurence nodded in agreement, gave his feet one last waggle to triple-check that the diving fins weren't going to fall off for no reason, then waved. He stepped off the platform and landed heavily in the water, but the wetsuit protected him from the cold, and he bobbed back up to the surface to test his breathing apparatus one last time.

He gave Mikey and Rufus the OK sign, and started his dive.

His plan was to follow the anchor chain down so that he didn't go off-course, so he swam around to the front of the yacht until the chain was in sight, then tilted downwards.

Laurence hadn't a whole lot of scuba experience, and it had been a few years since he and Ethan last went diving together. Bits and pieces were coming back to him as he descended, like adjusting his buoyancy control device, and to pinch his nose and equalize his ears every few feet so he didn't destroy his eardrums. The deeper he swam, the more he remembered why he hadn't gone back to diving; it required patience, and patience hadn't been one of Laurence's defining traits when he was younger. Hell, he could still struggle with it from time to time, but he was getting better. Learning to control his gift of stealth had forced him to work on it.

The deeper he went, the darker it got, and the more life he encountered on his way down. He'd brought a flashlight with him, but doubted he'd need it. His eyesight was already picking out stingrays swimming in the distance, and as the minutes crawled by he started to make out more of the ocean floor.

It was a whole different world, with rock formations and whole forests of seaweed swaying in the currents. The anchor chain disappeared into strands of kelp.

Laurence grit his teeth around the mouthpiece, but he couldn't afford to let his irritation get the better of him. Whatever the spell he was searching for was attached to was in this kelp forest somewhere, and he needed to move carefully to avoid getting snagged on any of it.

He pressed on and eased his way through the canopy. The kelp wasn't densely packed — he could slip between strands — but here and there it clumped together, and he wanted to avoid those areas the most.

Fish scurried out of his way. Seals messed around in the forest, chasing each other like they were having the time of their lives.

Laurence reached the seabed and started his search. The area was rocky, encrusted with layers on layers of barnacles, anemones, and weird shit that looked as though it might grab him if he got too close. Small fish nibbled at it all, grazing like cows in a field and utterly uninterested in the diver overhead.

There were all kinds of nooks and crannies, and none of them were glowing, which didn't help. In the end he resorted to the flashlight just to double-check holes, but a vibration from his wrist made him check his dive computer.

Shit. He'd already been down here forty minutes. Another ten and he'd need decompression breaks on the ascent.

Come on, he urged silently. *Where is it?*

There!

Something glinted in the flashlight beam and he pushed himself closer.

There was a box, no bigger than a jewelry box, covered in slime and barnacles and Goddess knew what else. The glint came from what little of a keyhole in the front remained that wasn't yet entirely obscured by organic matter.

Bingo!

At least, he hoped bingo, because the idea of coming back down here again did *not* appeal to him.

Laurence reached warily down into the crevice and fished out the box, fingers of his gloves slipping over it several times before he managed to dig the whole thing out. It was heavy, like it was filled with rocks, and he couldn't get the lid open.

His dive computer vibrated again.

Five minutes left.

Laurence turned off the flashlight and clipped it back onto his buoyancy control device, tucked the box under his left arm, and turned toward the sky.

Movement flashed nearby. That wasn't new, he'd been surrounded by wandering sea life for three quarters of an hour, but something about this particular motion tripped his danger senses, and his instincts flared into life. He twisted in the water, making an arc of himself so that he could turn to face the flash head-on and work out what had made it stand out.

All the seals had vanished.

Laurence's saliva dried up at once, and his heart thumped oxygen as fast as it could.

Where are the seals?

The movement was back. A streak of white flesh slunk between the kelp, and it was coming closer.

Shark. Shark! It's a fucking shark!

Laurence let out an explosion of bubbles as the panic hit him.

Idiot. Idiot! It's the middle of fucking summer! There are great whites breeding in their thousands in summer!

Every other shark in the area was harmless. But great whites? They'd eat someone just out of curiosity to see what they were made of, and all the seals had obviously decided not to try their luck with an apex predator in the area.

Maybe the bubbles were what drew the shark's attention, or maybe it was the way Laurence had turned in the water. Whatever the reason, the damn thing was coming straight at him now, picking up speed at a terrifying rate.

A second later, it put on a spurt and launched itself at Laurence, and its jaws opened wide.

Laurence screamed so hard that he lost everything in another cloud of wasted air, and the last thing he saw before it was all taken away was rows upon rows of fericiously sharp teeth.

3 4

QUENTIN

Freddy drove them home while Quentin kept Angela safe and comfortable in the back seat. She grew tired of playing with Windsor after a while and nodded off, but he didn't dare release her from his hold lest it distressed her.

It was distressing Freddy, that was certain.

When they'd driven to La Jolla earlier to drop Ellie off on Quentin's insistence — he was not about to leave her in a car in summer, not even for a few minutes — Freddy had been relaxed, even chatty. But now he was silent, laboring under a storm cloud of his own making.

Quentin sympathized. This must be one of Freddy's worst fears. He was so tightly controlled that the thought of losing all that he was had to be hitting him hard.

To Quentin, the notion of forgetting everything was almost appealing.

If only he could pick and choose. But one look at Angela made it abundantly clear that selective losses were no longer on the table.

If you had learned magic...

What?

What if he *had* learned magic? They had already established that if he'd returned home long ago — or never even left — he might be a competent magician by now, but he would never have met Laurence. Worse, his bride would be selected for him, and then he would be made to produce heirs.

And then, if his first-born showed no magical talent...

He closed his eyes and clenched his jaw, trying to tamp down on the sick sensation in his gut.

His father insisted that Quentin was the one being selfish, but how could he *not* be, when the alternative was beyond despicable?

Perhaps selfishness was what it took to touch freedom.

He felt the car slow, and then stop, and made himself open his eyes.

They were home, but of course, neither of them had a remote for the garage.

"You really should do something about this," Freddy grumbled. It was the first thing he'd said in half an hour.

Quentin eased his phone free from his jacket pocket and texted Flynn. "I blame the landlord, personally," he murmured.

At least that got a small snort of amusement out of Freddy. Hopefully that meant his funk would be lifted soon.

Flynn responded quickly, and moments later one of the garage doors opened. Freddy reversed into the garage and, once he'd parked, hopped out of the car to greet Flynn and draw him back into the house.

With the coast clear, Quentin was able to focus on gently easing Angela from the car. Windsor hopped up to his shoulder and leaned over to gently preen her hair.

"What's going on?" Felipe asked, but soon he wasn't alone. Every teenager in the house was cramming into the doorway, pushing and shoving to try and look over Felipe's shoulder, and if Quentin didn't get a lid on things quickly, they'd make enough noise to wake the dead.

"Just a small, ah… emergency…" he said softly. "Please, I would rather not wake her." He carried Angela toward the teens, and raised eyebrows slightly as he nodded to the doorway. "May we come in?"

"Ow! That's my foot!"

"Hey! Elbows, Felipe!"

"Who is she?"

Quentin tried so hard not to roll his eyes as he carried Angela through to the living room and laid her down on the couch, all while Grace, Pepper, and Ellie tried to mug him from the knees down. "Could someone fetch me a blanket, please?"

There was some more teenage jostling, and eventually Clifton seemed to have become the nominated blanket-fetcher. He dawdled out of the room, but his footsteps on the stairs suggested he'd switched to a speedier pace once he was out of sight.

Quentin checked who he had left. Myriam, Mel, Estelita, Lisa, Kimberly, Soraya, Felipe, all three dogs, Windsor, and Mia. Good god, virtually the entire household. He noticed that Mel had had a chance to clean up and switch to fresh clothes, and it transpired that her hair was actually a light strawberry blonde beneath the hoodie. She was warier than the other teens, too, which was wholly justifiable in Quentin's opinion. She had only met him this morning and he was already bringing unconscious women home with him.

"All right," he murmured as he gestured for the teens to find themselves seats. "This is Angela, and I'm afraid she's lost her memories."

"How?"

"What?"

"Are *we* going to lose our memories too?"

Myriam fluttered her hands soothingly to the teens. "Shh.

Why don't we let her sleep, and find somewhere else to talk this through?"

"The yard," Mia said, gesturing to the patio doors. "Let's go."

She herded the teens outside just as Clifton returned with the blanket, so he urged Clifton to follow, and wrapped Angela in it until he was satisfied that she was snug. Only then did he release his telekinetic hold, and he eased it away slowly, hoping not to disturb her.

The maneuver was a success.

"Stay with her," he murmured to Windsor. "Call me if she wakes, all right?"

Windsor clacked his beak. "Yes."

"Thank you."

He headed out into the hot, bright afternoon and shielded his eyes from the sun until he found shade by a hedge, and then he did everything in his power to explain the situation.

THE HOUSEHOLD SWUNG into motion after that. Soraya and Kimberly went out to buy supplies just in case Angela wasn't able to chew food or use the loo. Myriam, Estelita, and Lisa volunteered to help Quentin take turns in caring for Angela and keeping her safe. Clifton volunteered too, but Myriam pled the case for having women do the majority of the care in case any intimate needs arose, and Clifton agreed to cover Estelita's chores for her instead.

Mel kept quiet throughout, but Quentin could see her watching everything, listening and observing. It was sensible of her, especially as she had barely been in this house a few hours and already been presented with the chaos it could lead to, but she did not run. Instead she offered to take care of the dogs and keep them out of the way.

Soon everything was settled enough for Quentin to take a shower and switch into fresh clothes, and then he was able to face more time downstairs.

Flynn was occupied in the kitchen, preparing dinner if the sounds and smells were to be believed, and when Quentin re-entered the living room, Freddy was present, and Angela awake.

"How is she?" he asked softly as he returned, closing the door after himself to ensure a little privacy.

Myriam nodded. "She fussed a little when she woke up, but she was hungry. She seems to be doing okay with meal replacement shakes, but it's not a long-term solution." She gazed up at him from her seat on a couch, her hands in her lap, and there was a worried frown around her eyes.

Quentin looked to Angela, who had been relocated to the floor so that she could safely play with a soft toy Soraya must have bought for her, and his heart ached. This was so utterly awful, and poor Angela had no idea it had even happened. All any of them could do was protect her until Laurence found and disposed of the spell which had done this, and then began the task of attempting to restore what had been taken.

You should have learned magic.

He pushed the intrusive thought away. If he had, how would it help? Angela needed care, and it was every bit as vital a task as chasing down hidden sigils. If Quentin learned magic, he would not be here, looking after someone who was incredibly vulnerable, in her moment of utmost need.

No. He could not chastise himself. He would have the courage of his convictions, and he would do something important with his life, because leaving Angela alone was not an option.

"It is not," he agreed. Then he turned to Freddy. "Are they any nearer?"

Freddy raised his head. "I believe so. It seems as though

whoever trapped Lethe went to quite some lengths to make sure their sigils could not be broken. The spell is anchored to something at sea. They've had to hire a yacht to reach it. Laurence is diving as we speak."

Quentin blinked. He knew Laurence liked to surf, but diving?

Freddy must've seen something in Quentin's expression, because he added, "Laurence insists that he's used scuba equipment before. I'm sure it won't be long now, don't fret."

"How far out to sea are they?"

Freddy shrugged. "Within sight of the coast. It's not deep sea diving or anything, but they did have to travel down to the Mexican border. They'll be *fine*, Icky," he added, raising his hands. "What are we to do, hire another yacht and chase them down?"

"Welcome to our lives," Soraya said, sounding flippant. "We sit around all day worrying about you and waiting to see if you come home in one piece."

"It's not *that* bad," Estelita insisted.

Soraya just sniffed.

"You're absolutely right." Quentin tried to shake off his concern. Even if he *was* there, what use would he be? Absolutely none. He couldn't even swim, let alone use underwater breathing apparatus.

Laurence knew what he was doing, and Angela needed Quentin more right now.

He calmed himself so that he could focus on the task at hand, and he was reasonably comfortable with the situation right up until the moment Windsor started screaming bloody murder.

35

LAURENCE

THE BOX TUMBLED OUT OF HIS GLOVED HANDS, AND LAURENCE lost sight of it because there was no way he was taking his eyes off the enormous shark that would reach him in less than a second.

With no time to think, all he could do was hand himself over to his instincts, and trust them completely.

The shark was on him, and all his gut came up with was *punch the shark.*

So he did.

This won't work, it can't work, that thing has got to be two thousand pounds!

His fist landed right on one of the shark's eyes and the shark jerked aside at the last possible moment, so late that it bumped against Laurence as it flew past.

Laurence gulped down air and twisted to keep his eyes on the beast, but the damn thing had already started to turn, alarmingly graceful for its size.

It wasn't giving up.

He couldn't keep punching it.

Laurence spread his arms wide and *pushed.* He shoved his

life force out in all directions, reaching for the kelp forest. It was all he had, but it would have to be enough.

As the shark began to pick up speed again, Laurence commanded the kelp to move. It was slow at first, fighting the underwater current, but he put everything he could into it and the kelp lurched toward the shark.

Some threaded around its head, blocking its line of sight. Some snagged tail or fins, slowing the monster until more kelp could arrive.

The dive computer began to buzz in earnest.

Not now! I'm busy!

Laurence didn't want to kill the shark, but what choice did he have? The thing was intent on eating him, a fist to the eye hadn't stopped it, and Laurence was very against dying.

Some sharks suffocated if they weren't swimming. Laurence didn't know if the great white was one of them, but the sooner he got out of here, the quicker he wouldn't have to find out. He coiled more kelp around the shark, and dove to the sea floor to recover the box he'd dropped.

He could feel the pull against the kelp, the way it stretched and thrashed against his energy as the shark writhed, but so long as it didn't break free, Laurence didn't care. He snatched the box up and adjusted his buoyancy control to shoot up to the surface as fast as he dared.

The dive computer's buzzing grew increasingly angry. Laurence ignored it.

Breathe. Breathe!

His brain screamed at him. Or was it Windsor? The closer Laurence got to the surface, the more he felt Win's panic mirroring his own, like he was able to hear now that he wasn't one whole second from being eaten alive.

There was nothing he could do to reassure Windsor. Laurence literally wasn't out of the water yet, and the shark still thrashed in the weakening kelp below.

Breathe!

If he didn't breathe, he could damage his lungs with an uncontrolled ascent, he knew that much. He hadn't strayed too far over his time limit, so all he could do there was pray that the dive computer used really conservative estimates, because Laurence was *not* stopping until he was out of the water. No way.

The water overhead grew lighter, brighter, and he saw the hull of the yacht in the distance. Laurence turned toward it and swam with all his might, but so much of his energy was outside of his body, fighting a shark to give Laurence time to escape.

For a moment, he sagged, and rose through the water like something was hauling him up, but he shook his head and took another breath, then focused everything he could on reaching the boat.

The kelp started to slip through his hold. Adrenaline turned his muscles to jelly and his mind to mush, and it was all he could do to keep swimming.

Just keep swimming. Just keep swimming.

Laurence didn't have the energy to laugh, not even a little, as his brain replayed a cartoon fish's advice over and over, a mantra for survival.

The shark slipped free.

Laurence snarled, and the bubbles he left behind were almost furious, like they were angry at him for losing control over the kelp.

A blot appeared in the bright blue, sinking into the water from the hull of the yacht and accelerating toward him, and for a moment Laurence was utterly confused at the lithe, almost naked shape streaking toward him.

Quen?

That was dumb. Quentin couldn't swim. He wasn't even on the boat.

Rufus.

The witch had no breathing gear, no wetsuit, and apparently no fucks to give, because he came powering through the water toward Laurence, and was on him in seconds. Rufus grabbed Laurence around the waist, and propelled them both toward the waiting boat, adding his own strength to Laurence's.

Together, they made the few, final feet until Laurence's head broke the surface.

He couldn't stop here. He had no way to know where the shark was now, but it would outpace him in any race in water.

Rufus leaped out of the sea and onto the boarding platform like a carp chasing a fly, and he turned to grab Laurence's arm and drag Laurence up.

Laurence heaved himself as far as he could, and dropped the box onto the boarding deck so he could use both arms. With Ru's help, Laurence was finally free from the ocean in another couple of seconds, but he didn't stop there. He scrambled up onto the rear deck and pulled his mouthpiece out. "Shark," he gasped to Ru, the only explanation needed.

Rufus grabbed the box and jumped up after him, then yelled to Mikey. "Get us out of here!"

Everything ached. It could be failure to off-gas on his way up, it could be the fight for his life, it might even be both, but all Laurence could do was sag against the table and heave for breath as the yacht kicked into action.

He didn't want to look back, to see if the shark was chasing them, but he couldn't help it.

Behind the yacht's wake, where they'd been only seconds ago, the tip of a fin was already sinking from view.

I help! I help! I come!

I'm okay. Win, it's okay. I'm okay. I'm safe.

Laurence closed his eyes as his hands trembled in his lap,

but after a couple of minutes, he managed to string a coherent thought together.

"Why'd you come get me?"

He heard Rufus' snort. "One huge psychic game of telephone." When Laurence didn't answer, Rufus explained. "Windsor lost his shit, so Freddy told Mikey you were in trouble."

Laurence grunted. It made sense, but he was too exhausted to come up with a coherent reply.

All he could do is rest for now, and hope he hadn't done himself any lasting harm with his fast ascent.

MIKEY PUSHED the yacht hard on their way back. Laurence figured now Mikey knew how far they were from the marina, he was more willing to burn fuel. That or he wanted to get the hell away from sharks.

It made the ride bumpy as the hull slammed into wave after wave, every bump accompanied by a thud that *almost* had rhythm but not quite.

Laurence's gut didn't stand a chance, but he puked into a sink rather than risk leaning over a handrail.

They made it back to their dock in less than an hour. Rufus and Mikey worked together to make sure they'd moored properly, and then they sat on the rear deck with the encrusted box in the middle of the table.

Laurence had shed everything but his wetsuit. Rufus had managed to put clothes back on.

Mikey was the first to speak. "So do we open it?"

"It's locked," Laurence said.

"And even if we had picks, the lock is probably fucked by now." Mikey scratched his chin. "We don't mind damaging what's inside, right?"

"It would be good if we can open it without damage first." Rufus frowned at the box. "We need to identify the caster, and I can't do that unless I can see the magic."

"Which is inside the box," Laurence concluded. "Okay. Easiest solution is Quen. He can pop it open without wrecking it."

Laurence waited for either Mikey or Rufus to come up with a better — or, at least, quicker — idea, but they both nodded in agreement.

This did mean he had to move at last, though.

He grit his teeth and pushed himself to his feet, but now the yacht was only bobbing softly on the sheltered water, he was a lot less queasy. He'd had an hour to recover his strength, too, so now all he felt was tired instead of utterly depleted, and he finally had the energy to peel his wetsuit off and switch back into pants and t-shirt.

They carried the rental scuba gear to the truck, tossed it all in the back, and then crammed into the cabin so Laurence could drive them up to La Jolla.

LAURENCE WAS BARELY OUT of the car before Quentin was on him, hugging him tightly as though reassuring himself that Laurence was alive.

"Sorry, hon," Laurence croaked. He slipped his arms around Quentin's waist and hung on. It felt safe at last, being home and in his arms, and Laurence allowed himself a moment to revel in that sensation. "I'm okay."

"Windsor frightened the life out of us," Quentin breathed against Laurence's jaw. "Thank goodness you're all right. Freddy says that it was a shark?"

Laurence nodded. "Yeah. Damn, they're stealthy for their size. It was nearly on me before I spotted it."

Quentin seemed reluctant to release him, but Rufus stepped up beside them both and cleared his throat, then offered Quentin the box. "We need you to open this," he said bluntly.

Quentin peeled back and tore his attention from Laurence so that he could look at the box, and his nose crinkled slightly, but he reached out to take it regardless of how disgusting he clearly found it. The crinkle remained firmly in place as Quentin carried it out of the garage, holding it as though it might shit itself in his hands.

Laurence followed, and managed to catch Windsor before the bird could crash into his chest. He hugged Win as Quentin led them through to the living room, ignoring the delicious smells emanating from the kitchen which nearly dragged Laurence off-course.

The only people already in the room were Myriam and Angela. The faint clatter of cutlery and chatter of teens from through the wall told Laurence where everyone else was, though Freddy soon joined them in the living room and took a moment to squeeze Mikey's hand.

"So, can you do it?" Rufus said to Quentin.

Laurence rolled his eyes. There was on-mission and then there was just rude. He made his way to his mom and hugged her, careful not to squash Win between them, and he whispered, "How's Angela holding up?"

Myriam bobbed her head a little. "Freddy's making it easy to know what she needs and when. We're taking turns keeping an eye on her, feeding her, all the essentials. Do you have something?"

"Yeah. Maybe. I hope." Laurence peeled back and gestured to the box.

Quentin perched on a chair with a side table next to it, and he settled the box down. He drew out a handkerchief to wipe muck from his fingers.

"Well?" Ru huffed.

"I am *working*," Quentin replied testily.

It was then that Laurence noticed all the little things out of place in the room. Crooked lampshades. Pillows that weren't on the same seats as yesterday. Missing lightbulbs. A cracked patio door.

He grimaced. Quentin must've gone nuclear when Win started panicking, and here he was now doing his very best to pop open a box a minute after Laurence got home.

"You don't look like—"

Rufus cut himself off as the box lid flew open, flinging specks of grime and water across the carpet. Quentin remained intent on wiping his hands, and showed absolutely no reaction to having succeeded at his task.

Rufus grunted, which almost sounded like an apology.

"Thanks, babe," Laurence said, just to make it clear that at least someone in this room appreciated Quentin's efforts. He squeezed Quentin's shoulder as he moved closer to the box, and leaned over to peer into it.

The box was full of water. Some had leaked out onto and across the table, and was dripping onto the floor, but the rest remained. There was very little growth inside, though. With no water flow and no nutrients, Laurence figured nothing would be able to survive in it for long.

There were tiny sigils etched around the inside of the box, scratched into the plastic by something sharp. And mostly submerged in the remaining water was a glint of metal, a blob of silver which revealed itself — when Laurence dipped his fingers into the cold water and withdrew it — as a heart-shaped locket on a tarnished chain.

For spells to remain active for years which, judging by the state of the box, these had been, the objects they were anchored to had to be relevant to the spell being cast. A locket made perfect sense for locking away memories, but the box?

Laurence wasn't so sure. He beckoned Rufus away from Quentin and pointed to the sigils in the box's lid.

"That's sorcery, right?" He frowned at Ru. "I can't see any magic."

"It's very simple." Rufus came closer and added, "The spell. It's…" He tailed off, then reached for the locket. "Give me that."

Laurence handed it over and chose not to pass comment on Rufus' manners. "Sure."

Ru poked at it with a thumbnail until he managed to force the locket open, and he grimaced.

Laurence frowned. This spell *did* have a weak, barely-there glow, a dim red which only really became visible against the silver in Rufus' palm, and the sigils for it were almost microscopic scratches in the metal. They were the same style of geometric designs he'd had to make the locating talisman with rather than the more fluid sigils he would use himself.

"Fuck." Rufus slammed the locket down on the side table and stalked away, his hands clenching into fists.

Laurence grit his teeth and followed. "What? What's wrong? This *is* what we need, right? We just break this, and everyone can get their memories back."

"Yes," Rufus said thickly. "That's the spell. I figure the one in the box was probably a booby trap to stop the box being recovered. I'd have to do some research to be sure."

"Then what's the problem?" Laurence reached out and grabbed Rufus' shoulder. "Ru! What is it?"

"The spells!" Rufus spat the words as he span to face Laurence. "The *spells*."

Laurence let go of him and gazed into his eyes. "Uh huh," he prompted.

"They're hers." Rufus raised an arm and extended it toward Angela, his face reddening with slow anger. "She did this, Laurence. We've been chasing ghosts this whole time. The magic is hers, it matches everything on her house, it is *her magic*." He sucked in a breath, then sagged, as though all the fight had suddenly evaporated. "She did this to us to make us forget her. She's the killer, Laurence. She murdered my parents."

Laurence turned slowly to stare at Angela, who was playing with a soft toy on the floor, her back to a couch. She was smiling, entertained by whatever thoughts were running through her head, and utterly unable to tell them why she'd done any of this.

His shoulders slumped, and his mouth dried up.

Laurence almost got eaten by a shark for nothing, and the killer had wiped herself clean. She couldn't tell them why she'd killed Paula and Todd Grant, why she'd chosen to spare Rufus, or why she would rather reduce herself to a baby than admit to any of it.

So what if they'd finally found the murderer? All they had were more questions, and the only person who could have answered them yesterday couldn't today.

Laurence fumbled his way to an armchair and sat heavily as everything slipped through his fingers. His deal with Rufus was done, and Ru probably wouldn't teach him any more. Angela couldn't teach him either. If he wanted to learn more magic he'd have to start his search for a teacher all over again, and with nothing to offer in return.

But worst of all, they'd never know why *any* of it had happened. All they'd done was wasted their time, energy, and money on a wild goose chase.

"Fuck," Laurence groaned.

"Fuck," Windsor agreed.

36

LAURENCE

THE ROOM WAS SILENT FOR BARELY A SECOND BEFORE LAURENCE heard a soft scrape, and looked toward it.

Rufus had scooped a lamp off a table, and was tugging on the cord to pull it free from the wall.

Laurence blinked and straightened in his seat. What the hell was Ru doing? He wasn't here to steal the fixtures, surely?

Rufus weighed the lamp in his hand, and then whirled it toward Angela's head, with fury flourishing across his face.

He never made it that far.

Everyone leaped to their feet at once — everyone but Angela, who seemed blissfully unaware that she'd come within inches of having her skull caved in.

Quentin was first up, and judging by the way Ru was snarling and wrestling with the immobile lamp, he was the one who had stopped it reaching its target. "You are going to want to reconsider this course of action," he murmured, an undercurrent of threat mingled in with his light tone.

Freddy was on his feet in a flash, too, darting to Angela's side, looking about ready to punch Rufus in the face to protect her.

Laurence sucked in air and tried a more diplomatic route. "Ru. You can't just murder her, man."

Rufus spat at the carpet and let go of the lamp, glaring daggers at Quentin as he took a step back. "No, apparently not."

Myriam eyed the lamp and reached out, and Quentin sent it gently into her outstretched hands. She quietly returned it to the table, and dipped down to plug the cord back in.

Laurence gestured to the box and locket. "We've got work to do. We fix this, and then we work out what really happened. What's the point of attacking Angela? None of us know why she did this or what exactly she's hiding, and if anything happens to her we'll *never* get to the truth." He raised his chin angrily, and added, "And that's what I promised you, Ru. The truth. I told you: once I start a hunt, I don't stop. I will *not* let you get in my way."

He couldn't help but flash his teeth briefly, even though Rufus could probably use magic to turn him inside-out if the witch wanted to, and Laurence tried to stay calm, to ignore the low-level panic at his whole magical education getting wiped out in an instant.

Rufus stared back at him, his hands curling so that his fingers were like claws, his whole body leaning forward ready for a fight even though he had to know that it was futile.

"Rufus," Myriam said gently.

It felt like this standoff could go on forever, but in the end, Rufus relaxed his hands and stood up straight. A curl lingered in his lip a moment longer before it, too, was smoothed away. "Then what's your solution?"

Laurence didn't want to take his eyes off Rufus for even a second. "Quen, can you destroy the sigils?"

The shadow that was Quentin stepped slowly away from Angela. "I can try," he replied. "Michael, would you be so kind as to take these outside, please?"

Mikey glanced to Freddy, then nodded, and picked up both items. He carried the box carefully so as to not spill more water onto the carpet, and Quentin went with him to open the patio doors.

"Let's go," Laurence said.

Rufus licked his lips and gave Angela another look, but his shoulders stooped and he followed Mikey out through the doors.

Windsor hopped from Laurence's shoulder and glided down to Angela's knee, delighting her with his arrival. Myriam and Freddy remained with her, and both nodded to Laurence, an unspoken agreement that they'd protect her.

Laurence nodded back and set off into the yard.

It was a beautiful evening, hot without being *too* hot, the sun low enough in the sky that it dipped below the hedge which separated the back patio from the rest of the yard.

Mikey put the box and locket down where Quentin asked him to, and stepped well back, and the locket raised from the ground to hover over the water in the box.

Nothing really seemed to be happening.

Rufus let out an aggrieved huff and planted his fists on his hips. "What are we waiting for?"

Quentin didn't respond.

Laurence opened his mouth, but the next breath he took was of noticeably cooler air than the last one.

The temperature was sinking. Laurence was the first to shiver, but Mikey and Rufus soon followed.

Then Laurence's breath misted in front of his face. Frost formed across the leaves of the hedge.

The locket developed a white-red glow to it. The chain twisted and then fell free, landing in the water with a *plop* and a soft *hiss*. Only then did Laurence realize where all the ambient heat was going.

Quentin was going to melt the locket.

The locket darkened and then folded in on itself, and followed the chain into the water, which hissed aggressively around the dumped metal.

"I assume that was enough?" Quentin asked, as though funneling metal-melting heat out of the air was no big deal.

The temperature around them bled back toward normal. Cooler than it had been to start with, but they were no longer freezing in the height of summer.

Laurence looked to Rufus. "Did that do it?"

Ru stepped in close so that he could lean over the box and peer into the water. "Yeah," he said, his voice thick and uncertain. He stepped back. "What about the box?"

"Considerably easier," Quentin replied as the box tore itself into splinters, shedding the remaining water across the patio.

Rufus grimaced. "That did it."

"Great." Laurence crossed his arms tightly and tried not to let anyone see just how fucking horny for Quentin he was right now, because Goddess, Quen just melted silver and ripped wood apart like it was child's play, and Laurence wanted to drag him upstairs. He cleared his throat and did his level best to behave himself. "I guess nobody's just suddenly remembered everything?"

Rufus and Mikey glanced to each other, then both shook their heads.

"Me either," Laurence muttered. "Okay. That's the next job. We get our memories back. *Then* we figure out where to go after."

"You can't protect her from me forever," Rufus said.

"I won't have to." Laurence rolled his eyes. "Once she's got her memories back she'll be perfectly capable of defending herself."

"You don't have any evidence that Angela did anything other than save your life," Quentin interjected calmly, gazing up at Rufus with a hard glint in his eye. "If you are willing to kill on nothing more than an assumption, you are not the person I thought you to be."

"Oh?" Rufus squared up and stepped in closer. "And who did you think I was?"

Laurence took a breath to try and step in, but Mikey gave a brief shake of his head, and Laurence wondered whether that was Mikey's doing, or Freddy using Mikey to communicate from inside the house.

"I thought you were honorable," Quentin said simply. "Willing to do what was right, even if it meant doing things which made you uncomfortable. You have helped Laurence and me on many occasions, above and beyond simply teaching him in exchange for the very thing he is doing for you now. Despite your surly nature, you are a good person at heart, Rufus. Or, at least, that is what I believed up until you attempted to murder a helpless human being." He raised an eyebrow, showing measured disapproval, as though scolding a naughty toddler.

"She killed my parents!"

"Until you are able to prove it, she did no such thing." Quentin turned away and headed back inside without another word, pausing only to brush his hand against Laurence's fingers on the way.

"He can be a crushing bore at times," Freddy said from the other side of the doorway, "but he's not wrong. Now do come in, we need to fix this memory nonsense."

"But you can do that, right?" Laurence turned away from Rufus and raised a hopeful eyebrow toward Freddy. "Now Lethe won't bother us any more?"

Freddy's expression said it all. His lips were tightly pressed, and his brow furrowed. "I should be able to for us, certainly. But not for Angela. I can't undo that level of damage. It's as though there's nothing even there."

"Then just fix us," Rufus said, and Laurence could almost

hear a shrug in his voice. If ever a tone had conveyed *I don't give a fuck*, this was it.

"No." Freddy gave the sweetest smile, then turned his back on Ru and disappeared into the house.

Rufus stepped after him, but Laurence got in his way and put a hand on Rufus' chest. "Wait." When Rufus tried to interrupt, Laurence added, "Shh. Just a minute."

Something was tugging at his attention, and he had to let go of right now to allow the memory to surface.

In a moment's silence, it obliged, and Laurence was taken back to the hospital cafeteria, but it had been him who suggested Freddy restore their memories that time, and Ru who wasn't interested in that route.

Because Ru had a different idea.

Laurence blinked as everything slotted neatly into place, and he gazed into Ru's eyes. "What did you mean about going over Lethe's head?"

The witch said nothing, but Laurence wasn't going to let himself be deterred. Not when they were so close to all the answers.

"There's another god, isn't there? Someone above Lethe who could give us all our memories back. Who is it?"

"There are a hundred ways—" Rufus began.

"Dude, come *on*, stop fucking around," Laurence butted in. "Let's just do it properly, get our memories, get Angela's memories, and then we'll have all the answers you asked me to get for you. Right?" Laurence lowered his hand so he could cross his arms loosely, and offered up an easy smile. "Who is it?"

If Rufus meant to fight him, Laurence would find another way, but the witch's fingers slowly relaxed, and he rolled his eyes. "We have to go back to Hades and drink from the pool of Mnemosyne. But we need a password to get past Hades' staff."

Laurence nodded. "And how do we get that?"

Ru threw his hands up, exasperated. "It's probably in a book somewhere."

"Or we ask Lethe," Myriam suggested gently.

Everyone still outside turned to look at her, and she gave a wry smile.

"You *did* just free her," she murmured. "She may look kindly on you for that."

"Great!" Laurence clapped his hands together. The suggestion felt right, and his instincts yelled at him to run with it, so he was done messing around. They'd fix this nonsense, find out why Angela cast the spell in the first place, and then if Ru wanted to try and kill her that was his problem. Laurence had plenty of time to work out whose side he wanted to be on in that shitshow. "What do you need? Just a Sharpie? Somewhere big enough to fit us all in?"

Rufus' jaw was doing that thing, where a muscle twitched almost in time with a heartbeat, as his eyes narrowed thunderously. But in the end he sighed and nodded. "Yes. Whoever wants their memories back is going to have to get inside the circle."

Laurence eyed the patio, but the gaps between slabs would mean that a circle couldn't truly form, so he gestured toward the doors. "Great. Let's go upstairs and get this done."

Myriam and Mikey filed inside, and Laurence smiled sweetly at Rufus until Ru did the same.

No more Mr. Nice Hunter.

LAURENCE

It took a little organizing to get everyone who needed to be there up to the gym while also keeping out a horde of freshly-fed and inquisitive teenagers, but Myriam did a great job of answering all the kids' questions while keeping them out from underfoot.

Quentin was able to move equipment away from the center of the room so that Rufus had space, and Freddy carried Angela upstairs while Windsor kept her entertained. Rufus used his Sharpie to ruin the gym's beautiful flooring, and Laurence was impressed that Freddy didn't even raise an eyebrow at the damage to his property.

After ten minutes — and a lot of double-checking information on the internet so that Rufus could adjust his spell correctly — everything was ready.

"Okay. Everyone in who's coming," Rufus muttered, casting a glare toward Angela. "Everyone else can go."

Frederick stepped into the circle, still holding Angela in his arms, and kept as far from Rufus as the circle permitted while watching him like a hawk. Mikey stood beside him without a moment's hesitation.

Myriam pursed her lips, then drew herself to her full height and followed, moving closer to the center, placing herself between Rufus and Angela.

Laurence was about to join her, but he paused. "Just wait, okay?"

"For fuck's sake," Rufus growled.

"Thirty fucking seconds, Ru." Laurence tried not to fling any rude gestures toward his teacher, then slipped outside and quickly took Quentin's hand. "Hey."

Quentin took his attention from the teenagers who seemed to be orchestrating a sit-in out in the hallway like they were protesting being excluded, and gave Laurence a strained smile. "Darling."

"We won't be long." Laurence leaned into kiss Quentin's cheek, since going for the lips right now would probably be too much for Quen to handle. "No need for ambulances, okay?"

Quentin dipped his head and squeezed Laurence's fingers. "We'll be right here," he murmured. "Good luck."

Laurence fought the urge to make some light quip. Quentin was under enough pressure staying this close to powerful magic, and Laurence didn't want to add to Quen's discomfort by making him worry. Instead, he simply said, "Thanks. We'll be back soon."

He dipped back into the gym and closed the door after himself, then hurried across the floor and into the circle. "Done."

"Glad you could make it," Rufus muttered. "Everyone lay down."

Laurence winced faintly as Ru began his incantation. He had no idea whether Rufus would ever get over this sulking, and he wasn't eager to find out if the answer was 'no.' Ru might be the best source for magic education Laurence had any access to, but he'd spent the last decade holed up in a private realm with very little real-world experience, and no pressing need to go get any. No job, no social expectations, no obligations, just a stack of books and total safety.

Yeah, Laurence really needed to find another option, but it would have to wait until they got back from Hades.

A blink and the house was gone, replaced by the rolling hills, the ominous cliffs, and the sluggish river which Laurence was extra sure he wanted nowhere near his mouth. He checked around himself and did a headcount: Ru, Mom, Freddy, Mikey, Angela, Windsor. All present and butt naked, most with a sense of wonder or curiosity in their gazes, since Laurence and Rufus were the only ones here who hadn't drunk from Lethe to leave. Everyone but Angela slowly rose to their feet, and Freddy crouched to scoop her into his arms and keep her tucked in against his broad chest.

Nobody seemed distressed by having left all their clothes behind, which was a relief.

"Okay, we're looking for a pool, right?" Laurence beckoned to Windsor, and the raven flew across to perch on his wrist. "Where is it?"

"In the palace of Hades," Frederick said. "By a poplar tree."

Laurence nodded to Win. "Go find me a palace, and stay out of trouble."

He launched the bird into the air, and Windsor cawed excitedly as he beat powerful wings and hefted himself higher and higher.

When Laurence turned his attention back on the group, he found Rufus giving Freddy the stink-eye, and Laurence couldn't help wondering whether it was some irritation that he wasn't the only expert on Greek mythology in the room right now. Ru had to be so used to being the only book-smarts person around, which was made a whole lot easier by his refusal to talk to just about everyone, and maybe he was getting a bit of a paradigm readjustment.

"You're the one who gave Laurence that translation spell," Ru said.

Freddy quirked an eyebrow. "Correct."

"Where'd you find it?"

"That information is confidential."

"Your father?"

Freddy simply smiled and said nothing, not even to deny Ru's claim, and Laurence stepped in before Rufus could keep throwing himself at the rock and expecting it to give way.

"C'mon. We can't stand here waiting. If the pool is in Hades' palace, where's that gonna be? On top of this mountain?" Laurence pointed to the rock the river flowed from. "Have we got to climb a mountain?"

"Probably," Rufus grunted.

"Unclear," Freddy said.

"Cool, awesome, amazing. Totally A-Okay." Laurence paused as the river began to slosh around, and as Lethe emerged from the waters, he approached her so that nobody else could screw everything up.

"Hunter," she intoned. Her clothes were still dripping into existence as she stepped onto the bank of the river, and the black ringlets of her hair settled into place over her shoulders like a frozen cascade. "Philosopher," she continued, as she looked past Laurence to Rufus. As her gaze slowly passed across the crowd, she added, "Trickster."

Laurence turned to try and follow her gaze and work out who she meant by that, but it could've been anyone, so he returned his attention to her. "Lethe. We're sorry for returning, but we're hoping we've released you from the spell, right?" He gestured to the group behind him. "We can try and get our memories back and won't end up here again?"

"That is true," Lethe murmured. She folded her hands together loosely and returned her gaze to Laurence. "You seek Mnemosyne."

It didn't sound like a question, but Laurence nodded anyway. "Yeah. I mean, if that's okay?"

"Do as you wish." Lethe didn't seem particularly interested, and maybe she wasn't, now that she didn't have to do anything. "You will fare well if you possess the password for Hades' staff. It will save you speaking with him directly."

"Yeah." Laurence winced slightly. "We don't have it."

Lethe's murky gaze drifted across to Angela and settled there a while, to the point where Laurence really wasn't sure whether their conversation was over, but then she said, "You have freed me. I will give you the password."

Laurence blinked in surprise. He didn't respond right away. He was well out of his depth in this Otherworld, and didn't know the rules. If he accepted her help, did he owe her anything, or was she repaying a debt to him that would be even once they were done here?

"Okay," he said, carefully.

She eased her gaze back to Laurence. "You must speak truth," she finally said. "Tell them who you are and why you are there. Tell them that you are the son of earth and sky. They will allow you to pass. But once you leave Hades, you may never return while you remain alive."

Laurence swallowed weakly. He was vaguely aware of some myth about a guy trying to rescue his wife from Hades, but he looked back before they got free and doomed her. Lethe's warning sounded every bit as foreboding even though Laurence had no intention of ever coming back here, so he gave a serious nod and fervently hoped it'd never matter. "Thank you. I don't want to sound rude, but hopefully we'll never meet again."

"May you find what it is that you seek," she said. "I thank you for removing my bindings."

Lethe turned her back on them all and sloshed back into the river, her body falling apart far faster than it had assembled, and she was gone before Laurence could say another word.

"Well," Mikey breathed, "that didn't sound ominous."

"Agreed." Myriam clicked her tongue. "Still, we're here now. Best do what we came to and then leave as quickly as we can."

Palace!

Laurence swiveled toward the mountain, the direction he sensed Windsor's excitement to have come from, and he groaned.

Of *course* they had to climb the mountain. Otherworld *loved* mountains.

"Okay," he said as he struck a line toward the cliff face. "Looks like we're going up in the Otherworld."

He ignored the protests at his terrible pun and led the way, treading a path he'd already walked once before and praying to the Goddess that it would lead to a different outcome this time.

38

LAURENCE

Path!

Laurence slowed to a halt and held up his hand to let everyone know he'd meant to do it, then closed his eyes. *Show me.*

Yes!

When Laurence opened his eyes again, he was sharing Windsor's body and gazing down on land which seemed almost normal, if he ignored the ominous chasm off in one direction which even Windsor couldn't see the bottom of from high in the sky.

He could, though, see the top of the group approaching the mountain, and Windsor banked lazily to show Laurence a route which wound gently up the side and directly toward the buildings on top, including a pool, which Laurence figured was the one they were here for.

Got it, he said to Windsor. *Come back.*

Yes, Windsor agreed.

Laurence withdrew to his own body and turned to face everyone while he waited for Windsor to return to his shoulder. "Win's found us what looks like a pretty good path up," he explained. "So we don't have to try any naked mountaineering."

"Yeah, I keep meaning to ask," Mikey piped up. "Why *are* we naked?"

"Because we're not physically here," Laurence said. "It's only our minds."

Mikey glanced up to Freddy, who didn't say a word.

Windsor finally dropped down onto Laurence's bare skin, so Laurence set off again, trekking as fast as he dared, and glancing over to his mom now and then to check she was doing okay. She seemed wistful, her attention drifting across the world around them as she followed, and Laurence finally asked, "Are you okay, Mom?"

Her lips twitched into a sad smile, and she nodded to him. "Only dwelling on the irony that I finally visit an Otherworld, and it isn't the right one."

Laurence slowed so that he could take her hand and hold it, hoping he could comfort her just a little, because he knew damn well what she meant.

This wasn't Annwn, and Eric wasn't here.

"Of all the luck, right?" Laurence said softly.

"Beggars can't be choosers," Myriam said, just as quietly.

"We'll be home again soon," he said. All they had to do was walk, drink, and wake up in the safety of their own home, and that would be that.

She glanced up at him and her fingers tightened around his, and only then did Laurence truly understand how afraid she was.

"I promise," he added.

Maybe he shouldn't have said it, but he didn't care. His mom needed to hear it.

IF IT WASN'T for the eerie lack of a sun in the light sky, or the occasional flying thing on the horizon which Laurence wasn't totally convinced was a bird, he could have easily tricked himself into believing they were out on a pleasant, mid-afternoon hike.

Naked.

Laurence was glad Quentin hadn't needed to come along, because if the magic necessary to get him here wasn't enough to trigger an episode, all this nudity would've absolutely done it. He ached at not having Quen by his side as they climbed a mountain in Hades, but there was no need for Quen go through something traumatic just so Laurence was more comfortable. He'd deal with it, get home, then this would be behind them. Besides, he didn't have time to dwell on the weirdness. He had to keep his shit together for his mom, who had never been through anything like this in her life before and was still holding up like a champ.

He had no idea what he'd ever expected Hades to be, but this place didn't seem so bad. The mountain was covered in healthy trees and shrubs, the air was faintly salty like they were near the sea, and there didn't seem to be roving gangs of horrible monsters waiting to devour them on the path. The group had settled into a quiet rhythm on their ascent, with no bickering or chit-chat, and Angela had fallen asleep in Freddy's arms.

It took maybe eight hours of constant walking to reach the top. It was hard to tell. The light never changed, nobody got tired or thirsty, and nobody needed a piss. Laurence didn't even know whether his grasp of time was as coherent as usual without any external frames of reference, but when the trees thinned out and the ground gently sloped to become level, he picked up the pace, eager for it all to be over.

The palace covered the entire mountain-top.

The group halted and fanned out so that everyone could

see what sat ahead of them, and Laurence felt his mouth drop open in sheer awe.

Everything was so bright. He'd always figured that ancient statues were always marble or some other grey-white stone, and so were clothes, walls, and who knew what else, but the palace laid out in front of him was alive with color. White walls, columns, and plinths were capped with blue and gold, or held statues so lifelike that Laurence had to scrutinize them to make sure they weren't moving. Ornamental trees added bold clouds of green, and red roofs stood out against the blue sky. People wandered along wearing draped cloth of a rainbow of colors, all held in place with gold clasps, and none of them seemed at all bothered by the new arrivals.

"No defensive outer wall," Freddy said.

Laurence blinked.

Freddy was right. The path led directly to the palace grounds, without a wall or a gate in their way.

"I guess they've got nothing to defend against, huh," Laurence mused.

"Hades is powerful enough to keep the Titans imprisoned forever," Rufus said. "Who's going to storm his palace?"

"Us, apparently," Myriam said dryly.

Laurence licked his lips and then stepped forward. He took it slowly at first, and once his feet were off bare earth and on cool, smooth street tile, he picked up the pace a little, but nobody here objected to his presence or screamed for guards even once they did notice him. Some eyed him with curiosity, others with a welcoming smile, and everyone's afterlife seemed far more important than the arrival of a bunch of pale-skinned nudists.

"Which way?" Rufus asked.

Laurence checked several buildings to get his bearings, then pointed off toward his left. "It should be past those steps."

They started off toward the broad, almost glistening steps

which were lined with a mix of cypress and olive trees, and the group felt like it unclenched its collective ass-cheeks. Maybe that was just Laurence's imagination, but everyone was looking around with more curiosity than the subdued terror that had sustained them through their climb, and they were spreading out a little more, becoming less of a tight knot and more of a tour group, with Laurence as their guide.

"From my somewhat limited understanding," Freddy said, keeping a low voice, "gods require believers, yes?"

Laurence nodded. "Yeah."

"And gods of various underworlds last longer, due to having a stock of believers on hand to sustain them, yes?"

"Yeah." Laurence gave him the side-eye, because he knew exactly how Freddy had come by this knowledge, and it wasn't through conversation or books. It was from constantly dipping in and out of Laurence's mind, usually without permission.

"But is the point of an underworld not to effectively launder a soul and allow it to return to Earth?" Freddy tipped his head toward some people. "You can't tell me that there are enough believers in Ancient Greek faiths to sustain all of this, but none of these people have gone, either. Isn't that some sort of problem?"

Rufus shrugged. "Ancient Greeks didn't think everyone got reborn. People who had earned eternal paradise get a whole island off Hades all to themselves, to enjoy forever."

"Ah, yes. The Fortunate Isle?" Freddy nodded thoughtfully. "But what about here?"

"A lot of Greek faith viewed other realms as equally busy as Earth." Rufus scratched idly at his waist, like he'd briefly looked for a pocket to put his hands in and disguised the movement badly when he didn't find any. "There's a part of Hades for imprisoning Titans, an area for punishment, an area for wandering around without your memories for all eternity if you don't drink from the Lethe, or an area for wandering around in pretty good but not quite paradise if you keep your memories. Maybe you get to come up here to the palace if you want to, or once your punishments are done, or because Hades needs some admin people around to manage it all." He sniffed. "It's not my pantheon, to be honest."

"I see, I see." Freddy pursed his lips. "Regardless, these people are being withheld from the natural cycle of things, are they not?"

Laurence looked down as the texture of the path changed under his feet. They had stepped onto a mosaic section depicting hunters chasing down wild animals, and as they began to climb the stairs while Rufus did his best to respond to Freddy's endless questioning, the mosaic section chased up the walls alongside the steps.

Was Freddy distracting Rufus from something, or was he genuinely interested in the answers to his questions?

"Bambi," Myriam whispered.

Laurence looked up. With three more steps to go, he could see past the columns and statues. They lined cloisters, which themselves lined a huge yard with gently sloping lawns and — in the center — a pool the size of a hot tub with an absolutely massive poplar tree overlooking it.

Between Laurence and the pool, the people had stopped and turned to face him. It was the most attention he'd received from the dead since they'd stepped onto the palace grounds, and it was unnerving.

We're the only living souls here.

Laurence cleared his throat faintly. He had no idea whether they were in danger or if the worst these souls could do was toss them out of Hades, but if they *were* ejected, there was no coming back. They'd have to recover Angela's memories some other way, and who knew how long that would take, or whether Rufus would even try to help.

A woman in a burgundy robe stepped forward. Her hair was long and almost black, and rested over her shoulders in loose curls which spilled from a beautiful azure clip. Her skin was bronze, with light creases and wrinkles, and her eyes were hazel. She offered him a welcoming smile, but there was wariness in her gaze.

"Where do you mean to go?" She asked it as if it was a casual question from a stranger offering to help with directions, but that wariness told Laurence there was more under the surface, and he wasn't going to take the risk that this wasn't how password exchanges went in Hades.

"I am Bambi Laurence Riley, and I am here to drink from the pool of Mnemosyne to restore memories lost to the waters of Lethe. I am the son of earth and sky," he replied smoothly, hoping he didn't sound like a total idiot. "We are all here to do this, and nothing more."

The caution melted from her gaze and her smile finally reached her eyes. "Welcome. Please, come with me."

The assembled crowd parted for her, forming a tunnel of colors which led directly to the yard beyond while also subtly denying any other path, and she led the way toward the mirror-flat surface of the small pool that held all their answers.

Laurence quickly checked that he still had everyone with him, then quashed any lingering concern and followed her.

39

FREDERICK

There were a multitude of calculations to be made here, and Frederick brought up the rear of the pack to give himself more time to work through them all.

It was abundantly clear that Rufus intended to murder Angela and didn't care that she was not in any fit state to defend herself right now. Even though Rufus was magically shielded from Frederick intruding into his thoughts, his actions had spoken so loudly that there was hardly any need to worry that Frederick might have missed a vital clue.

Frederick had spent a great deal of time suppressing Angela's disorientation and discomfort until it had proven safest for her to make her sleep through this ordeal, and now that they were close to being able to recover everything she had lost, he did not want to allow Rufus the slightest opportunity to take that from her.

He hardly needed to dig deep to understand why he found her situation so upsetting, why he felt so compelled to keep her safe. While he was no therapist, he knew his own mind better than anyone else could, even though he rarely admitted it to himself, and being faced with a situation which could rob him of everything he had worked his whole life to achieve was pure horror. From Laurence's memories of Angela, he suspected she would feel exactly the same way.

There was more to it than that, though. Right now she was little more than a newborn, and children deserved every ounce of protection he could afford them. He may have failed to shield Icky, but a part of him knew he held himself to an unattainable standard there; they had both been children. What was Frederick supposed to have done?

He was an adult now. In control of his own gifts, and armed with knowledge and a very flexible set of morals.

Laurence still wanted to trust his teacher, but Frederick did not, and he would not allow Laurence's naivety to get them all killed. Or, worse, stranded in Hades for eternity.

Frederick, as he had pointed out many times, had the benefits of a classical education, but he knew that very few Americans understood the meaning of those words. Learning languages like Latin and Ancient Greek was only the beginning, because those were merely tools used to gain access to untranslated texts.

As a child, Frederick took those texts to be perspectives on the human condition, but now that he was here, he was extremely grateful to have a wealth of information at his disposal which Laurence lacked, and which Rufus — if he even knew it — was not providing.

There was more to Mnemosyne than recovering the memories they had lost, and Frederick had puzzled over what to do with that information throughout their entire hike, because he suspected only one of them would be able to take full advantage of what was on offer, and it absolutely must not be Rufus.

He eyed the reflective water ahead and reached out to Michael's mind.

I will need you to volunteer to drink first.

Michael showed no outward sign of having heard him, gazing around in wonder which wasn't at all feigned. *I'll do it. Why, though?*

I need to know whether we return to our bodies the moment we drink, he replied, *or whether we remain until we are all restored.*

He watched Michael run through all the options in his own thoughts, which was immensely satisfying. The boy had gone from smart but shambolic to a keen mind in barely over a year, and Frederick hadn't tired yet of waiting for him to think things through.

Kind of a fox, chicken, and river situation, Michael realized.

Precisely. If we wake up in the real world the moment we drink, then we cannot allow Rufus to drink first. He might choose to destroy the sigils and abandon the rest of us here to enact his revenge on Angela. I need you there waiting for him, ready to stop him, if that is the case. Enlist Icky's aid if necessary, but those sigils must *remain intact until we are all home.*

And if I'm still here after I drink? Michael asked.

They were already descending steps on the other side of the cloister, into the lush, sculpted garden.

Then we have a different problem, Frederick answered.

He knew Michael wanted to know what that problem was, but Frederick wasn't sure that now was the time to share it. The fewer variables up in the air the better, especially when half the people around him were using magic to keep him out of their minds, and that magic had stuck with them into Hades.

It was a pain in the arse.

Worse, because he couldn't communicate with Laurence without Rufus overhearing, he couldn't explain any of this *to* Laurence. Not until they began drinking and found out whether it meant disappearing from Hades one by one.

"Quench your thirst," the dead woman who led them to the pool said to Laurence. "May you find what you seek."

And then she left them there, walking away across the short grass and back to the cloister.

Laurence stopped at the pool's edge and looked down at it, then turned to face them. "I guess we just use our hands?"

Frederick eyed the pool. It was about large enough that they could all stand in it if they were willing to become best friends, but it was difficult to gauge the depth. The surface was like a mirror, and the tree looming over it distorted the ability to see what lay underneath. It could be a puddle, or it could be a sinkhole, and the only way to find out would be to test it.

"I'll do it," Michael said. He didn't hesitate, and he didn't bother waiting for anyone to agree. He stepped out of the group, leaving Frederick's side, and approached the pool. "That way we'll see how it works, right?" he added as Laurence raised eyebrows at him. "I'll try it, and we'll see whether I start remembering anything."

Frederick appreciated his cunning. Michael didn't mention the risk of waking up at all, which prevented Rufus from cutting in.

"Are you sure?" Laurence pushed hair back from his forehead as he regarded Michael. "I don't mind—"

Michael raised his hands. "Not being funny," he cut in, "but what if it does some weird shit? You and him—" he pointed to Rufus "—are the only people who know a damn thing about any of this, and if this pool fucks either of you up, we're all screwed. But me? I don't got any powers or magic, or even knowledge. I'm basically along for the ride. So let me go first, and we'll make sure this is safe, okay?"

Oscar-worthy, Frederick thought. He didn't share it with Michael. He didn't want to shower the boy in praise until later, when they could get back to that bed he'd promised before all this went to pot.

"It's a good point," Myriam said. "But what if it's dangerous?" She glanced to Frederick as she asked, and while her mind was beyond his reach, he suspected that she was fishing for something.

Frederick tilted his head faintly. "And if it is? We're stuck here unless we drink, yes? Or we leave and achieve nothing, I suppose." He met her gaze, doing his level best to distill *trust me* into the furrow of his brow and the set of his lips, and hoping that her intuition would fall on his side.

On all their sides, really.

Myriam's eyes narrowed ever so slightly, and then she returned her attention to Michael. "Then I will go next."

"Mom!" Laurence burst out.

"Bambi," she countered, with a no-nonsense tone that made Frederick's heart ache for the mother he'd already lost. "Mikey is right. If anything happens, you and Rufus are our only hope, so if everything goes well with Mikey, I'll go after him."

Do it, Frederick sent to Michael, *while they are distracted.*

All right. Wish me luck.

I'll wish you much more than luck.

Michael crouched at the edge of the pool, moving quickly and quietly, made easier by being stark bollock naked. He dipped his hands in and sent ripples across the surface which destroyed the illusion and enabled glimpses into the pool itself, then scooped water toward his mouth and guzzled it down before anyone could stop him.

"Mikey!" Laurence sprang toward him so fast that Windsor launched from his shoulder to avoid falling off, but his hands passed through thin air.

Michael had disappeared.

There was a moment of stillness while everyone else

processed what had happened and figured out whatever it might mean for their own machinations, and then chaos erupted, and all Frederick could do was hang back to keep Angela from becoming a pawn in whatever idea Rufus was about to come up with.

40

QUENTIN

Flynn had offered to bring him a chair while he waited outside the gym all night, but Quentin refused it lest he doze off.

The children certainly had taken themselves away to bed after the first hour or so, leaving him with the dogs and his thoughts. And when the dogs also fell asleep at his feet, only his thoughts remained.

There was no knowing how long this might take, and since nobody had emerged from the closed room by midnight, things were clearly going to drag on, so Quentin eventually caved and settled down cross-legged on the floor across the hallway, his back to a wall, so that he could meditate.

Whether that meditation had became sleep wasn't entirely certain, though he suspected that it had, because when Estelita arrived it startled him awake.

"No news?" She spoke softly and crouched down to fuss the dogs.

"No." Quentin unfurled himself and began to stretch, easing out several cricks and cracks from various joints. "Would you mind feeding the dogs and letting them outside?"

"Sure." She smiled as she stood, but it was a worried, strained thing. "I can't hear anything in there, other than breathing."

Quentin nodded to her. "It's all right. These things take as long as they take, alas. All we can really do is wait for them to wake up. But they will."

Estelita bobbed her head, still not looking entirely reassured, but she encouraged the dogs to follow her, and Quentin nodded to them to go.

Clifton came next, still wearing his pajamas.

"Did you get *any* sleep?"

Quentin laughed faintly and shook his head. "Possibly?"

"You gonna have breakfast?"

Quentin hesitated.

"I'll bring you something," Clifton said easily, walking away to the stairs.

From there it was a to and fro of teenagers as they woke up, came by to check in on him, and then headed away to have breakfast before they came back again until — finally — everyone was crowded into the corridor.

"This is totally normal," Mel declared.

"No, it pretty much is, though," Soraya said.

"Hanging around in a corridor waiting for people to wake up after they've gone to fairyland or wherever?" Mel pulled a face.

"Not fairyland," Quentin murmured. "Otherworld."

"Yeah, okay, whatever." Mel huffed. "Well, I can't stand around here all day, I've got shit to do with my life."

"Oh?" Soraya grinned. "Important shit?"

"Yeah." Mel sniffed.

"Sounds cool."

"Yeah."

Mel lingered, though, her arms crossed as though she was present under great duress, before she added, "Okay. Bye.

Nice meeting you I guess." She paused. "Unless that Neil Storm thing is still on?"

"Oh, you have *got* to come with us for that!" Soraya grabbed Mel by the shoulder. "He's going to rent a helicopter, we're going out to the desert, we're going to practice our gifts and he might bring his sister along—"

She got cut short by yelling from inside the gym.

"Quentin? Quentin! Get in here!"

It was Mikey, and he sounded panicked.

Quentin was jolted more fully awake in a split second, and the teens managed to get out of his way as he slammed through the doors and into the gym.

Mikey was the only one awake, and on his feet, another yell dying in his throat as he saw Quentin. Instead, he jabbed a finger toward Rufus. "You've got to stop him moving before he wakes up, or he'll kill Angela!"

Almost the entire room was covered in circles and sigils, like those in Freddy's hospital room but on a far grander scale, and with bodies neatly laid out in spaces made for them.

The sound of teenagers clamoring into the room behind him was muted. Dull.

Myriam's eyes opened, and she sat up quickly, looking around herself and then to Mikey. She followed his outstretched finger to Rufus.

"Oh," she said. "Ah, of course."

"Are you doing it yet?" Mikey sounded increasingly desperate. "Quentin?"

Quentin crinkled his nose, but did as he was asked. He reached out and did what he could to minimize his contact with the spell itself and only coil his telekinesis around Rufus' body, allowing him enough space in which to breathe, but immobilizing his limbs.

"All right," he breathed. "I have him. Why? What happened?"

"We're having to drink from this pool one at a time to get out of Hades," Mikey blurted, rushing himself. "Freddy sent me ahead to try and get you before Rufus wakes up, 'cause if Rufus wrecks this spell before everyone else drinks, they get stranded there. Maybe forever. You can't let him do anything until they're back."

"Metal," Clifton whispered.

"How long will this take?" Quentin tried to keep his voice steady, but the fact was that he was in esoteric contact with a powerful witch who was about to be *very* angry at him, and Quentin had no idea whether physical restraint would be enough.

The panic began to stir, somewhere deep inside himself. A distant scream, struggling toward the surface.

"Not long," Myriam assured him. "Just another—"

Quentin felt Rufus push against his hold before the witch opened his eyes.

"What the fuck?" Rufus strained against the telekinesis even harder, but got nowhere with it. He snarled and looked toward Mikey, then to Quentin. "You," he hissed.

"We're just going to wait until everyone is home," Quentin murmured, trying his best to fight the terror clawing its way toward his throat. It wasn't terribly easy, not with a crowd of onlookers, a large spell right in front of him, and half a bagel settling uncomfortably into his stomach. "Then I can release you."

"Let me go, right now, and I'll pretend this never happened," was Rufus' counteroffer.

"What, so you can kill everyone?" Soraya snorted. "Not gonna happen."

"You think I need to be able to *move* to do that?" Rufus stopped fighting, and laughed. "*Libérer—*"

Time seemed to slow to an absolute crawl before Rufus even finished his sentence. Before Quentin's brain identified the language as French, before the spell was completed, before the universe could act on whatever it was Rufus was doing, it stopped.

It *listened*.

Magic.

Rufus was casting some sort of spell. Quentin knew it. *Felt* it. Year after year, abuse after abuse, he understood that sensation so deeply in the very fabric of his being, and it was happening right in front of him, and he was *touching it*.

Darkness blossomed into existence at the edges of Quentin's vision and rushed toward Rufus. Wind tore through the room.

Oh god. Oh god. Not now. Not now!

"*—le colo—*"

Quentin couldn't think. His brain was attempting to shut itself down, but if he let it, if he did nothing, Angela would be stranded in Hades.

So would Laurence.

He reached out and adjusted his hold, slipping tendrils of his gift into and around Rufus' mouth, holding it still. His jaw, his tongue, his skull, all gripped firmly in place.

"*-ooooooghhhhh!*"

Time snapped back into motion. The spell fizzled and died.

The darkness rushed closer until there was nothing left but Rufus and Quentin's contact with him.

Rufus screamed. Pure, murderous, wordless rage poured out of him, carrying threats even though Rufus couldn't put them into words.

Hold on, Quentin urged himself. *Just one minute. That's all they need. Please!*

But then the blackness consumed Rufus, too, and Quentin was gone.

41

LAURENCE

Laurence froze like he could just turn thin air back into Mikey if he didn't let go of it, but it didn't happen.

This was good though, right? Drinking would send them right back home, never to return.

Yes! Windsor circled through the air to land back on Laurence's shoulder. *Home!*

"I'll go next," Myriam said.

"Better if I go." Rufus walked around her.

Alarm bells rang in Laurence's head, though he couldn't pin down exactly why, but he chose to act on them rather than wait. "No, let's think this through." He forced himself to move, to reach out and put a hand on Ru's shoulder, to try and hold him back while his brain caught up.

He could strand us here, he realized. *If he gets home before us, all he has to do is fuck with a sigil and we're screwed.*

Would Rufus do that? Screw them all over just to get his revenge on Angela?

Rufus ground his teeth and glowered at Laurence. "Let go of me."

"Sorry, man." Laurence lifted his hand away, but out of the corner of his eye he saw his mom dip a hand into the pool.

What *was* it with everyone?

Freddy was silent.

Everything slid together like sun peeking through clouds.

Freddy absolutely thought Ru would destroy the spell, given half a chance. That's why Mikey had gone first, to get home before Rufus could.

"Look," Laurence breathed, trying to rush words out before Rufus could steamroll him. "Windsor says Mikey's gone home, so this is safe, right?" He pointed to the pool. "So why don't we just take it one at a time, get ourselves home, then see what Angela has to say?"

Myriam disappeared.

Laurence refused to bat an eyelid in case he gave anything away.

"Freddy, why don't you go next?" Laurence murmured.

"I can't." Freddy sounded resigned. "Angela doesn't know how to drink, or even that she needs to. I must wake her and then make her do it, or she might drown. I have to be the last to leave."

Laurence shook his head. "I can stay with her."

"But you cannot make her swallow liquid that hasn't come via a teat," Freddy said, so quietly that he'd obviously already thought this all through. "It doesn't matter which order you all go home in, but I cannot leave until Angela has."

The twinge of fear in his tone wasn't reflected in his stoic features, and Laurence blinked at him.

This was the second time in as many days that Freddy had been willing to potentially sacrifice himself just to help others.

Mom must've really chewed him out!

He felt Rufus' movement at his side, and looked back in time to see him vanish.

"Fuck," he breathed. He crouched by the pool and dipped

fingers into it, desperate to get home before Rufus could do anything.

"Laurence, stop," Freddy said, suddenly stepping up to Laurence's side. "I sent Michael ahead to fetch Icky. Rufus shouldn't be able to lift a finger until we get back."

The water was cool around Laurence's skin, not cold, and ripples bounced gently back and forth across its surface. The urge to drink was almost overpowering, but he tried to hang back, to listen, because Freddy obviously had a plan like he always did, and for once he was actually willing to share it.

"Okay," Laurence said, glancing up at him. "What is it?"

"Mnemosyne isn't only the goddess of memory," Freddy said, speaking quickly. "She's also a goddess of time, of oracular visions. There is potential here for you."

Hours of trekking up a mountain, and Rufus hadn't mentioned this *at all*.

Laurence's lip curled. "Potential how?"

"Drinking these waters might sharpen your oracular gifts," Freddy explained. "They might not. I don't know whether cross-contamination from different pantheons might spell disaster. But in theory if you drink more than you need, it might — and, I stress, *might* — make it easier for you to control your visions."

Laurence considered it, but not for long, because the mental image of Rufus finding some magical way to overpower Quentin while they dithered here trying to make decisions about metaphysical shit Laurence didn't know anywhere near enough about to inform his choices was really strong.

"Okay," he said. "How do I drink more than I need?"

"That I don't know," Freddy said. "But on observation, everyone else has disappeared once they have terminated contact with the water."

"I've heard weirder ideas."

Laurence put a foot in the pool. He had no idea whether it was disrespectful, and he wasn't going to wait long enough to find out. He crouched down and scooped his hands together, then gulped down as much water as he could, diving his hands back in for a second scoop as soon as he was done. It was cool and it was delicious, and it reminded him strongly of the water from Avalon; the kind of pure waters that hadn't been found anywhere near where Laurence lived in thousands of years.

He hadn't vanished yet.

Freddy stepped into the pool alongside him and gently crouched down to lower Angela into the water, and her eyes drifted open. Without any sound, she began to scoop water more slowly into her own mouth, drinking little slurps while Freddy concentrated on whatever effort it took to make her do it.

There was a balance to be struck between gorging himself recklessly on water that might just cancel his own gifts out and leave him blind to the future and leaving Rufus enough time to beat Quentin somehow, so Laurence quit after his fifth mouthful and stood.

"You sure about this?"

Freddy nodded. "Go. Stop Rufus. We'll be back as soon as we can."

Laurence nodded, stepped out of the water, and crossed out of Hades altogether.

HE FELT wind against his face and ruffling his hair, and knew before he opened his eyes what it meant.

Rufus was screaming, furious, and possibly trying to be heard over the hurricane.

Laurence saw ceiling, and he turned his head carefully to

get his bearings, just in case any gym equipment was flying through the air.

Myriam and Mikey were on their feet but hunkered down, still in the circle. Rufus was pinned to the floor and angrily straining against nothingness.

Scattered around the edge of the circle were Quentin and the teens. The doors were shut, and Laurence heard barking from the other side.

Windsor popped into existence, squawked, and fought his way toward the edge of the room so he could grab onto a treadmill and hold tight.

Quentin wasn't looking great, if Laurence was honest. He was white as a sheet, his whole body rigid, eyes wide. But he had to still be present, even if he wasn't saying anything, otherwise Ru would be able to move.

"I could zap him," Mel yelled over the noise of Ru screeching.

"Hold that thought," Soraya said. "Might not be a bad idea!"

"Ru," Laurence called out. "What's wrong?" He sat up slowly, but kept his head as low as he could, just in case. Nothing *seemed* to be coming their way yet, but he wasn't willing to take any risks.

Rufus snarled. His eyes swiveled toward Laurence, but he didn't — or couldn't — speak.

Laurence searched for Angela, but she wasn't awake yet.

He wouldn't be able to play dumb for long.

"Quen?" Laurence licked his lips, then pushed himself to his feet, careful not to disturb any of the sigils around him. "Baby, can you look at me?"

Rufus snarled again.

"This takes time," Laurence snapped at him. "Did you threaten him?"

Rufus stared at him with all the lethal hatred of a caged panther.

"You threatened him *with magic?*" Laurence rolled his eyes, putting on a show of frustration that wasn't wholly made up. "We're going to need to talk when all this is done. Quen, baby, can you look at me please? It's okay. I'm right here."

Quentin's gaze dragged itself from Rufus and toward Laurence agonizingly slowly.

"I need you to calm down, okay?" Laurence gave an encouraging nod and maintained eye contact. "Just take a breath, Rufus isn't going to hurt you."

Rufus made a sound like he *really* disagreed with that statement.

Laurence threw up his hands and rounded on Ru. "Well, okay. If you're gonna make it clear to him he can't trust you, what do you expect?"

Angela gasped and sat bolt upright, and her hands flew to her face, then down her body swiftly, eyes widening with horror.

Rufus stopped fighting.

Motherfucker. Laurence felt something inside himself finally give in and die.

Rufus *had* intended to kill her while he could.

It took a few more seconds for Freddy to sit up, his features utterly set in stone. "It's all right, Icky," he said, so softly that Laurence wasn't sure Quen would hear it. "You can let go now. You're safe. We're all safe."

Quentin collapsed, and Soraya and Clifton caught him before he hit the ground. The winds cut out with him, and Estelita and Felipe warily got off the pile of practice mats after holding them down through the storm.

Rufus scrambled to his feet and raised his hands, words in Old English already spilling from his lips.

Angela snapped her own hands up, and said something abrupt, sending a flare of red out into the world which shimmered the air around her like a cocoon when whatever Rufus did bounced off it.

"Stop!" Laurence raised his hands and leaped in between them. "Goddess, Rufus, *stop!* I know you want revenge, but take a look at yourself, man! And I mean a real, good, hard fuckin' look at what you're doing!"

Rufus jabbed his finger against Laurence's chest, his face twisted with fury, eyes ablaze with it as it threatened to consume him. "She killed my parents, and I am *not* going to let you, your ridiculous boyfriend, or anyone else get in my way!"

"I didn't kill them," Angela wheezed.

"You're lying!" Ru's voice cracked. He sounded on the edge of tears.

Laurence felt for Ru, he really did, but he wasn't going to step aside. There wasn't any proof, not a shred of evidence that wasn't purely circumstantial, and his instincts screamed at him that Rufus was wrong, that all his assumptions were a mistake, and that letting him hurt Angela was out of the question.

Even if Laurence didn't know anywhere near enough magic to stop him.

"I didn't kill them," Angela repeated. "But I know who did."

LAURENCE

"Everyone just stop." Laurence held up his hands, then began pointing to people in turn as he issued instructions. "Freddy, Mikey, get Quen to bed. Clifton and Lisa, take the dogs out into the yard and let them calm down. Estelita, go check on Martin and see if Mia is with him. Felipe, Kim, Soraya, straighten this room out and get all these marks off the floor, or cover them with mats if you can't. Mel, I know this is asking a lot when you don't know us, but I'd really appreciate it if you could help out in here." Finally he indicated Rufus and Angela. "You two, with me. Downstairs, now."

Windsor flew back to his perch on Laurence's shoulder as almost everyone got to work, and Laurence opened the doors wide so that he could move around the dogs while they barreled into the room to check out what all the noise had been for.

He didn't wait to make sure he was being followed. If Ru started a fight, Angela would fight back, and Laurence was beyond caring right now whether or not she handed him his ass.

What was the point of asking a Hunter for the truth, only to ignore it?

Laurence heard footsteps following him down the stairs, but he didn't pay attention to who it was until they were in the living room, and he was satisfied to see that it was Angela and Rufus, and neither of them were singed or cursing or otherwise bickering.

"Okay. Sit down." Laurence waved a hand toward the couches, but he remained standing beside an armchair, and crossed his arms. "You both got your memories back, right? We did what we went there to do?"

Rufus' lip curled and he paced around the outer edge of the room to reach a couch, but he only sat once Angela did, on another couch as far away from her as possible.

"Yes," Angela said. Her voice was more settled, but quiet, and she folded her hands together on her knees. She was subdued, withdrawn, which was way more emotion than she usually showed.

"Great." Laurence slowly sat on the arm of the chair and looked to her first. "What happened to you? We came to see you, but you'd forgotten everything. Did Lethe do that to you?"

"It wasn't her fault." Angela licked her lips briefly. "It was a condition of the spell she was under. It wasn't enough to remove certain memories, there was also a failsafe in case anyone became too persistent in trying to recover them."

Laurence gnawed the inside of his cheek a moment, then huffed. "We know you cast the spell that bound Lethe," he murmured. "You don't need to dance around that."

She eyed Laurence a moment, then nodded. "Of course. To destroy the binding you at first had to *find* it. But how? I threw it off a whale-watching ship years ago. I even booby-trapped it to stop it being recovered."

"Yeah, I got chased by a shark, and I'm waiting to find out

whether I end up with any side-effects from my high speed escape. Thanks for that." He crinkled his nose as the rows of jagged teeth flashed through his mind. "Why'd you do it? Why did you go to all the trouble of protecting Rufus from the crash, then making us all forget you? Making *yourself* forget *us*?"

"I would have thought it was obvious."

Rufus jerked his chin toward her. "So that nobody knew you were the killer."

Angela huffed softly. "So that nobody *thought* I was the killer. If you remembered me, you'd remember the bear. If you remembered the bear, you'd remember what I said when I gave it to you, and you'd reach the reasonably logical conclusion that I'd killed them, but I didn't, and I swear to you on my own life I didn't know they were going to die. I didn't know anything bad was going to happen at all."

"Then why the bear?" Laurence prompted softly, trying to keep things calm before Ru could explode again.

"I was manipulated into it." She turned her gaze away, toward the windows. "I liked Rufus. We were friends. He was..." She tailed off weakly and then swallowed. "He was my *only* friend. And he could use magic. He was a couple years younger, but we got along, and he was the only person my father approved of me speaking to."

"Your father," Rufus repeated.

Angela shrugged and spared Laurence a brief look of regret before she faced Rufus. "He knew I liked you, so he said I should practice my magic by making you some charms to protect you in case anything happened. He showed me how to make the ones I didn't already know, he let me buy whatever I needed that I didn't already have for it, and I thought it was a good idea. Who wouldn't want to protect the people they—" She paused abruptly, then finished with, "Care about."

Laurence nodded as he listened. "Then you gave Rufus the charms, and his parents died the exact same evening."

"I was relieved Rufus survived," Angela said. "I thought it was such luck that I'd given him the bear on the exact same day the crash happened. I was so stupid. I figured, what if he didn't take it everywhere like I said he should? What if he left it home and something bad happened? How *fortunate* he had it with him because I'd only just handed it over."

Laurence noticed her knuckles whitening, her cheeks turning pale, as her voice strained.

"And then I realized he'd blame me," she continued. "Because that's what I would've done. If I got handed a lucky charm that allowed me to survive a fatal crash on the *day* of that crash, I'd be so suspicious. And I realized my father had used me. He'd used my feelings, my emotions, to make me do what he wanted, and if people came looking for me they might find *him*, and more people would get hurt. So..." Her hands finally parted, spreading, palms up while her elbows remained on her thighs. "I figured if I forgot too, he couldn't use those feelings against me ever again."

"That's dumb," Rufus muttered.

"I was fifteen and I just worked out my dad had murdered my only friend's parents," she snapped. "I had nobody. I couldn't face you, I couldn't face *him* knowing what he'd done, and I didn't have anyone else I could trust, so I did what I could. I figured out how to wipe the memories I wanted gone, and then I did everything I could to disappear from my own life."

Rufus looked doubtful, but at least he'd shifted from murderous at last.

Laurence drew his thigh up onto the arm of the chair and hung his forearm across it. Ethan would've mocked him for bisexual sitting if he'd been here, but thankfully neither Angela nor Rufus seemed to have an opinion on it. "I don't suppose you know why your dad would want Todd and Paula dead?"

"No." Angela clasped her hands together again. "Nor why he would want Rufus to survive. If there was a purpose to that plan, either he's already achieved it, or it's still in motion. I try to have as little to do with him as possible, but he *does* call on me now and then, and it's safest for me to just do what he asks until he lets me go."

"Calls on you for what?" Rufus leaned forward, which was the first sign he showed that he might believe what she was saying at last.

"Information. Tasks." Angela looked toward Laurence again.

Laurence sucked in air and raised his head so that he'd be as calm as he could be when he dropped the bombshell. "Her father made her reach out to me, to offer to teach me magic."

Confusion creased Ru's brow. "When?"

"This year."

"And you said no?"

Laurence shook his head. "No, I said yes, because I thought it would be a good idea to make more connections, meet more people who could use magic. I thought it'd be a chance to either make a potential ally, or find out whether she was a threat."

"But I was already teaching you," Rufus said. And then he scowled and stood. "You were trying to renege on your deal."

Laurence scoffed at him. "No fucking way. I made a promise. An oath. I swore to you I'd help you, and we both knew it'd be a while before I was ready to do that, because whenever I look through time I see horrible shit and we *knew* I'd have to watch your parents die. I still agreed to do it. I'm not an oathbreaker."

Windsor cawed loudly in agreement, affronted on Laurence's behalf, and he spread his wings out.

Ru eyed the bird.

"Shit!" Windsor declared. "Shit fuck bugger arse bastard!"

"Goddess, Win!"

"That bird is awful!" Angela agreed.

Rufus' scowl softened faintly.

Laurence couldn't help himself. He burst out laughing.

Angela joined in.

Rufus huffed and crossed his arms while the rest of his posture loosened.

It felt like a weight lifted from Laurence's chest. All the stress of the past couple days bled out of him like he was a popped balloon, and he slid down to sit in the chair, leaving one leg draped over the arm. Windsor hopped up onto the back and preened himself, fully aware of how clever he was, whether or not he'd intended this to happen.

"This isn't over," Rufus muttered.

"No," Laurence agreed. "It's way from over. We need to find out why her dad killed your parents, and we need to deal with him."

Rufus nodded. "Okay. Let's—"

"Nuh-uh." Laurence held up a finger in the air. "Stop right there."

Ru eyed him.

"Her dad's a warlock," he reminded Rufus.

Angela lifted her head. "And he's watching both of you."

"And I am going to need to get a *lot* better at magic before I face off against another warlock, 'cause the last one nearly killed me." Laurence eyed Ru. "What was that spell you tried to attack Angela with upstairs?"

"Just a basic hex." Rufus sniffed. "It was the fastest thing I could pull off given the circumstances."

"Great. I'm gonna need to learn it. What else do I need?"

"I am horrified on a daily basis by your lack of perception

magic," Angela mused. "You rely on your senses because they are better than most, but they are not enough."

"Frankly, if you're going to be running around stabbing everyone, the very least you need is a blade you can summon from anywhere," Rufus said.

Laurence knew he shouldn't be shocked to hear what Ru had been holding out on him, but it felt like a jab anyway. The amount of times he'd had to scramble around for a makeshift weapon because he didn't want to get caught with one on him, and he could just *summon* one?

"Okay," he said with care. "What else don't I know how to do yet?"

Angela shrugged. "With your gifts, you should also consider binding some plant life to you so that it can be summoned for your use in an emergency."

Rufus nodded slowly, and was tapping out numbers on his fingertips as they both spouted ideas. "Some wound resistance, too. He gets injured a lot."

"He does?" Angela nodded. "Healing spells?"

"He regenerates swiftly."

"Swift *enough*?"

"Hmm." Rufus counted off another finger. "He also relies on natural stealth, but there are magical options which could aid him."

Laurence felt like he was watching a tennis match, head turning back and forth as they bandied ideas between them.

He'd been wondering whether or not making some rainclouds was too much, but here were his teachers — at each others' throats half an hour ago — hashing out a martial training plan for their mutual student as though it was a new and exciting thought exercise.

It was overwhelming.

"Whoa, whoa," he breathed, hopping to his feet. "I'm not the fighter. That's Quen. I just—"

"Stab gods to death," Rufus deadpanned.

"Gods?" Angela stood. "He'll need a better knife."

"I had Carnwennan," Laurence reasoned. "But it was on loan for a specific daemon. I had to give it back."

"That's a shame, but Carnwennan has a very limited purpose." Angela smiled slightly. "If your enemy is not a hag, it's less useful."

"Wait. If your dad is a warlock," Rufus said, "how is it you're a sorcerer?"

"You'd have to ask him. I'd ask, but then I'd owe him something, and I already owe enough debt for raising me, and he would *love* for me to be indentured to him." She shrugged. "I figure he had me learn sorcery so he could hide behind me."

Laurence's eyebrows lifted and he sat up properly, then decided to stand, since everyone else was doing it. "How do you mean?"

"Warlockry does not look like any other magic. It leaves visible scars on the universe, and once you recognize them, you will spot a warlock from his workings alone. He dare not allow anyone to see his magic if he wishes to remain hidden, so he collects other magic-users and has them do his bidding with their knowledge and power. Until they are of no further use."

"Then what?"

"Then he kills them," she said simply.

Laurence bit his lip briefly.

Was that why he'd killed Paula and Todd, but spared Rufus? Was it why he was watching Laurence, too?

It was creepy as hell.

He shuddered and pushed it aside for now. "Okay, look. I need to go check on Quen, he should be coming round soon. After that I can give you both a ride home, or you can stay here a while, or—"

They snorted at him.

"These wards are not sufficient," Angela said.

"I've been away from my sanctum for too long," Rufus chimed in.

"Yeah, yeah, I get it. I'm too shitty a wizard for either of you," Laurence teased with a grin. "Fine. Wait here, I'll go check on Quen, then I'll take you home. And… thanks. Both of you."

"For what?" Rufus blinked.

"For not fucking killing each other and leaving me with more bodies to bury."

"Wait, what?"

"*More* bodies?" Angela frowned at him.

"Later, later!"

Laurence hurried out of the living room and straight upstairs, and did everything he could to forget the image of Dan's destroyed, wooden face.

43

FREDERICK

MICHAEL OPENED THE DOOR TO THE BEDROOM SO THAT Frederick could carry Icky inside, and he closed it after without being asked to.

Frederick settled Icky on top of the sheets and checked that he was still breathing, then backed away to the windows and looked outside. The sky was glowing with a soft sunrise, and the stars faded, too dim to be seen from so far away for another day.

He drew his phone to check the time.

They really *had* spent all night in Hades climbing a bloody mountain.

Michael stepped up alongside him and shoved his hands into his pockets. "Who knew going to Hades would be hours of hiking followed by a panicked scuffle for our lives?"

"Anyone who has read the classics."

Michael nodded faintly, and they were both quiet a while, until he said, "Are we going to talk about it?"

"About what?"

He knew, of course, because he lived in Michael's head rent-free. And there was little use hoping that Michael wouldn't say it out loud, because Frederick had just *invited* him to, after a year of encouraging him to be more assertive.

"About you falling apart after a few hours alone in a cave." Michael's voice trembled with contained anger, but it was fear which was controlling his thoughts.

Frederick took a slow breath, then let it out in an equally slow sigh.

It was hardly his proudest moment, now that he remembered it. But it had been utterly impossible to know how long he had been there, and it transpired that total sensory deprivation was a very effective method of torture.

He glanced across to Icky, still well and truly unconscious, then frowned at Michael.

"Yes."

Michael gazed up at him, searching his gaze for any hint of a lie, then jerked his chin up. "When?"

"After," Frederick murmured. "We need to head back to Arizona, to find out what the Marlowes have decided, and to decide what to do with Delaney. Then we will talk. I promise."

"I'll hold you to it," Michael declared. Only then did he take his hands from his pockets and reach for Frederick's waist instead.

He drew Michael in for the hug they both needed, though Frederick wouldn't usually admit such a thing even to himself.

The rest of the house was absolutely chaotic. Those whose minds he could reach were jostling back and forth between truth and lies, and he couldn't help but nose in to find out that the teenagers were on the brink of telling Flynn everything and the adults were struggling to stop them without arousing too much suspicion themselves. Frederick had honestly thought it would take longer than a handful of days for someone to let the butler in on the secret, but he'd overestimated the ability of young adults to keep quiet to people they liked, and they'd obviously taken to Martin already.

"And after that?" Michael finally asked.

Frederick shrugged. "Whatever you want."

Michael leaned back and lifted an eyebrow. "No, really though. Do we go home? Do we stay in the US?"

"That depends on—"

Delaney sat in a Starbucks, charging his laptop while he sipped from an empty reusable cup to pretend he still had a drink to nurse. Rain sluiced down the windows in whole sheets, rendering it next to impossible to see outside, to figure out what country he was in, let alone the city.

Frederick blinked several times, but this was not a memory. At least, not one of the past.

He looked over Delaney's shoulder, to the laptop's screen, and found nothing too incriminating, although the date in the top right corner was a year away yet. The boy was editing another of his interminably dull videos, which was undoubtedly why he needed to abstract electricity from a coffee shop. Frederick followed the cable to the wall, and the power sockets Delaney had found looked American. People at the counter were speaking English with American accents, too.

That narrowed things down to a continent, at least.

Frederick studied Delaney more closely. He looked older, less healthy, with dull skin and dull eyes, and his clothes were slightly musty.

Was Delaney unhoused?

Evidence. His brain automatically craved evidence. Proof. Data. So Frederick began to search his surroundings for everything he could glean.

There, by the counter. The rows of merchandise.

The area-limited mugs.

Seattle.

Frederick returned his attention to Delaney. What was he doing in Seattle? And, more importantly, why was Frederick seeing any of this?

Delaney closed the laptop and checked his phone. He stuffed the empty cup into his backpack and unplugged the laptop to slide it in there too. Either he'd got tired of waiting, or it was time to go.

A dark splash of red hair caught Frederick's eye, and for one horrifying moment he thought Michael might be in this vision, but the man hurrying toward Delaney and looking like a drowned rat was shorter, and had hazel eyes.

"Mr. Delaney?" he said, with a Bronx accent. He thrust his hand toward Delaney, and Frederick spied fingernails painted a stormy grey. "I'm sorry I'm late, I got held up."

Delaney eyed the hand, then clasped it tightly. "Basil Irwin," he said. "I've wanted to meet you for ages. I thought you were going to blow me off."

Irwin laughed, a bubbly sound that was utterly disarming, and he flapped his free hand through the air like a fan. "No way. A story like this? I flew in from the Big Apple for you! You want coffee?"

Frederick's gaze shifted to the ring on Irwin's finger. The one which he knew from Laurence's memories glowed blue, but didn't look remotely unusual to Frederick's eyes.

"I'd love one," Delaney said. "Just a flat white, if that's okay?"

"Stay right here, I'll go get it, and see if I can shed some water while I wait." Irwin crinkled his nose with his bright smile, then danced away to join the line.

Delaney sat back down, fished out his computer, and entered his password, then opened up a wealth of files in readiness for the meeting. They were all neatly organized in folders, files named with dates and subjects, and Frederick felt a dawning sense of horror.

Cameron Delaney wouldn't stop. Not unless someone stopped him. Because all those files weren't just about Icky anymore.

He'd expanded his net. He had files on Laurence, on Frederick, on the children, on just about everyone's extended families...

And he had a file on Irwin.

This was a trap. Irwin had flown all the way to Seattle, and it was a trap.

"Frederick!"

Michael was shaking him by the shoulders, terror pouring out of his mind like a waterfall, and Frederick was so disoriented that it took him a second to cram all the pieces of this particular jigsaw puzzle together.

Then he grabbed Michael's arms. "Stop!"

Michael froze, and waited for further instruction.

"Stop," Frederick repeated, more softly. "I'm all right." He straightened up, as if standing tall could reassure everyone present, but Michael was too smart, and Frederick knew himself too well. "It appears that a hunch I had was correct," he added. "But that will have to wait, too."

Michael pursed his lips, debating how to prod at Frederick some more, but the door opened before he could get words out.

This isn't over, Michael thought.

I concur, I assure you. Frederick slid the words into Michael's mind, then spoke out loud to Laurence. "He hasn't stirred."

Laurence hurried to the bed and sat by Icky's side, taking his hand and clinging to it. "Yeah, I didn't expect him to," he said. "Thanks for keeping an eye on him."

"Of course. And Angela?"

"Managed to talk Ru out of trying to kill her," Laurence sighed. "But now he's set on killing her dad instead."

"Well, if he's lining up fathers…" Frederick said with only a hint of a joke.

"Yeah, tell me about it." Laurence nodded grimly. "Hey. Quen? I'm right here, baby. It's safe. Take your time."

Frederick lowered himself into a chair, and Michael sat in the other, across the little table from him. His attention was on Frederick, giving Laurence and Icky some space while also making it very clear that he was annoyed.

After you left Hades, Frederick explained in silence, *I did what I could to give you enough time to fetch Icky and explain what needed to be done. But once Rufus was gone, I explained my hunch to Laurence.*

What hunch? Michael sat completely still, ignoring Laurence's soft murmurs to Icky.

That drinking more than he needed from the water would boost his oracular powers. The Ancient Greeks believed that seeing through time was a function of memory. Visions were simply memories uncovering themselves. Thus, Mnemosyne is a goddess of time and of oracles, as well as of memory.

He waited for Michael to chew on that, and enjoyed watching him reach the correct conclusion after turning it over and examining other possibilities.

You also drank more than you needed, and now you can see the future?

So it would seem. Frederick did his best to not seem smug, but really, he *was* rather pleased with himself. *It may take some experimentation to perfect, and certainly might never be as useful as Laurence's own gift, but it's another tool in the box.*

Michael ran over some more options, wondering whether this might be a blessing or a curse, and trying to figure out how this could be applied to keep them both safe, but in the end his response was, *Smart.*

"There he is!" Laurence's voice was gentle, warm. "Hey, baby. It's okay. You had an episode."

Icky sat up slowly while he assessed his surroundings, then he checked himself over, which Frederick found entirely understandable. The poor boy spent his entire childhood waking up to exciting new injuries. The analysis was undoubtedly ingrained by now.

"It's all done," Frederick assured him. "You saved Angela's life. That's all you need to know."

"From?" Icky blinked at him.

"Rufus."

Icky's eyes narrowed. "I see."

"It's okay," Laurence interjected. "Ru's over it."

"Oh, good," Icky said lightly. His sarcasm rang like a bell to Frederick's ears, but he wasn't sure whether Laurence would catch on.

Laurence snorted and kissed his cheek, then hopped to his feet. "Okay. I've got to drive Ru and Angela home, then I'll be back, and I can answer any questions then."

"I think you might be a little tied up later," Frederick said, intentionally going for the double entendre.

Laurence turned bright red and cleared his throat. "What? Why?"

Frederick pointed downward. "While Icky was out, and you were chatting, your teenagers have spilled the beans to Mr. Flynn."

"They did *what?*" Icky stumbled off the bed and did his best to straighten his clothes quickly.

"What? Why? Why didn't anyone stop them?" Laurence rushed for the door and grabbed the handle.

"Your mother and Mia did try their very best." Frederick raised his hands to protest his own innocence, lest Laurence get any funny ideas. "But he was bound to find out sooner or later."

Laurence narrowed his eyes at Frederick, then hurried out of the room, and Icky was about to follow.

"Wait, will you, Icky?" Frederick pried himself out of the chair and wandered toward his brother. "Just a second."

Icky looked like a spooked cat, his hair unkempt and his jaw unshaven. He paused, all angles and limbs. "What is it?"

Frederick caught up with him and gazed into his eyes. It

was, as always, deeply unsettling to stand in front of someone he couldn't read, but Icky had always been so, and that made no difference to what Frederick had to say.

"I don't know how long it's been since I last told you this," Frederick murmured. "And I don't want it to be as long before you hear it again." He reached out and drew Icky into a tight hug, wrapping himself around that stick-thin frame as though he could protect it with his bulk alone, even though it had never worked before. "You are my brother, and I love you."

Icky sighed as he sagged against Frederick, and grudgingly returned the hug. "I adore you, Fred. Stop being an arsehole."

"I don't think that I can," he said.

"Bollocks."

Frederick pulled back and frowned faintly. "You have titles in Otherworld, do you not? You and Laurence? Warrior, Hunter."

Icky frowned at him, but nodded. "That is correct."

"Mmm." Frederick grimaced at him and stepped away. "Alas, so do I."

Icky crossed his arms, but raised a finger to his lips as his brows furrowed in thought. "May I ask what it is?"

"You may, but you might not like the answer." Frederick ran fingers through his hair, but he knew he was fidgeting, so he dropped his hands to his sides after.

"Come on, Freddy, spit it out."

"Trickster," he said.

They stood in silence while Icky mulled it over. He took time with these things. Frederick was well used to it, and no amount of poking could speed him up.

"Not *all* tricksters are bad," Icky finally concluded.

"Most are not," Frederick agreed. "But it's a fine line."

Icky shrugged. "Well, then you'll just have to apply yourself, won't you? Make sure the line you walk doesn't harm the ones you love."

Frederick eyed him. "When did you get to be remotely wise?"

"When I stopped drinking. Now, if you'll excuse me, I likely have to go prevent a riot."

Frederick inclined his head and Icky slipped out of the room like an eel, leaving him alone with Michael once more.

"Home?" Michael suggested.

Frederick nodded. "Home, and then back to Arizona. We have something to take care of."

Bugger whatever Icky eventually decided about Cameron Delaney. Frederick had made his decision.

He would not allow the future he'd seen.

44

MYRIAM

It had taken the teens all of ten minutes to eat their breakfast, and another ten seconds to start debating whether or not to fill Martin in on their secrets with all the subtlety that only teenagers could manage.

Ultimately, Estelita and Felipe had tripped over each other to be the ones to come out with it, all while Mia and Myriam did their level best to stop them, but what could they do? They were standing before a tidal wave with their hands up, asking it to think for a moment.

Martin, the poor boy, had showed very little sign of believing any of it, even though the girls went into great detail about their own gifts and then begged for help in removing Sharpie ink from wooden flooring. They might even have retained some level of plausible deniability up until the moment Bambi came skidding into the kitchen with his hands held high.

"I can explain everything!" he gasped, his cheeks pinked by the burst of speed.

Windsor flapped his wings with excitement and hopped across to a chair closer to Bambi.

Martin raised the teapot. "Tea?"

"No, I'm… Yeah. Actually. Tea. Thanks. Look, Martin, whatever they've told you—"

"Which is everything," Mia sighed. "He hasn't even been here a week!"

"He deserves to know if he's going to be living here," Soraya insisted.

Martin poured tea for Bambi and passed it across with only the slightest trace of bewilderment around the set of his lips, the crease of his brow. "Rubbing alcohol," he finally said, "is the best way to remove Sharpie ink from wood. If you show me the problem area, I can take care of it."

"Which is why we had to tell you," Estelita said. "There's a lot of it, and it, um, kind of looks exactly like a huge magical ritual took place, so… Better to just come out with it, right?"

Bambi groaned and gulped a mouthful of tea. "Couldn't we have had a day to rest before we caused *more* trouble, though?"

Myriam reached for her coffee and drew it closer. "What's done is done," she said quietly, feeling out the words as she spoke them. "We can only move forward, never in reverse." She looked to Bambi. "Is Quentin all right?"

"Yeah." Bambi helped himself to some toast. "Freddy wanted a quick word with him, but they'll be down soon."

Myriam nodded thoughtfully.

So far, Freddy seemed to have taken her words on board. He was putting himself on the line, doing what he could to help out, even getting into trouble with a god to give them the information they'd needed to solve this problem.

But he had still tortured her son, and what was done was most certainly *not* done. Not quite.

Not until Freddy came clean to Quentin about it.

He was taking steps on the right path, but it remained to be seen whether he would be able to stick with it, or whether the temptation of forks in the road would be too great.

And where did that leave her?

Myriam still had a shop to run, a farm to maintain, a community to care for, and staff to pay. She couldn't drop her whole life just to become the conscience on Freddy's shoulder whenever he had the urge to do something foolish. She had already raised one child, she was not going to take on another.

No. She was a priestess, and that meant offering counsel was part and parcel of her role, but Freddy was outside her community, and he had no right to expect free therapy from her. She had already given him a reading and shown him his choices. The path he took now was up to him.

Is that fair?

She sipped the remainder of her coffee while the banter of teens faded to background noise.

Fairness was too nebulous a concept to rely on. Myriam much preferred justice; the removal of the barriers which produced inequity.

What, then, was the barrier here?

She needled away at it as Quentin entered the kitchen and launched another round of apologies and explanations.

Freddy's situation was, through history and genetics, unequal. He couldn't divest himself of his gifts, but he *could* work to challenge his own privileges.

Did he even understand the need to do that, or would that lack lead to him giving up and choosing the wrong path? And was it Myriam's responsibility to give him that information if he was not ready to hear it?

She idly watched Quentin as he patiently listened to the teenagers in turn, then shared his own thoughts, and asked their opinions on them. A man who had only just regained consciousness due to his own mental health struggles, and yet here he was setting his own fears aside to help others work through theirs.

A man who, when she had first met him, was a classist snob of the highest order.

Myriam finished her coffee, but kept the mug in place so she could work out her thoughts a little longer without attracting attention.

Quentin was the family that Freddy needed. He had changed, grown, and the kind but firm leader buried inside him had begun to flourish. He was the one who should be guiding Freddy, not Myriam.

Satisfied that she had her answer, Myriam finally put her mug down and smiled to Bambi to catch his eye.

Bambi noticed, and turned to face her, his eyebrows raised in an unspoken question.

"I should take Ellie home," Myriam said, speaking softly so as not to disrupt the rest of the room. "And then rest, I think. It's been a long night." She patted herself down for her phone, then tapped out a text to Ethan, adding, "I'll see if Ethan can run the store today."

"I can swing by after I drop Ru and Angela home," Bambi said. "Touch base, make sure everything's okay."

"That would be wonderful, dear. I would appreciate it."

"Sure thing." He smiled as he came over to lean in and kiss her cheek. "I'll probably crash and burn after lunch, though. I can't promise to stay there all day."

"I can go to the store," Soraya said, peeling away from the other conversation. "That way Laurence can just do his taxi run and come straight home."

"Ooo, I can go with you," Estelita agreed.

"We can all go!" said Lisa.

Quentin blinked as the discussion about Martin was abandoned en masse. "I could go along," he offered to Myriam, "to keep them from wrecking the place."

"You need to get back to Neil," Soraya said to him, "tell him we're still on for that helicopter ride even though we couldn't do it yesterday."

"I did inform Mr. Storm that you would contact him as soon as you were available," Martin agreed. "With your apologies, of course."

The energy in the room was lifting rapidly, and Myriam smiled. Everything was settling into a new path — a *good* path — and she felt far more at ease.

"Thank you, Soraya," she said. "I would appreciate it. Let Bambi get his beauty sleep."

"Let him get home so they can start bo—" Estelita began, but then a whole chorus of teens yelled at her and drowned her out.

Laurence blushed so hard that even the tips of his ears turned pink, and he coughed into his fist. "Okay," he said loudly. "I'm going. I'll see you all later." Then he leaned in to hug Myriam tightly, and added, "Merry part, Mom."

"Merry part, dear," she chuckled, squeezing him back.

Yes. She had no doubt that there were still clouds on the horizon. After all, her original reading about Rufus hadn't changed; he and Bambi *would* part ways on some core disagreement sooner or later. But that time was not now, and Myriam could rest easy for the time being.

When the time came, she would be ready.

45

___

QUENTIN

The house was quiet now. Myriam had left with Ellie, to go to the farm. Frederick whisked Michael away with a promise to return once he had taken care of business in Arizona. Laurence was off driving Rufus and Angela back to their respective homes, and Soraya had taken the girls south to see The Jack in the Green. Clifton and Felipe were at work.

Quentin had gone on his morning run with the dogs, and Mia had joined him since the gym was unavailable for her morning routine while Flynn cleaned it. After, he shut himself away in his bathroom.

He remained under the thundering shower long after he had finished washing, even though he knew that water — ironically — was very drying for skin. It almost lulled him to sleep on his feet, but he did feel something else. Something old that he was afraid he might have lost, that he thought Marlowe had taken from him.

He felt *alive*.

Quentin didn't doubt for one moment that this could be a fleeting sensation for now, but it afforded him a measure of hope that he was still in his own head somewhere, peeking out from the smothering lack of energy he felt most days.

He was sure that he had done very little but apparently — from what Mia had told him during the run — he was able to pull out all the stops and hold Rufus at bay. Even though he had very little sleep, even though the circles and sigils all over the gym's floor had given him the screaming heebie-jeebies, and even though he had ultimately had an episode because of it all, he had succeeded, and Angela was alive.

He clung to that. It was something to add to the notes in his phone, to discuss with Violeta during their next appointment, because it was evidence of the one thing she had assured him of right from the start; that he *would* begin to get better. With time, and work, and consistency, his mental health might never be perfect, but it could become more manageable, and he could live a life that he enjoyed. One that he could be proud of.

A life with a future.

He *was* good enough. And, yes, there was always room for improvement, but he would do his very best. If his best was not sufficient, then he would simply have to accept that not all situations were under his control, or even his *to* control.

It was a bitter pill, and one which might not stay down for long. He would probably have to keep swallowing it.

Much had lapsed since the Marlowes took him. He hallucinated his father, he failed to follow through on promises he'd made, and his interest in intimacy had waned more than it had waxed. He owed the teens a trip to Disneyland, as well as this helicopter ride with Neil they were clamoring for, and he needed to be far kinder to himself for his own shortcomings.

That was an easy decision to make. It was the follow-through which proved harder than he could have imagined.

Quentin turned the water off and stepped out of the

shower, then went through the usual routine. Pat dry with towel. Shave. Brush teeth. Comb hair. Apply cream to scars. So many scars. Check face for signs of aging. Fret over whether or not that's a grey hair or just reflected light. Sunscreen. Moisturizer. Fingernails.

Everything was as perfect as he could possibly make it, which meant that it was good enough, and he could let go of the things he could not change.

He gazed at his reflection, confronting himself with it and having a small debate over how he felt about it this particular morning, and he had to admit that — for once — it felt all right. Familiar. Comfortable. *His*.

The bedroom door opened and closed, and Quentin snatched up a towel in a heartbeat, but a few seconds later he heard Laurence's voice from the other side of the bathroom door.

"Quen? Are you in there, hon?"

Quentin let out a sigh of relief. "I am." He unlocked the door, opened it, and only then realized that he still had the towel in his hands, where it was least effective.

Laurence smiled easily at him and leaned against the doorframe. He was unkempt and unshaven, and even though he likely hadn't slept in two days, still looked remarkably upright despite the darkness under his eyes. "How are you feeling?"

"Better. Thank you." Quentin turned away to drop the towel into the laundry hamper, which earned him a wolf-whistle.

"Nice ass," Laurence commented.

"How fortunate," Quentin replied, "as it is the only one I have." He returned to the door and placed a hand against Laurence's chest to gently steer him back into the bedroom. "Now that it all seems to have calmed down, perhaps we can catch up?"

"Yeah," Laurence said, sounding distracted. "Uh." He cleared his throat. "It's fine."

Quentin quirked an eyebrow at him, then continued on to the walk-in wardrobe. "I'm not certain that was any kind of explanation."

Laurence gave a frustrated little huff and tailed him to the closet, to lean against that doorframe instead. "I can't believe you're going to get dressed. That seems really unfair."

"I thought it best to ensure that Mr. Flynn really was all right, after having everything dropped into his lap first thing this morning, and I am not about to do that without clothes." He glanced to Laurence and noted the gentle, lingering flush in his cheeks and the brightness of his eyes, and found that he was not immune to them today. Quentin rested his hands on a drawer for a moment, then added, "But we are tired, and — to all intents and purposes — have the house to ourselves, so I would not be averse to undressing again after that is done."

Laurence lit up with a broad smile. "All right. Well, uh, so we went to Hades and we had to climb a mountain, then all we had to do was drink from this pool to get our memories back, but then we realized Rufus was probably going to try to kill Angela if he made it back first..."

Quentin nodded as he selected clothes and began to dress himself. "I vaguely recall Mikey saying something to that effect. What will you do about him?"

"Mikey?" Laurence blinked.

"Rufus," Quentin clarified. "He exposes himself to you, he's willing to kill with very little evidence, and he's about to drag you along on his quest for vengeance." He glanced toward Laurence and raised his chin. "I do not trust him."

"Yeah. You and me both, hon." Laurence pushed disheveled curls out of his eyes, and they stuck up into the air instead. "But I made a promise, and I have to see it through. Angela's dad might be a warlock, sure, but until we have proof he's the killer, Ru's just going to get into even more trouble if I don't help him."

Quentin tugged a shirt on and fastened the buttons while he debated how to proceed. Laurence clearly meant to adhere to his word, which was no bad thing, but Quentin could not allow him to face a warlock alone, and that would mean changing the course of his therapy. Violeta was focusing on trying to get the hallucinations under control, but Quentin would need to tackle his fear of magic if he was to be of any use.

He nodded slightly, as much to himself as to Laurence, as he reached his decision. "Very well. But please, darling, be careful. You are barely touching the surface of all of this and already you are encountering wards you cannot see beyond, and gods who have altered your memories. This is a warlock who not only knows that people with gifts exist, but also how to protect himself from them. From us." Quentin tucked his shirt in, then fastened his trousers. "I don't like it."

Laurence's gaze lingered where Quentin's hands had so recently been, then he sighed and dragged them upwards. "Me either." He paused, wetted his lips with the tip of his tongue, and added, "How'd you melt that locket?"

Quentin blinked at the change of subject and attempted to poke his brain into jumping tracks along with it. "All that was required was the destruction of a single sigil, so I funneled as much heat as I could into as small an area as I was able, then crushed the metal once it was malleable enough. I am not certain that I actually *melted* it, *per se*—"

"It was hot," Laurence murmured.

"By necessity, yes—oh." Quentin realized a moment too late that Laurence did not mean temperature. "It was?"

Laurence huffed and threw his head back, making a noise like he was gargling air. "Urgh, babe, how can you go through life totally unaware of how fucking sexy you are?" He turned away and headed for the door, raising his arms in playful defeat. "Just wake up sexy, get dressed sexy, play the piano sexily, breathe in and out in a sexy way, it's *constant* hotness and then you go get *even hotter*." He snorted as he wrenched the bedroom door open. "Unfair."

Quentin tailed after him, pausing only to take his phone from the charger and drop it into the pocket of his trousers before they left the room. "If I am not effortlessly hot day in, day out, then how can I possibly hope to attract the attention of a man so utterly beautiful as yourself?"

"I *am* stunning, it's true..." Laurence laughed as he grabbed Quentin's hand on the way to the stairs. "You can flatter me some more if you want, I don't mind."

They would speak to Flynn, and then Quentin could reschedule things with Neil, and after that there would be time to take Laurence to bed and do whatever they wished together.

"Very well," he said. "Have I mentioned your eyes lately?"

"Go on, I'm listening."

Quentin laughed softly and showered Laurence with compliments as they headed downstairs, hands clasped tightly together, and the sense of being alive began to linger.

46

———

LAURENCE

Laurence mostly just listened while Quentin talked to Martin. They were both being super British about everything, so the entire conversation was an exercise in dancing around the subject while acting like everything was completely normal, all while Martin insisted on saying shit like "my lord."

Eventually, Laurence cleared his throat and gave Quentin the stink-eye, to which Quentin blinked and lifted his eyebrows.

"Quentin is sufficient," he said smoothly to Martin, as though he'd intended it all along.

"Noted, sir," Martin said.

Laurence finally sighed and leaned forward to study Martin. "You're taking this all pretty well. Are you *sure* everything's okay? Forget about all that protocol stuff, all the stiff upper lip. Why do you want to fly halfway around the world to do laundry and serve rich people?"

Quentin's eyes grew wide, like Laurence had just committed cultural murder.

Martin was utterly unruffled. "Butlers are in high demand. I had my pick of principals."

"Of what?"

"Employers," Quentin translated.

"Okay. Then why us?" Laurence frowned, struggling to comprehend not only why anyone would voluntarily take a job like this, but also why Freddy had insisted that Martin was the right butler for them.

"Because I believe that you are good people, sir."

There was more, Laurence was sure of it, but he also suspected that hammering away at Martin's professionalism would just cause friction, and maybe even lose them the butler completely.

Freddy was right. They *did* need help around the house. So maybe Laurence just had to suck it up and accept the assistance that was right in front of him, willing and capable and unfailingly polite about it all.

Laurence nodded to himself. "Okay. But if there's ever anything you want to talk about, just let me know."

"Of course, sir," Martin said smoothly.

Now that was *definitely* a lie.

HE GOT Quentin back upstairs as fast as he could and shut the bedroom door behind them. Even Windsor was locked out, busy cursing at seagulls out in the yard, and the peace and quiet was immense.

"So how about we rewind a little, back to the part where you were naked?" Laurence leaned back against the door, feigning casual.

Quentin laughed softly and backed toward the bed, reaching a hand toward Laurence in open invitation as he went. "Perhaps we could move forward, instead, to a time when we are *both* naked?"

"Hmm. That's an intriguing proposal." Laurence rubbed

fingertips through his stubble — though at this stage it felt more like it was thinking about stepping over the line into beard — as if he was mulling it over. "I'd love to subscribe to your newsletter."

Quentin's eyebrows lifted in amused confusion. "I don't have one, darling."

Laurence chuckled and hurried toward the outstretched hand. He grabbed it and drew Quentin in for a slow, luxurious kiss, and grinned as Quentin's arms settled around him. "Maybe that's for the best. Can you imagine the state the world would be in if everyone had access to your secrets? Nobody would ever get any work done. They'd just lay around in bed all day, fucking, taking their sweet time with each other." He traced his lips along Quentin's jaw, lips brushing toward his ear and relishing the rare texture of bristle against them. "Nothing else to do but touch each other, suck each other, make each other come," he added as little more than a whisper against Quentin's skin.

"That sounds terrible," Quentin croaked as his fingers slid up below Laurence's t-shirt and made contact with bare skin.

"Your secrets getting out, or the fucking?" Laurence grinned as he tugged Quentin's shirt free of his pants and made light work of his fly.

Quentin didn't answer, but he was still present, which meant Laurence had succeeded in breaking his brain in the right way. The fun way. The way that reduced this man who seemed to eat dictionaries in his free time into an incoherent mess of sounds.

They undressed each other slowly, taking their time. Quentin's fingers ran smoothly across Laurence's skin, and Laurence held Quentin wherever he knew those scars were least sensitive, until Quentin fell back onto the bed and Laurence sank down over him.

It became something simple and carefree as Laurence

kissed Quentin from collarbone to neck to lips, with his whole existence devoured by Quentin's dancing fingertips and his soft moans. His body covered Quentin's almost completely, and their cocks slid together in the heat they made together until it consumed them both.

Laurence sagged, utterly spent, and let his lips rest against Quentin's jaw. He might even have dozed off briefly; he couldn't be sure. He didn't want to let go of the sense of peace that had settled deep into his bones, but it eventually receded, cold air seeping into the spaces around them and touching sweat until it forced Laurence to pay more attention.

Quentin's eyes were closed, his features so relaxed, yet with the faintest glimmer of satisfaction in his lips.

Laurence slowly propped himself up on one elbow so that he could gaze down at Quentin and take him in more mindfully, allowing himself to pay attention to everything from individual hairs in Quentin's eyebrows to the fine lines in his lips and the way that the darkness of his hair made his skin look ethereal. When Quentin slowly opened his eyes, Laurence gazed into them, watching the minuscule muscles of his colorless irises adjust to the amount of light in the room.

Quentin's smile broadened. "Hello," he breathed.

Laurence chuckled. "Hey, baby. Caught me staring, huh?"

"Nobody could fault you for it." Quentin gazed up at him, not shying away, and seemed to drink him in every bit as much as Laurence was taking the time to do to Quentin. "I love you," he added, his voice softening, hands finding their way to Laurence's hips and resting there.

"I love you too, Quen." He dipped in to steal another kiss, and let it linger a while before the cool air reminded him where he was. "Shower or bath?"

"Mmm." Quentin seemed to consider it, his lips pressing together faintly while his gaze drifted, then he returned his attention to Laurence. "I fear if we get into a bathtub I might fall asleep before we make it out again."

"Yeah. Agreed." Laurence started the process of peeling himself off Quentin and tried his best not to laugh at the absolute mess they'd made — of the bed, and of each other — as he offered Quentin his hand. "I know you only just got out of one shower, but I hope you realize it was worth it."

Quentin eased to his feet with all the poise of a man not currently drenched in sweat and stickiness, and waved his free hand dismissively. "Of course it was."

They went into the bathroom and Laurence marveled not only at Quentin's ass, but also at how relaxed and accepting of his body he seemed to be today, with little effort made to hide himself or divert Laurence's attention elsewhere. If it lasted through the nap they were about to take, Laurence could be in for one hell of an evening.

He grinned to himself as he entered the shower after Quentin and did his best not to think about the future.

For now it was just the two of them, enjoying the luxury of time together, and neither of them needed anything more.

47

LAURENCE

AFTER A DAY SPENT CATCHING UP ON LOST SLEEP AND AN evening spent fucking everywhere from carpet to closet, another night of sleep should have put Laurence back on some kind of regular schedule. He still felt a little jet-lagged, but the night before had worn him out in the best possible way, and he spent his sleep more like a rock than a log.

He should, he figured, be fine to go to work today. After, he could check in on Angela and Rufus, and they could all start coming up with a more accelerated training program for Laurence than the one he'd been dawdling along with for the past year.

Not that he had anyone to blame but himself for that.

Laurence kissed Quen farewell when Quentin went out to take the dogs for their morning run, but instead of heading straight to the Jack in the Green, he took Windsor away to his den on the top floor. He meticulously checked on the plants decorating the room, from the ferns to his hydrangeas, and plucked any dying leaves free. He made sure they were well-watered and healthy. Then he lowered himself to the ground before his altar and set about checking it over, neatening it, and cleansing his workspace.

As the scent of smoldering sage drifted though the air, he placed his athame beside the raven feather on his altar, and closed his eyes.

"Beloved ancestor. Master of the wild hunt, king of the forest, lord of ravens, I offer you my sacrifice and I seek your counsel. Mighty Herne, I bear your blood in my veins. May your hunt be fruitful, and may life always follow death."

Laurence rested his hands in his lap and enjoyed the quiet for a brief moment as the sage smoke mingled with the fresh earth of his plants and the perfumes from their early morning blooms. He wasn't sure whether Herne would respond, but that was okay. For once, he was making a social call.

The odor of earth transformed slowly, and the perfumes were replaced by the damp, heavy scents of mosses and trees. Laurence heard the cheerful chirps of birds foreign to his ears, though growing less so every time he came to Otherworld.

He opened his eyes slowly and smiled as Windsor hopped across to demand petting from Herne, who took the bird in his enormous hands and held him with delicate care.

"Merry meet, Bambi," Herne said with a smile. "You are well-rested!"

"Merry meet, Herne," Laurence answered with an easy laugh. "I am. You're well?"

Herne dipped his head slightly, which sent his antlers forward enough that trees moved aside for them. "You seek counsel?"

"I worded that badly." Laurence stood and brushed strands of grass from his butt and the backs of his legs. "I was more offering companionship for a while. You once said none of your children speak to you, and I—" he spread his hands "— don't know whether you meant, like, as *family*. I don't wanna be the relative who only ever calls when they want something."

"Ahh." Herne stood too, but didn't worry about the leaves littering his furred thighs. He loomed over Laurence, Windsor so small in his grasp, and grinned. "Would you like to hunt?"

Laurence's eyes widened. Was Herne offering, or just making conversation?

There was only one way to find out.

"With you?" he breathed.

"Yes." Herne chuckled.

Laurence struggled to find words. A rush flooded him, warming his chest and sweeping through to his fingertips, his toes. His heart picked up the pace, sensing a thrill, while his eyes pricked with tears from clashing emotions which fought to break out of him and make him cry with joy, with love, and with hope.

"I'd be honored," he whispered. He didn't trust himself to try to speak any louder than that, or he knew he was going to cry.

He was totally going to be late for work.

HERNE SHOWED him how to use a bow and arrow, though Laurence would need to get far better at it before Herne allowed him to use them on a living target. He taught Laurence a few things about using a knife, from where to cut to cause the fastest blood loss with the least damage, to how to skin a rabbit, and Laurence felt a lot more at ease with such things now than he did when Herne had first skinned rabbits for them to eat.

They chased prey and caught it, and then they propped it over an open fire and talked while the rabbits cooked. Laurence told Herne about Hades, and Herne regaled

Laurence with stories of life before the Romans had invaded the British Isles.

Sooner or later, though, Laurence would have to go home. The veil was weak enough this time of year for him to spend a while in Otherworld without using magic to arrive, but eventually he'd be ejected again, and he might as well choose to leave gracefully instead of get dragged out into the real world with things unsaid and moments lost.

He took a deep breath and raised his chin toward Herne. "I used to think I wasn't a killer, and now I am. But I'm going to start hunting soon. Another warlock. And... I don't know. I guess I need to work out how to prepare myself for that. To know that I'm setting out with the *intention* of killing him. I mean..." Laurence huffed softly. "That's murder. Actual murder. Premeditated, considered, and everything." He tilted his head. "How do I do that? How do I accept *murder*?"

"Mmm." Herne looked up to the ravens in the branches above them, who Windsor had joined long ago and was chattering with. "I am no god of justice, or of human morality, Bambi. I don't know how to guide you in this. Are you sure that it is murder you seek to achieve?"

"Yeah, of course. I mean... I guess?" Laurence frowned and sat forward, raising a knee to rest an elbow on. "Rufus is looking for revenge."

"Then why is Rufus not the one to execute his vengeance?"

"I..." Laurence paused and mulled it over.

Why *was* he acting like he was going to be the one doing any killing?

Because I usually am.

But this isn't my fight.

He grit his teeth as the answer slowly crept up on him now that he'd bothered to ask the question. "Because this Harrow guy is a proxy, isn't he? For the warlock I couldn't kill. For Quentin's father."

Herne slowly turned to regard Laurence, with no trace of judgment or of disappointment. His gaze was kind, but firm. "That does not seem just at all."

"Yeah," Laurence agreed. "But Harrow *is* a killer..." He paused again, then rubbed his forehead. "Angela says he's a killer. We're *assuming* murdered Ru's parents, though. We need proof."

"You do," Herne agreed. "But you must also be prepared for what to do with your proof once you have it, whether that evidence supports his guilt or his innocence."

Laurence nodded. Little fragments of this image were shifting into place as he began to interrogate the very premise of his goal, and it wasn't lost on him that he was paying for therapy that Herne was offering for free.

Still, his therapist was available during winter, unlike Herne.

"Get proof, figure it out from there," Laurence said with a nod. "Prepare for the worst, just in case." He glanced to the knife they'd used to skin the rabbits, and made a mental note to ask Mia whether she could teach him to use one properly in a fight. "Got it. Thank you."

Herne smiled and reached toward the trees, and Windsor swooped down onto his arm, ready to receive more attention. "Take care, my child. Always pay close attention to your environment. The prey never exists in isolation."

Laurence opened his eyes to the last wisp of smoke drifting free from the sage that no longer smoldered, and he took a deep breath.

"The prey never exists in isolation," he repeated to himself.

Herne obviously felt it was necessary advice, so Laurence did what he could to internalize it, to make it stick, and then he tidied up the offering dish and made sure everything was neat before he went to work.

48

FREDERICK

FREDERICK WAS AT WHAT HAD LATELY BECOME ONE OF HIS LEAST favorite places: outside the Maricopa County Fourth Avenue Jail. Again.

Hopefully this would be the last time.

He also occupied one of his most favorite places: the inside of Michael's mind. This way they could speak privately without fear of outside observation from either the past or future, or — perhaps more importantly — being scried upon by any magic user Frederick might choose to upset at any moment. He could no longer assume that the talisman he wore could protect him against all magical eventualities, not when Rufus was the source of the spell Laurence had used.

Everyone had ulterior motives, of course, but Frederick no longer believed that Rufus' aligned with Icky's safety.

"If you can see the future now," Michael mused as he, too, watched the doors of the jail, "does that make you safer, or does it just put you in more danger?"

Frederick snorted in amusement. Michael was always worrying about him — and, to be fair, this concern had been further fueled by Frederick's hospital stay — but so rarely about himself. "I suppose the easiest way to find out is to look into the future. But that way lies madness, I suppose. I do not wish to become paralyzed by possibilities. It's a tool, just like any other, and one must always select the right tool for the job at hand."

Michael nodded as he mulled it over, and it was especially pleasing to watch him ponder the possibilities of having gained such a power himself, only to discard the idea as a horrible one. If Michael were given the opportunity to obtain any gifts, it certainly wouldn't be one where he could rewind and rewatch all his past mistakes.

"I'm sorry I bit your head off," Michael said at last. "The first time we were in Hades. I got scared, because if something happened to you that was bad enough to scare *you*, I knew it had to be terrifying."

Frederick pursed his lips and leaned back in his seat a while, ruminating on how to respond to Michael's statement. The boy was surrounded by people with powers beyond his wildest imagination, any one of whom could kill him in an instant, but Michael was almost used to that in a sense; he had lived his whole life surrounded by people with very different power, whether it came from a uniform or a gun, and knowing that any one of them could murder him on the spot and get away with it had been a daily fact of life.

What had shaken Michael was seeing his shield against that world falter. And now that they both remembered it, it would need to be addressed.

"You had good cause," Frederick assured him. "You were out of your depth, and I was not in a position to protect you from that."

Michael grunted softly. "Yeah. But I was in the wrong. I shouldn't have gone off at you when you were vulnerable, and it won't happen again."

"And in return I apologize for frightening you." Frederick

frowned slightly. "I'm afraid I thought I was losing my marbles. Perhaps we could…" he hesitated briefly. "*Both* work on accepting that I might not always be perfect."

Michael made an indecisive sound. "Mmm, I dunno. I don't think either of us are ready for that kind of big brain thinking yet."

Michael was right, of course, but Frederick was hardly about to admit it. Not while he was waiting to pick up Cameron Delaney so that he could put a new plan into motion after already having agreed with Laurence that he did not need to act alone. Laurence was also correct, but if Frederick brought him in on this, he'd be asking Laurence to lie to Icky, and that was unreasonable.

No. That might put unnecessary strain on their relationship. Either Laurence would agree and lie, which would hurt when Icky inevitably found out, or he would not agree, and Icky would try to stop Frederick for doing what had to be done.

"Here he is," Michael murmured.

"I shan't be long."

Frederick folded himself back inside his own body and exited the car. He approached Delaney with a polite, professional smile and an outstretched hand. "Mr. Delaney. I apologize for the length of time it took to secure your release."

Delaney narrowed his eyes, but he took the hand anyway. Not that it mattered. It was already too late for him, he simply didn't know it yet.

He would, soon enough.

"You look kinda familiar," Delaney said. "Have we met?"

"Not that you'd recall," Frederick said smoothly as he sunk barbed hooks into Delaney's mind. "Do come with me. I have a car waiting."

He led Delaney to the car and made the boy get inside before Delaney was even aware that his body was moving without his say-so, and once the car pulled away, entrusted his body to Michael's care so that he could do what needed to be done.

Delaney gasped as the car vanished, replaced by his rather disappointing university dorm room.

"What the…"

"My name is Frederick d'Arcy," Frederick said, cutting him off before he could complete his inane thought. "Earlier this year you enlisted the aid of Katharine, Stephen, and Adam Marlowe with the express intent of kidnapping and interrogating my brother, Quentin."

Gurgles of terror began to churn Delaney's gut. Frederick felt each and every one as they percolated through Delaney's body and seized his chest in an iron grip.

"Where are we?" Delaney babbled. "We were in a car, now we're in my dorm, but we didn't drive here, Phoenix is like six hours away from San Diego, how did we get here?"

"We aren't here." Frederick flashed a menacing smile. "And you never will be again. You did nothing to stop the Marlowes once you realized that you were not in control of the situation, Mr. Delaney. Your only interest was in saving your own skin."

"What do you mean never will again?" Delaney's voice raised with his growing terror. "Who *are* you?"

"My brother believes that you deserve a second chance."

Delaney swallowed tightly and leaped at the lifeline. "I do! I swear, I—"

"I disagree."

Frederick wiped the dorm room away and replaced it with the interior of a private jet, with Delaney seated across from himself, and a world of bright clouds outside the windows which rose and fell below them like mountains.

Delaney grabbed the arms of his seat and yelped in shock.

"All that time you squandered," Frederick drawled,

"chasing non-existent ghosts. What wasted potential. Fortunately, I'm here now."

"None of this is real," Delaney said, trying to convince himself that he was safe. "I'm imagining it. This is all just a dream, you're a figment of my imagination…"

"I'm telepathic, we're inside your mind, I am in full control, and I can read your memories. There is no lying to me, Mr. Delaney, no attempting to reframe what you did or how you intend to move forward. I was impressed by the breadth of information you managed to assemble about my brother."

That's where I know you from! Delaney connected the dots at last. He'd seen Frederick during his dirt-digging explorations into Icky's private life, but then promptly attempted to convince himself that he was still making this all up and seeding his own nightmares with real-world information.

Frederick had no interest in allowing Delaney to convince himself that he still had any control over his own life anymore.

So he put a stop to it.

Delaney was disoriented a moment while his train of thought was thoroughly derailed and then crashed and burned, far beyond his reach.

"What do you want?" Delaney licked his lips, and looked up at Frederick with a much more profound, more pleasing sense of horror radiating from him.

"You have excellent detective skills, even if you do draw the wrong conclusions and decide that ghosts are a rational explanation for whatever you find." Frederick rolled his eyes. "I am going to put those skills to good use."

Delaney stared at him. "What if I don't want to work for you?"

"Perhaps I was not clear." Frederick crossed his legs and leaned back, making himself more comfortable in the imaginary chair. "I *am* going to put your skills to good use.

You belong to me now, Mr. Delaney, until such time as I see fit to release you. If you behave yourself, if you do as you are instructed without fuss, I will allow you to retain your memories, and even that deplorable personality you think is such an asset to you. I will, of course, install safeguards to ensure that you cannot reveal this to anyone."

Delaney let out a slightly manic laugh. "You don't *own* me!"

"Oh, I really do." Frederick issued another cold smile. "And I have the ability to mold your mind as I see fit. If you fight me on this, I'll simply burn your memories to the ground and build a far more amenable Cameron Delaney from the ashes."

Delaney screamed and launched himself out of the chair, then ran around the inside of the made-up airplane like a blue-arsed fly for a few minutes, banging on walls and doors and zipping back and forth from cockpit to bedroom as he burned off his panic.

Frederick entertained himself by molding the clouds into animal shapes until Delaney ran out of steam.

"Sit down."

Delaney threw himself angrily back into his chair and glowered at Frederick. "What do you want me to do?"

Frederick put both feet on the carpeted floor and leaned forward until his elbows were on his knees, and he was much closer to Delaney's face. "You are going to track the Marlowes for me," he said. "You are going to keep tabs on them so that they do not disappear off the face of the Earth. And while you do that, you will backtrace their lives. I want you to find out where they've been every year since they were born, and I want you to build a database of each and every one of their victims. They have tortured and murdered their way across this country, Mr. Delaney, and I require the evidence. You're going to find every body with injuries indicative of being jabbed repeatedly by that bloody pricker of hers, every missing person who had strange things happen near them before they were never seen again, and every single scrap of proof that can build a more complete picture of the total scope of their crimes."

Delaney blinked slowly while he struggled to comprehend the size of the task he was being given. "That could take *years*," he breathed. "What about my studies? My degree?"

"The university has already booted you out; they're hardly about to take you back. You have no education, debt that you cannot repay, and a family who will be very disappointed if you show your face too soon. Ultimately that path leads to destitution, so you really have nothing better to do with your time." Frederick waved vaguely to the windows. "With me, you have access to a lifestyle you would never afford on your own, and your every need will be catered to. All *you* have to do is work."

Delaney slumped back, mind still reeling from everything Frederick had hit him with. "And then you'll let me go?"

He sounded so very hopeful.

"Well. After that there will be one more task. But *then* I'll consider letting you go."

"Yeah?" Delaney squeezed his hands together. "What is it?"

"Once we have the evidence," Frederick said smoothly, "I will need you to carry out the sentence."

"Wh—what?" Delaney shook his head. "I don't understand."

Frederick leaned back and steepled his fingers together as he unveiled the final part of his plan.

"You're going to kill them, Mr. Delaney."

EPILOGUE

RUFUS

LAURENCE MIGHT HAVE HAD A POINT WHEN HE WHINED — repeatedly — that Rufus needed an index system, because now that Ru needed something very specific, he had to sift through stacks of books to try and find it.

If he even had it.

He *had* to have it. There were spells to protect from telepaths, which meant that witches had butted heads with the gifted before and bothered coming up with protection, but telepathy wasn't Rufus' problem at the moment.

Psychokinesis was.

He'd known for ages what Quentin was capable of, but until he'd been the target of the lunatic's powers, Rufus hadn't fully understood what it meant. Now he did. He'd learned the hard way that Quentin would stop him *speaking* if he wanted to, and Rufus couldn't let that happen again. Every spell he carried, every imbued item he ever left the house with required a trigger, and every single one of those triggers was either a motion, a phrase, or a combination of both. They had to be. He couldn't risk unleashing a spell by accident, with a slip of his tongue or a wave of his hand. They needed to be intentional, the kind of thing he wouldn't say or do otherwise.

Rufus was *this* close to ending the curse that had plagued his family since before he was born, and he was not going to let some jumped up crazy British psychopath stop him.

Laurence would arrive soon — not that he was ever on time — and Ru would have to teach him things. How to cast spells that would wait for their trigger. How to hide weapons in plain sight. All the magic Rufus took for granted, that he'd been taught ever since he'd learned to speak, was new to Laurence, and that meant Ru could contain the damage, keep Laurence's field of study narrow, and make sure his student didn't get in his way. So long as Angela didn't screw things up, it would be easy.

Laurence didn't think, he didn't ever put two and two together until it was too late, and he sure didn't work hard at anything. For his whole life he'd relied on luck, and by the time Ru had what he wanted, Laurence would probably have run out of it.

No. Quentin was Rufus' number one problem. For all his intensely obvious levels of insanity, he was also occasionally perceptive, capable of stringing information together and reaching decent conclusions, and far too powerful even if he did refuse to use the magic his warlock father had gone to all the trouble of bestowing on him.

Angela was downgraded to Rufus' second most pressing issue. He'd have to work with her for the time being now that he'd lost his window of opportunity, but he could circle around and take care of her later on, once Laurence killed her father. Rufus would just have to make nice and act like the whole attempted murder thing was over and done with.

Here we are.

He stopped his search and skim-read the spell, then took in the notes which accompanied it.

Rufus would need some of Quentin's blood, but that shouldn't be too hard. Quentin got into a lot of scrapes. All Ru had to do was wait for another one, then mop up the mess.

Rufus closed the book, weighed it in his hand, then carried it with him as he pulled on the hidden latch which would swing out one of his bookshelves and allow him into the small room beyond. He couldn't risk Laurence finding this spell, so while it didn't technically belong with the dangerous books, it would do for the time being.

He felt a lot better now he had a plan.

He'd just have to make sure the Hunter didn't sniff it out.

*~ Inheritance continues in **Runes of Fall** ~*

ACKNOWLEDGMENTS

Remember when Sigils of Spring came out and I thought 2019 had been a hell of a year?

Apparently I shouldn't have said a bloody word!

We don't need to hear about how 2020 was a wash, or how 2021 somehow got even worse, or how 2022 has handed over its beer and waded in already.

Instead I'd like to thank everything that helped Spells of Summer (finally) happen, including:

- My dog, for being the absolute cutest. I will not accept questions at this time.
- Anyone in the UK who lets me use their hot tub.
- Becca Syme, author coach to the stars, for her gracious assistance.
- Dom and Rob, both awesome.
- Meg, for being the best editor anyone could wish for.
- Apple, for replacing my hard drive when it collapsed and attempted to eat Spells of Summer before it was even edited.
- Dropbox, for making sure Spells of Summer didn't get eaten.
- Ed and JuJu Bug, for being the best.
- Fofo, without whom none of these books could have happened.

Spells of Summer was largely written to the dulcet tones of UNKLE, Mesh, Ladytron, and The Prodigy.

See you later this year for Runes of Fall!

ABOUT THE AUTHOR

AK Faulkner is the author of the *Inheritance* series of contemporary fantasy novels, which begins with *Jack of Thorns*. The latest volume, *Spells of Summer*, was released in 2022.

AK lives just outside of London, England, with a charismatic Corgi. Together they fight crime and try not to light too many fires on the way.

Find out more at akfaulkner.com

Sign up for the *Inheritance* newsletter at discoverinheritance.com/signup

INHERITANCE

Season One:

Jack of Thorns

Knight of Flames

Lord of Ravens

Reeve of Veils

Page of Tricks

Season Two:

Rites of Winter

Sigils of Spring

Spells of Summer

Runes of Fall

Visit discoverinheritance.com to learn more about the characters and world of Inheritance, and sign up to the newsletter.